IMPERFECT PARADISE

BOOK ONE OF THE CHANDLER CONNECTION

IMPERFECT PARADISE

BOOK ONE OF THE CHANDLER CONNECTION

Debra Ann Pawlak

A Place In Time.Press • Beverly Hills, CA

A Place In Time.Press
8594 Wilshire Blvd., Suite 1020, Beverly Hills, CA 90211
310 428-1090 or info@aplaceintime.press

A Place in Time.Press
8549 Wilshire Blvd. Ste. 1020,
Beverly Hills, CA 90211
310 613-8872
e-mail:info@aplaceintime.press
Website: aplaceintime.press

Cover Design & Layout:
Cheryl Du Bois & Christopher Staser, brandweaver.tv

Library of Congress Cataloging-in-Publication Data is
available on file.
ISBN: 979-8-9893814-3-2

WOMEN'S FICTION
Printed in the United States of America
Our books may be purchased in bulk for promotional, educational, or business use. Please contact your local bookseller or the publisher: aplaceintime.press

First U.S. Edition 2024

For Linda Wells,

Who started this journey with me more than twenty-five years ago.

If I could choose a sister, it would be YOU!

OTHER BOOKS BY DEBRA ANN PAWLAK:

FARMINGTON/FARMINGTON HILLS

BRUCE LEE

BRINGING UP OSCAR, THE MEN AND WOMEN WHO
FOUNDED THE ACADEMY

CO-WRITTEN WITH CHERYL BARTLAM DUBOIS:

THE SECRET HEROINE SERIES:

SOLDIER, SPY, HEROINE, A CIVIL WAR NOVEL

THE REVOLUTION: CAPTAIN, PIRATE, HEROINE

THE REVOLUTION II: SEER, SPY, HEROINE

Website:
aplaceintime.press

CONTENTS

CHAPTER ONE

I*'m not sure where I went wrong or how I ended up married to a man who chooses whiskey over me. If that's not bad enough, Frank took my wedding band right off the dresser yesterday and pawned it, along with his ring—all for some booze, I'm betting. He promised he'd get them back, but maybe I don't want mine any more. I'm at a crossroads, but which path to take? I have no one here to confide in so I'll claim the blank pages in this journal as a safe place to unload the disjointed thoughts that keep running through my head. If I write them all down, maybe they'll eventually come together and make some kind of sense. If I'm lucky, I might even find the person I used to be—or at least the one I used to like.*

Bright tropical flowers and palm trees resting in oversized clay pots transformed the hotel's crowded ballroom into a Hawaiian village. Waitresses in grass skirts, wearing leis made with real flowers, donned skimpy coconut bras to complete their look. They carried trays filled with fancy food and their permanent California suntans shimmered under the soft lights. I'd never been to Hawaii, but I didn't think it looked quite like this and I was pretty sure our fiftieth state didn't reek of cigarette smoke.

Idly fingering my long string of dime store pearls, I glanced at my watch—nine-thirty. I'd been nursing a glass of Reisling for over an hour. Frank had disappeared as was his custom and it would be hours before my husband resurfaced with alcohol on his breath. I thought about leaving without him, but changed my mind. How would he find his way home after downing who knows how many shots? Maybe a walk outside would kill some time and clear my head. At any rate, my smoke-filled lungs would certainly be grateful for a dose of fresh air.

I weaved my way across the dance floor, dodging couples so absorbed in each other that they didn't notice me. I stepped into the hotel lobby and when I opened the outside door leading to the gardens, a rush of cool air met me head-on just as a man's voice startled me from behind.

"Leaving Paradise so soon?"

Whirling around, I collided with a stranger. He took a quick step back, neither of us realizing that he had somehow hooked up with my pearls. With a sharp tug, beads spewed to the floor, rattling and bouncing around us like hail.

"I'm so sorry!" he gasped. "I didn't mean to—."

"It's okay." I found myself looking up into a pair of striking blue eyes.

"But your necklace—"

"It's fine, really. Just some silly white pieces of plastic pretending to be pearls. Mikimoto would be laughing if he were here."

"Then it's a good thing he's still in Japan." The handsome stranger smiled and I found myself smiling back.

"And it only proves that Paradise isn't all that it's cracked up to be."

"Let's not be so hasty in judging Paradise." He tilted his head to one side and looked me over. "I'm sure I've seen you there."

"But I've never been to Paradise." I tried to suppress my smile, but it didn't work.

"That's funny," he said as his blue eyes held mine. "One time when I was imagining Paradise, I saw you under a palm tree, and another time I saw you on the beach and once I'm positive I saw you eating an apple in the garden. Then there was the time—"

"Okay!" I laughed despite the cheesy line and I took a really good look at him. Something about that dark, curly hair and those blue eyes seemed vaguely familiar. Where had I seen him before? Another party, maybe? No, I'd never have forgotten those blue eyes; somehow I knew this man. "Have we met before?"

"I told you," he replied with a sigh. "Several times. In Paradise."

"And I told you I've never been there."

"How about a walk and I'll try to refresh your memory?" He offered me his arm.

"I won't be very good company." I hesitated, not quite sure whether I should encourage his attention.

"Let me be the judge of that." He tucked my arm in his and pulled me outside toward the hotel gardens. I thought better of it, but those blue eyes were intriguing, not to mention his cologne—a subtle earthy fragrance that reminded me of amber mixed with a trace of musk. Besides, the night air was refreshing and what harm could there be in taking a walk? The scent of roses overwhelmed the other flowers planted along the pathway while miniature nightlights cast a fairy-like glow across the lavish landscape.

"Are you a regular at these parties?" he asked as we strolled along.

"I'm not much of a party person." I didn't know how to explain my situation.

"I'm usually not a party person either, but I'm doing a friend a favor by being here tonight."

"Are you meeting someone?"

"Actually, I am." He glanced at his watch. "And, lucky for me, she's late."

"Are you sure we haven't met before?" I asked him again. "Because it seems like I know you—and don't tell me we've met in Paradise."

"I was just getting around to that," he said as we walked. "I was hoping you'd remember the time we met at Paradise Park. I pushed you on a swing in the moonlight."

"It wasn't me." I shook my head with a grin.

"Yes, it was. I never forget a pretty face and I've been looking for you ever since. You see, it started to rain and I gave you my coat and—"

"There you are, darling! I've been looking everywhere for you." A drop-dead gorgeous blonde with upswept hair, wearing a revealing green dress, cut lower than should be legally allowed, quickly made her way toward us. "I'm sorry I'm so late. Antoine was running behind again and you know he's the only man who understands my hair."

The stranger rolled his blue eyes at me before turning to face her. She threw a disapproving look my way and then boldly kissed him right on the lips. "Who's your friend, Peter?"

"This is Miss Eden and we've been discussing the finer points of Paradise. Isn't that right, Miss Eden?"

"That's right, *Peter.*" I nodded, pleased to finally know his name. "And the point is *I* have never been there."

"Well, Miss Eden," he answered with the most wicked grin. "Something will have to be done about that."

The blonde yanked him away. Obviously, she wanted him all to herself. She certainly had nothing to fear from me. I had no business picking up with strange men no matter how intriguing they were. Still, those familiar blue eyes and dark curls nagged at me, as I tried remembering where I'd seen him before.

Frank came home periodically. Sometimes, he'd stay for a few days and then he'd be gone for a bit—on a bender, I suppose. I hate to admit it, but I liked the peace that embraced the house when he wasn't home. His erratic appearances were unpredictable except for Saturdays when he would always show up, insisting we attend some party somewhere so he could make connections and find work. I went along to appease him, but it was pointless. No one would hire a drunk, but he didn't want to hear that.

As the only working member of our household, my days were filled with writing assignments leaving little time for much else. There weren't many freelance technical writers in the mid-seventies so once I got my name out in the corporate world, work wasn't hard to find. Training manuals, job aids, and reference books were my specialty with an occasional newsletter or questionnaire thrown in the mix.

I rarely turned the television on during the day, preferring to work with the music of Sarah Vaughn, Louis Armstrong, or Frank Sinatra playing in the background. While I still appreciated a good song by Stevie Wonder or James Taylor, there was something soothing about those old tunes. The classics were my one indulgence—something I inherited from my mother. Growing up near Chicago, Mom surrounded us with those romantic melodies whenever she graded papers after a day of teaching high school history. She claimed they brightened her mood and, as a result, helped her students get better grades.

Most evenings, I was alone and I wandered through TV land, looking for an opportunity to lose myself in a world of black and white. The colorless company of Bette Davis or Humphrey Bogart was always welcome. I much preferred a visit from old Hollywood to the tension Frank brought with him when he wasn't sleeping it off.

A few nights after the hotel party, I was home by myself looking for Clark Gable or Spencer Tracy, or even better, both, when I remembered a new show that had debuted the week before—something about a fireman. I'd caught the very end of the first episode. Maybe I'd check it out—only this time from the beginning.

Settling on the couch with a magazine, I planned on half-reading and half-listening to the TV. A loud mix of sirens and trumpets announced the beginning of *Fire in the City*. I glanced up from the article I was reading and forgot to breathe. There they were—those fascinating blue eyes staring back at me! It was the man I'd met at the party! My magazine slipped unnoticed to the floor and for the next hour, Peter Chandler held my undivided attention.

The following Saturday, Frank appeared out of nowhere clutching a party invitation as usual, demanding that we go. Like always, I insisted on driving. Frank behind the wheel was not an option. We rode together in silence to a beachside estate where a Caribbean bash—complete with calypso music, tropical drinks, and women in flowered sarongs—was set up on the sand. After the standard greetings, Frank grabbed a drink and left me alone to contemplate my sorry state of affairs.

Stretched out on a lounge chair with a piña colada in a pink plastic glass, I watched as the cool night air pushed the partygoers toward the house. Not feeling very social and glad I carried a shawl, I preferred the beach where I could just hear the music that was now playing inside. The calypso beat had been replaced with the smooth sounds of Motown mixed with a little rock and roll. I found it ironic that such a beautiful setting was wasted on someone as unhappy as me.

"Miss Eden! There you are! I've been looking for you!"

"Peter!" I sat straight up, my drink spilling in the sand.

"You remember!" His blue flowered shirt matched his eyes perfectly making me wonder if he'd worn it on purpose.

"I do." I couldn't stop smiling no matter how hard I tried. "But you should have told me who you were."

"I did tell you!"

"No, your blonde girlfriend told me."

"She's not my girlfriend." He rolled those blue eyes. "And to make things even clearer, last week I was Peter Chandler and so far that hasn't changed."

"But, you never mentioned—"

"*Fire in the City*?" He finished my sentence for me. "I didn't think it was important. The show's only been aired twice, and if it gets cancelled, I'd rather you didn't know."

"But that's why you looked so familiar. That's where I saw you before."

"Good—the mystery's solved." He held out his hand. "How about a dance?"

"I don't want to go inside."

"Neither do I." He pulled me to my feet and as a silky melody played, Peter held me a little too close. I tried pulling back, but he kept a firm grip on my waist. Soon the scent of his cologne filled my head and I gave in, relaxing in his arms. He wasn't exactly Fred Astaire, but he was a good dancer and even though I hated to admit it, something was happening here—something that put every one of my five senses on high alert. When the song ended, he didn't seem to notice, as we kept moving together in our own slow rhythm.

"The music stopped," I whispered.

"I still hear it." He gave me a quick spin as another tune began.

This man was different—self-assured and funny. He certainly didn't take himself too seriously. He never even mentioned *Fire in the City* again. Best of all, his blue eyes were beguiling. As our second dance ended, I suddenly wondered why he was alone. "Don't you have a date tonight?"

"If you can put up with me, I have a date. How about a drink?"

I had no business being anybody's date. I'd come here with my husband, but right or wrong, I had this handsome man all to myself—at least for a little while. I liked the way he made me feel. Was it so wrong to simply enjoy his company for an hour or two?

The next Saturday when Frank insisted on partying, I didn't protest. As soon as we arrived at the iconic Capitol Records building, I perched on the sidelines. There was no particular theme tonight, but hundreds of gold records were on prominent display touting songs by such big hitmakers as the Beach Boys, Paul McCartney and Wings, and Natalie Cole—just to name a few. Tuxedoed waiters carried trays of champagne and a fully-loaded dessert bar offered tempting treats topped off by a chocolate fountain that released a sweet, but subtle fragrance. None of it, however, interested me.

Tonight, instead of looking for my husband, I found myself looking for Peter Chandler. He'd been on my mind all week. No matter how hard I tried to put him out, he simply wouldn't go.

A couple of hours passed and Peter had yet to appear. Feeling a bit guilty, I scolded myself for even thinking about him. He must have a million things going on. The third week into the new television season, the critics gave *Fire in the City* mixed reviews, but they all agreed that Peter was someone to watch. If ratings were any indication, however, the public resoundingly approved. From here on in, I kept telling myself, my encounters with Peter Chandler would be limited to his weekly television series.

Bored and a bit disappointed, I wanted to go home. When the band took a break and the canned music played, I surveyed the room hoping to spot Frank. Maybe I could talk him into leaving early tonight.

"I hope you saved a dance for me, Miss Eden."

The unexpected sound of that quiet voice made me shiver and Frank was no longer a thought in my head.

Several people interrupted our dance to congratulate Peter on the show's success, but their intrusions disturbed him. "It's a little too crowded in here. Are you up for a walk—maybe once around the block?" My common sense once again ran out on me and I linked my arm through his as we left the building.

"Whatever happened to that blonde you were seeing?" I asked once we were outside.

"She's still at Antoine's. It takes weeks for her to get completely made up. She probably has another ten days or so before they let her out again."

"That wasn't very nice." I couldn't help but giggle.

"Maybe not." He admitted with a shrug. "But it's true."

"So you don't have a date tonight?"

"To be honest, I was working late and I wasn't sure that I would make it at all."

"I'm glad you did." I wanted to pull back the words as soon as they left my lips. What was wrong with me? I had no business flirting with anyone, but whenever I was around this man, my good judgment went AWOL.

That night, driving home with Frank, my mind reeled with thoughts of Peter. Feeling guilty, I looked at my husband dozing in the passenger seat in his typical drunken state. I had promised to spend the rest of my life with him, but this Frank was not the same easygoing man who proposed two years ago in Central Park. I never promised anything to a drunk. My head hurt all the way home as I tried sorting through all my jumbled feelings. After I parked in the driveway, Frank was too drunk to come inside. He spent the night in the car. He probably didn't even remember the ride home.

Fire in the City took off and Peter right along with it. The show was in its fourth week when pictures of Peter began appearing on magazine covers and in the newspapers. Happy or not, I was a married woman with a troubled husband who needed my help. I had to stop thinking about Peter Chandler. After all, we'd only met a few times in very public places. He never once asked for my number or tried to contact me outside of the party circuit. We never shared more than a dance, a drink, and some casual conversation. Come to think of it, he didn't even know my name. He always called me Miss Eden. Besides, if he weren't already, Peter would soon be a bona fide star. He certainly didn't need a married woman like me screwing things up for him. At the outside chance of running into him for the fourth week in a row, I'd have to tell him the truth—I wasn't free to see him. Besides, he'd have no problem finding someone else to practice his charm on.

The following week's chosen spot was a chic country club in Bel-Air. I'm not sure how Frank wrangled that invitation. The room carried a fall theme with lots of reds, golds, and browns. Scarecrows stood between pumpkins and bales of hay that were scattered about. Within minutes of our arrival, Frank disappeared. This time I didn't even see him leave. Several couples enjoyed the dance floor. With a pang of guilt, I wished that Peter and I were among them. Wanting to get away from those happy couples, I decided on a walk around the flower garden just outside. Maybe I could find some refuge in the darkness.

Wandering through the maze of bright colors and fresh scents, I came across an inviting park bench surrounded by miniature mums. Taking a seat, I closed my eyes in an effort to clear my head. Staying in this marriage wasn't an option, yet I still couldn't bring myself to leave. I had to know in my heart that I'd tried everything to get Frank the right kind of help. Maybe talking to him just once more would do it. Maybe I could find a way to get through to him.

"A penny for your thoughts, Miss Eden?" Peter stood directly in front of me, arms folded, intently watching.

"I don't think so, Peter." I avoided his eyes, knowing full well that I was wrong for even talking to him.

"Would you take a nickel or maybe a dime?"

"Not even a quarter." I shook my head.

"Gee, I was really hoping you'd be glad to see me," he replied.

"That's just it—I am glad to see you, but I shouldn't be. There are a lot of things you don't know about me."

"But I do know." His voice grew quiet. "I know you're Darlene Donahue and I know you're married to a lousy drunk. I also know you deserve better."

I focused on the ground, not daring to look up at him. "When did you find out?"

"Right after we first met."

"But you never said a word."

"I was waiting for you to tell me."

"I'm sorry." I took a deep breath before I let myself finally look at him. "But we really shouldn't spend any more time together."

"Why not?" He remained standing with his arms crossed. "We haven't done anything wrong. We've never even been alone together. Not really. We enjoy each other's company. What's wrong with that?"

"You have a career to consider and being linked to a married woman like me could be disastrous for you."

"Let me handle my career." His eyes grew stern as he settled next to me on the bench. I watched in silence as he plucked a purple mum and placed it in my hand.

"Look at me, Darlene." He gently lifted my chin. "Can you honestly say that you want me to leave?"

It was no use. There was no arguing with those damn blue eyes so I just shook my head.

"Talk to me," Peter prodded, taking my hand in his. "Tell me how someone like you ended up with a man like Frank Donahue."

It took a moment for the words to come, but when they started, they tumbled one over the other. "I met him back in New York. He played drums in a house band on Broadway. You wouldn't know it now, but he was so different in Manhattan. We used to be happy, but then he got a job offer to play with a new band here in L.A. I was disappointed, thinking that he'd be moving across the country, but he asked me to marry him. He told me that he wanted me to come along for the adventure."

"Only it wasn't quite the adventure you had in mind, was it?" Peter, still holding my hand, encouraged me to keep talking.

"It all fell apart once we got here." I sighed, feeling the tears well up. "Six months later, the band broke up and my charming husband turned into a bitter, angry stranger. He started drinking and now there are times he doesn't come home for days. I have no idea where he is or what he's doing. I'm afraid that my New York Frank will never come back."

He looked me over for a moment and hesitated before speaking. "Why don't you wear a wedding ring?"

"Frank pawned it."

"He pawned your wedding ring?!" Peter seemed shocked. "What kind of man does that?"

"He pawned his, too." I thought about moving my hand, but I didn't. "It doesn't really matter. All we do is fight. I've tried talking to him, but he won't listen. He claims I'm the one with the problem, but he's obsessed with making connections. He honestly believes he'll meet the right people at these parties. He thinks dragging me along will help his chances, but I know that no one will ever hire him as long as he's drinking. He doesn't see that though."

"You can't help someone who doesn't want help."

"But he's still my husband and I feel like I owe him something."

"You owe yourself more."

"Maybe if we'd stayed in Manhattan things might be different. I suggested moving back there, but that made Frank furious. According to him, returning to New York would mean admitting failure." I twisted the mum in my free hand to keep from shaking.

"So I should thank Frank." Peter brushed my cheek with his fingers. "For bringing you here and making you stay."

I gave a shrug and wiped a stray tear with the back of my hand. "Maybe I should have listened to Sydney."

"Sydney?"

"My best friend back in New York. She never liked Frank much. She tried to talk me out of marrying him, but I thought maybe she just didn't like musicians."

"How does she feel about actors?" Peter wanted to know.

"The subject never came up." I forced a smile.

"Would you like a drink? I could sure use one."

I took the time to compose myself before he returned, carrying two White Russians.

"So, Peter Chandler," I said as he handed me a glass. "What deep, dark secrets do you have?"

"You already know my deepest darkest secret, Miss Eden. I'm an actor."

The next Saturday night, Frank and I headed to yet another soiree. "How come you stopped arguing with me about these parties all of a sudden?" he demanded once we were in the car, his voice thick with alcohol.

"Would it make a difference?"

"No, but it makes me think that there's something else, or maybe *someone* else?"

"What are you getting at, Frank?" My insides turned cold. I was sure Frank had never seen me with Peter, but then again maybe he had.

"I'll tell you one thing, *Mrs.* Donahue." He gripped my arm. "If I find out you're cheating on me, you'll regret it for the rest of your life."

"Let go, Frank." I tried to keep control of the car. "You're drunk and you're hurting me."

"I haven't come close to hurting you yet." It wasn't the first time he'd threatened me and I chalked it up to his inebriated state.

"You need help."

"I need a job. Everything will be the way it was if I could just get a gig. Maybe tonight's the night. I'll find a job tonight and we'll be back on track."

We arrived at a large estate in West Hollywood. I don't remember who lived there exactly; maybe I never knew in the first place. There were so many people that it was impossible to keep track of Frank, or he of me. Tonight, I was glad that it would be easy to avoid him—especially since part of me wanted to spend more time with Peter, but a couple of hours later, I was still alone. Either Peter was working late again, or he finally realized that spending time with me was not such a good idea. I could hardly blame him.

I'd given up all hope of seeing Peter Chandler that evening when he suddenly appeared with a very serious face. "I need to talk to you, Darlene."

"About what?"

"Not here. Will you come for a ride with me?"

"Peter, I can't just leave."

"Even if I promise to bring you back before anyone notices you're gone?"

My first reaction was to say 'no,' but once again, my good sense deserted me—a pattern, that when it came to Peter, was starting to establish itself. Against my better judgment, I agreed. Frank would never miss me anyway.

On the way out, we passed by a large den where several men and women lay on the floor—out cold. Needles and pipes were strewn across a wooden desk. It was the first time that I thought about drugs. Could Frank be doing drugs in addition to drinking? The thought was chilling.

Peter had left his black Jag parked near the front door where the valet attendants were gathered.

"Nice car." I noted the white leather interior and fully loaded dash.

"It's not mine. It's on loan to me from the studio."

"Nice perk."

"I've been worried about you," he said as he turned the car around. "How are things with Frank?"

"The same."

"He hasn't hurt you, has he?"

"Is that what you wanted to talk to me about?"

"No." Without another word, he drove for all of ten minutes to an out-of-the-way spot where he turned the engine and the headlights off.

"Peter, what are we doing here?" Battling butterflies took over my stomach. What had I gotten myself into?

"Am I making you nervous?" he asked with a grin, obviously amused by my jitters.

"You are making me incredibly nervous!"

"You could have said no."

"Maybe I should have."

"I'm glad you didn't." He grew serious. "We need a little privacy and I couldn't think of a more private place than this."

"Okay!" I sputtered. "You've got my attention so I suggest you start talking because talking is all you're going to get."

"Darlene! Do you think I brought you up here to—" Peter stopped mid-sentence and laughed. "Honey, I'm afraid I'm a little too old to be making out in a car." He abruptly grew serious and leaned in a little closer to me. "But if you insist, I could try to be accommodating."

I pressed my lips together to keep from laughing at how ridiculous he sounded.

"Geez, Darlene!" Peter went on with a shake of his head. "I offer my services and you laugh?!" With a dramatic gesture, he threw his head back and placed his hand over his heart. "You, Miss Eden, have single-handedly bruised my delicate ego. It will never be the same again."

"I'm sorry!" I put my hand over my mouth trying to stifle the giggles that were climbing up my throat.

"Maybe I should rethink my proposition." He folded his arms and frowned.

"What proposition?" I asked, still trying not to laugh.

"I had this crazy, mixed-up idea that you and I might have a little chemistry here and I thought maybe we could put it to good use. What do you say, Darlene? Are you game?"

Chapter Two

Frank was too drunk to notice the script I carried home tonight. He barely managed to crawl inside the house before passing out across the bed, but I can't sleep. Peter's crazy idea was just that—he thinks we should work to-gether. The actress originally scheduled for filming dropped out due to some sort of medical emergency and they are scrambling for a replacement. I know I shouldn't do it, but Peter wants me to call a lady at the studio on Monday—someone named Helene Williams. This whole thing seems pretty far-fetched, but he turned on those blue eyes and talked me into trying. Peter Chandler doesn't play fair.

I'm a technical writer—not an actress, but I did belong to the drama club in high school for four years. My teachers always encouraged me by saying I had a knack for the stage. I never did take it seriously and I'm pretty sure I never will. If anything comes of this, it will be a one-off kind of thing.

The script is thick and my curiosity is getting the better of me so I'll probably be up with my nose buried in the pages all night—not that I'll ever do it. Besides, I have no business even thinking about Peter Chandler. What's gotten into me and why does my good sense jump ship every time I see him? Regardless of what Peter thinks, I'm sure this Helene Williams person will send me straight home before the director yells, "CUT!"

It was a two-parter, which explained the size of the script. Part One opened with a fire and Peter's character, James Dakota, on the scene. A young woman, Gina, (supposedly my part) is trapped inside a burning apart-ment building. In typical TV fashion, James saves her, but she isn't happy about being rescued. Terminally ill, Gina feels that his heroics are just a twisted trick of fate. Despite her condition, which she keeps secret, they fall in love. During an emotional scene, she finally tells him the truth, which ends Part One. Part Two picks up with the same scene and James' reaction to her news. He leaves in a disturbed state, but soon returns, telling Gina he loves her. The story continues with Gina's declining health, her struggle to live, and James' dilemma over his inability to help her. It was seventies television at its best.

I could hear Peter saying every line, but me as Gina? Not even credible! Still, the thought of seeing him almost every day for two weeks made the whole idea very tempting. That is so wrong, but with Frank out of work, we could use the money. Writing manuals paid the bills, but there was never enough for any extras. A new stereo would sure enhance the crooning of Tony Bennett and then there was that oak desk I'd been eyeing at Sears.

When I pulled up to the studio gate that Wednesday morning, the guard checked his list and found my name. Before he let me in, however, he picked up the telephone. "This is Harvey at the front gate. Could you please let Helene know that her guest is here?" There was a pause. "Yes, I'll tell her where to park." He turned to me with a surprised look. "That's odd. Helene is coming down to meet you herself. I probably shouldn't be asking, but how do you know her?"

"I don't," I told him with a shrug. "I have no idea what she even looks like."

"You can't miss her," he said with a smile. "And good luck to you today!" He then gave me parking directions and I was on my way.

After I parked, I pulled out my script and read over the scene once again while I waited. My nerves were getting to me and I began questioning my sanity for agreeing to do this screen test at all. I was busy scolding myself for letting Peter Chandler talk me into this mess when a fifty-something black woman wearing teal-colored cat's-eye glasses and sporting long dreadlocks pulled up alongside me in a golfcart. "Hop in, Miss Eden."

"Helene?" I hesitated, not quite sure who she was.

"That's right." She smiled before narrowing her eyes. "And never, ever forget that I saw Peter first."

I slid next to her not quite sure what to say. Lucky for me, she just kept talking. "Peter asked me to meet you this morning and get you ready for the screen test. You know, hair, makeup, wardrobe. It's all about what the camera sees." Her medium build leaned into me. "And I'm telling you up front that Peter and I have a thing going. Everyone around here knows, he's off-limits and any woman who tries to come between us is looking for trouble. Are we clear?" Before I could answer, she smiled again and extended her hand. "By the way, it's nice to finally meet you, Miss Eden—I mean Darlene. Peter never mentioned you were a pretty little thing. He always leaves out the details. He knows how jealous I am."

Helene left me with the hairdresser, promising she'd be back in an hour. *An hour?! What could possibly take an hour?! Do I look that bad?* A stylist washed and curled my hair, and then it was on to make-up. From there, I went to wardrobe where Helene had picked out a pair of blue jeans, a pink cardigan with matching pink socks and white tennis shoes. This was a costume? It wasn't much different from the way I normally dressed.

While I waited for Helene to return, I took a good look in the mirror. My shoulder length brown hair, normally straight, was flipped up on the ends. The streak of eyeliner made my brown eyes larger and rounder. I hated to admit it, but I kind of liked the subtle changes. When Helene reappeared, she smiled. "Not half bad. Maybe Peter was right. What do you say we give this thing a shot?"

Back at the soundstage, Helene was handed a note. "It never fails." She crumpled the paper. "Peter is running late. They're still filming out back. Normally we'd use a stand-in for a screen test like this, but Peter insists that he wants to do it himself so make yourself at home." She pointed toward several chairs and a coffeepot. "Help yourself if you'd like a cup. Waiting seems to be the name of the game around here. You better get used to it."

Even though Helene's voice nattered on, I had stopped listening at 'You better get used to it'. I'd already been at the studio for ninety minutes and the last thing my sensitive nerves needed was caffeine. The size of the soundstage was overwhelming and everywhere I looked, I saw various people performing various jobs. How does anyone get used to this inner sanctum of chaos? I should be on my way home by now—the screen test a bad memory—but we hadn't even begun. Maybe this was a sign for me to run and never look back.

Just as I was planning my escape, Peter appeared wearing his fireman's uniform. Under the black soot that covered him, his blue eyes sparkled. "I'm sorry you had to wait. I've been saving old folks from a nursing home fire, and even in a crisis, you can't rush the elderly. Give me ten minutes to clean up."

"I think you need more than ten minutes," Helene piped up before I could muster a word.

With a wink at me, Peter turned, leaving footprints across the floor. Black dust trailed after him. He reminded me of Charlie Brown's cohort, Pigpen, who was always surrounded by a perpetual cloud of dirt.

"On the positive side, we always know where to find him," Helene said as she watched him go, then she turned to me. "Would you like to run your lines with me?"

"I think I'd just like to run," I said with a sigh.

The set was sparse, but resembled a hospital room with a cameraman, a lighting man, and a second unit director all waiting to begin. They showed me a piece of tape on the floor and asked me to stand on it while they set up. This particular scene had Gina being discharged from the hospital after the fire. She doesn't know it, but James Dakota is about to drive her home.

"Are you nervous?" Peter finally returned, dirt-free, in jeans and a T-shirt.

"Of course she's nervous," Helene answered for me. "We had a long talk this morning and I set her straight. She knows all about us now, but I'm a little disappointed that you didn't tell her we have an arrangement. I'll overlook it for the moment, but tonight when you come to my place, we'll go over the rules again and this time, you'll take notes."

"I'll try and do better." Peter bussed her cheek and she laughed as she claimed a spot behind the camera.

"I don't know what I'm doing here," I quietly confessed to Peter after we quickly read our lines together. "I'm way out of my league. The high school drama club doesn't even come close."

"Just follow my lead," he whispered. "They are looking for chemistry and I'm pretty sure we have it."

Chemistry?! We weren't supposed to have any chemistry! Peter Chandler was off-limits and his remark certainly didn't relieve my anxiety. If I made it through the next several minutes without fainting, falling, or having a breakdown, it would be miraculous. To this day, I can still play that scene in my head.

INT. TYPICAL HOSPITAL ROOM – DAY

Gina, dressed to leave the hospital, is packing a small bag which lays open on the hospital bed, when James Dakota, in casual clothes, enters the room and startles her.

> GINA
> What are you doing here?

> JAMES
> I heard you're being discharged so I thought I'd come by and drive you home.

> GINA
> You shouldn't have bothered. My mother's already on her way.

James looks uncomfortable.

> JAMES
> Actually, your mother's not coming.

Gina grows impatient

> GINA
> What do you mean?! She was here last night and she said she was picking me up.

James looks even more uncomfortable.

> JAMES
> I talked to her this morning. She told me I could bring you home. She even gave me directions.

Irritated, Gina abruptly turns her back to him and resumes packing while James moves closer.

> JAMES
> I know it's just part of my job, but I did risk life and limb

> to pull you out of that fire.

Gina, now angry, continues packing.

GINA

Maybe you wasted your time.

James moves closer to Gina.

JAMES

I don't consider what I do a waste of time.

Gina is startled.

GINA

Look, I'm sorry. Really, I am. It's just not a good idea for you to be here.

JAMES

Your mother seemed to think it was a fine idea.

GINA

My mother should mind her own business.

James places his hands on Ginn's arms.

JAMES

Give me one good reason why I shouldn't drive you home.

I was through as soon as he touched me—that last line of dialogue reduced to nothing.

"I'm waiting," Peter prompted me. "Give me one good reason why I shouldn't drive you home."

It was hopeless, my head was empty. "I can't do this," I finally sputtered.

"Cut!" A voice sliced through the air. "Good job, Darlene, very good job. Let's try it again from the top."

"Like I said." Peter grinned, but didn't let me go. "Nothing to it."

"But I screwed up."

"No you didn't—just trust me."

"I did trust you and now I'm on the verge of cardiac arrest!"

"Do you need CPR?" he asked. "When I went to fireman school, I aced mouth-to-mouth resuscitation."

"You never went to fireman school."

"But I taught James Dakota everything he knows."

I pressed my fingers against my lips, trying not to laugh, but it didn't work. The giggles erupted.

We shot the scene two more times, but it never got any easier. On the second go-round neither of us could manage a straight face. I think Peter was trying to calm my nerves, but it didn't work. We took a ten-minute break and tried to compose ourselves. Mercifully, we wrapped it up after take number three. I was pretty sure I needed a tranquilizer by the time it was over.

Helene stepped out from behind the camera. "That's it for today, Darlene. We'll be in touch, and you'd do well to remember—Peter is mine." She put her arms around his neck and with a sideways glance at me, she kissed him, and it was more than just a friendly peck. "My place. Seven o'clock. Be on time—and don't forget the uniform."

"I'll make sure it's nice and clean," Peter called after her as she walked away.

"I prefer dirty," she hollered without looking back.

"Who is she, Peter?" I had to ask.

"She's the head of casting around here and she's the reason I got this job in the first place. I asked her to take care of you today. It's not everyone who gets the full Helene Williams treatment."

"And do you get the full Helene Williams treatment?" I asked, trying to understand what I just witnessed.

"If you're asking do I sleep with her—no!" Peter laughed and shook his head. "But if you stick around long enough, you'll get used to her. She's really made of mush, but don't tell her I said so. She'll deny it. Now how about lunch?"

"Do you think we should?"

"I don't see why not. People eat lunch everyday. It's a common practice. Besides, Helene gave me her blessing."

"But I don't want to cause any trouble for you."

"With Helene?"

"With Helene or anyone else."

"So you've told me. Do you like Chinese? Because I know a little

Chinese place where no one could possibly spot us."

Peter didn't exaggerate when he used the word 'little'. Wu's Room had exactly eight booths and four tables. Small, but appealing, the place was decorated in the traditional Chinese red and black with gold trimmings. Peter was a regular customer and the waitstaff greeted him by name. Even the cook came out of the kitchen to personally take our order.

Peter unfurled his red napkin. "If you like it here, we'll come back when you film the show."

"How can you be so sure I'll be coming back?" I remained skeptical, positive I had screwed things up, majorly.

"I read the director's face. He liked what he saw, and so did Helene. Besides, I know when I'm right about something, but I have been wondering what Mr. Donahue has said about it."

"He doesn't know. He hasn't been home all week."

"Where is he?"

"I have no idea. I only wish he'd come around long enough to talk."

"Talk about what?"

"I want a divorce." I was shocked by my own words. It was the first time I'd said them out loud.

"Congratulations! You're in!" Helene telephoned me later that week. "There's a page on his way to your house right now. He's got a contract for you to sign and an application for a SAG card. Fill everything out and I'll take care of the rest."

"Are you positive they really want *me*?"

"The camera doesn't lie. You and Peter are quite an item. Everyone here is buzzing about the test tape. It kills me to say this, but if there isn't something going on between the two of you, there should be."

My delight soon turned to dread as Frank pulled in just ahead of the messenger. He accepted the package as I watched from the side door. As soon as the page left, Frank tore open the brown envelope. Loud and reeking of liquor, he stormed inside the kitchen waving the papers in front of me. "What the hell is this?"

"I-I found out about it today." I stood in the middle of the kitchen, not quite sure what to say.

"Don't lie to me, damn it!" he roared. "This just didn't happen! All of the parties we go to and *you* get the gig?! Would you care to explain, Darlene?"

"It's a part for that new television show, *Fire in the City*."

"That's Peter Chandler's show, isn't it?" He stopped, and for a moment seemed almost rational. "You've been seeing him, haven't you?"

"No, Frank. I haven't been seeing anyone."

"Stop lying to me, Darlene! I've heard the talk and this proves it!" He ripped the paperwork into little pieces and threw them at me like confetti. "That's what I think of your contract!" In a rage, he paced up and down the kitchen. "And if Peter Chandler knows what's good for him, he'll keep his hands off you!"

"I don't know what you've heard, Frank, but you're wrong! I've only met him at a couple of parties that *you* made me go to!"

"No wonder you stopped arguing about those parties." He drew himself up over me. "I'll ask you one more time. Have you been seeing Peter Chandler?"

"No, Frank, I haven't."

"You're lying!!" he railed, louder still. "And you've been lying to me for weeks!!" He snatched the toaster from the counter, yanking the plug from its socket causing a spark, and lobbed it across the room. "And it hasn't been only parties, has it?" He threw the coffee pot just past me and it shattered against the wall. "You've been seeing him when I'm not here, haven't you?" The electric can opener came whizzing by my head. "He's probably been in our house and, for all I know, in our bed!" The blender came flying toward me and clipped my right shoulder.

"Stop it, Frank! You're drunk!" I screamed back at him. "You're always drunk and I can't live with you anymore!"

"So that's it." He stepped closer to me. "All your talk about 'Frank get help; I'll be there for you, Frank' was nothing but lies!"

Before I realized what was happening, he lifted his hand and with one swift motion, he hit me for the very first time, sending me reeling to the floor.

"When I get through with Peter Chandler, he'll be sorry he ever looked at you!" Frank stormed out. The entire house shuddered as he slammed the side door behind him. I sat there momentarily dazed, gasping for breath. Frank had knocked the wind right out of me.

I hardly slept all weekend fearing that Frank might come back. Even though I'd been icing it, the bruise on the side of my face remained swollen and sore. My once happy-go-lucky husband was now violent. Still shaken Monday morning, I was on my third cup of coffee and trying to work on a reference manual for keypunch operators. Frank Sinatra played in the background, but today the music that usually helped me focus didn't seem as soothing. After I swallowed a couple of Tylenol hoping to ease the ache in my jaw, Helene called. "We never got the contract back, Darlene. Is everything all right?"

"Everything's fine," I lied.

"Then what happened? Peter thinks you changed your mind."

"No, I haven't changed my mind."

"Then where's the contract? Your husband signed for it. Didn't you get it?"

"Not exactly."

"Is there something wrong?"

"N-no. I'm in the middle of an assignment that's due at the end of the week so I'm a little pressed for time and I mislaid the paperwork."

"Not a problem. I'll send someone over later today with another set. I'll have them wait while you fill it out. They can bring everything back here and I'll personally finalize the arrangements. Are you sure you're all right?"

"Yes and I'm really sorry about the inconvenience."

Within two hours after the page left with the signed contract, Peter called. "I need to see you, Darlene."

"I can't." I touched the bruise on my cheek.

"Wu's Room at seven." He didn't seem to hear what I said.

"I have an assignment to finish," I tried again.

"If you're not at the restaurant when I get there, I'll come straight to your place."

"But Peter—" The click of the telephone stopped me cold.

Self-conscious about how I looked, I tried covering the bruise with make-up and dark glasses. By the time Peter arrived at Wu's, I was sipping hot tea in an effort to keep my hands from trembling. Without a word, he waved off the staff and slipped inside the booth next to me. He lifted my chin, removed the glasses to get a better look at the damage, and then flinched at what he saw. "Frank?"

I could only nod my head, as the words seemed to stick in my throat and the tears spilled over.

"Let's get you out of here." Peter threw a few bills on the table and pulled me to my feet. The next thing I knew we were in his car heading toward Pacific Coast Highway.

A little past Malibu, Peter pulled into a lonely lookout area and for the first time since we started our drive, he spoke. "How many times has Frank hit you?"

"Just this once." My voice shook no matter how hard I tried to control it. "He found out about the contract and he was so mad he tore it up. He said he heard rumors about us, but when I tried to explain, he wouldn't listen. He got madder and madder. If he finds out we're together—"

"I don't give a damn what he finds out." Peter opened the car door and came around to my side. "Let's walk."

A little stone wall separated the beach from the parking lot and after we stepped over it, I began shivering from the brisk night air. Without a word, Peter draped his leather jacket over my shoulders. There was something comforting about the warmth of his coat, along with the rhythmic sound of the waves as they rolled to shore. Clouds covered the moon and the stars and I was grateful for the darkness. Peter took my hand as we walked along.

"Our messenger came back to the studio this afternoon and told Helene that you looked like you might be in some trouble. She called me right away."

"I wish she hadn't. I'm fine."

"You're hardly fine, Darlene. Frank is out of control and next time it could be worse. You need to get out of there."

"I don't have anywhere to go."

"Come home with me."

"I can't drag you into this."

"I'm already here. Did you call a lawyer?"

"I need a little time."

"Time for what?" He suddenly stopped and I could hear the irritation in his voice.

"Time to talk to my husband, Peter. If I up and file for divorce, it might push him over the edge."

"He's already over the edge, honey." Peter's voice rang with impatience. "He. Hit. You." He paused after every word for emphasis. "You need to end it and if you won't leave the house, at the very least change the locks because if Frank ever touches you again, he'll answer to me, and I can promise you one thing—when I get through with him the damage will be permanent."

CHAPTER THREE

I've spent the last two weeks on a writing binge. I need to wrap up three jobs before I start working at the studio. My high school drama teacher would be proud, but I still can't believe I agreed to film a television show. Even though I've been studying my lines in between writing booklets and manuals, I'll never be ready to face a camera. I haven't seen Peter since our walk on the beach, but he phones twice a day—once in the morning and once at night to make sure I'm all right since I didn't take his advice and change the locks. Frank, on the other hand, is avoiding me. He makes it a point to come home when I'm not here, leaving telltale signs of his presence such as a raised toilet seat or a dirty towel on the bathroom floor. He hasn't even surfaced with his weekly party invitations. Maybe he feels bad about hitting me or maybe he's on another binge. Whichever it is, I wish we could talk—the whole reason why I didn't call a locksmith yet. I want Frank to come home because I can't spring divorce papers on him without a warning, but at the same time, I can't go on living in the wake of his turbulence. Maybe I'll give it a couple more days before I call a lawyer and then I'll change the locks.

Come Monday, I was due in make-up at seven a.m. sharp. Scrambling out of the house, I left my script on the kitchen table. Halfway down the driveway, I remembered it and scurried back inside. Flustered and lacking sleep, the few lines I could recall were hazy. How would I survive the day, let alone the next two weeks?

Helene and her golfcart once again greeted me in the studio parking lot. "Good morning, Darlene. Are you ready for day one?"

"I'm a nervous wreck." I noticed a script tucked under her arm as I clutched mine.

"Don't be. Around here, we keep it simple. Whatever happens in front of the camera is just work. Off-camera, Peter's mine and as long as you remember that, you'll be fine."

"I read the script a hundred times," I said with a loud sigh. "But I can't remember my lines and now I'm having a hard time remembering my name."

"I hope you didn't study too much." Helene shoved her script at me as I slid into the seat next to her. "Here's the latest. I marked today's scenes."

"But I studied the lines in this one!" I held my script out in front of me, my stress level soaring.

"Stop fretting, hon. There'll be plenty of time to look it over after we make the rounds." She made a wide U-turn as I tried to keep my sanity in check. "Come on. Let's get you picture perfect."

In between Helene's steady chatter, my hair was restyled and my make-up removed, then reapplied. Lastly, I changed into bell-bottom Levis and a UCLA T-shirt. Overwhelmed, I hovered near Helene despite her never-ending monologue as we made our way to the soundstage.

"Peter has got to be here somewhere." She looked around, but didn't spot him. "Why don't I introduce you to the crew?"

They made me feel welcome, all promising to help me get through the first day with as little pain as possible. I got plenty of advice that morning:

"Don't be afraid to ask questions."

"It's okay to make mistakes."

"Relax and have some fun with it."

"Don't let Peter rattle you. He's a perfectionist."

I was already rattled and I hadn't even seen him. Helene showed me to my dressing room and slipped me a key. "This will be home for the next two weeks. It's not much but make yourself comfortable."

The perfectly square room was small with a brown leather loveseat and miniature coffee table. A white vanity with three drawers and a mirror occupied one corner. The diminutive chair that sat in front of it looked like it belonged to someone under seven.

"Feel free to come here whenever you can." Helene prattled on as I laid my purse in the vanity's bottom drawer. "I'm sure there'll be times you'll want to escape the madness. Now, how about we find that handsome fireman of ours?"

My sweaty palms kept telling me that I didn't belong here. It took all my self-control to keep from dashing off. After managing one long, deep breath, I followed Helene down the hall. She peeked inside a partially open door that had Peter's name on it. "Look who I found."

"I was wondering when you'd get here." Peter sprang to his feet as we stepped inside. "Are you all settled in?"

"I think so." My heart rat-a-tatted like a mobster's machine gun. I was sure everyone within one-hundred feet could hear it.

"Don't forget about us." Helene frowned at Peter, putting her hands on her hips. "Miss Eden may be a little younger, but I have all the experience."

"Don't worry, I'll keep him in line." A man with glasses and a receding hairline, appeared in the doorway as Helene turned to leave.

"These two are trouble," she told him as she walked by. "Call me if you need back-up."

"Darlene, this is our director, Gene Sutherland," Peter introduced us. "We let him think he's in charge around here."

"Don't listen to him." Gene extended his hand. "He'll put all kinds of ideas in your head if you let him."

"He managed to get me here," I muttered.

"Are you nervous?" Gene smiled, knowing full well I was.

"I'm way past nervous. I'm bordering on hysteria."

"It'll get a little easier every day—I promise. By the end of the week, you'll be a pro." He turned to Peter. "See you in five."

We were alone. Peter looked at me for what seemed like a long time. Finally, he smiled.

After a quick table read, mostly for my benefit, I pretty much did whatever Gene told me to even though I found Peter very distracting. Remembering what to say, where to stand, what to do, and how to do it took all my effort. I had no idea that memorizing lines would be the easy part.

Over lunch at Wu's Room, Peter briefed me on what to expect that afternoon. He explained how some days might be longer than others depending on the complexity of what we were filming. If technical problems arose, that could delay things. No matter what, he emphasized, we had a schedule to keep and if that meant working late—that meant working late—Sundays included.

"No more shop-talk," Peter declared once our lo mein arrived. "Let's talk about you."

"I'm a very boring subject. What else do you want to talk about?"

"I want to ask you if you made that call to your lawyer."

I nodded in reply.

"Good!" His face relaxed. "Has Frank gotten the divorce papers yet?"

"I didn't file for a divorce." I felt awkward telling him. "I filed for a legal separation."

"Darlene, you're sending me mixed signals. You said you wanted a divorce. Is your marriage over or not?"

"It's been over for a long time, but I can't just spring a divorce on Frank with no warning. He isn't stable. I don't know what he might do. Once he gets the paperwork, maybe he'll come home. All I want is a chance to talk to him and end it face-to-face."

It was pretty clear that Peter did not understand, but Frank and his precarious mental state worried me. Filing for a separation was the only way I could live with myself.

Tuesday was a little easier and by Wednesday, my confidence was building. I didn't look at the dailies, but Peter did and he liked what he saw.

Thursday morning, we worked on a scene that had Gina and James coming home from a date. Peter still rattled me, but Gene was a prince. He knew I was nervous about James kissing Gina as the scene ended. During rehearsal, he teasingly told Peter to save the kiss for the camera. I tried not to think about it.

That's the other scene I can still play out in my head:

INT. APARTMENT HALLWAY – NIGHT.

James and Gina stop outside her door. She takes a key from her purse and

James pulls it from her hand and unlocks the door. Gina steps inside block-ing the entrance.

GINA

Thank you.

JAMES

That's it? Thank you?

GINA

What is it you want?

JAMES

Let's see. This is our fourth date and you've never once invited me in. I want to see what you're hiding in there.

GINA

Komodo dragons. Hundreds of 'em and they don't like strangers.

JAMES

I'm hardly a stranger so I don't think the Komodos would mind if I come in for a coffee.

Gina nervously walks through the apartment set into the kitchen with James close behind. She glances at the kitchen counter where several bottles of medication stand. (Later, a close-up of the meds would be cut into the scene so viewers would understand that Gina was worried about James noticing them. He doesn't. He is too busy watching her.) Gina turns the water on and reaches for her coffeepot. As she fills the pot, James, standing right behind her, reaches around, takes her wrist and pulls the coffee pot from under the water. With his other hand, he reaches around the other side of her and turns the water off.

JAMES

Forget the coffee.

Gina sets the pot in the sink and looks up at him over her shoulder.

GINA

I thought you wanted—

James turns Gina around to face him.

JAMES
What I really want is this.

For one brief moment, Peter hesitated and those blue eyes gripped me. He was way too close and there was nowhere to go. I couldn't catch my breath as our lips barely touched and then reality replaced fantasy as he pressed his mouth firmly on mine. Overwhelmed by the feel of his fingers in my hair and the scent of that now familiar musky cologne, I curved myself into him, liking the way he made me feel. Peter pulled me even closer. Caught up in the moment, I gave in to him, slipping my arms around his neck while that kiss grew even more intense.

"Cut! Cut!" From somewhere far away, an annoying male voice kept booming. "Cut! Cut!" That damn voice wouldn't go away. "Peter!" he continued to shout. "What the hell, Peter?!"

It was Gene's voice that jolted us back to the present and Peter let me go. We both stood there looking at each other stunned by what took place as we realized we were inside a sound stage, standing in front of a crew. I wanted to fall through the floor and disappear. *Where was a good magician when you needed one? With a simple wave of a wand, we both could have vanished.*

"Take a break!" Gene called out to the crew as he strode over to us, whispering to Peter. "I'm not sure *what* just happened but take Darlene to her dressing room and get back here—on the double. We need to talk."

Peter never let go of me as we left the set. He pushed me inside the little dressing room. "Don't go anywhere."

I sat in front of the vanity, catching my ghostly reflection in the mirror. That kiss had sucked the breath right out of me. No man had ever made my good sense run amok like that. What should have been a private moment turned into a public spectacle, caught on camera no less, and I couldn't blame it all on Peter. I was a willing participant. Shocked at myself for losing control, I never heard Peter come back.

He placed his hands on my shoulders, making me jump. "Are you all right?"

"I'm not sure." I looked from my ghastly reflection to his more composed face.

"I never should have let that happen." He pulled me to my feet. "But

I won't apologize for kissing you. I felt something out there and I'm pretty sure you did, too."

"Yes, I felt something out there." I hesitated for a moment. "And then every thought in my head walked out and stayed out. Peter Chandler, you ought to come with a warning label."

He laughed and wrapped me in his arms. "I've been wanting to kiss you for weeks, but I honestly forgot where we were and I really am sorry."

"Is Gene upset with us?"

"A little upset with me, not you." Peter said with a shrug. "Next time—I "

"Next time?" I gasped and in one-tenth of a second, I sped from shock to panic as I realized we never finished filming the scene. "I can't go back out there!" I pushed away from him. "Everyone must think we're lunatics!"

"I am crazy about you." He grinned. "But I think they've all figured that out by now."

"It's not funny, Peter!' I poked his shoulder.

"Look, honey, it's no secret that you've been going through a rough patch, and I can't hide my feelings anymore. They've all noticed."

"This isn't good, Peter. In case you've forgotten, I'm still legally married."

"I haven't forgotten, but that doesn't change the fact that we have to get back to work. No one wants to be here until midnight. Let's walk out there together and I promise it will be fine. Do you trust me?"

"No, I don't trust you. I'm not sure I trust myself!"

"Even if I promise not to kiss you like that again?"

"Never, ever?"

"As long as the cameras are rolling." He gave me a squeeze. "But once I get you alone, all bets are off."

Chapter Four

*P*eter kissed me right in front of everyone. I don't think he meant to—at least not like that. It just happened and now I can't pull myself together. Getting involved with another man is the worst thing I could possibly do right now. I'm still married to Frank, but tonight when Peter kissed me like that for the second time, my good sense ran out on me again and I kissed him back!

Visitors swarmed the set that Friday. Some looked familiar and some didn't. Peter happened to be in wardrobe when John and Eric Cox, the brothers who produced *Fire in the City*, appeared for the first time that week. They looked like brothers—both slightly built with thinning blonde hair and both sporting rimless glasses. I was sitting off in a corner, talking with Gene about an upcoming scene when they arrived so he introduced us.

"We had to see for ourselves," John spoke first. "You and Peter are the talk of the lot."

"We hear things get pretty hot around here," Eric agreed. "On camera and off."

"Darlene's pretty new to all this." Gene attempted to save me. "We're trying to go easy on her."

"If I were you, Darlene," John spoke up, "I'd be careful."

"Very careful," Eric added with a nod as the two of them walked away.

"I'm so embarrassed." I quietly confessed to Gene once the brothers were out of earshot.

"Don't be—especially around them. The Brothers Grimm are different, but they're good at what they do. They dreamt up *Fire in the City*."

"Did you just call them The Brothers Grimm?" I couldn't help but laugh.

"That's what everyone calls them," he said with a grin.

"Will they be back?"

"Sooner or later. We all hope it's later, much later."

"Gene, I really am sorry about what happened yesterday."

"I know." He reached over and patted my hand. "But this place is like a small town and when things happen, it doesn't take long for word to get around. I'm hardly surprised that people keep coming by to see the girl who stopped production on the James Dakota set."

I idly fanned the pages in the script I was holding. "I hope you weren't too hard on Peter yesterday."

"But it was my job to rein in the fireworks and, to be honest, the way Peter looks at you, I shouldn't have been surprised."

"I just ran into The Brothers Grimm." Helene seemed to pop out of nowhere, but her face was one I welcomed. "Were they looking for Peter?"

"I think they were just looking." Gene shrugged.

"They ought to leave Peter alone." She frowned. "He's doing a terrific job at making them look good." She turned to me, shaking her head. "I heard there was a situation yesterday—very unprofessional. Understandable, but unprofessional. Darlene, you're treading on my territory." She looked at Gene. "Can I borrow Darlene for a quick cup of coffee?"

"Go on." Gene nodded. "I'll send for you when Peter gets back. He shouldn't be much longer."

With steaming Styrofoam cups in hand, Helene and I retreated to my dressing room where we both put our shoeless feet up on the coffee table. Now that I'd gotten used to her, I liked Helene. She'd taken me in and I was grateful.

"About yesterday," she scolded, "may I remind you that this is a business establishment?" She leaned in closer. "But tell me something. Did it happen again—I mean after hours, of course."

"It did," I admitted with a smile. "And thankfully no one yelled 'CUT'!"

"I knew it!" She looked me over with a serious eye. "I knew you passed my test."

"What test?"

"Remember the first day you came here?" Her demeanor softened as she sipped her coffee. "I kissed Peter right in front of you and you never even blinked. I knew right then and there you were good for him. Not as good as I am, of course, but I'm sure we can come to some sort of understanding. Big things are coming his way. He'll need someone. Are you up for the challenge?"

"I don't know." I looked down into my cup. "My mind doesn't seem to work the way it should when it comes to Peter."

"Then don't think about it—let things happen the way they're meant to."

"You sound like my mother. She's a firm believer in fate."

"Smart lady." Helene took another swig of coffee. "Sometimes we have to let life take over and see where it leads."

"And you think that this is one of those times?"

"It could be—if you let it."

"But I hate to drag Peter into the mess I've made. You know my situation."

"A mere technicality." She idly traced her finger around the rim of her cup. "What—or should I ask who—is it you really want, Darlene?"

"I'm not sure." I sighed placing my empty cup on the coffee table. "I feel like I owe something to Frank. He needs help."

"And Peter?"

"Peter scares me." I glanced away from her.

"Why is that?" She picked at the rim of her cup.

"Whenever he's around, I seem to forget who I am."

"And just who are you?"

"I've always been the good girl. You know, play by the rules, dependable—never let my emotions get ahead of me. But when Peter comes along, that good girl disappears and there's a stranger in her place who can't seem to focus."

"You're being too hard on yourself, hon." Helene gave me a motherly smile. "You're in a difficult situation and there are no easy answers, but I know Peter pretty well and something keeps telling me that the two of you—"

"The two of us what?" Peter appeared in the doorway wearing his fireman garb complete with helmet and boots.

"The two of us have a thing for a man in a uniform." She winked at me and stood up. "Peter, if I ever have a fire at my house, I'm calling you instead of the fire department."

"I wouldn't do you much good," he told her.

"Oh, yes, you would." She threw her arms around him. "We'd start an even bigger fire and that first one wouldn't matter!"

An entire week had gone by since I started the separation proceedings and I still hadn't heard from Frank. Anxious to know whether he signed the papers, I called my lawyer who assured me that Frank had gotten the package, but hadn't responded. Maybe he was too drunk to figure it out.

I soon forgot all about Frank, as Peter and I were busy working on that depressing scene where Gina tells James she's dying. There was a lot of dialogue to learn and, to make matters worse, the writers kept changing it. Peter and I rehearsed our lines in his dressing room with an open door so anyone who walked by could see we were really working. There was no sense in fostering any more trouble. A sharp knock on the wooden door-frame broke our concentration.

"Doug!" Peter smiled at the tall, well-dressed man who stood in the doorway. He wore a dark navy-blue suit, with a light blue shirt.

"How nice of you to remember me!!" He paraded into the room and promptly removed his print tie. "I just got out of court and I'm starving. How about lunch—on you—or do you have a previous engagement with Miss Eden?"

"Would it matter if I had?" Peter rolled his eyes.

"Not at all. I think it's high time I met Miss Eden. You do know who I'm talking about—the one who shut down production the other day."

"This is Miss Eden." Peter gestured toward me. "And how did you hear about that? You don't work here."

"Unlike you"—Doug leaned toward Peter—"I get around."

"You mean you get in trouble."

"You're the one in trouble, my friend. I don't think lips ever locked like that on the Barretta set."

"I hope not. Barretta works with a bird."

"For your information, I got a call from Barretta and he wants Miss Eden to replace the bird."

Peter shook his head in exasperation while Doug and I looked each other over. He was handsome in a studious sort of way with his light brown hair cut close and rounded glasses that protected a pair of hazel eyes.

"In case Peter hasn't mentioned me, I'm Doug Lassiter and I think you should know that the bird has already gone to the union with a complaint against you."

Peter closed his script with a loud bang. "Didn't you say something about lunch?"

Doug drove us to a nearby deli where Peter caused a stir when he walked in. "That didn't happen the last time we were here," Doug muttered as we sat down.

"Shows how much you know." Peter picked up a menu.

"I talked to Art and Angie last night." Doug snatched the menu from Peter's hands. "They're getting a big kick out of seeing you on TV."

"That's because they always liked me better." Peter grabbed the menu back from Doug.

"Don't listen to him." Doug looked my way. "My folks take in strays. Peter is no different. He just eats more."

"I gain at least ten pounds every time I go to Michigan."

"Maybe you should start dieting. Art and Angie want you to come home for the holidays."

"That would be nice." Peter smiled, obviously pleased with the invitation. "I'll give them a call."

"So how long have you two known each other?" I asked after we ordered.

"Too long," Peter sighed.

"We met at NYU," Doug elaborated. "Peter was always in trouble and I was always saving him. That's why I studied law. Once Peter decided to be an actor, I figured I better focus on the entertainment end so I could keep an eye on him. I could tell you stories…"

"Exactly why I never mentioned you to Darlene in the first place."

"Admit it." Doug narrowed his eyes. "You were afraid she'd fall for me."

That depressing scene we'd been working on was soon forgotten as I giggled through lunch. I liked Doug Lassiter. He had a warm smile and friendly eyes, not to mention a quick tongue. Through their silly conversation, I gleaned that Doug did indeed work at an entertainment law firm where he represented Peter—his first major client. Meeting Doug got me to thinking. Even though Peter knew almost everything about me, I didn't know the first thing about him.

After lunch, Doug dropped us off at the studio. As he drove away, he rolled his window down and hollered, "Don't worry about the bird, Darlene. I'll make him settle out of court."

On Sunday afternoon, we took advantage of our only day off and headed for Pacific Coast Highway looking forward to a relaxing drive and a walk on the beach.

"You seem awfully quiet," Peter said once we were on our way.

"I've been thinking."

"That sounds like trouble."

"Who are you, Peter Chandler?"

"You know who I am."

"No, I don't. You know everything about me, but you've never told me anything about yourself. You never even mentioned Doug. Meeting him made me wonder what else you haven't told me."

Peter didn't say another word as we drove up the coast. Maybe I had crossed some imaginary line. I wondered where we were going in this relationship—if we even had one.

Peter pulled into the same scenic overlook we'd been to before. Once again, it was deserted. We sat in silence on the little stone wall for several minutes before heading down toward the beach. The water sparkled in the bright sunlight while white-capped waves collided with the glistening black rocks. There was a slight breeze and it was chilly, despite the afternoon sun. I was glad that I had grabbed my jacket.

"I don't want to scare you off, Darlene." Peter finally spoke as we walked along the water's edge.

"Why? Were you a professional hit man before you started acting?"

"Not that I remember." He grinned for the first time. "But I'm not sure what you want to hear."

"I want to hear everything—right from the beginning."

"The beginning was in Brooklyn. We lived there while my father served in the war. He saw action in Japan and came home with a Purple Heart and a pretty good limp. He and my mother started an ad agency on Long Island and eventually we moved there."

"We?"

"I have an older sister, Carmen. She still lives back east and she's married to a doctor. They have two boys." He stopped walking and pulled out his wallet to show me pictures of his nephews. "Bobby is four now and Timmy is two. I haven't been home since Timmy's christening. I'd like to be more than a long-distance uncle, but going home isn't an option right now."

"Why not?"

"Let's just say my dad and I don't quite see eye to eye on things." He put his wallet back in his pocket and we continued our stroll.

"What about your mother? I'm sure she misses you."

"I'm sure she doesn't miss all the arguing. It's better if I'm not there—less stress for her. That's why I lived in Manhattan after college. I worked in the theater for a while—just small roles all off-Broadway. That's where I met Helene. She was in the audience one night and came backstage. She gave me a business card and made me promise to look her up if I ever came to L.A. I owe her everything. She got me the audition for *Fire in the City* and fought hard for me. If it weren't for her, Donny Osmond might be playing James Dakota."

"Donny Osmond?!" I giggled at how silly that sounded.

"Only because Marie wasn't available." Peter took my hand with a grin.

We walked a little further in silence before I asked him how he managed to avoid going to Viet Nam.

'That's a story!" Peter replied. "Doug and I decided to do some white water rafting on the Colorado River during spring break one year. The rapids were really rough—class five if I remember correctly—and the raft we were in hit some rocks. The guide lost control and the whole group of us were flung into the water. We each rode the rapids on our own."

"That sounds terrible," I told him.

"It was pretty scary and when it was over, five out of the eight of us, including the guide, needed surgery."

"How bad was it?" I asked.

"Not as bad as it sounds," he said with a shrug. "But it did keep Doug and me out of the military."

We talked until the sun began its descent and I finally got a sense of this man and he learned that he could trust me.

"Did I cover everything?" Peter wanted to know as the cool night air sent us back toward the car.

"There may be one more thing."

"What's that?" He opened the passenger door.

"Was there ever anyone really special to you?" I slid inside the car.

"I've never been married if that's what you mean." He seemed more relaxed than he had before as he bent over the open car door. "But I did have a major crush on Marilyn Monroe when I was a kid only she never returned my calls."

"Marilyn doesn't count. I'm talking about a real girlfriend."

Peter closed the door and walked around the back of the car. Maybe I had pushed a little too much. He got in on the driver's side, a pensive look on his face. "There was a girl back in New York. I wanted to marry her, but it didn't work out."

"I'm sure she's sorry now."

"It was a long time ago. It doesn't matter anymore. Since then, I haven't been serious about anyone until I met you." He turned the key in the ignition. "Darlene, I'm not sure what to do here. The timing is off. There's so much going on in my life right now, I wasn't planning on throwing a woman in the mix. I have so many commitments, I can't possibly make another one without some serious fallout."

"I'm not asking for a commitment. I'm not ready for that either."

"So where do we go from here?" he asked.

"Dinner might be nice!" I smiled.

When we reported to the studio for our second full week of filming, we picked up where we left off with that dreadfully depressing scene. It took everything out of me and I was glad that I wasn't needed on the set until late in the day. Planning to stay in my dressing room and regroup, I didn't expect a visitor—a young man with a very official-looking package. Maybe, Frank had finally signed those separation papers.

As I opened the oversized envelope, my heart mis-stepped. 'Decree of Divorce' boldly flashed across the top of the paperwork. The words, "irreconcilable differences" shouted from the page.

Stunned, I could hardly breathe as I tried to keep my hands from shaking. *Get yourself together, Darlene. You can't fall apart here.* I stuffed the papers back into the envelope and shoved them inside the top vanity drawer. I would deal with all of this later.

The rest of the day was a struggle. I tried putting the divorce papers out of my mind and concentrate on the job at hand, but the headache that was starting to take over wouldn't let me. My lines wouldn't come out the way they were supposed to. My timing was out of sync. Preoccupied, I couldn't even remember whether I should move to the right or to the left. I must have stepped out of camera range a dozen times. Afterward, Peter followed me to my dressing room.

"Do you want to tell me what's going on?"

I couldn't talk about it, not yet. I needed some time to come to terms with the fact that my marriage had failed miserably. I thought I had already accepted it. I thought I was ready to move on, but the finality of those papers left me numb—except for the pain that crept up the back of my head.

"Darlene." Peter tried again. "Did you even hear what I said?"

"I'm sorry, my head is killing me and I'm really tired."

"Something's off with you, Darlene."

"I told you I have a lousy headache!" My insides felt like they belonged to a stranger, but I didn't mean to snap at him like that.

Weather conditions were not cooperating for the scheduled 'fire' that Tuesday. With a blustery morning, Gene felt it was unsafe for us to film. We switched Tuesday's schedule for Wednesday's, postponing the fire by one day hoping for less wind. Peter and I said very little to each other as the morning progressed. Even the crew noticed the coolness between us. I blamed it on my still aching head.

Peter went to lunch with Doug. I stayed behind so I could read through the divorce papers alone. I'd left them at the studio overnight because I wasn't ready to face them. Alone in my dressing room, I studied each page looking for answers, but found none. Not wanting to prolong the process, I signed the papers and returned them to the envelope hoping it would jar some kind of emotion inside of me. Nothing—just this nasty headache still gaining strength. I laid the envelope on the coffee table and stretched out on the couch hoping to catch a nap.

"Darlene?" Peter knocked. "Are you in there?" The door slowly opened and he came in with a white carryout container. "I brought you something from Wu's."

I slowly sat up holding my head. I couldn't keep this from Peter any longer, but I just couldn't say it so I picked up the envelope and held it out to him. "I got these yesterday."

He put the takeout container on the coffee table and took the envelope I offered. As he leafed through the pages, I watched his face hoping to read his reaction, but there was none.

"You should have told me." He stuffed the paperwork back into the envelope.

"I'm sorry. I just couldn't talk about it." The words gushed out. "I never thought Frank would turn around and do this."

"But you said you wanted a divorce."

"I do, but I was so sure that once he got the separation papers, he would call. All I wanted was a chance to talk."

"To end it or to fix it?" Peter folded his arms and gave me a stern look.

"To end it, of course."

"Are you sure about that?"

"I'm positive."

"Convince me."

"I don't love Frank!" I took in a sharp breath. "I love you."

Chapter Five

*A*m *I possessed?! I told Peter I loved him with the divorce papers still in my hand! At first, I swore there was a ventriloquist in the room, but it was me! The words raced from my mouth before my head could stop them. Worst of all, I meant it. God knows, Peter only complicates things, but it's not like I planned it.*

I should have been a better wife or tried harder to get Frank to see a doctor or, at the very least, gotten him to AA. I guess I wasn't strong enough or tough enough. Maybe it was my fault he started drinking in the first place. I don't know. If only we could have ended it face-to-face, this whole thing might be a little easier. Who am I kidding? Since when was a divorce easy?

Wednesday's weather conditions were ideal for the fire scene. I wasn't sure what to expect as we drove to the back lot in a golfcart, where the technicians were preparing the fire. This fire business bothered me, but I couldn't say why exactly so I kept my uneasy feelings to myself. I didn't expect to find paramedics and an ambulance standing by, which did nothing to alleviate my nervousness. Peter assured me they were always present in case of an emergency.

We only needed a few minutes worth of film: Peter rushing inside the building and carrying me out. The rest would be taped back at the sound-stage where close-ups and dialogue could be captured under more controlled conditions. A few special effects would be added in later.

"We're only going to shoot this once," Gene promised. "We'll work with whatever we get." He nodded my way. "This should be easy for you, Darlene. You're knocked out. You don't have to do anything, but lay there and let Peter do all the work."

After we were both sprayed down with black soot, we took our places inside the empty building and the technicians lit the flame bars. Despite the intense heat, the fire wasn't all that close and there was very little smoke. As Gene instructed, I lay on my mark on the floor. Peter picked me up and then whisked me outside while three cameramen, with handheld cameras, trailed after us.

It didn't take long at all. Once Gene yelled cut, the technicians literally turned off the fire. We hadn't noticed The Brothers Grimm who must have arrived after filming started.

"Peter, you really need a stand-in for this sort of thing." John Cox frowned.

"You get hurt," Eric chimed in, "you shut down production."

"We've had this conversation a thousand times and it never seems to go anywhere, now does it?" Peter brushed soot off his uniform with one hand and, with his other hand pulled me toward the golfcart that would carry us back to the soundstage.

"What's their problem?" I asked. The brothers had once again aroused my curiosity. "Why do they always give you such a hard time?"

"I don't think they get out much and they're a wee bit jealous because sometimes I get the girl." He grabbed a yellow towel that was in the back of the golfcart, rubbed the smudges off my face, and then wiped his hands.

"Be serious.' I took the yellow towel from him. "Why are they always so upset with you?"

"Because I wasn't their first choice for the show. It was Helene who wanted me for the part. I hear she pretty much threatened them with her evil eye."

"They must know by now she was right." After attempting to clean my hands, I tossed the now-dirty towel back into the golfcart and tried to smooth my hair with my fingers. "The brothers may have created *Fire in the City*, but you're the reason they have a hit on their hands."

"It doesn't matter. I just do what I think is right for the show because I'm the one on the firing line. People will credit me if the show's successful or blame me if it's not."

"And who else would take on this kind of dirt?" I said with a grimace as we climbed back into the golfcart.

"Dirt is only one of the pitfalls." Peter rolled his blue eyes and gave a loud sigh.

Saturday was my last day on the set. Gene left an oversized bouquet of sunflowers in my dressing room. Next to them stood a crystal vase overflowing with red, yellow, and white roses. Before I even read the card, I knew the roses were from Peter.

> *Darlene,*
> *Today may be the last day we work together,*
> *but it's only the beginning of our real story.*
> > *Love,*
> > *Peter*

Our final scene ended on an upbeat note as we finished filming early. A bright sun kept the crisp fall air from being too cold, so Peter and I planned a walk on the beach. It was becoming one of our favorite pastimes. Before we headed up Pacific Coast Highway, however, I took my flowers home, setting them on the coffee table in the living room. They brought warmth to the house—something that hadn't been there for a good, long time. I slipped Peter's card in my purse just in case Frank came around. There was no point in making matters any worse.

By the time we arrived at what I now thought of as 'our spot' on the beach north of Malibu, it was late afternoon. As usual, the place was deserted. A dazzling sparkle that hurt our eyes floated across the ocean as the water reflected the bright sun. We wandered in silence until the wind picked up just enough to send us back to the car. As we watched the sunset from the warmth of the Jag, we agreed on dinner—a takeout from Wu's Room and then back to Peter's place.

That evening marked the first time I'd been to the small, fully furnished, ranch-style house in Topanga Canyon that Peter had been renting since he originally moved to L.A. two years ago. Filled with earth tones, it looked like a typical bachelor's dwelling. Inside, there was a small, but efficient kitchen with avocado appliances, an oblong living room with orange shag carpeting and a tiny yellow bathroom sandwiched between two bedrooms—one brown, one rust-colored.

Once the fortune cookies were read, we settled on the couch while Norma Shearer, a.k.a. Marie Antoinette, was about to lose her head. Before long, she also lost her audience as I nestled into Peter's arms. His warm breath caressed my skin as his mouth slid down the side of my neck and then back up again. Really alone for the first time, I welcomed each probing kiss until one after the other, they grew a little more demanding and I was suddenly afraid of my own feelings.

"Peter, wait." I drew back. "I'm not sure I'm ready for this."

"I am," he whispered, his lips on mine.

"Please, Peter." I tried again. "Let's not rush this. I-I need to catch my breath."

"You weren't worried about your breath a minute ago." His eyes narrowed.

"I'm sorry. It's just that whenever I'm with you I always jump in head-first. I never seem to stop and think about what I'm doing."

"Darlene, you picked a fine time to stop and think!" He threw his head back on the couch and closed his eyes.

When Peter took me home that night, he went inside first, making sure nothing was out of place. I followed, stopping in the kitchen long enough to set my purse on the table. "Darlene!" Peter gasped as something caught his eye in the living room. I hurried through the kitchen while a sick feeling filled my stomach.

Mangled sunflowers and crushed roses lay twisted amidst water and shattered glass. My flowers! My beautiful flowers! Horrified, I knelt down and fingered the damaged petals. "How could Frank do this?"

"It's late," Peter gently pulled me to my feet. "We'll come back tomorrow and clean this mess up. Now, get your things."

"Peter—"

"Get your things," he repeated firmly. "There is no way in hell I'm leaving you alone in this house."

"But, Peter—"

"No, buts!" He folded his arms sternly, looking down at me. "The way I see it, you have two choices here: one—you come home with me, or two—I stay here with you. As it stands right now, number two would be a very bad pick because if Frank shows up while I'm here, he won't walk away. So that leaves number one—now, get your things." He noticed my hesitation. "You can sleep in the second bedroom, if that's what you're worried about. It doesn't matter. What matters is getting you out of this house. Now, get your things."

"I'll go to Doug's tonight if you want me to," Peter offered once we were back at his place and he had put my bag in the second bedroom.

"Don't be silly. You shouldn't have to leave your own house." It was after three a.m. We'd been up almost twenty-four hours and we were both exhausted. "It makes no sense for you to drive around the city at this hour because of me."

"Then, let me know if you need anything." He kissed my forehead rather quickly and left me alone. I changed and crawled into bed, planning to get a good night's rest and have a clearer head in the morning. But rest didn't come. Sleep was out of the question. Peter was too close.

I got up, thinking I'd watch TV in the living room. I'd keep the sound low so I wouldn't disturb Peter. He'd probably fallen asleep as soon as his head hit the pillow. The surprise was on me, however, when I found him lying on the couch, among a myriad of blankets, staring at a soundless TV.

"I didn't wake you, did I?" He seemed just as surprised to see me.

"No, I couldn't sleep." I stood there staring at those blue eyes.

"Do you need something?"

"I think I need you." I leaned over letting my lips linger on his. He kissed me back, taking his time, then stopped.

"Let's not start something we can't finish."

Without a word, I slipped off my robe. He slowly looked me over and then gave me one last chance to change my mind. "Are you sure?"

I pushed the blanket aside and climbed on top of him. As Peter pulled the blanket back over us, my lips settled on his with a long deep kiss—a kiss that asked for so much more. It wasn't the first time we kissed like that, but it was the first time I started it.

That night, I gave myself to him in a way that had never happened with Frank. I'd always kept an element of control during our lovemaking—aware of what was happening at all times. With Peter, it was different. Lying against him, thinking no longer mattered as I gave in to a spontaneous passion for the very first time. Every intimate touch and eager kiss aroused us more than the one before. I wanted him and he wanted me. It may have been reckless, but I abandoned myself in his arms and whether I wanted him to or not, Peter Chandler took my breath away—our bodies responding, each to the other, until we'd both had enough.

Later that morning and still on the couch, I woke up relishing the secure feeling his warmth offered until I remembered that I was the one who started it! I'd never, ever done anything like that before! I no sooner told him I wasn't ready and then I just offered myself up! *What in the world is wrong with you, Darlene? Did you misplace your mind? It's those damn blue eyes! There is no other explanation!*

Shocked at what I'd done, I quietly moved away from Peter's grasp. His eyes opened and he pulled me closer with a kiss that stirred me up all over again. I had to look away in order to compose myself.

I sat up, pressing the blanket around me, and I began to babble. "Peter, I don't know what got into me. I couldn't sleep in the other room. Then I thought I'd try the couch, but you were here—"

"I live here, Darlene," he interrupted.

"But I've never been with a man—except Frank, and—"

"Are you having second thoughts?" He interrupted me again.

"I don't know what I'm having," I yammered on trying not to look at him. "Whenever I'm with you, I do things and I feel things I'm not sure I should."

"You came to me, remember?"

"But I never do that sort of thing!"

"And you think I do? Honey, I don't make love to a woman if I don't feel something for her."

"But maybe emotions were running a little too high last night." The words kept spilling out as I left the couch still clutching the blanket. "I feel like I've been on a runaway train these last few weeks. I'm so mixed up about everything and, Peter, you make me crazy. First, I talk to you when I shouldn't; then I walk with you when I shouldn't; then I dance with you when I shouldn't; then I kiss you when I shouldn't—"

"Whoa! Hang on there, Darlene." Peter interrupted me for the third time, slipped on his shorts, and followed me across the room. "Honey, maybe I haven't said it the way I should, but I love you. All those parties we met at? Did you think it was a coincidence that we were always at the same one every single Saturday?"

"Wasn't it?"

"Of course it wasn't. Well, maybe the first one, but after that I made tons of phone calls every week trying to find out which one you were going to be at so I could be there, too. I even got Doug to help me."

"You mean, you were coming to all those parties just to meet me?"

"Darlene, I really thought by the third week you were on to me."

"But there had to be hundreds of girls at those parties. Why would you pick me?"

"Because there we were in Paradise, and you looked so sad. I got curious so I followed you."

"And you broke my pearls."

"Even Paradise isn't perfect." He put his arms around me and laid his forehead against mine. "But after that night, I couldn't stop thinking about you." His lips brushed my cheek, then gently moved across my mouth, and down the side of my neck. "I still can't." I could feel myself giving in to him again, no matter what my head was saying. Maybe I'd regret it later, but for now, I nestled against him and the blanket slipped from my shoulders.

"Let's take this to the bedroom," Peter whispered as he lifted the blanket back over me, all the way to the top of my head. "I'll unwrap you like a present."

"Peter?" Doug startled us as he called from the kitchen. "Are you awake?" He barged into the living room, carrying a small brown bag.

"Hold that thought." Peter sighed as I buried my face in his shoulder, still gripping that blanket.

"Maybe I should have knocked," Doug said, coming to a fast halt.

"Maybe you should have." Peter frowned at him, keeping me close.

"But I never knocked before."

"Maybe you should start."

"But I always come by on Sunday mornings for coffee," Doug protested, holding up the bag. "I brought bagels. Darlene, I'm sorry—I only brought two. I had no idea you were here. I'll share my bagel with you. I know for a fact that Peter won't share his." He stopped, looking a little perplexed, when I didn't answer. "That is Darlene, isn't it?"

"Of course, it's Darlene!" Peter sounded exasperated.

"It's hard to tell with that blanket over her head."

"Will you please leave?!" Peter clenched his teeth.

"Not until I get some coffee and from the looks of things, I'd say you don't have any brewing. Don't mind me. I'll just go in the kitchen and put on a pot. Darlene, do you like regular or decaf?"

"Darlene likes Kona coffee." Peter glared at him. "Maybe you could swim to the islands and get her a cup."

"Someone didn't get enough sleep!" Doug declared as he walked away.

I slowly picked my head up. "Is he gone?"

"For now."

"Does he always walk in like that?"

"He does." Peter sighed. "I obviously made a huge mistake when I gave him a key."

CHAPTER SIX

Sleeping with Peter may not be the smartest thing I've ever done, but I can't seem to help myself. The first time it happened, he caught me off guard! I never meant to do it, but there he was lying on that couch and those blue eyes reeled me in! I never had a chance! After Doug left on Sunday, it happened again and that time, I plunged right in headfirst—never hesitating or questioning what I was doing. As for second thoughts—I don't have any, no matter how many times it's happened. What is wrong with me? Better yet—who am I? The old Darlene would never sleep with a man without giving it some serious consideration or at least a little hesitation. Then again, that 'good girl' didn't know Peter Chandler. He must think I'm easy and, evidently, I am—at least when it comes to him. It's those damn blue eyes, throwing me off-kilter every single time. Either this divorce is playing games with my head or the dynamics of working with Peter simply pushed us together. Maybe I've completely lost my mind. Yep, I think that must be it. Darlene, your mind has skipped out on you.

Peter had been putting in painfully long hours so I thought a quiet Thanksgiving dinner at his place would be perfect. I invited Doug who, holiday or not, was always happy to have a home-cooked meal. I tried not to think about Frank, but, as I was grocery shopping a few days earlier, I could have sworn I glimpsed him in the parking lot. When I turned back to get a second look, he was gone. Who would have ever thought that on Thanksgiving Day, we would be in the middle of a divorce and I would be involved with another man? Marriage meant happily ever after, at least I used to think it did. Instead, I changed the locks to keep my soon-to-be ex-husband out. That way, I could safely work at home during the day and stay with Peter at night. Of course, it was all only temporary until I found a place of my own, but I never imagined that my life would take such a sharp U-turn so quickly.

Thanksgiving morning, I got up early and left Peter sleeping. He'd gotten home late the night before, exhausted. Most nights, we seemed to eat on the fly and since I had pretty much stopped cooking for Frank, it had been a while since I'd put together a big meal—something I actually enjoyed doing. I liked being in the kitchen and I wanted the holiday to be perfect.

I planned a traditional Thanksgiving dinner with a small turkey, complete with stuffing, fresh cranberries made with vodka, and all the customary trimmings. I also decided to bake some dinner rolls and, to top it off, I reluctantly bought a pumpkin pie. As much as I liked to bake, I always fell short—unlike my mother's pies, which were legendary in Naperville, especially her peach pie. One day, I'd ask mom for some pointers. Until then, store-bought was my safest bet.

I treated myself to a cup of coffee before I got started. The cranberry sauce was already done and the stuffing put together, but I had to make sure that the turkey was in the oven on time so we could eat at a decent hour. After that, I started on the dinner rolls. The dough needed a little extra time to rise.

I was kneading it in a large mixing bowl when Doug came by a little after noon toting a bottle of wine for dinner and a colorful autumn bouquet for me.

"Smells good in here," Doug said. "You never told me you were related to Betty Crocker."

"A distant cousin of mine," I replied while washing the flour off my hands. I took the bouquet from him and laid it in the sink. "Thank you, but you didn't have to bring me flowers."

"You deserve a whole florist shop for putting up with Peter. Where is the old firefighter, anyway?"

"He's not up yet." I searched in the cupboard for a vase. "He worked half the night."

"Won't he have a couple of weeks off at Christmas?" Doug opened another cupboard door and pulled out a tall beer glass.

"That's what he tells me." I continued rummaging through the kitchen cabinets.

"And have you made any plans?" Doug filled the beer glass with water.

"We haven't had much time to talk about it." I tried the cabinet under the sink. "But I really need to go home and see my mother for a few days.

Peter mentioned something about going to Michigan to see your folks and I thought maybe he might want to see his family."

"The last thing Peter needs right now is a visit to Long Island." Doug shoved the flowers inside the beer glass. "I wouldn't press it if I were you."

"Do you always put flowers in beer glasses?" I watched as he set it on the table.

"It never came up before." Doug shrugged, helping himself to a bottle of beer from the refrigerator. "But I guess things have changed a bit since Peter has a lady in his life."

"What about you?" I checked on the turkey before returning to the dough. "Is there a lady hiding somewhere in your life?"

"Nope." He searched the junk drawer and spotted an opener.

"Why not? A handsome lawyer like you? I'd think pretty girls would be lined up in droves waiting to go out with you."

"Pretty girls can be a lot of trouble." Doug's voice held a hint of bitterness as he popped off the bottle cap. "I know. I married one."

"What happened?"

"I caught her cheating in the backseat of my car and now I prefer the single life."

"She must have been an idiot." I punched down the dough and then covered it with a clean dishtowel before washing my hands again. "I was the idiot." He paused to take a swig before claiming a seat at the table. "Peter warned me about her, but I wouldn't listen. I was in love. Six months later, she was loving someone else. I was minus a bride and a car."

"So now you've given up on women?" I sat down across from him, ready for a break before the potatoes needed peeling.

"Pretty much and I like it that way."

There was something about Doug that made him easy to talk to. He was good company. Some woman, somewhere, was sure to turn him around. As we continued to talk, I boiled a pot of salted water and dropped the now-peeled potatoes in while keeping an eye on the clock, wondering how long Peter was going to sleep. It was close to two-thirty when we finally heard the bedroom door open and Peter wandered into the kitchen wearing only his jeans.

"Darlene, why did you let me sleep so late?"

"We were having fun without you," Doug teased, but he looked at Peter with a serious eye. "You should have stayed in bed a few more minutes. Darlene was about to run off with me."

"People don't run off with you," Peter said with a grin. "They run from you." He turned to me. "Do I have time to shower before dinner?"

"If you make it quick."

"Don't be surprised if we're gone when you get back," Doug called after him. Once the bathroom door closed, Doug gave a loud sigh. "Peter looks terrible. If they remake *Night of the Living Dead*, he could play the lead zombie and he wouldn't need any make-up."

Our quiet dinner went well and my stuffing garnered rave reviews. It was my mother's recipe and the first time I had tried to make it. We all agreed that the dried fruit mix I added was the game changer and of course, the vodka-laced cranberries were a major hit. The store-bought pumpkin pie was only ok, but neither Peter nor Doug complained, especially after I served it with a healthy dose of fresh whipped cream. The ringing telephone interrupted our dessert. It was Peter's sister, Carmen, and after a brief conversation, he went for the Tylenol.

"You ok?" Doug asked.

"Let's just say, it's a good thing I live in California and the rest of the Chandlers live in New York—my sister included." Peter dismissed the subject. He seemed withdrawn as the three of us sat at the table with our pumpkin pie. This was not how I wanted our holiday to end.

"I should call Art and Angie," Doug said as he pulled the phone with its long cord to the kitchen table. As soon as his folks found out he was at Peter's, they wanted to talk to him. Doug held out the receiver. "Art and Angie are on the line for you."

That brought a genuine smile to Peter's face. "Hi, Mom. Hi, Pop." I was surprised at how easy their conversation flowed as Peter grew more animated. He assured them he wasn't working too hard, no matter what Doug said, and promised to see them over the holidays.

"And if it's okay, I'd like to bring Darlene so you can meet her."

"Great!" he continued. "I'll call you as soon as we have our plans firmed up."

Doug seemed to know just what to do to make things right and I was grateful to him. By the time they hung up, Peter's mood had lightened considerably.

"Do you want to call your mother?" Peter pushed the phone toward me.

"No, she's out of town with friends. I talked to her last week."

"And you didn't tell her what's been going on, did you?"

"Not yet, but I will."

I had been putting off that call to my mother for a while now. How would I tell her about the muddled mess I'd made of things? We'd barely talked these past few months, always keeping our conversations brief—just enough time to let her know I was okay and to hear that she was okay. I didn't want her worrying. And what do I say to Sydney? She must have seen something I missed because she had told me a hundred times not to marry Frank. And then there was Peter. How could I ever explain Peter to them when I can't explain him to me! I had never even told mom or Sydney about filming the show. That certainly would have started a conversation I wasn't ready to have.

Shortly after the holiday, I took my name off the lease of the house that Frank and I had been renting, and moved into an apartment about a half mile from Peter's place. It was small, but partially furnished with two bedrooms and one bath. The balcony had a street view and there was enough room for a bistro-type table and two chairs. The galley kitchen was a little cramped, but the dining area was roomy and held a wooden table with four chairs. There was a blue plaid couch in the living room, with a pine end table on either side and a silver pole lamp that needed brighter bulbs. In front of the couch sat a narrow coffee table that was quickly littered with my latest work projects. A console television stood against the opposite wall. It certainly wasn't the Taj Mahal, but it fit my budget and I was determined to make it as cozy as possible. It would just take a little time.

Now that I'd moved, I had no choice but to tell my mother and Sydney about the divorce. There was no getting around it anymore, but I was having a hard time making myself call them—especially my mother. When all the trouble began between Frank and me, I hadn't kept in touch the way I should have. I didn't want them to know how my marriage had collapsed and how I had totally failed as a wife. Trying to figure out exactly what to say to them kept me up at night.

I wondered whether Frank would continue paying the rent for the house we lived in—something I had always done—or maybe he'd leave the premises. If he left, I hoped he would have somewhere to go. My head told me that Frank was no longer my problem, but my conscience kept telling me that I could have done more. I should have been a better wife, or at least a more loyal one, but after Frank hit me, it changed everything.

The first Sunday I was in the apartment, I cooked dinner for Peter and I also invited Doug, who was quickly becoming one of my favorite people. He made me laugh and, even though he was technically Peter's friend, I knew he'd be there for me if I needed him. Still living among boxes, I made sure that my kitchen was functioning, complete with a crockpot and other wedding gifts that I knew Frank would never use.

"Darlene, are you sure you don't have any sisters at home?" Doug asked over homemade brownies and ice cream.

"My mother's single."

"Speaking of your mother, you haven't talked to her yet, have you?" Peter threw me a frown and I shook my head in reply.

"How about if we clean up while you call her?" Doug offered.

There was a telephone in my bedroom, but I opted to use the one next to the couch in the living area. I thought talking to Sydney would be easiest so I dialed her number first and, at the same time, I prayed she wouldn't be home. Unfortunately, she was. The moment she said 'hello,' I felt tears welling up. I'd rehearsed the words over and over in my mind a million times, but now I couldn't recall one of them.

"Hey Syd!" I braced myself for the conversation to come. "I'm sorry I've been so bad at keeping in touch, but a lot has been happening here."

"Are you okay?" she asked.

"I am now," I answered. "And I wanted to let you know that I moved. I have a new address and phone number."

"When did you and Frank move?"

"*We* didn't. *I* moved."

"Where's Frank?"

"I'm not sure. We're not together anymore."

"Not together?!" she gasped. "What do you mean not together?"

I told her everything—even the part about Frank hitting me. The only detail I left out was Peter.

"Are you sure you're all right, Darlene?"

"Yeah, now that things are a little more settled, I'm fine, but it was kind of rough going for a while there."

"Have you thought about coming back to New York? You could stay with me. It would be like old times. Maybe you could even get your job back. I can ask around tomorrow morning—"

"No, Syd," I interrupted her. "I'm not coming back to New York."

"Why? If you're not with Frank, what's keeping you in L.A.?"

I hadn't intended to tell her about Peter just yet, but my silence answered for me.

"You're seeing someone, aren't you?" she asked.

"Yes, but it all happened so fast, I didn't want to say anything yet."

"I knew it!" she declared. "Come on, Darlene. It's me, Syd! Spill it and start with his name."

I hesitated for just a second before answering. "His name is Peter Chandler."

"No, Darlene. That's the guy from *Fire in the City*."

"Yep, that would be Peter." I nervously twisted the phone cord with my fingers.

"Are you sure we're talking about the same Peter Chandler here?"

"Believe me, Syd, there's only one."

"Darlene, what are you thinking?! An actor?!"

"I know how it sounds, but I didn't go looking for it."

"Come on, Darlene! Your divorce isn't even final and you take up with an actor, no less?!"

"I tried to put on the brakes," I said in my defense. "I honestly tried, but slow doesn't work when it comes to Peter."

"How serious is this between the two of you?"

"Dead serious," I replied and then went on to tell Sydney the whole story, starting with how we met.

"Did you even hear yourself?" Sydney demanded. "You met an actor at a party, worked with him for two weeks, and now you're an item?"

"Don't ask me to explain it because I can't."

"I can," she said with a sigh. "The hamster in charge of your brain is on vacation."

My mother was next. As I dialed the phone for the second time that evening, my stomach tightened, but as soon as I heard Mom's voice, I ached for her arms. She knew something was up, so I took a deep breath letting it all out at once. I told her everything I had just told Sydney, except for the part about Frank hitting me, and, of course, I left out Peter. I didn't give her a chance to say one word. When I finally finished, there was a moment of silence and then she quietly asked, "Has Frank ever hurt you?"

"No," I lied.

"Thank God." She breathed a loud sigh of relief. "I knew something wasn't right. I kept hearing it in your voice, but I could tell you didn't want to talk so I didn't press it, but honey, I've been worried sick about you."

"It's all over now and I'm fine."

"Why don't you come home for a while? Let me take care of you."

"I can't. Not now."

"Why not?" she demanded, then her voice changed. "What aren't you telling me, Darlene?"

"Trust me, Mom. I need to handle things my own way. I just wanted you to know." How could I explain leaving Frank and meeting Peter in the same conversation? It certainly had not gone well with Sydney.

"Darlene, what's going on with you?"

"Nothing, Mom. Please don't worry. I promise you, I'm fine."

"Darlene, you're keeping something from me. Maybe I need to come out there."

"No. There's nothing you can do. I'm ok. I'll call you next week and I'll see you at Christmas."

I felt kind of bad leaving our conversation on such a sour note, but I couldn't bring myself to tell her about Peter. I knew the day would come, but not now. Sydney was pretty sure I had lost my mind. I was beginning to wonder if she might be right, but when I walked back into the kitchen that evening, I took one look at Peter and knew that, trouble or not, we were somehow connected.

In a very short time, Peter Chandler had settled himself into my very bones and there was no undoing it. Even if I tried, I would never find a way to get him out of my system—whatever the future held. But was that a good thing or a bad thing? I couldn't decide. *Explain that to your mother, Darlene!*

Chapter Seven

I love my apartment even though Peter can't quite understand why I didn't move in with him. He clearly would have preferred it that way, but he respects my decision. I tried to explain that I really need my own space—especially with the divorce still pending. I worry about publicity. The last thing Peter needs right now is bad press because of me so I try my best to stay in the background.

Fire in the City is turning into a huge success, much bigger than even the brothers had hoped. In reality, it's Peter's achievement. He's the one people want. In between filming the show, reporters covet interviews, photographers demand pictures, fans ask for autographs. He's become a talk show favorite. There are agents and publicists to deal with. I've been wanting to see that new Jack Nicholson movie, One Flew Over the Cuckoo's Nest, *but going out with Peter is difficult. People won't leave him alone.*

We've fallen into a routine of sorts. While Peter is at the studio, I work at home, currently tackling a large assignment that involves rewriting a five-volume training manual for the telephone company. Most evenings we spend together either at my place or his. With his long work hours and so many other demands on his time, I usually end up with the 'tired' Peter. I don't mind, but I can see that all this bedlam is wearing on him. The holiday break won't come soon enough.

As Christmas drew near, Peter's schedule grew even more hectic. The relentless demands of the series forced him to keep a frantic pace. He squeezed in interviews and photo sessions during breaks in filming. Merv Griffin and Johnny Carson couldn't get enough of him. Mike Douglas wanted him to co-host his show, but at the moment, flying to Philadelphia for a week was out of the question. Audience reaction was wildly enthusiastic, but the dramatic change in lifestyle was taking its toll. Peter was exhausted.

Sometimes, his mother or his sister called. They only added tension to the tiredness. He never mentioned their conversations, but as soon as he hung up, he'd complain of a headache and go searching for Tylenol. It got to the point where I made sure that if I was there, I answered the phone. If Joyce or Carmen was on the line, I'd simply tell them that Peter wasn't home—whether he was or not. I was sure they knew better, but I didn't care. I was the one that had to deal with the fallout after they hung up. I was the one worrying about him. Peter always called them back the next day from the studio. That way, he wouldn't have a lot of time to talk. By evening, their conversations would be mostly forgotten.

Publicly, Peter handled himself well. His keen sense of humor always shone through. He delighted reporters with funny stories, and charmed photographers with his intriguing blue eyes. If he'd had time to travel, he could have been booked for weeks. Of course, The Brothers Grimm encouraged all of this no matter the cost to Peter. It was great publicity for their show. They grew irritated with him if he declined an invitation, but Peter seemed to know when he'd had enough. Even when he pushed himself, if Peter thought he wouldn't be at his best, he simply said no, whether the brothers liked it or not.

Privately, I saw a different Peter. When we were alone, he seemed overwhelmed by all the attention. He was frustrated by the lack of privacy when we went out. Wu's Room had become our safe place since no one really bothered us there, but our 'dates' became fewer and fewer. If I didn't cook, takeouts became the norm. My biggest concern was the utter exhaustion. Many nights, he'd come home after work and fall asleep on the couch, sometimes too tired to eat. I especially worried when I knew they were filming fires. Being tired on those days could be disastrous.

"Darlene, this is all so unfair to you," he told me one night after yet another long day at the studio. We had just finished a very late dinner and were cleaning up the kitchen.

"What's unfair to me?" I asked as I closed the dishwasher.

"All of it." He leaned against the counter, his arms folded. "You deserve better than a guy whose life is spiraling out of control at warp speed. None of this is normal, Darlene. We can't go anywhere or do anything without a million and one interruptions, and to be honest, even if I could take you somewhere, I'm too damn tired to do it. Some days, I feel like I'm barely hanging on."

"Then hang on to me." I slipped my arms around his neck. "I've got you."

"But you shouldn't have to." He laid his forehead against mine. "You deserve better."

"But you are all I want," I told him. "Even if you come with a few minor glitches."

"Is that what you call it?" He suppressed a smile. "A few minor glitches?"

"Problems? Complications? Snags? Obstacles? You pick. I don't care. All I know is I love you, Peter Chandler, whatever it is you come with."

The studio was planning a huge holiday party at the Chataeu Marmont before Christmas. Peter repeatedly told me that he had no interest in going, but the brothers were pressuring him, so during one of our Sunday walks on the beach, he asked me to go with him. I knew that coming out as a couple would happen eventually, but I was hoping my divorce would be final first.

"Do you really think we should?" My stomach lurched at the thought of being seen with Peter at such a public affair.

"Why not?" He stopped walking as the wind picked up. "Everyone at the studio knows anyway."

"But my divorce is still pending." I pushed the hair out of my face. "And, as many times as you've been asked, you haven't ever given anyone a straight answer about us."

"Maybe it's time I did." He took my hand and we continued walking despite the chilly air that the wind brought in. "Look, honey, I never talk about you in an interview, because I know you don't want me to, but maybe we should officially meet the rest of the world."

Meeting the world wasn't important to me, but Peter had a sixth sense about the media. This seemed important to him, so I had to trust his judgment. If he thought we should go public with our relationship, then that's what we'd do. It wouldn't be the last time I deferred to Peter when it came to the press. Nor would it be the last time I would have to steady my nerves and convince myself we were doing the right thing.

The holiday party was a formal affair so with Helene's help I bought a new floor-length, black dress with silver thread running through it, causing it to shimmer in the light. It was sleek-looking, yet festive, with a turtleneck and long sleeves that buttoned at the wrist. Helene said it reminded her of some up-and-coming designer named Armani. I had no idea who she was talking about, but I took her word for it.

I went to Peter's place late that Saturday afternoon to get ready as a car was picking us up there. He was still at work so I put my things in the second bedroom where I would be out of his way once he got home. He didn't get there until six-thirty. "Darlene?" He dashed by not stopping to look. "Are you in there?"

"Yes, and you're late!"

"I only need a few minutes to shower and change. Are you almost ready?"

"Just about."

I heard the water turn on in the shower. In less than twenty minutes, Peter emerged in a dark suit looking like magazine material with hardly any effort. I, on the other hand, had spent over an hour on hair and make-up alone, and was still not satisfied with the end result. As I unhooked a locket my mother had given me, Peter knocked on the doorframe. "All set?"

"As soon as I put this on."

He stepped inside the bedroom and I noticed a small blue box in his hand. "I was hoping you'd wear these tonight."

I laid my locket on the dresser and opened the blue box. Inside was a single strand of Mikimoto pearls that made me gasp. I slipped them around my neck and Peter fastened them. They looked elegant against my black dress. "They're beautiful, but—!"

"No buts," Peter interrupted me as he looked over my shoulder with a satisfied smile. "Just replacing the old ones."

As we stepped out of the car in front of the Chateau Marmont, cameras flashed like strobe lights, momentarily blinding us. Clutching the small black bag I carried, I squinted at the hotel entrance, which seemed awfully far away. Reporters and photographers converged on us. Different voices called Peter's name. His hand tightened around mine as he kept moving forward, smiling, and talking all the way, but I couldn't make out all of the words because of the noise. It took forever to reach the doorway, but once inside, things were much quieter.

"Why didn't you warn me that we would be bombarded like that?!" I tried catching my breath.

"I knew the press would be here for some publicity shots, but I had no idea it would be like that!"

"Peter, I hope this wasn't a mistake." I was having doubts again.

"Honey, I love you. There's no mistake about that, and tonight, I don't care who knows." He put his arm around me and we headed to the ballroom. After a few deep breaths, I said a silent prayer to St. Elmo because I felt like one of his sailors who was lost at sea.

The Chateau was a holiday delight—decorated with oversized Christmas trees, life-size toy soldiers, and brightly wrapped boxes with enormous bows. A model train weaved in and out among the trees, while an intricate gingerbread house, complete with little men, sat in the center of each dinner table. Several large wreaths decorated the walls and huge silver bells hung from the ceiling. The waiters and waitresses wore red and white uniforms topped off by Santa hats as a band softly played holiday tunes. The festive atmosphere did little to instill the Christmas spirit in me, but I was happy to see Helene waving when she saw us walk in.

Dressed in a chic red pantsuit with shiny black patent leather heels, she wasted no time throwing her arms around Peter and kissing him squarely on the lips. "Darling, how about if I borrow one of those Santa hats for later?"

"How much later?" Peter grinned good-naturedly.

"I was thinking Christmas Eve at my place. You could come down the chimney and be a naughty Santa."

"Santa isn't supposed to be naughty." Peter gave her a serious look.

"My kind of Santa lights up the tree without plugging it in." Helene ran her fingers through his curls and gave him a wink. If you know what I mean."

She took Peter by the hand and led us to a table where Gene Sutherland was already seated with his red-headed wife, Leeanne. I hadn't met her before, but she looked older than Gene and I sensed something off between the two of them. Maybe it had something to do with the four empty martini glasses sitting in front of her, but I couldn't be sure. Even worse, The

Brothers Grimm, along with their platinum blond dates for the evening, rounded out the dinner table. The brothers grew grimmer once we arrived and their ladies took an obvious interest in Peter. I was beginning to see why he hadn't wanted to come here in the first place. Christmas party? It was more like a holiday hazard. And the night was still young.

After dinner and a few more martinis, Gene and Leeanne went home. Neither seemed very social and I found that odd. Gene had always been so pleasant at the studio. The Brothers Grimm took their dates to the dance floor while Peter was asked to speak with one of the few reporters who were allowed inside. It seemed to me he was always working, but that left Helene and me alone at the table with a few minutes to catch up.

"Things look like they're going well between the two of you," she commented as Peter left the table. "But I have to admit I was a little concerned when I heard you were getting your own place."

"I couldn't stay with Peter indefinitely." I kept an eye on him as he made his way across the room.

"That's where we're different, hon. I wouldn't let him out of my sight."

"I just need my own place. It's got nothing to do with how I feel about Peter." He disappeared as a group of glamour girls swarmed him.

"So how do you feel exactly?" Helene followed my gaze. "Last time we talked, you weren't so sure."

"I feel a little awkward," I admitted as my insecurities surfaced.

"Are you worried about other women?"

"That plus a hundred other things."

"Like what?" she asked.

"For starters, I'm technically still married yet here I am with Peter. He seems to think it's okay, but I'm not all that comfortable with it and to tell you the truth, Helene, I'm not even sure what he sees in me. The women he knows are gorgeous. You see them, and we both know, I can't compete with all of that."

"Gorgeous women are everywhere—especially out here." Helene nodded in their direction. "But I don't think you have anything to worry about. Peter never looks at them the way he looks at you."

I wanted to believe her, but deep down I wondered how long I could really keep Peter's interest. I hadn't thought about it before, but where would we be in six months or a year? Would it be only a matter of time before he moved on with someone else—someone who could hold his attention? Was I enough to keep him satisfied for the long haul or just a passing fancy? I tried shaking off the doubts. At least for tonight, he was mine. When he finally returned, we moved to the dance floor and flashbulbs popped.

"Peter," I whispered. "They're taking our picture again."

"They can take all the pictures they want." He pulled me a little closer. This was just part of the job to him and he was so at ease with it. Peter could definitely work a room, but I was more the wallflower, shrinking-violet type and all that attention made me nervous. I still felt uneasy, but I closed my eyes, laid my head against him, and let him lead.

As our dance ended, another reporter tapped Peter on the shoulder. "Could I have a word with you?"

"Only if the lady doesn't mind." Peter looked at me.

"Go ahead. I think I'll go find the restroom."

"You have five minutes." I heard Peter telling the man as I went back to the dinner table to retrieve my purse.

Helene was just returning from the ladies' room herself. "It's at the top of the stairs. Come on, I'll show you. It's kind of stuffy in here anyway."

"What's with Gene and Leeanne?" I asked her as we walked together.

"Nothing good," she replied. "Some women marry a man for a lifestyle they want. I'm pretty sure Leeanne went after Gene because he's a success-ful television director."

"How long have they been married?"

"Four years I think, but Gene's not moving up the ladder fast enough for her."

"That's too bad. Gene is an awfully nice guy."

"Exactly who the Leeannes in this world go after," Helene replied as we climbed a set of winding stairs. "Because nice guys, like Gene, are too nice to send those vampires packing. I never liked Leeanne and I certainly never wanted Peter to end up with someone like her. I'm glad you came along when you did."

"I'm glad you approve." I grinned as we walked toward the ladies' room.

"I don't exactly approve," she said with a sigh. "I did see Peter first, if you remember, and I have much more experience with men. It comes with age, you know."

It suddenly occurred to me that she was alone. "Why didn't you bring a date tonight?"

"I thought we were sharing Peter."

"We can always share Peter, but don't you have any other gentlemen callers?"

"Listen, honey, after being married to a magician, a deadbeat, and a doctor, I'm through with men—except for Peter, of course."

"Why? What happened?"

"The magician liked to disappear with his assistant and the deadbeat bounced one too many checks. He ended up in the big house."

"What about the doctor?"

She slipped her arm around me and smiled. "He decided he liked nurses—male nurses."

Despite her unlucky love life, I felt fortunate that she had taken me under her wing. She was my lifeline when it came to adapting to Peter's world. I was a fish out of water as they say, and Helene always seemed to point me in the right direction. Whether she did it for me or for Peter, I wasn't quite sure, but either way I was glad she was there.

On our way back to the ballroom, Helene descended the stairs first and I followed. Halfway down, I noticed several reporters and photographers, who had been outside the hotel earlier, converging at the bottom of the stairs. "There she is!" one voice shouted and I turned in that direction.

"Mrs. Donahue!" a second voice called out. "Is it true Peter Chandler broke up your marriage?"

"N-no!" I shook my head confused. Flashbulbs were going off again, making it hard to see.

"Come on fellas!" Helene tried. "Leave her alone."

They ignored her and continued barraging me with questions. "Mrs. Donahue? You're still Mrs. Donahue, isn't that right?"

"You people are not supposed to be inside the hotel!" Helene shouted over them. "If you don't leave, I'll get security."

They paid no attention to her, but kept on. "Is it true you started seeing Peter Chandler while you were still living with your husband?"

"Were you sleeping with both of them?"

"Did your husband file for divorce because of your affair?"

"Did you even want the divorce?"

Helene disappeared. Where had she gone? It was my worst nightmare come true. All this bad publicity for Peter because of me. I took a few steps back up the stairs desperately trying to find Helene. I felt under attack as their callous questions continued and their cameras flashed nonstop.

"Tell us about your love triangle, Mrs. Donahue!"

"There must be something you can say about your marriage and your affair!"

"How long were you with Peter Chandler before your husband realized that you were cheating?"

"Did you leave your husband for Peter Chandler, Mrs. Donahue, or did your husband leave you first?"

I panicked, my heart racing. I didn't want to be here in the first place, but Peter insisted, and now, this brazen bunch was badgering me with personal questions I found disturbing. I scanned the area hoping there might be somewhere I could go to get away from them, but the only place I saw was the ladies' room, a good thirty feet away. As I turned in that direction, I stopped at the sound of Peter's voice.

"Darlene is my business, not yours!!" He was making his way to the stairs with Helene close behind, a worried look on her face. There was an entourage of security behind her. They looked like secret service agents in their black suits. She must have gone back to the ballroom for them.

"Outside now!" a guard bellowed above the din. "You don't belong in here!" The security men surrounded the pack of reporters, forcing them toward the entrance.

Shaken, I watched as Peter took the stairs two at a time, while Helene remained below with the security detail. "I'm so sorry!" I said as the tears welled up in my eyes when he reached me. "This could be so bad for you and it's all my fault."

"This is not your fault," Peter said firmly, slipping his arms around me. "They should have come to me."

"But Peter, they said some terrible things."

"I know, but pull yourself together, honey," he whispered. "We have an audience." The ballroom had emptied out and the party was now in the lobby, where everyone was trying to see what happened.

I quickly swiped at my tears and, at the same time, tried to keep my hands from trembling. "What do you think they'll say?"

"Whatever they want." He tucked my arm in his and we descended the stairs. "I love you, Darlene, and I honestly don't care what the rest of the world thinks." He abruptly stopped halfway down as something new struck him. "On second thought, there may be someone we need to worry about."

"Who's that?" I sniffed.

"Your mother! Maybe you should call her before her next trip to the grocery store. She may not appreciate reading the tabloids when they say that her daughter has taken up with some shady actor."

Like it or not, Peter had a point.

CHAPTER EIGHT

Peter was right after all. Since the Christmas party, we've had very little bad press, which mostly went unnoticed. We are now an official couple privately and publicly—although the 'public' part terrifies me. My mother is not convinced that I'm making rational decisions. I'm hoping that once she actually meets Peter, she'll understand. Thank goodness Christmas hiatus is here and he's already had a few days off. Even though it's last minute, we firmed up our holiday plans agreeing to spend three days, starting tomorrow, Christmas Eve, in Naperville with my mother. Then we're off to Michigan for another three days to see the Lassiters. Peter never once mentioned anything about visiting his own family. His parents aren't getting any younger and he needs to straighten out whatever's wrong while he still can. Every time I mention it, however, he promises to think about it, but that's as far as we get.

Since we're flying out in the morning, Peter and I exchanged gifts tonight. Out of everything I bought him, he especially liked the picture I gave him. Lucky for me, Helene pulled a few strings with some of the photographers she knew and got a picture of Peter and me dancing at the holiday party. I placed it in a silver frame with the words 'Every dance belongs to you' etched on it. It was nothing, however, compared to the pearl earrings that Peter gave me to match my necklace. I hear Mikimoto just opened a new store in New York. I'd love to pay him a visit sometime.

Unlike the stir that Peter caused at LAX, we went pretty much unnoticed as we disembarked at O'Hare. There was no snow on the ground, but the Windy City was awfully cold. We only wore light jackets so we welcomed the warm car that awaited us at the airport.

"You've been awfully quiet," I said to Peter once we settled inside the car. "Is something bothering you?"

"I keep thinking about whether I should go home for a day or two." Peter slipped his arm around me.

"I think you should."

Glancing at his watch, he quickly changed the subject as he always did when it came to visiting his folks. "How long does it take to get to your mother's house from here?"

"About forty minutes. Why? You're not worried about meeting my mother, are you?"

"Maybe, a little."

"You meet people all the time." I couldn't believe he was rattled.

"I don't meet your mother all the time and I'm already starting out on her negative side."

When our car pulled up in front of the house, a flood of memories rushed through me. This is the place where I grew up and for one quick second, I longed to be that carefree little girl again—playing in the backyard, doing homework in the living room, cooking with mom in the kitchen. So many happy memories inside that small red brick bungalow with its over-sized porch. A bright red awning hung over two chairs and a table, now covered by a heavy tan tarp for the winter. Mom, in a green sweater and jeans, must have been watching for us because she opened the front door just as we got out of the car.

"Go see your mother," Peter told me. "I'll take care of this."

I didn't realize how much I'd missed her until that moment. As we clung to each other in silence, I breathed in her signature scent—Chanel No. 5—and my mind drifted back to an earlier time when mom could magically kiss away each hurt and make everything better. For one brief instant, I let myself be her little girl again. I forgot the time; I forgot the cold; I even forgot about Peter who had paid the driver and was now shivering behind us with the luggage. His thin jacket was not doing a good job of keeping him warm.

He tapped me on the shoulder. "Darlene, it's a little chilly out here."

"Come on inside where it's warm." Mom kept one arm around me and with her free hand pushed open the front door. Home had never looked so good as we were greeted by mixed aromas that wafted from the kitchen. The living room was exactly as I remembered it—small and cozy with an overstuffed gray couch and a matching recliner. Her glass coffee table was covered with books and magazines—several of which had pictures of Peter. Two more stacks of books sat on an end table to the left of the couch. A small artificial Christmas tree graced the front window. patiently waiting to be lit up. The sight of the old ornaments made me think about the Christmases Mom and I shared in this house. Even though it was only the two of us, our home was always filled with love and an overabundance of laughter.

"Darlene, I'm so glad you're finally here." Mom took my face in her hands. "I've been so worried about you. Tell me how you are—and be honest."

"I'm fine, Mom." I wriggled away from her and slipped off my jacket. I took a good look at her while she took a good look at me. Mom never changed. Maybe her hair was a little grayer, but it still framed her face in a blunt cut that fell just below her ears. She always carried herself with a certain grace that I attributed to her many years spent standing in a classroom. Rarely did anything upset her, and her dark brown eyes were forever on the prowl for fun. How had I shut her out for so long? Those days were over, I promised myself. Never, ever again!

"I'd know you anywhere, Peter Chandler!" She held her hand out to him with a smile.

"It's good to finally meet you, Mrs. Wells."

"Call me Ruth," she told him. "I've been watching you on TV and I feel like I already know you."

"I hope you don't believe everything you see on TV."

"I don't, but I do like your show and you make a fine fireman."

"I try."

"I hope you're hungry," she said. "I've got all of Darlene's favorites in the kitchen."

"Did you make a peach pie?" I asked hopefully.

"That's for Christmas." She shook her head. "Tonight, it's strawberry cheesecake."

After a huge meal that started off with homemade chicken soup, Mom served up her strawberry cheesecake. I couldn't stop smiling as we sat around the table together. Conversation between the three of us flowed easily. Mom seemed to like Peter well enough, but then again, mostly everyone did. At least, they were no longer strangers. After dessert, Peter and I cleared the table, while Mom turned the Christmas tree lights on and then we took our coffee into the living room. Being with my mother revitalized me. I only wished that Peter would go home to his family so that he could feel the way I did. It was hard for me to understand that his parents might not give him the same kind of warm welcome.

Mom always watched the late news. It was a habit she'd gotten into when she started teaching high school. Although she was a history teacher, she began each day with a current news story. Her theory? Today's news was tomorrow's history. Just as the news started, Peter called it a night. "I think I'll let you ladies catch up on your girl talk. Darlene, have you seen my carryon? I don't remember taking it upstairs."

"I think it's still by the front door." Sure enough, it was and when I picked it up, it weighed way more than I expected. "What the heck is in here?"

"I can't tell you." Peter snatched the duffel bag away from me. "It's a secret mission involving national security, straight from the top."

"The top of what? Old Smokey?" I shook my head and reached for the zipper.

Peter pulled the bag away from my grasp. "Don't open it, Darlene. If you do, you could unleash a whole boatload of ugly and the world as we know it might end before we open presents."

"Really, Peter?" I tugged at the zipper pull. He squeezed his eyes shut and braced himself. "You have scripts in here!!" I hollered when I discovered several screenplays, neatly stacked.

"No, they're classified documents disguised as scripts. That's why President Ford personally asked me to handle this mission for the CIA. No one will ever suspect a thing."

"You are not supposed to be working!" I reminded him.

"It's not exactly working, it's reading, and I'm pretty sure there is something about the CIA in one of them."

"So you're going to read scripts over the holidays?"

"Come on, Darlene, you know that this is the only chance I've had." He kissed me on the forehead and then headed toward the stairs with his duffel bag in hand. "You realize that I'm going to have to report back to the president and advise him that you got into my bag. After that, I can't promise I'll be able to protect you from the foreign agents."

"No scripts tomorrow, mister," I yelled after him, ignoring his silly remarks, as he disappeared up the stairs. "It's Christmas!"

"I told you not to open it!" he hollered back.

"What was that all about?" Mom asked, once Peter was gone.

"He shouldn't be reading scripts. He's supposed to be on a break—a break he really needs. You can't imagine what kind of schedule he keeps."

"Is he looking to make a movie?" Mom patted the couch, indicating she wanted me to sit there.

"So he tells me." I settled next to her.

"Does that mean you spend a lot of time alone?" Mom wrapped one arm around me and I laid my head on her shoulder, enjoying her closeness.

"I do, but I don't really mind the alone time. I have tons of work to catch up on. I've even had to turn down a couple of assignments this month and I hate doing that. Besides I'm not totally settled in the apartment yet."

"What about Frank?" Mom asked, stroking my hair. "Do you ever hear from him?"

"Not one word. I'm not even sure where he is or if he knows why I really left him."

"Did you leave him because of Peter?"

"No, Mom, I didn't!" I sat up so I could look her straight in the eye. "Frank had his own set of issues and he drank way too much. I wanted him to get help, but he wouldn't, and I couldn't live with him anymore. I wish I had the chance to really explain things to him the way I wanted to."

"So you still feel like there's some unfinished business between the two of you?" My mother knew me so well it was a little disquieting.

"Even if I do, the divorce will be final next month so it doesn't really matter anymore." And with that, I dismissed the subject and laid my head back on her shoulder.

A light snow ushered in Christmas morning. When Mom woke me up for breakfast, Peter was already at the dining room table with a cup of coffee. He looked rested for a change while I was still getting used to the time change.

"Did you put your scripts away?" I yawned.

"Yes, I did. Just for you."

"How many did you read last night?" I took a seat next to him.

"I only made it halfway through the first one before I fell asleep."

"Maybe you should put that one on the bottom of the pile."

Mom came in from the kitchen carrying a platter of banana pancakes—another one of my favorites. "Peter and I have been getting acquainted this morning." Mom set the heaping dish on the table before she turned to him. "Would you mind getting the coffee?"

My mother quickly looked at me once he was in the kitchen. "We need to talk, Darlene." She turned back around just as quickly before Peter returned with the coffeepot. I looked at the two of them shaking my head, wondering what had transpired between them before I got up.

After breakfast, it was our custom to open presents. Among the things Mom gave me was a journal and a crystal atomizer filled with her favorite perfume, Chanel No. 5. I spritzed some on and smiled. Maybe Mom and I were more alike than I thought. She gave Peter a black leather wallet that he really needed and a large beer mug with 'James Dakota' etched on one side and a firetruck etched on the other. Peter thought it would make a great prop for the show, which delighted Mom. We bought her a watch set on California time and an airline voucher good for a round-trip ticket to L.A. whenever she wanted to come.

"Be sure you use that ticket," Peter told her.

"I will. I've been wanting to visit for the longest time, but I thought Darlene didn't want me there."

"Of course I want you to come. You can stay as long as you like. I have an extra bedroom in the apartment and we can go to all the places I can't take Peter."

"Like where?" she asked.

"Like Disneyland, the movies, the zoo, Knott's Berry Farm, you know—anywhere there's people."

"Going out has been kind of a hassle lately." Peter frowned. "Lucky for me, your daughter has been a pretty good sport about it."

"I can't even imagine what it must be like." Mom sympathized with a shake of her head.

"Come out to L.A." I encouraged her. "We'll leave Peter at home and hit all of the hot spots."

Mom's Christmas ham was like I remembered, served with all the holiday fare she used to make when I was little. She even cooked carrots glazed in a sweet, brown sugary sauce with a little whiskey thrown in for good measure. As promised, we were treated to her famous peach pie with a healthy scoop of French vanilla ice cream on the side. It was heavenly! Peter even went for seconds.

"Ruth, you outdid yourself with this pie," he told her as he pushed his empty plate aside.

"Mom's peach pie is a Naperville legend," I explained as I took my last bite. "Anytime anyone has a function, they request one."

"I can see why." Peter smiled. "Darlene, why haven't you made a peach pie like this?"

"Because I can't seem to get it right. My pies never come out like Mom's."

"You must be missing something." Mom grinned at me. "Remember how we used to do it? Before we dipped them in the boiling water, we'd line them up on the counter and kiss every single peach to make the pies sweeter."

"I haven't thought about that in ages!" I laughed. "But I'm pretty sure kissing the peaches won't make the pie taste any better."

"Not so fast, Darlene," Peter interjected. "I think you should try it. You might be surprised. Ruth, do you kiss apples when you make apple pie?"

"As a matter of fact, I do." Mom nodded as serious as she could be. "And when Darlene was little, she used to have to kiss me so the car would start. The key never worked on its own."

"I like the way you operate, Ruth." Peter cleared the dessert plates from the table and headed to the kitchen where he placed them in the sink.

I picked up what remained of the pie and followed him when it occurred to me that he had never called home to wish his folks a Merry Christmas. "Honey, don't you think you should call your mother before it gets too late?"

"Go ahead and use the phone in my room," Mom offered as she rinsed the small plates before placing them in the top rack of the dishwasher.

"I guess I should."

"It's too bad Peter's family gives him such a hard time," Mom said once we were alone.

"What do you know about Peter's family?" I was surprised at her comment.

"Peter told me a lot of things this morning." She continued rinsing the larger dinner dishes one by one.

"What exactly did he tell you?" I put the leftover peach pie in a round container.

"He told me about the show and how much things have changed because of it. He said it's taken a lot of getting used to. I get the impression that he was caught off guard by everything that's happened."

"That pretty much sums it up," I agreed, snapping the container's cover in place.

"Peter also said that you are the glue that holds everything together."

"I try, Mom. I do my best to make sure he eats something when he comes home, but most nights he's so exhausted, I barely get two words out of him before he falls asleep."

"Are you happy with a man like that, Darlene?" Mom stopped—plate in hand—to look at me.

"I can't imagine being with anyone else." I put the pie container in the refrigerator.

"But don't you think this all happened a little too fast? Maybe you should slow down a bit. Recover from your divorce before you get involved with someone else." She slipped that last dish into the dishwasher.

"Too late, Mom. I'm afraid slow and Peter don't mix."

"I get it, honey," she said, wiping her hands on a dishtowel. "He's handsome and he's charismatic, but what kind of life do you have?"

"Peter makes me happy." I tried to make her see. "And I can't explain it exactly, but we're connected somehow—like it's fate or something—I can't quite put my finger on it."

"Darlene, you know I'm a firm believer in fate, but at the same time, I think you should be careful with your heart."

"But I never gave Peter my heart. He just took it the first time I met him."

"I only hope he takes good care of you and your heart," Mom said with a sigh. "And I hope he feels that same connection you do."

"I think he does."

"How can you tell?"

"I can tell by the way he —"

"Darlene?" Peter called from the bedroom before I could say any more. "Can you come here a minute?"

As I rounded the corner into Mom's room, Peter held the receiver with his hand covering the mouthpiece. "My dad wants us to come to Long

Island. What do you think?"

"If you want to go, we'll go."

"Dad?" Peter put the receiver back to his ear. "We'll see you in a few days."

Chapter Nine

We're in the air heading east toward Detroit. Peter's sound asleep. He needs the rest and it gives me a few minutes to catch up in my journal.

I haven't been to Michigan in years. Mom and I went there a couple of times when I was a kid. We stayed on Mackinac Island where no cars are allowed. I remember riding in a horse and buggy and biking around the island. The second time we visited Michigan, we went to Greenfield Village and the Henry Ford Museum. I'll never forget seeing the bloodstained chair that Abraham Lincoln was sitting on when he was shot by John Wilkes Booth at the Ford Theater. It made quite an impression on my young mind.

Spending Christmas with my mother was exactly what I needed. I felt that old closeness rekindling between us and I swear never, ever to lose that feeling again no matter what happens. Reconnecting with Mom reminds me how much I've given up since moving to California. After all, a girl only has one mother and in my mother's case, she's only got one daughter. I'm not sure I convinced her about that connection I seem to have with Peter, but I hope she comes out to L.A this summer and sees it for herself. I hope Sydney comes to visit, too. I miss having a girlfriend and the fun we used to share. Now that Frank is out of the picture, I am through shutting them out.

I'm looking forward to seeing Doug and meeting his family. It's obvious that Peter prefers being with the Lassiters rather than the Chandlers. Now I'm not so sure about going to Long Island. Come to think of it, I'm not too thrilled with Peter at the moment either. He's still lugging those scripts around.

The flight into Detroit was a quick one—less than an hour. Doug and his brother, Carl, were waiting for us at Metro Airport. Carl was a younger version of Doug—right down to the glasses and hazel eyes. The Lassiters lived in West Bloomfield, an upper-class suburb just north of Detroit—about forty-five minutes from the airport. Art was a high-ranking vice president in the Finance Division of General Motors. He had worked his way up from the assembly line over a thirty-plus-year career. Angie had been a secretary at the same automotive company when they met, but she traded in her typewriter to be a stay-at-home mom once Doug was born.

Light snow was falling as Doug pulled into the large circular drive that safeguarded a prominent colonial gray brick home set on what looked like at least an acre of land. Several tall evergreens standing near the house were lit up for the holidays along with two live wreaths that hung on the double wooden doors. The entire scene looked like a Christmas card. It was just as cold in Detroit as it had been in Chicago, but once we were inside, a feeling of warmth greeted us. Peter stopped and looked around, smiling. "I sure have missed this place."

We were only as far as the spacious marble foyer where we hung up our coats in the front closet when a tall, sandy-haired woman appeared. "I thought I heard the door." She stopped for a second when she saw Peter, and then hastened toward him with a smile that would put the sun to shame.

"Mom!" He scooped her up, just as delighted.

"Art!" she called out as Peter put her down. "Art, Peter's here!" Doug's father rushed down from upstairs. He was an older version of Doug and Carl—right down to the glasses and hazel eyes. Art and Angie reminded me of bookends. Both long and lanky with similar coloring, I couldn't help but wonder whether married people really did grow to resemble each other if they stayed together long enough.

"Peter, it's been way too long since you've been home to see us." Art gave him a hearty hug.

"Out of the way, Art!" Angie pushed her husband aside. "I want to look at Peter. Doug says he's been working way too hard."

"You know better than to believe anything Doug says." Peter shook his head.

"You're too thin," Angie observed.

"That's why the TV camera adds ten pounds." Peter gave her a wink.

"Where are the girls?" Angie looked around. "Do Gloria and Tina know Peter's here?"

Giggles came from the top of the stairs. Two teenage girls also with sandy-colored hair and hazel eyes looked down at us. Both wearing the ugliest of ugly Christmas sweaters, they seemed a little shy and unsure of what to say to Peter now that he was on television.

"Come on down here, you guys!" Peter called out to them, but they didn't move. "Gloria! Tina!" He held his arms out. "Nothing's changed. I'm still Peter." They looked at each other and grinned before racing down the stairs, almost knocking him down in their excitement, both talking at once.

"People, please," Doug said in his best legal voice, speaking over the noise. "There's someone here you haven't met yet." Silence followed. Peter took a step toward me, but Doug held out his hand signaling him to stop.

Doug loudly cleared his throat and slung an arm around me. "Everyone, I would like you to meet my new girlfriend. We've never told Peter, but Darlene and I have been seeing each other for the last few months."

"You wish." Peter pulled me away from him. "Mom, Pop, this is Darlene. She doesn't even like Doug."

"You boys will never change." Angie smiled and gave me a hug. "Darlene, it's good to finally meet you." She turned to Carl. "Take Darlene's things upstairs to the guest room and, Doug, take Peter's things to your room."

"Why can't Peter take his own things upstairs?" Doug complained. "He knows his way around the house."

"Douglas, do what your mother says," Art spoke up.

"Dinner's almost ready." Angie was still beaming. "I made your favorite, Peter—city chicken."

"Petah, Petah, Petah!" Doug attempted a poor Bette Davis imitation as he lifted Peter's suitcase. "Can you try and remember who your real son is here?"

"We always liked Peter better than you," Gloria told her brother.

"Yeah, Peter used to take us for ice cream when we were little," Tina added.

"How about some ice cream after dinner tonight?" Gloria asked. "Will you take us, Peter? Please?"

"Please, Peter?" Tina joined her sister in cajoling him. "Please? We promise not to take too long picking out a flavor like we did when we were little."

"I remember you both taking forever to decide what you wanted and then you ended up getting the same flavor every time!" Peter laughed.

"Strawberry cheesecake!" Both sisters shouted and then the giggling started up again.

"Girls, leave Peter alone," Art admonished his daughters. "It's his first night here and it's the middle of winter for crying out loud."

"It's all right, Pop." Peter grinned, obviously enjoying every moment. "After dinner, ice cream it is."

Seated around the dinner table, the Lassiters were a boisterous bunch—everyone talking and laughing pretty much at once. In comparison, my mother's house had been so very quiet, but here, Peter blended right in as Angie passed the city chicken around the table. City chicken was a new one on me. Although it wasn't really chicken at all, but cubes of breaded veal and pork on a stick, I liked it and I liked seeing Peter forget about reading scripts, filming the show, and all the recent pressure he'd been under. He was genuinely happy here and it showed.

According to Art and Angie, Peter often came home with Doug during college breaks and they 'adopted' him. Doug, however, had a different version of the story.

"The truth is," Doug began, pointing an empty city chicken stick straight at me, "Peter followed me home uninvited and told my parents he was an orphan who lived on the streets. They fell for his sob story and let him stay.

Then he just kept coming back. There was no getting rid of him—even now."

"Are you through?" Peter shook his head and rolled his eyes. "Because the way I remember it, mom and pop tried to get rid of you."

"You see how he lies?" Doug sighed. "Never trust an actor, Darlene."

The word 'actor' triggered something because now the Lassiters began peppering Peter with hundreds of questions.

"Will *Fire in the City* be renewed next season?"

"Have you ever met The Fonz?"

"What's it like to be on television?"

"How do they make those fires look so real?"

"Do you think you'll make a movie?

"Do you know Robert Redford?"

"Where does Klinger get his dresses?"

It was obvious that Peter's success thrilled them as he barely answered one question before they were on to the next. I'd rarely seen Peter so animated and relaxed. After dinner, he kept his promise to take the girls for ice cream.

"Who's coming with us?" Peter extended the invitation.

"I'll go," Carl volunteered.

"What about the two of you?" Peter asked Doug and me.

"You take the children and go," Doug told him. "Darlene and I have plans."

"Peter, do you really think it's a good idea?" I suddenly had an unpleasant thought.

"What can happen at an ice cream parlor in West Bloomfield on a cold winter day?" He seemed surprised and a little irritated.

"The same thing that happens at the grocery store, the bank, and the drugstore," I reminded him.

"It'll be fine. No one will even notice I'm there. You worry too much."

One hour later, we were watching television in the family room with Art and Angie. Peter and 'the children' weren't back yet. I threw a worried look at Doug who glanced at his watch.

"If they're not back in fifteen minutes, I'll go look for them," he promised. "Peter's got my coat."

My uneasiness spread to Art and Angie. "They have been gone an awfully long time for ice cream," Art said.

"I'm a little worried," Angie admitted with a frown. "They should have been back by now."

"All right, I'm going." Doug stood up, shaking his head. "It's a good thing I'm a lawyer because Peter has probably gotten himself into trouble again. I hope this time it doesn't involve jail. Are you coming, Darlene?"

I nodded, but as I stood up to join him, we heard the front door open and loud voices came rushing down the hallway.

"You wouldn't believe what happened!" Carl was the first one in the family room.

"It was a riot!" Tina's eyes were wide as she followed her brother.

"It was worse than a riot!" Gloria was right behind her sister.

Peter, looking a bit disheveled, was the last one in. He held what was left of Doug's jacket out in front of him. The collar was ripped, the buttons were gone, and the pockets were hanging off. "Here's your coat."

"What the hell did you do to my coat?"

"I didn't do anything to your coat." Peter threw it at him.

"It wasn't Peter's fault." Carl tried to explain. "The place was crowded and there was some crazy lady in line ahead of us. She saw Peter and started screaming! Then everyone saw him and they started screaming. Then ladies started pushing and pulling on him!"

"Tina and I ran outside and flagged down a police car." Gloria picked up the story, just as excited.

"Yeah, the girls left Carl and me in there alone." Peter threw himself next to me on the couch.

"We were trying to get help!" Tina defended herself.

"So what did the police do?" Doug wanted to hear the rest of the story.

"Before or after they called for backup?" Peter rolled his eyes.

"Backup?!" I echoed.

"Yeah, backup," Peter repeated. "Two more police cars came before they could get us out of there!"

"Did you get your ice cream?" Doug was obviously amused by the whole episode despite the loss of his coat.

"NO!!" All four of them shouted at once.

For the next couple of days, we played it safe and stayed in. There was a lot of activity in the house and, consequently, a lot of laughter. Carl and the girls had friends coming in and out to meet Peter. Art and Angie fussed over him and he enjoyed every minute. Coming to the Lassiters was a good choice, despite the ice cream parlor incident. I only hoped going to Long Island would work out as well.

It was a good thing we landed at JFK Airport in New York. That same day there was a bombing at La Guardia and eleven people were killed. Details were sketchy, but it certainly shook us up so we were glad when we arrived safely at the Chandlers' place that afternoon.

If I thought that the Lassiter house was big, nothing prepared me for the mansion-like Chandler home. It was an oversized two-story house, very modern in appearance, with lots of windows. Painted white with beige trim, it stood alone on a hill and on the upper floor, there was a large balcony that overlooked the water, which was two blocks away. When the airport car stopped in front of it, I couldn't hide my surprise. "Is this where you live?"

"Where I used to live," Peter corrected me.

No one opened the door as we got out of the car and gathered our luggage. Tense, Peter rang the bell, but he broke into a broad smile when a well-dressed woman with manicured nails and perfect makeup opened the door. She resembled Peter, but her dark hair was straight and cut in a short bob. Her eyes weren't blue, but brown and her gold jewelry jangled as Peter greeted her with an enthusiastic hug and kiss.

"Darlene, this is my sister, Carmen."

She extended her hand without a smile. Already uncomfortable, I hadn't even gotten past the front door.

"Where is everybody?" Peter asked as we stepped inside an elegant foyer with a large crystal chandelier hanging from the ceiling.

"Daniel is home with the boys. They're napping, but they'll be here for dinner. Mom and Dad are in the den." Something was wrong here. Peter hadn't seen his parents in two years and they didn't even come to the door? My uneasiness grew. Carmen took our coats and hung them in the biggest front closet I had ever seen. It looked bigger than my bedroom back in Naperville. Carmen led Peter by the hand down a long hallway with some interesting artwork on the walls. I followed behind, trying to decide whether this was a home or a museum.

John and Joyce were relaxing in matching green leather easy chairs in front of the TV in a large den encased with built-in bookshelves and dark wood paneling. A rolltop desk made of oak, covered with paperwork, sat in one corner and a green leather sectional ran along the opposite wall. "Mom, Dad, Peter's here," Carmen spoke up. She didn't mention me, but she did excuse herself, saying she had to call home and check on the boys.

"Peter!" Joyce seemed genuinely happy to see her son, but only gave him a dutiful hug. She wasn't motherly at all—at least nothing like my mother who was always warm and friendly no matter who came to visit. Joyce's hair was white and pinned snugly on top of her head giving her a stern matronly look. There was no playfulness in Peter's demeanor like there had been when he greeted Angie Lassiter.

John never even got up from his chair, but looked over with mild interest, extending his hand—a simple formality, not the way a father should ever greet a child. "Glad you could make it home, son."

Peter shook his father's hand and then slipped his arm around me. "Mom, Dad, this is Darlene."

"Hello, Darlene," Joyce looked me over rather grimly. "I believe we've spoke on the phone a few times."

"Darlene." John now stood up, extending his hand to me. He was a tall, handsome man with salt and pepper hair. It was obvious where Peter had gotten his striking blue eyes. I took John's hand, trying to hide my bewilderment. What kind of welcome home was this?! Everything Doug told me about Peter's family ran through my mind on fast-forward. Maybe they didn't care about meeting me, but they should be ecstatic to see their only son. The Chandler dynamics were just plain weird to me. The formality. The distance. The lack of enthusiasm. Suddenly, our two nights in Long Island loomed ahead like an eternity. Coming here might not have been such a good idea.

"Peter, you can take your things up to your room and Darlene can have Carmen's old room," Joyce stated rather quickly.

"I'll help you," I offered—anything to get away. Peter and I returned to the hallway alone and silently picked up our bags. His room was the last door on the left down a long hallway.

"How many bedrooms are up here?" I wanted to know.

"Eight," he said with a shrug. "And four bathrooms if you're counting."

"Which one is Carmen's old room?" I looked around.

"Last one on the right--across from mine," he answered. "Put your things down and come on over."

"Where do your parents sleep?"

"They have a private wing at the other end of the hall." It seemed like a long way off from their children. Mom was never more than a few feet away from me.

I set my things down in Carmen's room. It didn't look much like a girl's room. As a matter of fact, it didn't look like anyone's room. That was the problem with the whole house! It appeared sterile and unwelcoming. There were no personal touches anywhere—no signs that real people lived here. I wandered across the hall to Peter's room. He was just standing in the middle of it looking around.

"What are you thinking?" I snuck up behind him, putting my arms around him.

"I'm thinking that I'm tired of waking up without you." He returned the hug. "Maybe we should have taken these last few days for ourselves."

"We're here now. Let's make the best of it, okay?"

He kissed my neck, then my lips, lingering a little longer than he should have.

Carmen's husband, the doctor, arrived in time for dinner with four-year-old Bobby and two-year-old Timmy. Dr. Daniel Vincenzo was about five foot nine with olive skin and a slight build. His jet-black hair and piercing black eyes screamed Italian. He had a friendly smile and greeted Peter warmly, but the boys, who looked exactly like their father, were shy. They didn't know their uncle and it took awhile for them to feel comfortable around him. Once they did, however, roughhousing with Peter became their favorite sport. The rowdier they grew, the more the boys liked it, and the louder they squealed. Bobby, being older, did most of the talking, while Timmy went along with whatever his big brother said.

Most of the dinner conversation took place between Carmen, Daniel, and Peter. Peter's sister and brother-in-law asked about the show and how things were going in Hollywood. Peter gave his standard answers, almost as if he were talking to reporters. I soon realized that they had no idea what was really going on with him. To be fair, Carmen did seem interested in what her brother was doing, but John and Joyce said very little. No one talked to me except Peter who tried hard to make me feel comfortable. It didn't work. The longer I sat there listening, the more bewildered I grew.

After dinner, we went back into the den. As Peter undertook another round of wrestling with the boys, Daniel's beeper went off, signaling an emergency at the hospital.

"That happens all the time," Carmen sighed, clearly irritated by the interruption. I thought about Peter's long hours and late nights and the ice cream parlor incident. His life had been dramatically altered yet his own family had no clue about any of it.

Once Carmen and her boys went home, I wondered what Peter and I were going to do alone with his parents for the rest of the evening. The suspense didn't last long. Peter brought his carryon into the family room and we settled on the green couch where he pulled out one of his scripts. John and Joyce sat in their matching chairs. Apparently, Peter planned on reading while his parents watched TV.

The evening dragged on, minus any conversation, until the late news began. Peter announced that he was going upstairs to read the last of his screenplays. Joyce got up next saying that she was going to bed. I had no intention of staying downstairs without Peter, so I got up, too. I couldn't wait to get out of there.

"I hate to watch the news alone." John said. "Do you think you can stay up with me for a while, Darlene?"

I jumped. Even though he was looking directly at me, I was sure he was talking to Peter, but I could have sworn he said 'Darlene'.

"Dad, Darlene's a little tired." Peter tried to save me.

"She can't be that tired," John spoke up. "Can you, Darlene?"

"I-I guess not," I sputtered.

Peter shrugged, kissed his mother good night, and left me alone with his father.

"I hope you don't mind putting up with an old guy for a while, Darlene." John uttered my name for the third time.

"No, not at all," I lied. We sat silently for several more minutes, staring at the television. What was the point in this? I could have been in bed, reading, sleeping, something other than sitting here with Peter's father who didn't seem very talkative.

"My son has quite a hit on his hands." When he finally spoke, John's voice startled me.

"Have you seen the show?" I couldn't think of anything else to say.

"Watch it every week." His answer surprised me. "Peter makes a pretty convincing fireman, but this acting's not a real job. There's no security in it and that's something I could have given him along with the business."

"It's what Peter does and what makes him happy." I thought about what I was going to say next. They already disliked me, so what the heck, I had nothing to lose. "You should be proud of him. Not many people achieve what he has."

"I am proud of Peter."

"You should tell him that."

"I thought maybe you would."

"Why can't you tell him yourself?"

"Peter and I don't talk. We're different. I don't understand him and he doesn't understand me."

"But he's your son, your only son. Your approval is the one thing that would mean the most to him."

"Peter's never needed anyone's approval for anything—least of all from me." John clicked the 'power' button on the remote turning off the TV. Evidently, our conversation was over, but I wasn't quite ready to end it.

"You're wrong about that, John." I was probably crossing the line, but I couldn't stop myself. "I know Peter. In spite of all of his success, he feels that he's never quite measured up in your eyes. It would mean a lot if you'd just talk to him."

"I've known my son a lot longer than you have." John frowned at me.

"Do you really know him? Do you have any idea what kind of man he is?"

"I know he's a lucky man to have someone like you taking up for him." John seemed amused. "You're even willing to tangle with his crusty old father. I'd say Peter was doing all right." He limped off, leaving me sitting there wondering what just happened.

The next afternoon, Peter and I left for Carmen's house in Joyce's silver Mercedes. He wanted to get there right after naptime so he could spend some quality time with his nephews. The Vincenzo home, a traditional Cape Cod, was much more inviting than the Chandlers' and not quite as large. There were several pictures of the boys, as well as framed photos of Peter, and his parents. Daniel must have come from a big family as I noticed a picture of him surrounded by what I assumed were six siblings and their parents.

As soon as the boys spotted their uncle, they were ready for some rough-housing and so was he. While Bobby and Timmy wrestled with Peter, Carmen slipped into the kitchen where I assumed she was prepping for dinner. I offered to help, but she refused. She still hadn't made me feel very welcome and I couldn't figure out why. I had only spoken to her a handful of times over the phone and each conversation was brief. Maybe she thought no one was good enough for her brother. Her cold, standoffish behavior made me uncomfortable. I decided to ask her about it so I followed her into the kitchen.

"Carmen, have I done something to upset you?"

She stopped what she was doing and turned to me. "Maybe I don't approve of my brother running around with a married woman."

"It was never a secret. Peter knew from the beginning that I was married, and if we're being honest, the marriage was pretty much over by the time I met your brother."

"So now you've latched on to Peter. Tell me something—what's in all of this for you? Are you after the money or do you like the celebrity status?"

"Neither!" Leeanne Sutherland immediately came to mind and I resented the implication. "Money is not an issue and that celebrity status you speak of comes with a lot of trouble." I told her about the ice cream parlor incident in Michigan.

"Was Peter all right?" For the first time, I heard concern in his sister's voice.

"He was, but don't think he's been having an easy time of it lately, because he hasn't. You can't begin to imagine the pressure he's under and the hours he works. I don't know how he keeps it all together."

"My brother seems fine to me." She pulled a stack of plates from an upper cupboard and set them on the table.

"But he isn't fine, Carmen. His life's not normal anymore. Everything happened so fast he's having a really hard time dealing with it.

"So where do you fit in exactly?"

"I try to give him a quiet place to come home to, somewhere he can escape all the madness."

She put her hands on her hips. "So you've appointed yourself Peter's guardian angel."

"If you mean do I worry about him—yes! And it's too bad that I seem to be the only one. He's always working, and he's exhausted most of the time. You have no idea what it's been like."

"Why should I believe *you*?"

"Because I'm there every single day and I see it firsthand." The words tumbled from my mouth. "I don't pretend to understand your family's nuances, but I'm telling you, Carmen, your brother is stressed, and just because he doesn't show it, doesn't mean he's okay. Ask him about it. Maybe if you showed a little interest, he might open up to you."

"I'm pretty sure Peter can take care of himself!" Her voice was sharp and I realized she had already made up her mind to dislike me. "He was doing fine before you came along and he'll be even better once you're gone."

"I'm not going anywhere!" I stood my ground.

She gave me the once-over before she spoke again. "Darlene, in case Peter didn't tell you, I will. He has a terrible track record with women so I wouldn't get too comfortable if I were you."

CHAPTER TEN

I *can't wait to leave Long Island even though I'm a little nervous about going to the airport after the LaGuardia bombing the other day. What in the world is wrong with people? I'll never get it.*

I'll never get Peter's mother or sister either. They don't like me and to tell the truth, I'm not too crazy about them. Carmen's words stung: "Peter has a terrible track record with women so I wouldn't get too comfortable if I were you." Did she say it out of spite or was there something more to it? Peter only mentioned one girl he'd been serious about in the past and he's never made me feel like I was temporary. Still, I can't help but wonder if I'm really enough for him and I didn't need Carmen adding to that worry.

Peter's father, however, is different. I can't quite figure John out. He's complicated with a tough exterior, but deep down I think he really wants to reach out to Peter. He just doesn't know how. It would mean a lot to Peter if his father would only talk to him—at least that's what I've been trying to tell John the last couple of days. I don't think he's listening though. Neither is Peter. They haven't exchanged more than two words since we've been here. So much for my unsolicited advice, but I had to try.

I can see that John is stubborn and a lot like his son. Maybe that's why I like him despite his gruff demeanor and for some reason, he seems to have taken a liking to me. One Chandler out of three—good going, Darlene!

"Darlene? Do you have a minute?"

Breakfast was over and I had just started up the stairs to pack my things when Daniel's voice stopped me.

I came back down to meet him at the bottom of the stairs.

"I have to get to the hospital, but before I leave, I wanted to apologize for my wife's bad behavior. I'm afraid she doesn't always have the best judgment."

"What Carmen does or doesn't do is not your fault." I was touched that he even approached me. "I wish we'd gotten off to a better start for Peter's sake."

"I'm not sure why Carmen has been giving you such a hard time, but I intend to find out."

"I think she disliked me before I even got here. Maybe because I was still married when I started seeing Peter."

"That's between you and Peter—no one else."

"I never claimed to be a saint, Daniel," I said with a sigh.

"I know my father-in-law doesn't say much, but he seems to like you just fine and you're certainly a step above most of the girls Peter used to bring home." He leaned in a little closer. "Don't tell Peter I told you, but he had quite a knack for finding women with their own agendas. You're not like that and I hope you don't let Carmen or her mother scare you off."

"They didn't scare *you* off." I suddenly realized that's exactly what Carmen had tried to do with her snide remarks.

"That's because they like having a doctor in the family." Daniel grinned. "Some days I feel outnumbered by the Chandlers so I could use a partner on the outside. Promise you'll come back?" He extended his hand with a smile.

"I promise." I shook his hand and smiled, too, feeling so much better than I did before.

As we waited in the foyer for the airport car to arrive, John silently watched his wife and daughter fuss over Peter. Bobby and Timmy stood sobbing at the front door, devastated at the thought of their uncle going away. They were inconsolable even though Peter promised he'd see them again as soon as he could. Their tears upset Peter who got a little teary-eyed himself.

"Tell your mother she needs to bring you to California." Peter lifted them up—one in each arm. They hung on his neck, not wanting to let go.

"Why can't you stay here with us?" Bobby demanded in a shaky voice.

"Stay!" Timmy nodded.

"Because I have to go back to work."

"Uncle Peter, are you a doctor like my dad?" Bobby wanted to know as he continued to snivel.

"Doctor!" Timmy echoed.

"No, I'm not as smart as your dad." Peter smiled. "But if you come out to L.A., I'll show you where I work. How does that sound?"

"It sounds okay, but we still don't want you to go." Bobby continued to cry, giving his voice a hiccuppy sound.

"No go!" Timmy shook his head.

"But if I don't go, I can't come back." He kissed them both on their tear-stained cheeks and tickled them for good measure before setting them down. They squealed, as Peter directed a stern look toward his sister. "Carmen, the boys are growing up and I don't want to be a stranger to them."

"I'll talk to Daniel," she promised and that seemed to satisfy all three of them for the moment.

When the airport car pulled up in front of the house. I reached for my jacket, but John grabbed it first.

"Darlene," he whispered quietly as he held my coat open. "I think my son's finally done something right."

"Thank you." I slipped my arms inside the sleeves. "But it's still not too late for you to talk to him. Tell Peter what you told me. It would mean a lot to him, John."

In a rare display of affection, he hugged me shocking everyone—even Peter. John then picked up my luggage and limped outside with his son.

Alarmed, Joyce looked at Carmen with a worried face. "Don't give them a chance to argue." The two women headed toward the door.

"Give Peter and his father a minute to talk." I stepped in front of them, which didn't earn me any brownie points, but I didn't really care.

We couldn't hear the words, but as the three of us stood watching, John shared a brief conversation with Peter before embracing him.

When Peter motioned for me to come outside, I thanked Joyce for having us. Neither she nor her daughter answered, but it didn't matter. While the rest of the family said their goodbyes to Peter, John hugged me one more time. "You're a good girl, Darlene. My son should thank his lucky stars and I hope one day, he'll be smart enough to make you a Chandler, too."

For the first time since I'd met him, John smiled.

Soon Peter and I were in the air heading west without incident despite our worries about airport safety. He was unusually quiet, but we had one last stop to make before going back to L.A.—San Francisco. It was Peter's idea. Home would have been fine with me.

The City by the Bay was damp and on the cool side when we landed. We tried hard to keep our plans under wraps, but people always seemed to spot Peter—and it only took one before the rest bombarded him. When we stopped inside the airport car rental office, Peter's presence caused a stir. I stood aside and watched as he tried to rent a car in between signing autographs, chatting with fans, and taking photos with people he didn't know. When we were home, he normally didn't mind so much, but today I could tell by the set of his jaw that he was anxious to leave. Once we threw our luggage in the small trunk, we headed south. It was drizzling when we arrived at an elegant, old Victorian-style, oceanfront hotel on Halfmoon Bay. Peter had booked an exclusive top-floor suite with five large rooms and a screened-in balcony that ran the entire length of the suite, overlooking the water.

Designed with coastal details, the living area held two aqua couches, several glass lamps, a coffee table, a television, two large paintings of the beach, and a ceiling fan with blades shaped like tropical leaves. A small kitchenette had all the amenities including a coffee pot, microwave, and refrigerator stocked with drinks. The bathroom, with its gold trim, had an oversized Jacuzzi that looked very tempting. All the faucets were made to resemble fish with water pouring from their open mouths when you turned them on.

An oak bed with four posters took center stage in the main bedroom along with two nightstands—each with an old-fashioned hurricane lamp on top. The matching dresser held a small television to one side of a large mirror. Three fascinating paintings of the San Francisco area as it looked before the 1906 earthquake hung around the room. There was another smaller bedroom with a second bathroom similar to the main bath, but minus the Jacuzzi.

Once we were settled, Peter grabbed a cold beer and we curled up on the small rattan couch that rested on the balcony. The air was chilly as a gentle rain continued to fall. We had hoped to take a walk on the beach, but the weather wasn't cooperating this afternoon. Instead, Peter took a large blue-and-white blanket that hung over the back of the sofa and wrapped both of us inside it. It must have been a combination of the steady rain and jet lag that lulled me to sleep. I woke to find him still gazing out at the water, a pensive look on his face.

"I could stay here forever." I cuddled even closer to him, happy that we were finally alone.

"Forever is an awfully long time." His fingers played idly in my hair, but I knew I didn't quite have his full attention.

"You've been preoccupied since we left Long Island. What's bothering you?"

He didn't answer right away, but kept staring out at the ocean. I wondered if he even heard me and then he finally spoke up. "My dad said he liked the show. I never even knew he'd seen it."

"Of course he's seen it. His son stars in the hottest television show of the season, and you honestly think he wouldn't watch?"

"You don't know my dad." Peter laid his head back on the couch. "He still wants me to come home and run the business with him, but that's never been what I wanted."

"Did he say anything else?"

"He did and that was even more surprising." Peter kissed the top of my head. "My dad said that whatever I do, I should hang on to you."

"Good advice!" I yawned, still feeling a little groggy.

We had dinner reservations at Scoma's on Fisherman's Wharf so it was back to San Francisco for the evening. Scoma's is a picturesque Italian place specializing in seafood and situated on the water. The manager took Peter's picture to hang on the wall along with the other celebrities who had dined there and then, at our request, seated us at a table in the very back of the restaurant. Other than a few heads turning our way, our dinner was quiet as the waiters did their best to make sure we had some privacy. Peter seemed more relaxed and the stone crab was delicious—not to mention the glasses of pinot noir I managed to empty.

We passed on dessert and instead paid a visit to the old Buena Vista, famous for its Irish Coffee. A lively crowd was already celebrating the New

Year when we walked in. As we made our way to the bar, no one paid much attention to us—until we sat down. While I enjoyed four Irish Coffees, Peter signed autographs and posed for pictures with several patrons. His one drink went pretty much untouched and I could see his patience was once again wearing thin.

"Let's get out of here, honey." He laid some bills on the bar and stood up, pulling me to my feet.

I immediately felt the effects of those four drinks plus the wine I had at dinner and clutched his arm to steady myself.

"Are you all right?" he asked and I nodded, afraid to let go.

As we stepped outside, I took in the cool night air, but still felt light-headed as we walked to the car.

"I'm sorry, Darlene," Peter said once we were in the Mustang.

"Sorry for what?" I blinked. Peter suddenly seemed a little fuzzy.

"All I wanted to do was take you out for a drink on New Year's Eve." He sighed as he started the car. "Sometimes I wonder why you even stick around."

"Because your dad said I should and I like your dad." My voice sounded a little louder than normal, but maybe it was just me.

Peter started the car and tried to keep from smiling. "Honey, maybe you should close your eyes while we drive back."

"But I'm not tired," I protested. "I had four Irish coffees."

"And it's starting to show." He shook his head with a grin.

By the time we got back to the hotel, I was pretty much myself. Still not tired, I stood staring out of the balcony's sliding glass door into the darkness. We'd be going home soon. That meant Peter would be back to work and our time together would once again be limited. We would have to somehow survive another three months of filming the show, and if Peter decided to make a movie, however long that might take.

"What are you so serious about?" Peter wanted to know as he came up behind me.

"Just thinking that I don't want the holiday to end." I leaned back against him, happy to finally have him all to myself.

He kissed the side of my neck, then stopped. "It's not midnight yet."

"What does that have to do with anything?"

"Rules, Darlene. We have rules on New Year's Eve. No kissing until the clock strikes twelve."

"That's a stupid rule." I looked up at him. "Besides, it must be midnight somewhere."

"It only counts here. Now, why don't you go and enjoy the Jacuzzi?"

"Are you coming?"

"No, I have other things to do."

"Peter, it's New Year's Eve. We're in a hotel. What else do you have to do?"

"You ask too many questions." He gave me a push and waved his hands. "Just go, go, go."

Maybe this Jacuzzi idea wasn't so bad after all. The steady noise from the jets was soothing and the swirling warm water, relaxing. I idly wondered about the silly rules Peter came up with tonight. No kissing before midnight? I'd never heard of anything so stupid, but he was insistent. My eyes felt heavy and just as I was dozing, I heard him call. "Darlene, come on out here."

"Maybe you should come in here."

"That's not part of the plan."

"What plan?"

"Come out and see."

I reached for the white terry cloth robe the hotel had left neatly folded near the tub. It was soft and felt good as I wrapped it around me. I opened the bathroom door and peeked around the corner. Frank Sinatra was crooning "What are you doing New Year's, New Year's Eve?" from a small record player that mysteriously appeared in a corner of the dimly lit bedroom. There were two empty champagne flutes perched on a dining cart. A large champagne bottle peeked out over the top of a wine bucket filled with ice. Next to the champagne was a small silver dish with a domed lid protecting whatever was inside. A vase filled with white roses waited on the nightstand. Peter stood against one of the bedposts, his arms folded.

"It's not quite Paradise, but it's the best I could do with a little help from room service." He picked up the champagne bottle and popped the cork. He then filled the two glasses and handed one to me as I tried taking it all in. Before I could say anything, he tugged on the bathrobe's collar. "Honey, why are you wearing this goofy thing?"

I looked down and realized the hotel bathrobe wasn't a very romantic choice—especially on New Year's Eve. "Give me a minute. I'll change." I turned to leave.

"Oh no you don't!" He laughed grabbing my arm. "You're perfect! I wouldn't have you any other way." He tapped my glass with his. "To us, Darlene. May our nights never be quite the way we picture them, and may every New Year find us closer than we are right now."

As we sat on the bed having our third glass of champagne, the phone rang. Peter answered, but hung up without saying a word.

"Who was that?" I asked as the room began to spin a little.

"A wake-up call," he replied, as I watched him walk over to the little cart and pick up the small covered dish. After flicking the lights off, he set it on the nightstand and reclaimed his spot next to me. "It's midnight, Darlene. Time to start the New Year off right."

"What's in there?" I pointed to the dish, feeling a tad woozy.

"Coconut cream pie." He lifted the lid, revealing an enormous piece. "I thought it might come in handy later—in case we work up an appetite."

"I couldn't eat another thing tonight." I shook my head even though it did look tempting. I could feel that last glass of champagne going to my head as Peter pressed his mouth gently against mine. I wasn't sure if it was that long drawn-out kiss or the drinks I had downed that made me tingle all the way to my toes.

Peter abruptly pulled back, and those blue eyes flickered with mischief. "You know, honey, if Helene were here," he mused as he glanced from me to the pie and then back to me, "she would be upset if we wasted a perfectly good piece of pie." He pushed me back on the pillows and then distracted me with another kiss, after which he promptly smeared a dollop of pie across my lips. I tasted the distinct flavor of coconut—and it was heavenly, but before I could utter one word, he lifted my chin and once again placed his mouth firmly on mine. His tongue made a quick sweep around my mouth.

"Peter Chandler," I gasped, trying to regain my focus. "Could you at least give a girl some notice?!"

"That was your notice!" He stopped momentarily. "And to make it even clearer—I'm just getting started." He placed another dollop at the hollow of my throat and went to work on that.

"What do you think, Darlene?" His lips once again wandered over mine.

"Should I keep going?"

"Only if you promise that every once in a while, you'll make sure I'm still breathing." My words came out a little slurred—at least I thought they did.

He murmured something that I didn't quite catch and then I felt another dollop of pie fall just a little lower than that last one...and so it went for a good little while until we were both spent and only scraps remained on the silver plate.

"Peter?" I asked, as he nuzzled my ear in the darkness.

"Hmmmm?"

"Am I still breathing?"

"I think so."

"I feel kinda sticky."

He slowly ran his hand down one side of me and up the other. "Yep, pretty sticky and I think you're still a wee bit tipsy, too."

"It's all your fault!" My tongue felt a little thick.

"I'll take full responsibility for the sticky part, but not the tipsy part— you did that all on your own."

"Maybe we should move our party to the hot tub." I pointed toward the balcony. "That would fix the sticky part."

"Darlene, you're brilliant when you're tipsy." Peter laughed.

"There's just one thing...I can't remember how to get there," I said with a frown and he laughed even harder.

We did move the party to the hot tub and it definitely helped with the sticky part. As for the tipsy part, I woke up on New Year's Day with a mean headache. I had never, ever drank so much in my entire life! My resolution for 1976? No more drinking wine, Irish coffee, and champagne all in one night—that only leads to trouble.

When we finally made it back to L.A., we went directly to my place where I put my roses in fresh water. I set them on the dining table and stood back to admire them. "These are the first flowers you gave me since the ones Frank ruined."

Peter's relaxed demeanor immediately changed. "What made you bring up Frank?"

"Nothing. I was talking about the flowers."

"No, you were talking about Frank." The irritation in his voice surprised me. "Do you still think about him?"

"How could you even ask me that?"

"Just answer me."

"The Frank chapter is closed. I thought you knew that by now. He was part of my past and I can't change that or pretend it never happened."

"Neither can I." His blue eyes flashed with a sudden annoyance I had not expected.

"Frank doesn't matter anymore." I shook my head, bewildered by the entire conversation.

"Tell me something." He took a step closer. "If Frank cleaned himself up would you take him back?"

"Where is this coming from, Peter? What makes you think that I'd ever want Frank back—sober or otherwise?"

"I need to know if Frank is an issue for us."

"Only if you make him one."

That night, I learned never to mention Frank's name in front of Peter again—not even when I got the final divorce papers a few weeks later.

CHAPTER ELEVEN

It's over! My divorce is final. I'm relieved, but there's a tiny piece of me that feels like I failed. I know that's ridiculous given how Frank turned into a self-destructing wreck, but I never entered into our marriage thinking that it would end like this. I only hope he gets help and then moves on with his life. The old Frank had a lot to offer. Maybe a new and improved Frank still will—for someone else, that is.

I haven't told Peter about the divorce only because I hate to mention Frank around him. It seems to set him off. I'm not sure why, but Peter doesn't handle the topic of my ex-husband very well. Our time together is so limited. There's no room for hard feelings or arguments. It's better for both of us if I don't say anything.

I was looking forward to summer hiatus, but now Peter's signed on to film a movie. I wish he hadn't. He could use the downtime, but obviously rest isn't part of Peter's plan. His birthday is a week from Sunday and I want to do something special.

The Friday before Peter's birthday, I surprised him with a large cake delivered to the soundstage with a little help from Helene. She met me there that afternoon and we found Peter in his dressing room looking over script changes. He was wearing his full fireman's regalia, and his black helmet sat on the floor next to him.

"Peter, Peter!" Helene shook her head. "There ought to be a law against firemen looking so good."

"What are you two doing here?" He was a bit startled to see us.

"I don't know about Darlene, but I'm here for a birthday special." Helene snatched his script, threw it on the floor, then plopped down on his lap and wrapped her arms around his neck. "Thirty-three sure looks good on you, Peter. If only I was twenty years younger."

"But I like a woman who knows her way around." He kissed her cheek.

She turned to me, still holding on to Peter. "If I were you, Darlene, I'd make him bring this uniform home."

"Don't give her any ideas." Peter sighed, shaking his head.

"Maybe us girls will have to walk over to wardrobe later and see what other uniforms might be collecting dust." Helene nodded at me, but pulled Peter closer. "You could be a cop or a sailor or even a ringleader at the circus. I've always wanted to try one of those."

"Are you ladies through?" Peter asked in exasperation.

"Darlene might be, but I'm just getting started." Helene shrugged and reaching for the black helmet, she set it on top of Peter's head. "There! What do you think, Darlene?"

"I kinda like it." I nodded. "But I keep going back to that ringleader. "

"With or without the whip?"

"Definitely without."

"Darlene, hon," Helene said with a dramatically loud sigh. "You have to think outside the box. That whip could make things interesting."

"You ladies are going to be the death of me!" Peter took his helmet off and placed it squarely on Helene's head. "Now suppose you tell me what you're both doing here."

We thought it best to show him so with Helene still wearing that black helmet, we took him to the soundstage where a birthday cake, shaped like a fire truck, awaited along with Gene Sutherland and the rest of the crew. The cake was a big hit with everyone—especially Peter. The Brothers Grimm showed up for a piece, but, as usual, barely spoke. The party didn't last long because everyone had to get back to work, but I think Peter was pleased. Before I left, I promised him something special on Sunday.

Sunday morning marked the beginning of a new month, February, and a new year, number thirty-three, for Peter. I got up as quietly as I could and slipped into the kitchen. After cooking up a batch of blueberry pancakes, I filled a carafe with coffee, placed everything on a tray, and headed back to the bedroom.

"Peter?" I whispered because I thought he was still sleeping. "Peter?"

"Is that you, Darlene?" He kept his eyes closed, but it was obvious he was awake.

"Were you expecting someone else?" I asked, trying to balance the tray.

"Would you be mad if I said yes?" He opened one eye.

"Maybe you'd like to wear these pancakes." I tilted my head to one side.

He sat up with a grin and scooted over to make room for me and my cache. "You're spoiling me, Darlene."

"That's the idea." I slid in next to him. "But don't get used to it."

"You mean this won't be a regular part of our Sunday routine?"

"No, it won't. You'll have to wait another year before I do this again."

"Then I guess I better enjoy it now." He loaded up both our plates and then turned serious. "Honey, do you realize that Friday was the first birthday cake I've had since I've been in L.A.?"

"You're kidding?! Didn't you celebrate your birthday?"

"Only if you count beer and pizza with Doug." He poured us both some coffee. "Speaking of Doug, how come he didn't come by this morning?"

"Because I invited him over for beer and pizza later—much later."

After we cleaned our plates, Peter looked over the empty tray with a frown. "Something's missing."

"What did I forget?" I couldn't imagine what he was talking about.

"Dessert!" was all he said as he picked up the bottle of syrup. "You forgot dessert."

"I never even thought about it." I shook my head, not quite catching on.

"That's okay. I've thought about it enough for both of us." He narrowed those blue eyes, still holding on to the syrup. "How about getting sticky again?"

"Ewwwwwwwwwwwwwww! Peter, no!"

"But's it's my birthday." He gave me his saddest face.

"We don't have a Jacuzzi." I reminded him.

"I could throw you in the tub afterwards."

"No!" I shook my head. "Absolutely not and don't even think those blue eyes of yours are going to talk me into it."

"Come on, Darlene, we had so much fun in San Francisco."

"That's because I had way too much to drink. You probably could have done whatever you wanted that night and I wouldn't have cared."

"Now you tell me!" He put the syrup down and moved the tray to the floor before turning back to me. "Okay, Darlene. You win. I got rid of it."

I slowly turned my head around and those blue eyes drew me in as usual. "How many times can a girl win in one morning?" I asked.

"I don't know." He shrugged, moving closer. "Let's find out!"

It was an unusually balmy day for February so we took advantage of the fair weather. That afternoon, I packed sandwiches and we drove up Pacific Coast Highway to our favorite spot near the ocean. As expected, it was pretty much deserted and the few random fishermen that were there paid little attention to us while we set up our own private picnic as far away from them as we could.

"Does it get any better than this, Darlene?" Peter asked quietly as we lay on our blankets staring up at the blue sky and listening to the waves.

"I don't see how." My eyes followed the arc of a lone seagull as it made its way over the water.

"If someone told me six months ago that *Fire in the City* would be the number one show of the season, I would have laughed. Then if they told me I'd have you to share it all with, I would have said they were crazy."

"Six months ago, I'd just about given up on everything and then you came along." I sat up, pulling a small package from the picnic basket. "Here, honey." I handed it to him. "Happy birthday."

He smiled, propped himself up on one arm, and opened the box. He pulled out a gold chain with an antique medallion hanging from it. A profile of St. Florian, the patron saint of firemen, was etched on the front while Peter's initials and the date were on the back. "St. Florian protects firemen," I explained. "Even if you're not a real fireman, it couldn't hurt to wear it while you're working."

"I wonder who it belonged to," he mused as he sat up to examine it, genuinely touched.

"Whoever it was, I'm sure St. Florian took good care of him. Now he can take care of you."

He carefully laid the medallion back in the box. "I know I don't say it enough, but I really do love you, Darlene." He took both my hands in his. "And I know I've been neglecting you lately. Will you let me make it up to you?"

"What do you have in mind?"

"Next month we'll be wrapping up the show for the season and I'll have a few weeks off before film production starts. What do you say we take some time for ourselves? I was thinking maybe Maui?"

"As in Hawaii?"

"I did promise to take you to Paradise," he said with a grin. "Unless, of course, you'd rather go to Burbank."

The two-part episode we filmed together aired the last two weeks in February. I had never seen the final cut so Peter insisted that we watch it together at his place. I didn't want to see it at all, but to pacify him I agreed. I wasn't happy when I found out he had also invited Doug to watch the first part with us. I busied myself in the kitchen with dinner in an effort to keep my mind off the show. I even threw a frozen apple pie in the oven for dessert. By the time Peter and Doug got there, Mom, Sydney, and the Lassiters had already called. Due to the time difference, they had seen the show and their kudos only made me more nervous. I was sure they were just being nice.

Once we cleaned up the kitchen and the dishwasher was running, it was time for *Fire in the City* to begin. Sitting between Peter and Doug, who each held a beer, my stomach churned and a slight headache started creeping up the back of my neck. Even my palms grew sweaty. I was used to seeing Peter on TV, but nothing could have prepared me for seeing myself.

I hated the way I looked. I hated the clothes they chose for me. I hated the hair and I hated the makeup. The hour dragged on so long that I was pretty sure the sun was about to come up. When the show finally ended, my nerves were frayed and it was all I could to breathe. "It was awful—the worst show this season. You should have picked a real actress instead of me."

"Don't be so hard on yourself," Doug spoke up first. "You two generate electricity. Anyone with two eyes can see that and it certainly came across on the show."

I took in a deep breath. "Did you just watch the same show I did?"

"Yes, and personally, I make it a point never to walk in between the two of you. The lightning that flashes when you look at each other could kill or permanently maim a person."

"I have no idea what he's talking about." Peter squeezed my hand. "But I'm pretty sure we pulled it off."

"You mean YOU pulled it off!" I choked as the phone rang. It was Helene who wanted us to know that the ratings had skyrocketed and the network switchboard was jammed with enthusiastic callers who could hardly wait for part two.

The next week when part two aired, it wasn't so bad. I made dinner for the three of us once more and calmly watched the show. I was even more convinced that anyone could have done a better job. This would be my first and final foray in front of a camera. No one—not even Peter—would ever talk me into doing something like that again.

When Helene called that night, Peter insisted I talk to her. "Darlene, the ratings were over the top, better than last week, if you can believe it. It's too bad there's not a Part Three!"

Part Three?! I couldn't have survived Part Three!

Come March, my biggest priority was deadlines. I doubled up on my work hours and finished what I had to before we left for Maui. While I was busy writing, Peter got busy growing a beard as soon as *Fire in the City* wrapped. He hoped that it might keep people from recognizing him so easily. Once I got used to it, I rather liked his new look.

Even though Peter continued to work on the movie's preproduction, the whirlwind he always seemed to live in, slowed dramatically. We saw more of each other, but I knew better than to get used to it. Eventually, things would pick up again and our time together would be limited. Until then, however, I looked forward to our trip to the islands where there would be no demands on either one of us for a change.

The moment we stepped off the plane in Hawaii, the intoxicating tropical breeze gave the island a magical feel. The greenery and the brightly colored flowers made it seem like a different world. If ever there was a Paradise, this had to be it. As customary as it was, we passed on receiving the lei greeting so as not to draw attention to ourselves. It seemed a small price to pay for some privacy. An airport car drove us to the Sheraton Hotel on Maui's Kaanapali Beach, where we had reservations as Mr. and Mrs. Peter Lassiter.

The bellhop led us to our suite on the Sheraton's top floor, and as Peter tipped him, the young man paused. "You look familiar. Have you stayed with us before, Mr. Lassiter?"

"No, it's our first time in the islands." Peter's answer satisfied him and he left without saying another word. As Peter closed the door behind him, we both smiled. I was starting to like that beard even more.

Everything in the room had a tropical vibe as pineapples and palm trees dominated the décor, giving our suite a vintage Hawaiian look. The best part was the oversized lanai with its rattan furniture and fabulous view of the Pacific framed by a row of graceful palm trees. The first thing I wanted to do was take off my shoes and head for the beach. Peter, however, was a bit more practical and ordered lunch.

"Are you happy, Darlene?" His serious tone caught me off guard as we finished our burgers and fries on the lanai.

"Do you even have to ask?" I gestured toward our picturesque surroundings.

"Paradise aside," Peter persisted. "Are you happy, Darlene?"

"Of course, I'm happy. Why would you even ask?"

"I wanted to hear it from you." He laid his hand on top of mine. "Sometimes, I feel like I've shortchanged you."

"I have never once felt shortchanged." I laid my other hand on top of his.

"Even on the days I can hardly catch my breath?"

"I thought that was why we came to Paradise," I reminded him. "So we could both catch our breath—at least for a little while."

That evening, we drove in to Lahaina for dinner and chose a seafood restaurant on the water. The place was crowded and as we waited for a table, I noticed one or two people watching Peter. I'm sure they were trying to decide who he was exactly, but no one approached us. Before the hostess led us to our table, she stared at Peter for a moment, but didn't say a word. It was the petite blonde waitress who took our order that recognized him. "You're Peter Chandler!"

"You caught me." Peter flashed those blue eyes at her. "But do you mind if we keep it between us?"

"Do people bother you a lot?"

"All the time."

"Not in my section," she promised, and we were able to enjoy a quiet dinner in a restaurant minus any interruptions. There were no autograph seekers, no picture takers, and best of all, no strange women—only a happy waitress who took her apron off and asked Peter to sign it before we left— proof that he'd been there.

We did all of the things tourists do in Maui. We snorkeled. We biked down Haleakala at sunrise. We even drove the winding road to Hana, stopping to take pictures along the way. We caught an inter-island flight to Honolulu where we visited Pearl Harbor—a sobering experience that touched us both as we stood over what remained of the *U.S.S. Arizona*. Another day, we flew over to the Big Island to explore Volcano National Park with its two very active volcanos, Kilauea and Mauna Loa. Each island was beautiful, but Maui and its magnificent beaches remained our favorite. Peter's beard turned out to be one of his better ideas. More often than not, we were just another couple spending time in Paradise.

The night we returned from the Big Island, a message from Doug was waiting at the hotel. He was the only person who knew exactly where we were so it concerned me. "I hope nothing's wrong."

"There's only one way to find out." Peter picked up the hotel phone and called him back. Other, than 'What's up, Doug?' Peter barely said a word. I watched most of the color drain from his face as he sat down on the bed, then I heard him say, "Are you sure? Are you absolutely positive?"

Something was wrong. I knew it. I could tell by the look on Peter's face. Whatever it was sounded serious enough to send us home in a hurry. When he finally hung up, he remained silent.

"What did Doug say?" I asked, even though I didn't really want to know. "What's wrong?"

"Emmy nominations were announced today and, according to Doug, *Fire in the City* is up for six of them."

"Honey, that's good news!" I gave him an enthusiastic hug. He looked at me with a rather dazed expression and I knew there was more. "What else did Doug tell you?"

"He said that I was nominated for best actor in a drama series."

"Peter!" I squealed in delight. "This is so exciting! We should celebrate!"

"Darlene, I didn't win it yet." He was still trying to grasp the idea.

"Winning doesn't matter. A nomination is huge!" I told him. "I think we should celebrate big tonight."

And we did just that by going to a traditional Hawaiian show—complete with fire dancers and hula girls. Afterward, we went out back behind our hotel where a bar, a band, and a dance floor were set up on the beach. An endless amount of champagne seemed to flow right in front of me and I downed one bubbly glass after another, not bothering to count. Evidently I had learned nothing from my exploits in San Francisco. By the time the band turned in for the night, my head was spinning. I steadied myself on Peter's arm as we rode the elevator back up to our suite.

"I think maybe you had one too many glasses of champagne." Peter grinned as he held onto me.

"I think it was about six too many." I put my hand to my head. "Peter, I'm so dizzy."

"I think the word you're looking for is tipsy—again." He laughed as the elevator doors opened on our floor. Once inside our suite, I stood near the door trying to decide where I should go exactly. "What's wrong, Darlene?"

"I'm not sure where we are." I blinked.

"We're in our hotel room in Maui." Peter tried not to smile. "And I think you need to lay down." I just stood there looking at him, totally bewildered so he picked me up, carried me straight to the bedroom, and deposited me on top of the bed.

"I don't want to get sticky tonight." I shook my head and my voice sounded funny.

"No, honey." Peter stretched out next to me. "I wouldn't think of it."

"I mean it, Peter!" Suddenly there seemed to be two of him. "No sticky business!"

"Darlene, I promise you, there is nothing in this room that could possibly make you sticky."

"You're sure?"

"I'm positive."

"Okay." I nodded, not really certain what we were talking about. "I thought we were cebelating."

"What?" Peter asked.

"We're supposed to be cebelating something. That's why I drank all the champagne."

"I think you cebelated enough for one night. You need some sleep."

"But I can't sleep here. There's something wrong with this bed."

"What do you mean?"

"It keeps whirling around like Dorothy's bed in Kansas. Are we in Kansas, Peter?'

"No honey, we're in Hawaii, remember?"

"Oh." I thought about that for a second. "But I'm afraid I might fall off the bed."

"Okay, honey." He sat up, pulling me against him. "Close your eyes and I'll hold onto you."

"Promise?" I clung to him as the bed continued to swing and dip.

"Yes, Dorothy, I promise."

That night we slept in our clothes on top of the covers.

"Ohmygod, my head hurts!" I moaned over coffee on the lanai the next morning. "Why did you let me drink so much?"

"Because you were so funny!"

"I don't know what got into me."

"Champagne got into you."

"Oh, Peter!" I hid my face in my hands. "You get nominated for an Emmy and we didn't even celebrate the way we should have."

"You cebelated just fine." He assured me. "But maybe tonight we can think of something better."

Champagne aside, I loved everything about the islands. The sunshine. The trade winds. The sandy beaches and the clear water. The lush greenery and the colorful birds of paradise, bright red anthuriums, and eye-catching plumeria. There was no end to the scenic surroundings. Best of all, I had Peter all to myself and, in my mind, that defined Paradise.

Our remaining vacation days went by way too fast. Before we knew it, we were spending our last evening on the lanai. "Do we really have to leave tomorrow?" I curled up on Peter's lap wishing it was our first night in Maui instead of our last.

"We have to go home sometime."

"Why?"

"Because home is where we live and we both have to get back to work."

"Do you think we can take the Maui magic with us?"

"It's got nothing to do with Maui, Darlene. It's you. You make the magic. You always have."

CHAPTER TWELVE

We're home!

I cried when we left Maui even though Peter promised that one day we'd go back. His beard was the perfect foil. Even though some people still recognized him, they were few and far between. Part of me hates that he will have to shave it off soon. I've gotten used to it and I especially like the cover it gives us. Somehow that Maui magic strengthened our bond, but I know it's only a matter of time before things spiral out of control again. That's the way it is with Peter and even Maui magic can't stop it. He'll start filming soon and I have deadlines looming. I'm also worried about the Emmys. They are coming up next month. Peter can simply don a tux, but I need something to wear. I'll have to talk to Helene. She always knows what to do.

"Movie mogul and aviation pioneer, Howard Hughes died today in a Las Vegas Hotel. The eccentric billionaire turned recluse was seventy…"

"Now, there's a movie!" Peter said as we listened to the late news about the death of one of the world's most peculiar and richest men.

"It's kind of sad." I frowned. "Imagine having all that money and no one caring enough to even get him a haircut."

"Or a manicure," Peter added. "I wonder how he ended up like that."

"I don't know, but maybe one day we'll find out if they ever make a movie."

The Hughes Phenomenon was still in the news when Peter began filming what everyone was now calling *Night Shoot*. In it, Peter plays Dex Reed, a softhearted con man that wheels and deals people, but ultimately ends up helping them because his conscience always gets the best of him. A lot of funny scenes have Peter interacting with completely different characters in a series of short vignettes that blend together into the main story. Dex Reed was certainly very different from his James Dakota character, which made everyone wonder how it would be received.

While Peter was preoccupied with *Night Shoot*, I focused on my assignments and what to wear to the Emmys. Thank God for Helene. She was an old hand at this sort of thing. When I called to ask her for help, she invited me down to her office so we could talk about it. Her secretary let me in and I found Helene sitting behind her oversized desk speaking with someone on the phone. She signaled to me that she would be done in a minute and then hung up.

"Always putting out fires around here," she said with a sigh. "Speaking of fires, how's Peter?"

"He's fine—busy with the movie."

"I hear it's going well." She made her way to the coffee pot that sat in one corner of her office.

"That's what he tells me."

"I haven't seen him since you two got back from Hawaii." She poured us each a cup. "And I have a plumbing problem."

"I'll have him call you." I grinned, accepting the cup she offered.

"You're such a good sport." She smiled as she sat down on the small red loveseat opposite her desk and made room for me. "So you're wondering what you should wear to the Emmys?"

"Yes." I nodded. "You helped me with that black dress at Christmas and I was hoping you'd point me in the right direction now."

"What are you thinking, Darlene? Something flashy? Something plain? Something daring?"

"I don't know." I shrugged. "People really only notice Peter, not me, no matter what I wear. Maybe it's silly to even worry about it."

"It's not silly at all." She sipped her coffee. "And I don't think you give yourself enough credit, hon. People do notice Peter, but when you're together, they see a couple who glow. It's kind of refreshing for a change—especially here."

"If you say so." I gave a shrug, thinking she was just trying to be nice. "But that doesn't help me figure out what to wear to the Emmys."

Helene looked me over with a serious face while she finished her coffee. "Stand up for a second."

I did as she asked.

"Now turn around nice and slow." A broad smile spread across her face and she removed her cat's-eye glasses. "I think I've got it, and if you like my idea, we can run with it forever!" Without any further explanation, she went to talk to her secretary and then returned, closing the office door behind her.

"Darlene, when you think of glamour who comes to mind?"

"Not me!" I shook my head. "What are you getting at, Helene?"

"Hear me out…I know you like the old movies so what if we pick an iconic dress from the classic era and duplicate it to fit you? Something maybe Audrey Hepburn might have worn, or Joan Crawford or Bette Davis? The sky's the limit and from here on in, you could channel an old movie star every time you go somewhere with Peter! What do you think, Darlene? This could really be a lot of fun!"

"I'm no glamour girl." I shook my head. "And I'd feel silly trying to be."

"So maybe we'll pass on Jean Harlow for now, but I bet we could find a dress that would suit you to a tee!" Helene grew more enthusiastic the more she talked about it. "Wait till my secretary gets back. I sent her down to wardrobe. I think they have some books with pictures of the dresses I'm talking about."

A few minutes later, the young lady returned with a whole stack of books. Helene and I sat together poring over them. I couldn't help but smile at the beautiful clothes worn by the likes of Katherine Hepburn, or Myrna Loy, or Norma Shearer. I was beginning to think Helene might be on to something, but it was Ginger Rogers who convinced me to do it. I fell in love with the light blue feather dress that she wore in *Top Hat* when she danced "Cheek to Cheek" with Fred Astaire. It was made of satin with long feathers that fell around the shoulders and then three more layers of feathers that hung just below the hips all the way to the floor. Fred hated that dress because it shed all over him, but Ginger insisted on wearing it and even called her mother to the studio to back her up. The ladies won the battle and her feather dress became one of the most famous gowns of her career. I wanted to wear that dress, but with a few minor modifications.

"Leave it to me, Darlene." Helene gave me one of her brightest smiles. "I'll get the costume department to copy this for you, but you'll have to be available for a couple of fittings."

"No problem," I told her. "Do you really think we can pull this off?"

"I know we can!" She laughed. "Just you wait! From here on in, you're going to these affairs dressed like a real star! Oh and Darlene, don't forget to tell Peter about my furnace."

"I thought you had a plumbing problem."

"No, I changed my mind. I think I'd rather have him heat the house."

I wasted no time renting *Top Hat* so I could study that feather dress. Without telling him why, I made Peter watch it with me—twice. I loved the graceful way the gown flowed, but by the time the Emmy Awards arrived in May, I was having second thoughts about that dress. Maybe it was too much or too crazy, but I had nothing to replace it with. After hair and makeup appointments, Helene dropped me off at the apartment. Nothing seemed right. I wasn't used to seeing my hair swept up. Maybe I should have worn it down. Maybe I had on a little too much makeup. Maybe the silver heels and purse were a bad color choice. *Maybe I should send Peter to the Emmys with Helene and stay home.* I had to take a few minutes and some deep breaths to collect myself before I got dressed. If I was this jittery, Peter must have been climbing the walls. I was glad that Doug was with him even though I secretly wished Doug would have had a date as he was going with us tonight, but he didn't.

When I unzipped the garment bag that held my dress, I took a good look at it. It had worked well for Ginger Rogers, but I was hardly one of Fred Astaire's dancing partners. How in the world had I let Helene talk me into this? No matter, it was too late to change my mind. I donned my feather dress and thought about all the glamour girls that would be at the awards ceremony tonight in their clingy gowns. *I hope Peter won't be disappointed when he sees me. He has no idea what Helene and I cooked up.* I slipped on my shoes and opened my jewelry box, taking out my necklace. Unlike Ginger's dress, my gown had a scooped neckline, one of the small changes I insisted on, so that I could wear my pearls.

When I got to Peter's house, I went through the side door and into the kitchen. Doug was rounding the corner minus his jacket. "Peter!" he hollered. "A gorgeous brunette just walked in. You better get rid of her before Darlene gets here!"

Peter came around the same corner and Doug shuddered. "Watch out! Lightning!" He rushed past Peter, leaving us alone.

Peter stood motionless and then whispered, "Turn around, Darlene." I did as he asked. The dress seemed to sway in its own kind of rhythm, but his expression never changed as he came toward me. "Now it all makes sense. Here I thought you liked Fred Astaire when you made me watch *Top Hat*."

"I do like Fred Astaire, but I'm not so sure about this dress, Peter," I confessed. "Helene and I got wrapped up in the idea of old Hollywood glamour, but maybe I could have made a better choice."

"Honey, you look perfect!" He smiled, giving me a whirl. "Maybe we should skip the Emmys and go dancing instead."

When the three of us arrived at the auditorium, I was still unsure about my dress even though Peter insisted it was dazzling. His word, not mine. A million flashbulbs went off all at once, blinding us. People screamed Peter's name. Microphones and cameras surrounded us. Peter talked to everyone at once. Gorgeous women were everywhere. Some I recognized, some I didn't. Other than saying a quick hello, Peter hardly paid attention to any of them. Doug and I did our best to keep up.

More reporters and cameras were inside the auditorium where a small stage was set up for photos. When it was our turn, we stepped up together and someone called out, "Hey Ginger! Where's Fred?"

"Fred couldn't make it tonight so I'm standing in for him!" With a smile, Peter lifted my hand above my head and twirled me around. The gown did its thing and flashbulbs popped.

"One more time!" another voice called, and Peter twirled me again.

"I've always dreamed of giving Ginger Rogers a spin!" He laughed and whisked me off the little stage.

A page showed us to our table where Helene and the brothers were already seated. Her face lit up when she spotted us. She was out of her chair and in Peter's arms in one sweep. Wearing a black pant-suit trimmed in sparkling silver, she looked classy as always. I envied her for being so at ease, but at the same time, I was grateful. Keeping up with Peter would be a whole lot harder without Helene.

"Darlene!" She winked at me. "I'll clean your house for a year if you let me take him home tonight."

"Sorry, Helene, tonight won't work. How about next Tuesday?"

"Only if he promises to show up in this tuxedo." She straightened his tie. "Oh, and Darlene, you don't look so bad yourself. Was I right about that dress or what?"

"It's not too much?"

"This is just the beginning," she said with a smile and then turned her attention back to Peter. "And I hope you have an acceptance speech prepared."

"Being nominated and winning are two different things," Peter reminded her.

"Not in your case. Name one other fireman on prime time that wears a uniform like you do."

"Wearing the uniform doesn't count in the Emmy department."

"Peter, I've been around long enough to know how to pick 'em, and I'm telling you that Emmy is as good as yours."

The brothers shook hands with Peter, their faces barely smiling. I thought it was odd that they didn't bring dates, but then again this was The Brothers Grimm we were talking about. Maybe they were worried about saving face if they didn't win or maybe they didn't want their dates to eye Peter the way the blondes that they brought to the Christmas party did. You never could tell with the brothers.

"What a couple of fun guys," Doug whispered in my ear. "I can hardly wait to spend the evening with them." I poked him with my elbow.

Gene Sutherland, who had directed most of the *Fire in the City* episodes, joined us and this evening he was also alone. I wondered where Leeanne had gone. Without her, Gene was more like the nice guy I had met at the studio. At least, he seemed relaxed. Wait staff made sure we had a steady supply of champagne. Finally, the lights dimmed, the music began and the 1976 Emmy Awards were under-way. Peter's icy hand held mine under the table until it was time for him to present an Emmy.

Peter, along with a redhead I couldn't quite place, gave out the award for 'best comedy series.' Her black dress was a little too tight as she pressed against him in a way that was a little too familiar.

"Who was your partner up there?" I wanted to know when Peter returned to the table.

"Rita Hayworth?" He gave a shrug.

"Do you think Rita could have gotten any closer to you?" I rolled my eyes.

"She tried backstage, but I outran her."

When the time came for the Best Actor Award, I just wanted to get it over with. If Peter won, that would be great. If he didn't win, what would really change? Absolutely nothing. We would still be go-ing home together, and he would still be working on *Night Shoot* over the coming months. I can't remember who presented the Best Actor Award that night or who else was in the running, but I clearly recall Peter's cold hand squeezing mine till it hurt. He looked perfectly calm as his name was read along with the other nominees, but his hand-holding technique gave him away, at least to me. As the envelope was opened, we all held our breaths.

"…and the winner is Peter Chandler, *Fire in the City*!"

The band began playing the theme music from the show, com-plete with sirens. As Peter heard his name, he squeezed my hand even tighter, and then let go. Everything happened quickly after that.

Cheers erupted from our table as Peter stood up. He took two steps toward the stage, but turned back. With a mischievous wink, he took my champagne glass and slid it in front of Doug. It was nothing more than a silly gesture that made me laugh.

He reached the stage and accepted his Emmy. "When I signed on for *Fire in the City*, I thought it was just another job and I would once again be an unemployed actor within a matter of weeks. Shows you how much I know."

Everyone laughed and after a brief pause, Peter continued. "There are a lot of people I need to thank for this, so I'll start with the crew and the Cox brothers who created and produce *Fire in the City*; Helene Williams who fought for me from the beginning—Helene, I probably owe you my first-born; Gene Sutherland, who directs most of our shows and likes sending me into those fires. On a personal note, I want to thank my family in Long Island—especially my dad who surprised me when he said he actually watched the show; and the Lassiters who always make me feel like I belong to them and yes, Doug, your folks do like me better. Finally, but most important of all, I have to thank a very special lady. Darlene, you not only make the world right, but you throw in your own brand of magic. Honey, I know putting up with me hasn't been easy, but somehow, you always keep the balance for both of us and thank you everyone for honoring me with this Emmy tonight."

"Darlene!" Helene leaned toward me. "Let me take him home tonight and I'll clean your house for two years."

"Not after that speech." I finally felt the tension ease. "Do you think Peter will be gone long?"

"He'll be awhile," she replied. "Every reporter in the world is back there and I'm sure they all want to talk to him."

He never did make it back before the award for the Best Drama Series was presented. That award also went to *Fire in the City*, which The Brothers Grimm accepted. They each had a list of people to thank, including Helene, but merely mentioned Peter because they had to—an obvious slight.

"Those two are going to get a piece of what little mind I have left!" Helene was livid. "They wouldn't even be here tonight if it weren't for Peter! They can't admit that without him, there would be no *Fire in the City*."

"You're right about that." Gene agreed. "The brothers ought to treat Peter like gold."

"It upsets me," Helene continued. "Everyone knows how I feel about Peter."

"And I feel the same way about you." Peter stood behind her, holding his Emmy.

She turned to look up at him. "Peter, the brothers—"

"I saw it."

"They make me so mad!" She fumed all over again as the Emmy Awards were coming to an end.

Peter reclaimed his chair, setting his Emmy on the table in front of him. "I'm not wasting the night worrying about The Brothers Grimm and neither should you. What do you say we head out of here?"

We left before the brothers came back. Helene had originally ridden to the awards with them, but Peter insisted she come with us to the studio party. In our limo, there was more champagne. We all had a glass to celebrate.

"How did it go backstage?" Helene wanted to know.

"Don't ask." Peter shook his head, setting his Emmy on the floor of the car.

"Why? What happened?" My curiosity was piqued.

"You won't like it." He wore a serious expression. "But I suppose I should tell you now while Helene and Doug are here to protect me."

"This ought to be good." Doug sat back with an expectant look.

"She's going to go for my throat." Peter looked at him, took a deep breath, and then turned to me. "Honey, I never even gave it a thought. You have to believe me."

"What did you do, Peter?" I narrowed my eyes.

"Helene, you know how you told me about the standard questions the reporters ask backstage after you win?" He shifted uncomfortably.

"Yeah, they pretty much ask everyone the same thing."

"Well, they didn't ask me." He sighed, tossing a sideways glance my way. "Every last one of them wanted to know why I took that champagne glass away from Darlene."

"What did you tell them?" I tried to prepare myself for what was coming next.

"I told them how you cebelated the nomination in Maui," he said rather quickly with a pained look. "And I told them I had a different kind of cebelation in mind for tonight."

"You did not!" I thought he had to be kidding, but he wasn't.

"They loved it, Darlene." He tried smoothing things over. "And I never once mentioned New Year's Eve."

"Peter Joseph Chandler!" I was horrified. "You better *not* have said anything about New Year's Eve!"

"She's using three names," Doug said, shaking his head. "That's never a good sign."

"What happened on New Year's Eve?" Helene asked.

"Darlene wasn't herself on New Year's Eve," Peter began with a grin at me. "She had a few too many Irish coffees that night and she got herself into a very sticky situation. She kept asking me if she was still breathing and then she thought the jacuzzi was on the lanai, but being the gentleman that I am, I pointed her in the right direction."

"Peter, you were no gentleman that night and now you're skating on very thin ice." I gave him the evil eye. "I suggest you quit while you're still ahead."

"Oh come on, honey." He slipped his arm around me. "I honestly didn't know they saw me move that glass, but you have to admit, what happened in Maui makes a great story. I'll save the New Year's Eve version for some other time."

"Helene, I changed my mind." I picked up Peter's Emmy and handed it to her. "You can take him home tonight and keep him."

The studio party was held at the Roosevelt Hotel. As we walked inside, I was still not happy with Peter. Despite his bad behavior, I couldn't help but smile, thinking about all the history behind this place and the glamorous people who came here before us—Jean Harlow, Douglas Fairbanks, Mary Pickford, just to name a few. The very first Academy Awards were even handed out here. Some people think the hotel is haunted by the likes of Marilyn Monroe and Montgomery Clift so I tried to pay attention to any shadows that might be lurking in the corners, but I never did see Marilyn or Monty that night.

As the four of us entered the ballroom, the band started playing "Cheek to Cheek". Smiling, Peter gave his Emmy to Helene and then pulled me onto the dance floor where we made one grand sweep ending with me in a dip. We were hardly Fred and Ginger, but we did have fun and even earned a brief round of applause.

"Still mad at me?" Peter asked with a grin as we walked toward the table where Helene and Doug were sitting.

"Peter Chandler, you are going to pay dearly for what you did tonight."

"I can't wait!" He laughed as he gave me one more twirl.

"Do you mind if I take Ginger for a spin?" Doug asked Peter before we even had a chance to sit down.

"As long you keep her away from the champagne." Peter replied and at the same time extended his hand to Helene for a dance.

When we returned to Peter's house in the wee hours of the morning, he insisted on a couple of more twirls in the kitchen before taking a deep breath. "Okay, Darlene, I'm ready to pay for telling that story, unless of course, you were doling out empty threats earlier."

"Listen, mister!" I yanked him by the collar. "You are still in trouble up to your eyeballs and when I get through with you tonight, you won't even know your name!"

"Do I get a last request?"

"What would that be?"

"This!" His lips traveled over mine and with that familiar feel of his fingers in my hair, I curved into him like always. Slipping my arms around his neck, I kissed him back.

"Darlene, you really do make the magic," he whispered. "Especially tonight."

"It must be the dress."

"It's got nothing to do with the dress." His lips brushed my ear. "It's all you."

I closed my eyes and tilted my head as he kissed the side of my neck. "Are you trying to make me forget I'm still mad at you?"

"Is it working?" he asked as he moved along to the other side.

"No," I murmured. "You're digging yourself in deeper."

And he laughed.

CHAPTER THIRTEEN

That feather dress turned out to be the best choice Helene and I could have made. Everyone loved it—especially Peter—and it turned our fabulous evening into a memorable night despite his storytelling, which I haven't quite forgiven him for! Helene even managed, once again, to get an 8 x 10 of Peter and me dancing. I swapped that picture with the first one from Christmas into what we began to call our 'Fred and Ginger' frame. Our picture and Peter's Emmy sit next to each other on top of his television.

Speaking of Ginger, Ms. Rogers penned me the kindest note, thanking me for breathing life back into her old feather dress and for remembering how hard she had to fight to wear it. I will treasure that note forever.

I also found out why Gene Sutherland came alone. According to Helene, Leeanne had left him for a more successful producer. It seems she's had her eye on this new guy for a while. Once he expressed a smidge of interest in her, she went after him with a vengeance, leaving Gene in the dust. He had to have seen it coming—everyone else did. Still a nice guy like Gene deserves so much better.

And now for the best news of all—my mother is coming for a visit later this month once the school year ends. I can hardly wait for her to get here. I wish she could stay all summer, but I'll settle for a few weeks. Maybe by the time she leaves, she'll finally understand what I've been trying to tell her—Peter and I are connected. Such a simple thing, but so hard to explain.

A few days before mom arrived, I still had a couple of manuals to edit and I worked on them for most of the afternoon. Peter had an interview scheduled after work that night and he was running late. He picked up a takeout from Wu's Room and showed up at my place well after nine. I could tell he was tired, but right after dinner, he had several script changes to study for the next day's shoot while I continued revising my manuals. I didn't use them often, but my dictionary and thesaurus were sitting on the coffee table in their usual spot.

Peter went to the kitchen for a beer. Before sitting back down, he inadvertently knocked the dictionary to the floor. The pages flew open and a small picture fell out. He picked it up and the color drained from his face.

"What the hell is this?" He shoved the photo at me. My stomach tightened as I saw that it was an old picture of Frank and me. Sydney had taken it one Sunday afternoon as we rode the carousel in Central Park.

"I didn't know that was even in there!" I pushed my manual aside, bracing myself for what I knew would be another Frank episode.

"What other remnants of Frank are you hiding around here?" His voice rang with irritation and his jaw clenched.

"Why would I hide anything? We've been divorced for months."

"Something you never bothered to mention to me."

"Only because you don't handle the subject of Frank very well."

"Can you blame me?" His voice went up a notch. "Your ex-husband is always turning up."

"Don't be ridiculous, Peter!" I tried, but before I could say more, he returned to his script and went into silent mode. I went back to my manuals and he left shortly after without so much as a good night. His moodiness usually blew over and things would once again resume their even keel—until Frank came up again to rock the boat. As much as I tried to avoid it, my ex-husband managed to surface every now and then, sending Peter into a tailspin no matter what I said.

Mom arrived the last week in June. School was out and the country was planning its upcoming two hundredth birthday party. I met her at the airport while Peter was working. Moviemaking was different than filming a television series. For the most part, his hours were a little more sensible. Most evenings, he was home early so he suggested taking Mom to dinner at a new Italian restaurant that opened on La Cienaga Boulevard. I preferred eating at home, but Peter wouldn't hear of it. He sometimes forgot the stir he caused when we were in public.

Even though we asked for a table way in the back, we had to walk through the restaurant to get there. A half dozen people approached Peter for autographs before we even sat down. It always irritated me, but my mother seemed amused. With a hundred interruptions during dinner, I was glad to finally be heading toward the car when a female voice called out to Peter in the parking lot. The three of us turned in time to see a tall platinum blond lift her blouse revealing everything she had. Peter was embarrassed, mostly because my mother was there.

"I'm really sorry about that," he said as we drove off. "Darlene was right as usual. We should have stayed home."

"I never expected that to happen." I was having a hard time believing it myself.

"There's a first time for everything," Mom piped up from the back seat.

Peter grew a little too quiet, which made me suspicious.

"You mean that wasn't a first?" I asked.

He still didn't answer.

"Has that happened before when I wasn't around?" The pitch of my voice went up.

"Once or twice." He stared straight ahead at the road.

Muffled laughter came from the backseat. "I'm sorry." My mother tried to stop giggling. "But Peter, if you could have seen the look on your face." Her laughter was contagious and I giggled along with her, but Peter just shook his head.

"It never ends." He gave a loud sigh and rolled his eyes. "Darlene, next time, let's order a takeout and you go pick it up."

As we had discussed at Christmas, Mom and I went to all of the places I couldn't take Peter. We visited Disneyland and the L.A. Zoo. We stood in the footprints at the Chinese Theater and had a drink at the Pig 'n Whistle. We went to Knott's Berry Farm and drove down to the Mission at San Juan Capistrano. We treated ourselves to two matinees: *All The President's Men* with Robert Redford and Dustin Hoffman and *Taxi Driver* with Robert DeNiro and an impressive little girl named Jodi Foster who seemed older than her years. We shared popcorn like we used to and had a box of jujubes that stuck to our teeth. I always picked out the cherry and grape-flavored candies and gave Mom the rest. Through it all, we reclaimed the closeness I had let lapse during those rough times with Frank.

One afternoon, we surprised Peter on the set, hoping he'd be free for lunch. Instead of Peter, however, we found Doug. "Darlene! Are you here to break things off with Peter?"

"Not quite. What are you doing here?"

"Peter promised to buy me lunch, but so far I haven't seen him. He's probably gone underground so he doesn't have to pick up the tab."

"You must be Doug." Mom extended her hand with a smile. "I'm Ruth, Darlene's mother."

"Ruth, I'm glad you're here." Doug took her hand in both of his. "Your daughter needs help. This whole thing with Peter isn't right. He's no good for her. I keep telling her to get rid of him, but she won't listen to me. Maybe she'll listen to you."

"Ignore him, Ruth." Peter came up from behind, swatting Doug in the head. "He's always been jealous because I saw Darlene first."

"A simple technicality." Doug gave Peter a shove. "It would never stand up in a court of law."

"Neither do you." Peter rolled his eyes. "As a matter of fact, I'm surprised they even let you inside a courtroom."

"Can we go to lunch?" I spoke up.

Peter checked his watch. "Can you give me fifteen minutes?"

"Exactly what I'm talking about." Doug threw his hands up. "Darlene, I would never keep you waiting." He turned to my mother. "Ruth, if you want to save your daughter from this wanton actor, we'll have to set aside some time to talk."

"How about dinner at Darlene's tonight?" she asked him with a grin.

Mom insisted on cooking and she wanted to treat us to one of her homemade peach pies, so after a quick stop at the grocery store, we headed back to my apartment with everything we needed. Once in the kitchen, I pulled out the ingredients while Mom filled a large pot with water and set it on the stove. She then lined the peaches up on the counter.

"Let's kiss them like we used to, Darlene," Mom suggested, and I didn't have the heart to say no. Before we dropped them in the boiling water, we kissed each peach one at a time.

"I wonder what Doug's like in court," Mom mused out loud as she dipped the peaches into the pot. "Is he ever serious?"

"Mostly he's not, but when he is, you'll know."

"Does he come around a lot?" She pulled the peaches out of the water almost as quickly as she dropped them in.

"He does, but he's Peter's best friend. They've known each other a long time."

"They're quite a pair." Mom smiled as she removed the fuzzy skin from the fruit. "And he seems to approve of you."

"I like Doug," I admitted as I watched her work. "And, now that I think about it, he's been a pretty good friend to me, too. I wish he'd meet someone who appreciated him, but Doug doesn't make things easy for a girl."

"Why do you say that?"

"Because his ex-wife did him wrong so now he puts up a wall. If a girl wants to get to know him, he won't let her."

"He doesn't seem to have a problem with you."

"I'm not a threat. I've got Peter so Doug doesn't need to put up that wall for me."

That evening, Doug arrived early for dinner. "Ruth, we still need to have our talk. Darlene is making a terrible mistake."

"Doug! Stop teasing my mother!"

"I'm not teasing your mother!" He gave her a wink, then checked all the pots on the stove and opened the oven. "Everything smells so good. Do we have to wait for Peter?"

"Yes, we have to wait for Peter."

"Darlene, one day when we have an entire minute, I want you to explain exactly what you see in him." Doug turned to Mom. "Help me out here, Ruthie. You need to convince Darlene that I am much better for her than Peter is. He works too many hours and he's crabby. It's six-thirty and where is he? Still working. I'm telling you, Peter is no fun anymore. You can't even take him anywhere. What kind of life is that?"

"No one's called me Ruthie since high school." Mom laughed just as Peter came in carrying a bottle of wine.

"Honey, was Doug sampling the cooking sherry again?" Peter bussed my cheek.

"I'm starving," Doug complained. "But Darlene insisted we had to wait for you. Where the hell have you been?"

"Some of us work." Peter set the wine on the table before he turned to my mother. "Ruth, you shouldn't listen to him. He's not well."

"Ruthie, don't believe a word he says. He lies about everything. That's why he's no good for your daughter, but we'll talk more about that *after* dinner."

As we sat around my dining table, Mom laughed till she cried. Peter and Doug were in rare form and once we finished eating, she placed her peach pie on the table.

"Ruth, you made my day!" Peter told her with a smile. "But I have to ask, did you and Darlene kiss the peaches?"

"Yes." Mom nodded as she served it up. "Each and every one."

After we had our fill of peach pie, Mom insisted on cleaning up the kitchen. "I'll help you, Ruthie." Doug wasted no time volunteering, and then he turned to Peter and me. "You two kids go on in the living room and put the television on, but if I hear any fighting, I'll come in there and turn it off. Do you understand me?"

"Do you think she's safe in there with him?" I had my doubts about leaving Mom alone with Doug once we were settled on the couch.

"None of us are safe as long as he's here," Peter said with a sigh.

At first things were pretty quiet, but within fifteen minutes, hysterical laughter poured from the kitchen. I looked at Peter and he looked at me. We shook our heads as the laughter grew louder. "What do you think is going on in there?" I asked.

"We don't want to know," Peter answered. "It could be terrifying."

Mom's laughter turned into shrieks as silverware clattered and dishes clanged. I started to get up, but Peter pulled me back.

"Don't go in there, Darlene. It's too risky. We're better off out here." He slipped an arm around me, as the racket continued for a good little while until Mom and Doug came into the living room. He had one arm slung around her shoulder and she was wiping her eyes.

"What was going on in there?" I looked up at them.

"Doug proposed!" Mom laughed so hard, she cried.

Peter closed his eyes and shook his head while I took a breath. "Doug, you cannot marry my mother!"

"Come on, Darlene!" He kept his arm around Mom. "Did you even taste that pie?"

"Pie or no pie, you cannot marry my mother!'

"Look, I know there's an age difference," Doug went on. "But as I told Ruthie, I'd be willing to wait until she is through with high school."

"Doug, my mother doesn't go to high school. She teaches high school."

"Then what's the problem?"

"Can you please help me out here?" I turned to Peter as Mom tried to compose herself.

"Maybe if we give him a piece of that pie to take home, he'll leave," Peter suggested.

"Ruthie, I could be persuaded to take some pie home, but I still want to marry you no matter what Darlene thinks."

The next morning, Mom and I lingered on the balcony over our first cup of coffee. "I can't remember the last time I laughed so much!" Mom said as a warm breeze blew past.

"You never know what Doug might say or do."

"He's a lot of fun." Mom nodded, still smiling. "But you were right when you said I'd know when he was serious."

"And when exactly was Doug serious last night? Before or after he proposed?"

"Before!" She grinned. "He said you're the best thing that's happened to Peter since he's been in L.A. and that includes getting the part of James Dakota." She paused for a moment. "But my mother's intuition tells me that Peter kept you from falling apart."

"I guess he did." I sipped my coffee and braced myself for what was coming next.

"You didn't have to go through all that alone." She reached over and brushed my hand. "You could have called and I would have been here."

"I didn't want you to know how bad things were. I didn't want you worrying, and then I met Peter and I wasn't sure what you would think of that."

"I'll be honest with you, honey, I had my doubts at first, but I'm glad he came along when he did."

"Even though we didn't take things slow?"

"I'm your mother, Darlene. I have the right to worry about you and yes, I wish you hadn't gotten involved as quickly as you did, but you're a grown woman and I want you to be happy."

"And if Peter makes me happy?"

"Honey, don't get me wrong. I like Peter. I really do."

"But?"

"But there is one thing that bothers me."

"What's that?"

"Frank."

"Frank?! What about Frank?"

"I mentioned him to Peter the other day, just in passing. I told him I was grateful that he was there for you when things got so bad with Frank. I never really gave it a thought, but he clammed right up. I didn't mean to upset him, but it was obvious I had."

"For some reason, Frank's name sends Peter into a nose-dive." I put my coffee cup down. "He can't seem to talk about Frank without getting angry no matter how many times I've told him that Frank is part of the past."

"Have you ever asked him why he gets so upset?"

"No. When Peter gets into one of his moods, he stops talking. Eventually, he gets over it, then everything is fine again—until the next time something reminds him of Frank."

"Why is that, Darlene?"

"I honestly don't know."

"Honey, I'm not trying to tell you what to do, but maybe you should ask him."

"And set him off again? I don't think so, Mom."

"But honey, if you don't find out what the problem is, you can't fix it."

"But if I don't mention Frank, then there's nothing to fix." I quickly dismissed what she said.

CHAPTER FOURTEEN

I drove Mom to the airport this afternoon. Seeing her off was hard. Most of all, I miss her calming presence. Ever since I can remember, she was the one person who always made everything better—whether it was a skinned knee or a lost doll or a broken heart. I wish she could have stayed another week or two, but Mom is meeting a group of teachers in Montreal for the final week of the Summer Olympics—more history in the making. She promised that next time she came, she'd stay longer. I don't think how long my mother stays matters. Saying good-bye to her will never be easy. Maybe one of these days, I can talk her into moving out here.

Oh, and the oddest thing happened after I dropped Mom off. I had to stop at the drugstore to pick up some Tylenol and as I was leaving, I noticed Frank parked across the street. It jarred me, but as soon as I spotted him, he started his car and drove off. This isn't the first time that I've seen him and it makes me wonder what he's up to. I don't feel threatened by him, but seeing him like that makes me uneasy. I certainly won't mention it to Peter.

My apartment was not the same the day Mom left. The quiet was too quiet and the emptiness she left in her place smothered me. I was glad to see Peter that afternoon especially when he announced that the *Night Shoot* filming was coming to an end. Of course, *Fire in the City* would be back in full swing soon enough and I truly dreaded what that would bring.

We drove up Highway One and took a walk along our favorite part of the beach late that afternoon. It was something we hadn't done since my mother came and I was looking forward to the peace it always brought after hectic times. Peter, however, seemed pre-occupied. He had barely spoke during the car ride and it was obvious something was on his mind. We sauntered along in silence until I couldn't stand it anymore.

"Honey, why are you so quiet? Is something wrong?"

"I've been thinking." He stopped walking and looked down at me. "Darlene, why don't you give up that apartment and move in with me? We spend practically every night together anyway."

"I know, Peter, but your place is so small."

"I'm not talking about my place." He hesitated for a moment. "I want to buy a house, Darlene. A real house—some place for us to settle down in. What do you think?"

"I thought things were fine the way they were." He caught me completely off guard and my stomach clenched as the sun tucked itself behind a cloud.

"But they could be better. We both could use a little more space, plus we'd be together."

"That would be a major change." I wanted to give this whole idea some serious thought. "Do you need an answer today?"

"Not really." He pushed my hair behind my ear as a gust of wind blasted around us. "Even if I hire a realtor today, it won't happen overnight. It'll still take some time before we find the right place and after that maybe some remodeling before we move in. Just say you'll think about it."

"Okay," I promised, unsure of how I felt. "I'll think about it."

Peter was dead serious about house hunting. He called a real estate agent that same week. His first choice of residence was Hollywood Hills and it was my job to work with the realtor and look at houses. Much to my relief, he didn't mention me moving in with him again. I liked having my own place and I liked the way things were between us. I didn't see a need for change. Besides, a change that big was kind of scary—at least to me.

Sydney planned to visit for a week in early August. I wished she could have stayed longer, but that was all the time she could get off from her copywriting job at the publishing house where we first met. I gave up my clerical job there when Frank and I moved to the west coast. Although we talked on the phone regularly, I hadn't seen her since I left New York, and I missed her. We'd had such good times in the Big Apple. We were even roommates for a while.

Sydney was the girl of many colors. She loved loud clothes and lots of jewelry. Compared to my conservative ways, we made an odd couple, but her outgoing personality drew me out of myself and we had fun together. Despite our differences, we both loved the theater, good books, and movies. We shared secrets and hopes, along with bottles of wine. I had not made any girlfriends in California—mostly because of Frank's erratic behavior. Now that he was out of the picture, I still shied away from people. Old habits are hard to break.

Before Sydney came, however, I had a ton of work to catch up on in between looking at houses—thankfully, there were very few on the market I thought I should see. After Mom's visit, I'd fallen behind on several training manuals and one small procedural book. Due dates were looming and, always deadline-driven, I went on a writing rampage. I stopped long enough on Peter's first day back to work to pay him a visit at the studio. The second season of *Fire in the City* was underway. Maybe this time around now that things were more established, it would be a little easier.

Before I found Peter, however, I spotted Helene as she whizzed past in her golfcart. She slammed on her brakes and backed up when she saw me. "Darlene! What are you doing here?!"

"Looking for Peter." I smiled, happy to see her. "I was just heading for his dressing room."

"Oh, I guess you don't know. Peter doesn't have a dressing room anymore. He's got his own trailer—a much nicer place. Hop in. I'll take you there."

She zigged and zagged a few times and then stopped in front of what looked like a tiny mobile home. Peter's name was on the door. "I'm not sure if he's here," she said as she knocked. No one answered. She tried the door, but it was locked. "Tell Peter to get a key made for you."

"I'll wait out here for a while. He can't be too far."

"How about some company?" Helene asked and we sat down on the cement step in front of the door. There was no shade and, with the bright sunlight, the warm air was a bit stifling.

"Are you ready for round two?" She wanted to know.

"I'm trying to brace myself."

"For the new season?" Helene stretched her legs. "Or the new house?"

"Peter told you he's looking for a house?"

"We had coffee this morning. He says he asked you to move in with him, but you haven't given him an answer yet. Any other woman, including me, would have had her bags packed and on his front porch by now. What's holding you back, hon? "

"It's a big decision and I'm not sure I'm ready to give up my own place."

"Would it make a difference if the word 'marriage' was part of the offer?"

"Not really. I'm happy with the way things are. I don't want to take any chances and spoil what we have."

"Life is full of chances, Darlene. We talked about that once before."

"I know, but I have to be sure that—"

Peter pulled up in his own golfcart, surprised, but pleased to see the two of us perched on the step. "Must be my lucky day. I have not one, but two lovely ladies sitting outside my door."

"I thought I'd surprise you, but I'm the one who's surprised." I stood up. "You never said anything about your new residence."

"I just found out about it this morning." He gave Helene an odd look before pulling her to her feet. "Come on in. I'll show you around."

Peter unlocked the door and pushed it open. The trailer had a small living area with a loveseat, television, and stereo. I smiled at the sight of our 'Fred and Ginger' frame resting on top of a tiny side table next to the couch.

"I planned to put our picture in my dressing room," Peter

explained. "And then I found out about this place." He passed a second odd look Helene's way and this time she rolled her eyes.

Next to the living area there was a little kitchen, with miniature appliances, and two barstools pushed under the counter. The very back housed a bedroom with one twin bed and a small nightstand. Adjacent to that was a bathroom complete with a shower.

"Are The Brothers Grimm planning to make you live here?" I asked.

"They're just trying to keep Peter happy, and it's about damn time," Helene quipped as she checked her watch. "Speaking of time…I've got a meeting this afternoon so I should be on my way, but first—" She put her arms around Peter's neck and, in her usual dramatic way, kissed him squarely on the lips. "Sorry, Darlene, I wanted to be the first one to christen James Dakota in his new home! You'll have to settle for second." And with that, she left.

"Second isn't so bad," Peter said with a grin as he slipped his arms around me.

"Maybe not." I pulled him closer. "But since I'm number two, I'll just have to try harder."

When Sydney landed, Peter was still filming the season's first episode of *Fire in the City*. She was a blonde at the moment and wore a long paisley skirt with lots of oranges, greens, and browns along with a white peasant blouse and bright red sandals. I tried to warn Peter about her unique look, but I don't think he quite understood until he saw her in person. After a quiet dinner at Wu's Room, we went back to my apartment. I made three big bowls of popcorn and we settled in front of the television with Grace Kelly and Frank Sinatra as they romanced their way through *High Society*.

During Louis Armstrong's rendition of "High Society Calypso" Peter brought up the one subject I dreaded. "Honey, have you heard anything from the real estate office lately?"

"No, nothing in the past week or so."

"House hunting?" Sydney asked.

"Yeah, I think it's time for us to have our own place." He nodded, looking directly at me.

"A house won't surface overnight." I didn't like where the conversation was going. "It'll take time to find the right one."

"I'm hoping we find the right one soon. I'd like to move in before the holidays."

"So tell us what's going on in New York, Syd." I abruptly changed the subject and, thankfully, it worked—or at least I thought it did.

As soon as Grace and Frank ended up together, Sydney yawned. "Either I'm getting old or jet lag is catching up with me. I think I'll turn in for the night. Travel days are the worst." She left us alone on the couch.

Peter flipped through the channels looking for another late movie, but I could tell by the set of his jaw that he was irritated. "I'm really having a hard time understanding why you don't want to move in with me, Darlene."

"I never said I wouldn't."

"But you never said you would." His blue eyes were piercing as he lifted my chin. "Honey, I'm not buying a house for me. It's for us."

"Do I have to give you an answer right this minute?"

"Why don't you tell me what's holding you back?"

"I don't know exactly. It's not that I don't want to, but—"

"But what, Darlene? Do you want to get married? Is that it?"

"No, that's not it." I heard my voice rise up a notch. "I'm not ready to get married again."

"Good, because with everything else going on, I'm not ready to get married either." Peter's frustration was obvious. "Buying a house and moving in together seemed like our best option. I honestly thought you'd be happy about it, but I see I was wrong."

"Peter, buying a house is a huge decision. If that's what you want, it should be for you—not me. I'm not saying I won't move in with you, I need some time to be sure it's what's really best for both of us."

"Being together is what's best for us—or at least I thought it was. Evidently you have reservations that I don't understand." Those blue eyes made it so hard to say no as he pulled me closer and his lips drifted to my ear. "You have to decide what it is you want. I'm buying a house, but I won't ask you to move in with me again. When you decide to do it, you can let me know."

Alone in the kitchen Sunday morning, I took two Tylenol with my first cup of coffee. My night had been restless with very little sleep.

"Headache?" Sydney appeared wearing some kind of psychedelic bathrobe with at least eight different colors sweeping through it. The sight of it made my head hurt even more, but still I was glad she was there.

"Nothing a little Tylenol won't fix," I said with a sigh. "Do you want some coffee?"

"I'll get it." She poured herself a cup. "I know it's none of my business, but I heard you and Peter arguing last night."

"I'm sorry if we kept you up." I apologized, feeling even worse.

"Did he leave?"

"No, he's still sleeping. Sunday is the only day he gets to rest."

"Good," she said, smiling. "If he didn't leave, I assume the two of you kissed and made up."

"We kissed, but I'm not sure about the making up part."

"Kissing is always a good start." She grinned and then grew serious. "Do you want to talk about it?"

"What did you hear?"

"Mostly just voices." She shrugged, putting her cup to her lips. "It was the tone I picked up on. I'm sorry, Darlene. You don't have to tell me anything if you don't want to."

But I did want to tell her. I needed someone to talk to. Sydney patiently listened while keeping our coffee cups full.

"Darlene, think about it," she offered after hearing me out. "Number one, the two of you spend almost every night together.

Number two, neither of you want to get married right now for your own reasons. Maybe buying a house is Peter's way of making some sort of commitment to you."

"I hadn't thought of it that way."

"But I know you and I can see you're afraid that such a big change might do more harm than good. Am I right?"

"Yes. Moving in with him could be a disaster and not moving in with him could be even worse."

"Has Peter given you an ultimatum?"

"Not exactly." I shook my head. "It's just that I never let myself think too far ahead. I try my best to live in the moment because whenever I think about the future, I can't help but wonder how long I'll really keep his interest. Whether I move in with him or not, what if he gets bored with me or if someone more intriguing or more exciting comes along, than what?"

"Why would you even think like that?" Sydney sat back in her chair. "Has Peter said something to make you feel like you're only temporary?"

"No, he never has. It's all on me. Deep down, I feel like I'm not enough for someone like Peter and at some point no matter what I do, he's going to realize it. If we're living together then that will make it all the harder."

"Darlene, you should be having this conversation with Peter, but I think you are way off base. I've only just met him, but he seems like a stand-up kind of guy. He wouldn't lead you on."

"Maybe not intentionally, but you know me, Syd. I don't have what it takes to compete with these glamour girls that live in his world."

"And you think that's what Peter wants? A glamour girl?"

"Maybe not today, but what about next month or next year? Then what?"

"Darlene, none of us can predict the future. We just do the best we can with what we know now."

"I don't know what to do, Syd, and it's eating me up inside."

"Good morning, ladies." I felt Peter's hands on my shoulders and

I closed my eyes wondering how much of our conversation he might have heard.

"Peter!" Sydney left her seat in a hurry. "Have some coffee! I'm going to shower."

He found his mug and filled it before sitting down in Sydney's now empty chair. "So you were talking to Sydney." It came out more like an accusation.

"She heard us last night." I looked down at the table.

"Arguing or making up?" He picked up his mug, taking a drink.

"Did we make up?" Somehow I didn't feel as if we had.

"I told you last night. I'm not forcing you into anything you're not sure about, but that doesn't mean I like it. When I asked you to move in with me, I never dreamed that you would have so many mixed feelings about it, but I meant what I said. I won't ask you again. I just wish you'd tell me what's holding you back."

"Do we have to talk about it now?" I asked, starting to feel even more uncomfortable."

"Darlene, what's going on inside that head of yours?" His demeanor seemed to change. "Are you still thinking you might get back with Frank?

"Frank?!" I couldn't believe what I was hearing. "No, Peter, it's not about Frank. It's got nothing to do with Frank."

"Then what's it about? What did you tell Sydney that you can't seem to tell me?"

"I'm afraid." I took a deep breath and gazed into my coffee cup. "I told Sydney I'm afraid of such a huge change and I thought things were going fine the way they are."

"I thought moving in together would make things even better."

"I know, but—"

"But what?" His voice rang with impatience once more.

"But sometimes I think you deserve a woman who has more to offer than me and one day you'll see that." I blurted out the words, finally admitting what was bothering me, but instead of feeling better, I felt worse.

"Darlene, why would you think that?" Peter reached across the table and took both my hands in his. "Honey, we're connected and no matter what happens, that's not going to change."

His choice of words made me catch my breath. It's exactly what I'd been trying to tell my mother for months. "Do you really feel a connection, Peter?"

"Yeah, I do, and I was pretty sure that you felt it, too. Was I wrong?"

"No, you're not wrong, but I never could explain it to anyone no matter how hard I tried."

"Darlene, I promised I wouldn't pressure you, and I won't, but whatever you decide, our bond will always be there, no matter what. I don't think we'll ever be able to totally break free from each other— even if we wanted to."

Chapter Fifteen

Breakfast in bed with Peter is one thing, but breakfast in bed with Doug is not quite how I planned to celebrate my birthday this year. He just showed up as Peter surprised me this morning with balloons, flowers, and a catered breakfast. Doug's birthday is today and mine is tomorrow so he thought we should celebrate together. Doug is a terrific birthday partner. This may be the start of a great birthday tradition. Oh, and Peter gave me a pearl bracelet to match my necklace and earrings.

Turning twenty-four isn't exactly a milestone, but my life has changed so drastically this past year, it feels like one. I'm ten years younger than Peter. That doesn't seem to matter much on most days, but sometimes, I wonder if it will.

I wish Sydney could have stayed until my birthday, but the week she was here was filled with some serious shopping and several lazy afternoons at the beach. Our nightly pajama parties centered around wine and frozen pizzas. As for Peter, he dropped by after work every night, but always went home shaking his head at our antics. Like my mother's visit, Sydney's was way too short, but once she left, I had to focus on work and house hunting, which now seems to be gearing up.

The presidential race is also in full swing. President Ford, who was never really elected in the first place, is up against a peanut farmer from Georgia. There's also a mysterious illness hovering over Philadelphia. They're calling it Legionnaire's Disease and I hope they get to the bottom of it soon.

The premiere for Night Shoot has been scheduled for Christmas Eve. I thought that was an odd pick, but who am I? Peter suggested it be held in New York City since his family is there. The powers-that-be seemed to like the idea and are searching out possibilities. I have to speak with Helene about a dress and I already have something in mind!

Even though I still had a few months before the *Night Shoot* premiere, I bought a VHS tape of *High Society* and sent it to Helene via Peter with a note to pay special attention to the "Mind If I Make Love to You" number. While Frank Sinatra crooned, Grace Kelly wore a full-skirted chiffon gown with a mesh neckline and sleeves. Colorful embroidered flowers started at her right shoulder and cascaded downward toward the knee. A delicate piece of matching chiffon cinched her tiny waist. It was simple yet elegant.

I did a little research and discovered that the dress was designed by Helen Rose who won two Academy Awards for Best Costume Design. She also created Princess Grace's iconic bridal gown. *High Society* was the last film Grace Kelly made for MGM before her move to Monaco and the studio gave her this dress as a wedding present. It was breathtaking and if it was good enough for Grace Kelly, it was good enough for me.

After Helene watched the movie, we made a lunch date and I met her at The Smoke House in Burbank—one of her favorite spots. She carried a large envelope that she set on the table.

"So you're thinking of Grace Kelly this time?" Helene asked after we ordered.

"I've been studying the dress she wore when she was dancing with Frank Sinatra by the pool. What do you think, Helene?"

"I think it's a great choice." She opened the envelope and inside was a picture of that dress. "But it's the same light blue color as the feather dress. That won't do."

"Could we change the color—maybe make it a light lavender or a mint green, or a pale pink?"

"We could." She seemed to consider it for a moment as she looked more closely at the photo. "I think the lavender might be best and what if we got rid of the mesh top? How about one strap over the right shoulder? The flowers could start there."

"That might work!" I took the picture from her and tried to imagine those changes. "I could wear my pearls. Peter seems to think they're lucky, but there's one thing…"

"What's that, hon?"

"My waist is nowhere near as small as Princess Grace's. Look at how little that sash is."

"You don't need to worry about that. When we get through with it, this dress will look perfect on you! Just think, Peter will have a real princess on his arm at the premiere! I told you we could have fun with this, but Grace and Ginger will be hard to top. Now, have you thought about the studio

Christmas party?"

"No," I answered with a sigh. "Peter never said a word."

"He'll have to make an appearance whether he wants to or not."

"How about just a regular party dress?"

"And disappoint everyone? Oh no, hon. We'll have to find something subtle that won't upstage Princess Grace. Let's think about it for a week or two. I'm sure we can come up with something."

I looked at several houses between September and October. None of them were what Peter wanted. It was a little discouraging in some respects, but in other ways, it was a relief. At least I didn't have to give him an answer about moving in yet. True to his word, he never mentioned it again and I certainly didn't bring it up. As a matter of fact, I tried my best not to think about it at all, especially with the Christmas party playing heavily on my mind. I didn't have a clue about what to wear and I wasn't convinced that old Hollywood was the answer.

Just before Halloween, I went to the studio's costume department to have my first fitting for the Grace Kelly dress. It was coming along nicely and the pale lavender color was a great choice. Afterward, I stopped in to see Helene, hoping she had some ideas for the holiday party.

"Darlene, I think I found it!" She seemed excited to see me as she began digging through her desk drawers. "I have a picture here somewhere. I've been meaning to give it to Peter, but I keep forgetting. Here it is!" She pulled a photo from her bottom drawer and handed it to me. "How much do you know about the silent era?"

"A little," I said with a shrug as I recognized Clara Bow, Hollywood's original "It Girl". She was wearing a sleeveless black dress, with a square neckline and a full, cocktail-length skirt fitted at the waist.

"That dress not only changed Clara Bow's life, but it started a trend."

"I thought Coco Chanel started that trend."

"She did, but on a much smaller scale. Once women saw Clara in that dress, it became a fashion statement. Before Clara, women mostly wore black to funerals. After *It*, the little black dress became a staple in evening wear."

"Who designed it?"

"Travis Banton. He worked at Paramount and he dressed the best…Carole Lombard, Marlene Dietrich, and even Cleopatra!"

"Cleopatra worked at Paramount?"

"Well, Claudette Colbert when she played Cleopatra. What do you think, Darlene? Is Clara Bow's little black dress brilliant or what?"

"I kinda like it." I nodded, studying the picture a little closer. "It's actually pretty simple."

"And it won't overshadow the Grace Kelly dress one bit."

"Let's do it!" I really did like the idea, but I was more relieved than anything else to finally figure out what to wear to the party. "I'd be so lost without you, Helene! I owe you big time."

"Could I borrow Peter for a few days?" she asked with a grin. "My electrical system is on the blink."

"I'm not sure he'd be able to help you with that."

"Oh hon, I don't want his help!" She shook her head as the waitress approached our table with lunch. "I'll light candles when he gets there and let nature take its course."

Next, I made my way over to Peter's trailer. He wasn't there so I used my key to open the door. I slipped my shoes off and turned on the television. Within the hour, Peter turned up covered in black soot, but before coming inside, he removed his fireman gear, boots, and hat, leaving them in a dirty heap outside the door. Underneath, his clothes were fairly clean, but his hands, face, and hair were filthy. I surprised him when I opened the door.

"What are you doing here?" he asked with a smile.

"I had some business with Helene."

"The thought of that is terrifying." He cringed and came closer while I took a step back trying to avoid him. "I've lost track of who comes up with what."

"She did mention an electrical problem. She wants you to come by, but she doesn't want you to fix it. She said something about candles and letting nature take its course."

"How about if *we* let nature take its course?" He took another step closer and I backed up again.

"You need a shower before any course is taken."

He quickly bussed my check as he walked past and I could feel the grime on my face.

"Yuck!" I protested, as I tried to wipe off the dirt with my hand, but only succeeded in smearing it more.

"Use this!" Peter tossed me a hand towel from the bathroom before closing the door.

"Peter Chandler!" I hollered just as someone knocked. "You better stay in there if you know what's good for you!"

"I see Peter got to you." Gene Sutherland grinned as he stood in the doorway with a script in hand.

"Sometimes I forget what a dirty job he has." I ran the towel over my face. "Come on in, Gene."

"I wanted to drop this off." He handed me the script as he stepped inside. "So what do you think of the trailer?"

"Definitely a step up from that dressing room." I laid the script on the small kitchen counter and folded the now-dirty towel in half before dropping it on the floor. "The brothers must have been feeling generous when they gave it to him."

"Oh, I thought you knew. It wasn't the brothers. It was all Helene. I hear she threatened to gouge their eyes out with an icepick if they didn't give Peter a trailer. They fought about it for weeks."

"Why am I not surprised?" I shook my head while Gene grabbed a can of soda from the dormitory-size refrigerator. For the first time, I noticed he was no longer wearing his wedding ring. Leeanne must have been gone for good.

"So what have you been up to?" He plopped down on the couch.

"Working, house hunting, and worrying about what to wear to the premiere in December, not to mention the Christmas party, which I totally forgot about because Peter never even mentioned it."

"That feather dress will be hard to top."

"I'm working on it." I perched on one of the barstools. "And what have you been doing?"

"Shedding my wife." His answer startled me. "Leeanne and her martinis are someone else's problem now."

"I'm sorry, Gene."

"Don't be. Everyone but me saw it coming. I think I'll keep away from women for a while."

"You just need to find the right woman."

"That's pretty tough to do in this business."

"Especially since Darlene is off the market," Peter said with a grin as he stepped out of the bathroom. He wore a pair of jeans and a shirt that he hadn't yet bothered to button. His hair was damp and a few unruly curls fell across his forehead.

"We're not all as lucky as the two of you," Gene noted. "Not everyone can be part of a golden couple."

"Golden couple?" I repeated.

"Yeah, you must have heard that. Ever since the Fred and Ginger thing that's what people have been calling the two of you."

"Have you heard that?" I asked Peter.

"Once or twice and I've never bothered to deny it—until now." He walked over to me, shaking his head. "Darlene, if you want to be part of this golden couple, you really need to wash your face."

I touched my cheek and black ash came off in my hand. Evidently, I'd missed a spot. "It's a good thing you dropped by, Gene. Otherwise, you'd be writing James Dakota out of his own show."

Finally, the day after Jimmy Carter won the presidential election, I saw the house I knew we would eventually call home. I fell in love with the two-story home the moment we pulled in the driveway. Set on five acres of a mostly wooded lot, there was an enormous backyard with a swimming pool, tennis court, and a large outdoor kitchen centered around a firepit. The tiled area could easily hold a couple of couches and chairs. There was a long driveway made of pavers leading to a four-car garage that couldn't be seen from the street.

The house itself was just over five thousand square feet and it seemed massive to me, but the classic Spanish-style design and red-tiled roof gave it an elegant appearance. Inside the double wooden doors was a large foyer with stairs leading to the second floor. To the right was a living area where a tiled fireplace took center stage. To the left was a den with built-in bookshelves. The large country kitchen was dated, but nice. To the left of the kitchen was a dining room and to the right, a family room with another fireplace. There was also a half-bath and a utility room on the first floor.

Upstairs, a large master suite included a bathroom, oversized walk-in closet, and an even bigger sitting area. A long hallway that overlooked the foyer led to four more bedrooms—two on each side of the hallway with a Jack and Jill bathroom in between them. All of the bedrooms were large with picture windows—one side overlooked the backyard while the other side had a street view. The house was set back on the lot and beautifully landscaped with flowering shrubs and a manicured lawn. There were only three houses on the block and they were spaced far apart, ensuring privacy. This particular house was in the middle.

As I walked through, I could picture Peter working in the den, watching television in the family room, and having dinner in the kitchen. Upstairs, I even saw children running down the hallway—two girls and two boys, each sharing a set of bedrooms and a bath. This was our 'happily ever after' house. I could feel it. I made an appointment for Peter to see it.

When we pulled up in front of the house on Sunday afternoon, Peter looked it over with a serious eye. Our realtor hadn't gotten there yet so while we waited we took a walk around the grounds. Peter seemed pleased with the outdoor kitchen and he especially liked the tennis court.

"I haven't played in a long time," he said out loud, but I think he was talking more to himself than to me.

When the real estate agent arrived, she opened the door and told us to go inside. "Take your time. Look around. I'll wait in the kitchen. You can let me know what you think."

We wandered through the downstairs before heading upstairs. Peter seemed to be analyzing every detail and it was hard to know what he was really thinking.

"Let's talk for a minute." He pulled me back into the master bedroom once we'd seen the entire place and I couldn't help but wonder whether he liked it or not. "Darlene, when you first saw this house, what did you think?"

"I thought it was nice. I really liked the yard and I liked the way it was laid out. What are you thinking?"

"It seems kind of big."

"It's not near as big as your parents' house on Long Island."

"That's definitely too big, but this house is homier and when I look around here, I see a place that we can grow into and make our own."

Without realizing it, I took in a sharp breath.

"I'm not asking you to move in, Darlene." He frowned at me. "But can you imagine having dinner in the kitchen and relaxing around that firepit? And just think about the kids that could fill these bedrooms? This house is made for raising a family, honey. And that's exactly what I want one of these days. What do you think, Darlene? Should I go for it?"

Although this seemed like the hundredth house I looked at, it was the only one Peter saw. He put in a bid and, the next day it was accepted. Once he closed on the house and it was really his, he wanted some major changes. With keys in hand, we visited the house soon after the closing. As we walked through each room, Peter had bigger ideas than even I had imagined.

He wanted the kitchen completely gutted and redesigned with all new appliances, a full bath added on the first floor, and a new fireplace built in the family room. He also wanted the main bedroom and bath remodeled from top to bottom, including the installation of a skylight and a jacuzzi. Because his schedule was so hectic, he put Doug in charge of all the construction. His only stipulation was that the house be completely finished by the end of March. He wanted to move in as soon as *Fire in the City* wrapped for the season. He never asked me to move in, but the time was coming for me to make up my mind.

CHAPTER SIXTEEN

*N*ovember is over and Peter has yet to slow down. Every spare moment away from the series is spent promoting the movie. With a Christmas Eve premiere set in stone, there will be no time off. I'm not sure how we'll make it to March. I guess we'll have to hang on one day at a time. One good thing, Peter has been too busy to mention anything about me moving into the new house. I'm still not sure what to do, but I'll have to make up my mind once the renovations are complete.

Most nights, Peter falls asleep on the couch and I throw a blanket over him before heading home myself. I have my own time crunch to worry about with several projects due before Christmas. We're both running at full speed on a collision course with the holidays. I can only imagine how President-elect Jimmy Carter must feel. Life on the peanut farm will never be the same.

Night Shoot *has generated lots of talk. Most people are surprised to find Peter in a comedy. They seem to think of him in serious roles because of* Fire in the City. *I haven't seen the movie yet. I'm waiting for the big night. It sounds silly, but I don't want to jinx it.*

Peter's family will be there—what better publicity could there be? I will try my best to avoid Joyce and Carmen, but I am looking forward to seeing John and Daniel. Of course, Sydney promised to be there, too, but I have to somehow squeeze in a visit to Naperville to see my mother. Peter assures me that we can fly from New York to Chicago in between Christmas and New Year's. If he can't make it, I'll go alone. I need a Mom fix.

First things first, however, and that Christmas party is sneaking up on us. I hope Clara Bow's black dress works. Peter has no idea why I made him watch her most famous film, It. He did get a kick out of discovering that a very young Gary Cooper was featured. I think Gary and Clara were actually engaged at one point, but his mother didn't approve of her. Most mothers didn't. Poor Clara always got a bad rap. I guess we have something in common after all—Peter's mother doesn't approve of me either!

The 1976 Christmas party was held at the Beverly Hills Hotel—another iconic place in Tinseltown history. Peter and I have come a long way since last year's party. Now divorced for almost a year, I no longer worried about what the press might say. There would always be rumors, but more often than not, I learned to dismiss them. Peter certainly paid little attention to what was bandied about by reporters. Occasionally, we were referred to as the *golden couple*. I'm not sure what that meant exactly, but Helene said it was because we were genuinely happy together and it showed. We were happy, but no relationship is perfect. I still hadn't given Peter an answer about moving in with him. His inexplicable irritation at the mere mention of Frank's name continued and, in the back of my mind, I always feared the day when a more intriguing woman would catch Peter's eye. All good reasons to live in the moment and not think about what an uncertain future might hold.

That afternoon, before the party, Helene treated me to a spa day and we had our hair and make-up done, as well as getting manis and pedis. She dropped me off at Peter's place so I could finish getting ready there. To my surprise, I found him already wearing his suit minus his shoes and tie.

"The car will be here in thirty minutes, Darlene!" He checked his watch.

"I know," I answered, rushing past him to the second bedroom. "I just have to put on my dress and my pearls."

We had made a few minor adjustments to Clara's little black dress. Helene thought a little beading here and there would catch the light, making the dress more festive and, unlike the original skirt that fell just below the knee, this one hit mid-calf. When I stepped out of the bedroom, Peter was finishing off the knot in his tie. It took him a moment, but a smile of recognition slowly appeared. "Is that the dress Clara Bow had on?"

"With a couple of changes!" I took a quick spin and the skirt floated around me. "What do you think?"

"I think I had absolutely no desire to go to this party—until now." He took me in his arms with a smile. "Only the 'It Girl' could change my mind."

"I have to admit it was Helene's idea, but I wasn't hard to convince. I'm not sure that anyone will even recognize a dress from the silent era."

"Don't worry about that," he said with a grin. "I'll be sure and let everyone know that my date tonight is the original 'It Girl', Clara Bow herself."

And that's exactly what Peter did. I think he had more fun with it than anyone else—including me. One reporter even asked who I was planning to be for the *Night Shoot* premiere. I shrugged my shoulders and smiled. Peter couldn't answer because he didn't know. I suddenly understood what Helene had been saying all along: Channeling a classic movie star was not only imaginative, but it also created an effective way to keep 'em guessing—Peter included!

After the Christmas party, people started speculating who I would be dressed as for the *Night Shoot* premiere. Peter found the whole thing amusing and pestered me to tell him, but I refused—even on the flight to New York.

"Come on, Darlene!" He tried his best before we landed at JFK on Christmas Eve. "Can't you at least give me a hint?"

"Nope!" I looked out the window so I wouldn't see those blue eyes staring right through me.

"Will you tell me if I guess?

"Nope!" I concentrated on the clouds as we began our descent.

"What if I threaten to tell the New Year's Eve story?"

"You do and you'll be going to your premiere alone." I glared at him, but then quickly turned back to the window before his blue eyes did any damage.

"At least, give me her initials."

"No, but if it's any consolation, you'll be the first to see my dress once I put it on."

"Darlene, you are the most exasperating woman I have ever met!" He put his head back on the seat and closed his eyes.

"Just my luck there'll be a blizzard tonight." Peter picked up the menu from room service. "Are you hungry? I am."

New York was bitterly cold with a few inches of snow already on the ground when Peter and I checked into the Waldorf on Christmas Eve. It was early afternoon and the gray winter sky didn't look promising. The movie premiere was scheduled for seven with a holiday gala back at the hotel immediately after. We turned the TV on hoping to hear a weather report.

Peter ordered lunch while I kicked my shoes off and stretched out on the bed, taking a good look at him. He'd lost weight and his handsome face was pale. At least the weather report was reassuring—only a few inches of snow were expected well after midnight.

"Are you tired?" I made room for Peter to lie down.

"I am." He propped himself up on one arm, looking down at me.

"You need to take better care of yourself."

"I don't need a lecture." His voice held a hint of irritation.

"I wasn't going to give you one, but there were days I wondered whether you would even make it to the premiere tonight. You're always spreading yourself too thin."

"I admit things have been a little crazy lately—"

'You mean crazier?" I interrupted him.

"I'll make it all up to you on New Year's Eve, I promise."

"Why do we have to wait till New Year's Eve?" I slipped my arms around his neck.

A knock on our door interrupted what was turning into a rather nice kiss.

"That can't be lunch already!" I sat up, curiously watching as Peter left the bedroom.

"Darlene," he called out a moment later. "There's someone here to see you."

"Syd?" I rounded the corner and then stopped dead in my tracks. "Mom, what are you doing here?!"

"She's doing me a favor." Peter smiled, obviously pleased with himself. "I need to fill up the theater and I have another two hundred seats to go. Do you have any cousins, Darlene?"

It turned out that Peter had called my mother and made the arrangements for her to come to New York. She was staying in the room next to ours—the nicest surprise of all. The whole enterprise was top secret, but I couldn't have been happier to see her. She joined us for lunch and then went back to her own room so she could rest up and get ready for the evening.

"I'm not sure how you did it!" I hugged him once my mother was gone. "But thank you!"

"You don't have to thank me," he whispered as his fingers played in my hair. "I couldn't ask you to give up your mother on Christmas."

Helene was in Arizona with her two sisters so she couldn't make the premiere. They were both married with large families. From what I heard, her nieces and nephews idolized her. She was the cool aunt who worked in Hollywood with real stars. She sent Peter a telegram wishing him good luck and at the bottom she told me to have 'a royal good time'. Peter had no idea what that meant.

By five o'clock, we were about ready to leave for the theater. Peter, as well as the rest of the cast, needed to be there early for meet and greets, photo ops, and a few last-minute interviews. I shooed him out of the bedroom so I could put on my dress. I didn't want him to see me until I was completely ready, but even the best-laid plans sometimes go south. The Grace Kelly dress was elegant, but when I slipped it on, I couldn't get the zipper all the way up.

"Darlene, can I please come in there and see what you're wearing?" Peter called impatiently through the closed bedroom door.

"I'm not quite ready!" I answered looking at myself in the mirror. "I need help with the zipper. Is my mother here yet?"

"No, but zippers are my specialty." Peter opened the door a crack. "Can I please come in?"

"Only if you promise to—" Before I could finish, he walked in, then stopped, studying my reflection from top to bottom. He didn't say a word.

"Peter, my zipper!" I reminded him and he promptly unzipped it.

"You're supposed to zip it up."

"But zipping it down is what I'm good at!" He kissed the side of my neck. "I thought you knew that by now."

"You're not helping here!"

"If I zip it up now, can I unzip it later, princess?"

"Peter Chandler, you are impossible!"

He laughed, zipped my dress up, and then started singing 'Mind If I Make Love to You'.

"Maybe you should leave the singing part to Frank Sinatra," I told him. "Just because you both have blue eyes doesn't mean you can carry a tune."

He stopped for a moment. "Wasn't the princess a little tipsy during that number?

"I believe she was."

"Are you going to get tipsy tonight?"

"No."

"We'll see about that," he said with a grin and began singing again.

Peter looked every inch the leading man in his new navy suit. I made sure his tie had a little of the light lavender color running through it to match my dress. I put on my pearls—necklace, earrings, and bracelet. As I stepped into my dark gray heels, Peter's mood turned serious. He pulled me close and laid his forehead against mine.

"I need a minute with you before everything gets started."

"Are you nervous?"

"I'd be lying if I said no."

"I've got my lucky pearls on," I reminded him.

"I hope they are lucky, but I keep telling myself that no matter how things turn out tonight, we'll still be coming back here together and that's what really counts."

"And if you behave yourself tonight, maybe when we do get back here, I'll let you unzip my dress."

"I'll keep that in mind, princess!" He finally smiled.

Mom, in a simple black dress, rode over to the theater with us. She was a little overwhelmed by the stretch limo, but even more amazed when she saw the reporters and photographers that were waiting for us. Flashbulbs popped and questions were thrown our way as we kept up a steady pace toward the theater doors. Surprisingly, Peter didn't answer any of them, but once inside the lobby, which was all decked out for Christmas, the real work began. "Peter!" someone called out. "Who's your date tonight?"

"Darlene couldn't make it." Peter pulled me along. "So Prince Rainier graciously allowed Princess Grace to come instead." More flashbulbs popped. The dress with its cascading flowers intrigued them all.

"How does it feel to have a real princess on your arm?" Another person asked.

"Don't tell Darlene." Peter gave a wink. "But I kind of like it."

"Did you know about the dress beforehand?"

"No, it was classified information—until the princess here needed help with her zipper."

After all the dress hubbub died down, Peter posed for pictures with the other cast members, while I stayed close to Mom. Sydney arrived soon after, wearing some sort of red-and-gold Chinese outfit complete with chopsticks in her hair, which was now dyed jet-black. I was hoping she'd have a date, but she didn't. "You look fabulous," she whispered as she gave me a hug. "But where's Peter?"

"Working." I nodded my head in his general direction. Several more people had arrived that I didn't know and they all wanted to talk to him. The atmosphere was quickly turning festive, but Sydney, Mom, and I stayed off in one corner chatting until the Chandlers arrived.

The lively dynamics changed when Peter's family entered the theater. Joyce and Carmen focused their attention on Peter. Their cool attitude toward me was expected, but John's open arms and Daniel's warm smile made up for them. Peter's family had never seen him in action and I wondered how they felt watching him handle the press. The photographers wanted some family shots so I stepped aside with Daniel, letting Peter take pictures with his parents and sister.

"I see you came back!" Daniel took my hand with a grin.

"I promised you I would."

"I like that—a woman of her word. Darlene, my wife really thought you'd be long gone by now, but you proved her wrong. From one outsider to another, I really am glad to see you!"

The lobby buzzed with excitement. More photographers. More reporters. More guests arriving. I finally spotted Doug and the rest of the Lassiters. Peter had no idea that we'd been plotting for weeks to surprise him.

"You're supposed to be in Michigan!" He pointed a finger at Doug.

"I figured if we didn't come you might be here by yourself." Doug was always pleased when he got one past his friend, but it was seeing the entire Lassiter family that really thrilled Peter. While Gloria and Tina giggled and Carl took in the pretty girls, Peter greeted Art and Angie.

"Mom! Pop! I can't believe you're here!"

"Art and I wouldn't have missed this for anything!" Angie beamed at him. "This is so exciting and we're so proud of you."

"Hey, remember me?" Doug pushed Peter aside. "Your eldest son?"

"Are you in the movie?" Art asked.

"I'm the one with the law degree and that makes me the brains behind this outfit," Doug answered.

"If we're discussing brains," Peter said. "I think you missed your appointment with the Wizard. Maybe you should call him and reschedule."

Doug rolled his eyes and then turned to me. "Darlene, you look terrific in that dress—much too nice to spend the evening with my sorry friend here."

"For your information," Peter spoke up, "this isn't Darlene. It's Princess Grace all the way from Monaco."

"Your majesty!" Doug gave a formal bow. "The resemblance between you and Darlene is remarkable. I can never tell the two of you apart."

"The real princess wears a crown." I gave him a hug and then whispered, "I'm so glad you and your folks made it. Peter never suspected a thing."

"How many times do I have to tell you…he never was the sharpest tool in the shed." Doug looked around the lobby. "Is your mother here?"

"Over there, talking to Sydney." I pointed them out.

"Ruthie!" Doug hollered, making his way over to her, pulling me along with him. "I need a date for tonight!"

"So do I!" Mom beamed when she saw him.

Leaving me with Sydney, Doug took Mom by the arm and walked her over to his parents. "This is Ruthie, Darlene's mother, and she's single!"

Soon after the Lassiters arrived, it was time to take our seats. In the darkened theater, Peter's icy hands gave him away. No matter how calm he appeared, he was nervous. We both were. "This is it, Darlene. They're either going to like it or they're not." He squeezed my hand until it hurt. "This could be my first and last feature film."

I concentrated on the movie since I hadn't seen it before. His blue eyes were made for the big screen. They dominated every scene he was in. Peter, on the other hand, concentrated on the audience. The script itself was strong, but with Peter's delivery and timing, it came alive. By the time the final credits rolled, everyone in the theater knew Peter had a hit on his hands. That night, I thought that he could do anything he set his mind to.

Back at one of the Waldorf's banquet rooms, the rest of the evening sparkled with dinner and dancing. Security kept the reporters away and we had fun. I had watched Peter struggle over the past few months juggling more than he should, so it was good to see him relaxed and enjoying himself. The Lassiters and the Chandlers had rooms booked for the night and Sydney decided to stay with Mom. Tomorrow, we were all gathering together for a Christmas brunch and a look at the early reviews for *Night Shoot.* By the time Peter and I got back to our room, the only thing we wanted to do was take off our shoes.

"Honey," Peter fell back on the bed. "Tonight was perfect—right down to the last dance!"

"You sound like it's over," I sat next to him.

"You mean it's not?"

"I seem to remember something about unzipping this dress—unless of course, you're too tired to help me out." I picked up the phone. "I could always call my mother."

"I'm not that tired." He sat up, took the phone from my hand and hung it up. He reached behind me, slowly tugging my zipper down. Next, he pulled the strap off my shoulder. "How about we make what's left of this perfect night unforgettable?" His arms felt strong and his kisses more intense than I remembered them being in a long time.

When I woke up Christmas morning, I felt like a steam shovel had rolled over me—twice. Peter was still sleeping so I lay there hoping whatever it was would pass. It didn't. It wasn't like me to get sick. I rarely even caught cold. Maybe it was something I ate. That was probably it. I hoped no one else was feeling bad. The thought of meeting everyone downstairs for Christmas brunch made me feel even worse. I thought maybe if I took a quick shower, I would feel better, but I didn't.

"Are you ok, honey?" Peter was still lying in bed when I came out of the bathroom.

"I feel really tired and my stomach is upset. I don't think I can eat anything."

"You were fine last night." He sat up. "What happened?"

"I don't know." I sat down next to him. "I didn't have that much to drink. Maybe a cup of caffeine will do the trick."

"You don't have to come downstairs. Maybe you should stay up here and rest."

"Peter, it's Christmas. Everyone's here and I don't want to miss it. I'm sure whatever it is, will go away, once I get something in my stomach."

But it didn't go away. When we got downstairs, all I could manage was a half-cup of coffee. I couldn't eat a thing. The smell of all that food sent me to the bathroom where I promptly upchucked the coffee. Mom came after me.

"Honey, what's wrong? You're white as a sheet."

"I'm not sure. I just don't feel good."

She felt my forehead and decided I didn't have a fever. "How much did you have to drink last night?"

"Not enough to make me feel like this," I answered. "I'm not hung over, Mom, but I feel like I picked up a bug."

"Let's go back upstairs. Maybe if you lie down for a bit, you'll feel better." Mom took me by the arm. "I'll let Peter know. Meet me at the elevators."

CHAPTER SEVENTEEN

ere it is Christmas and the first time, we're all together, I get sick. Mom reminded me that there's never a good time to be sick, but that doesn't make me feel any better. Whatever this is, it came on quick and I can't even think about eating. Hopefully, it's a twenty-four-hour bug that will be gone by tomorrow. When Peter came back to our hotel room, he brought the newspapers with him so we could read the reviews for Night Shoot *together. The majority of them were good. Almost all of the critics agreed that Peter had pulled a comedic trump card out of his sleeve. We would have to wait and see if the box office numbers agreed. Now if I could only get myself together and shake off this germ, everything would be okay.*

The Lassiters flew back to Michigan after our Christmas brunch, but before they left, Doug stopped in to see me. I had sent my mother back to her own room for some rest before we headed out to Long Island and Peter was in the lobby saying goodbye to the rest of Doug's family.

"You feeling all right, honey?" Doug asked, kneeling next to the couch where I was lying.

"I'm fine," I smiled up at him, genuinely touched by his concern. "But I'm sorry I didn't talk to Art and Angie this morning. It was so nice of your family to come. I know having them here meant a lot to Peter. Make sure you thank them for me."

"I will, but you just get better." He gave my cheek a pat. "I'll give Peter a call later to check on you."

"You don't have to do that."

"But I do." Doug's serious moment seemed to have passed. "I can't trust Peter to look after you. It's a good thing Ruthie's here. I'm going to run next door and ask her to marry me again—while you're indisposed."

The rest of us went to the Chandler home on Long Island that afternoon, but I still couldn't eat a thing. Joyce and Carmen were civil to Mom and Sydney, but pretty much ignored me. Bobby and Timmy took a little time to get used to their uncle again, but before long they were all wrestling on the floor. While the boys tussled and whooped in delight, John seemed to have his eye on me.

"We haven't had much of a chance to talk." He limped over to where I was sitting with Mom and Sydney. "Are you ok, Darlene?"

"I'm fine. I must have caught something and I don't want to pass it around."

"Can we talk for a minute?" he asked. Mom and Sydney threw me puzzled looks and I shrugged as John led me by the hand into his den.

"Darlene, I want you to know how sorry I am about the way my wife and daughter treat you," he began. "I've had words with both of them, but they seemed to have made up their minds about you and I'm not sure why."

"It doesn't matter, John. Don't apologize for them."

"I feel like I should." He sat on the green couch and motioned for me to join him. "Peter's brought girls to this house before, but not one of them measured up in my eyes—until you. No one knows better than me how difficult my son can be. You deserve a gold medal for putting up with him on a daily basis."

"He puts up with me." I gave John a smile. "So I guess we're even."

"I watched the two of you last night and I honestly can't remember seeing Peter so at ease. I only wish my wife and daughter could see it. Before you came along, there was always something restless about him—an edginess of sorts and it was probably my fault."

"Why would you say that?"

"Because I've given him such a hard time about the business and if I had my way, I'd still want him to come home. I never will under-stand his choices, but what I really want to know is why he's dragging his feet when it comes to you."

"Dragging his feet?" I repeated, not sure what he was getting at.

"I know it's none of my business, Darlene, but I thought by now the two of you would be planning a wedding. You've been together for over a year and Peter just bought a house, so I was hoping to see a ring on your finger for Christmas. If you don't mind me asking— what's the holdup?"

"I don't think either one of us is quite ready for such a big step."

"Why not?" he asked.

"I barely survived a bad marriage," I reminded him. "And Peter can't seem to juggle much more."

"So it's a mutual agreement to wait?"

"Yes."

"Darlene, I never had much luck trying to tell my son what to do, but I'd like to tell you that waiting for the right time isn't always the smartest thing. You two have something special despite what Joyce and Carmen think. Don't make a mistake and wait. A lot of things can happen while you're waiting, and I don't want Peter to break your heart because he can't make up his mind."

"Maybe one day we'll surprise you and since I don't have a father, I'd expect you to step in for the daddy-daughter dance."

He smiled, leaned over, and kissed my forehead. "You really are a good girl, Darlene. I hope Peter realizes how good and if he ever hurts you, he'll answer to me and I promise you, I won't go easy on him."

Peter was still concerned about my pale complexion and lack of appetite when I overheard him talking to Daniel as we were getting ready to leave.

"Stop worrying," I admonished him with a poke.

"I don't have anything better to do at the moment." He frowned at me.

"Find something." I frowned back. "I'll be fine in a day or two and I'm sure Daniel has a whole ward full of patients who are really sick and need him."

"Give it a few days." Daniel helped me with my coat. "If it's a virus, it should be gone by then. If it isn't, call me and we'll go from there."

When we got back to the hotel that night, I went straight to bed—exhausted from doing absolutely nothing. The next morning I still wasn't feeling better. Peter was taping an interview so Mom stayed with me, while Sydney headed home to her apartment. There was no sense in all three of us sitting around. Mom tried coaxing me into eating, but the thought of putting food in my mouth was too much. All I wanted to do was lay on the couch. I hadn't even gotten dressed when my mother offered me a few crackers that she had pilfered from the banquet room.

I was hungry so I ate them and my stomach seemed a little less queasy.

"Darlene," Mom said in her quietest voice as she settled next to me. "Is there a chance you're pregnant?"

"NO!" I almost shouted at her. "Why would you even ask me that?"

"Because of how you're feeling and the way you look."

"Mom, I have a virus and I don't look any different than I did before."

"I didn't mean to upset you. I just thought—"

"You thought wrong!" I promptly stood up, dismissing the whole conversation, and went to shower. I shouldn't have snapped at my mother like that, but where would she get such a ridiculous idea? Once I was dressed, I apologized to Mom before falling asleep on the couch—my head in her lap. When Peter returned, he wanted to call Daniel, but I wouldn't hear of it. It was senseless to make him drive all the way to Manhattan just because I was out of sorts.

By Monday, I still couldn't eat. Every time I tried, I ended up in the bathroom losing it all. This time, Peter didn't ask. He simply called Daniel who promised to come to the hotel later that afternoon. Peter had another interview scheduled so Mom once again stayed with me. We should have been shopping in Manhattan or seeing a play on Broadway. Instead, we were stuck in a hotel room listening to me whine—all of which made me feel even worse. I couldn't seem to shake whatever this was.

On his way back from the interview, Peter ran into Daniel in the hotel lobby. I was so tired I had fallen asleep on the couch in the middle of a movie my mother and I were supposed to be watching. Peter woke me up to let me know that his brother-in-law was there.

"How are you, Darlene?" Daniel asked, setting his black bag down.

"A little better, but I'm still feeling run-down and I still don't have an appetite."

"Do you mind if we use the bedroom so we can talk privately and I can take a look at you?"

"I'm sorry for dragging you out here like this, Daniel," I said after I closed the bedroom door. "I told Peter not to call you."

"Don't be sorry. We're the outsiders, remember? We have to take care of each other." He opened his bag and rummaged through it, pulling out his tools of the trade—a thermometer, a stethoscope, and a blood pressure cuff.

I sat down on the bed while he took my temperature and checked my blood pressure before listening to my heart. Everything seemed to be in order. He asked me about my symptoms and I answered his questions as best I could.

"Darlene, as Peter's brother-in-law, this is absolutely none of my business, but as Dr. Vincenzo, I do have to ask you—is there any possibility you might be pregnant?"

"Were you talking to my mother?!"

"No, of course not." He shook his head. "It's just a routine question."

"And the answer is no!" I once again dismissed the whole idea as ludicrous. "Absolutely not! We've always been careful! It has to be something else."

"It could be a million things—none of them serious, but just because you use protection doesn't mean a pregnancy can't happen."

"I told you, Daniel." I tried to keep my voice even. "I'm not pregnant."

"When was your last period?"

"Somewhere around the middle of the month."

"And when did you start feeling sick?"

"Christmas morning."

With a loud sigh, he reached inside his black bag and pulled out a package. I couldn't tell what it was and he didn't offer any explanation. I watched as he scribbled something on his prescription pad and then sealed the paper in a hotel envelope before handing it and the package to me.

"Wait until January tenth or so and then use this."

"What is it?"

"A home pregnancy test."

"A home what?!"

"They're not available to the general public yet, but they will be next year. An ob-gyn friend of mine has been testing them in his office so I asked him for one. He tells me that they're pretty accurate. Follow the instructions, and after you take the test, call me with the results—either way. And, until you know for sure, stay away from alcohol and any types of drugs including over-the-counter meds."

"Shouldn't you be prescribing an antibiotic or penicillin or something?" I asked him, just a little irritated.

"I don't want you taking anything until we are one-hundred-percent positive that you are not pregnant."

"I'm pretty sure I'm not." I insisted, now even more irritated.

"Humor me, Darlene," he said. "I only want what's best for you. If you're not pregnant and you're still not feeling better in a couple of weeks, there's a million other tests we can run, but until then, please do as I ask."

"Ok," I said with a shrug. "But I'm telling you, Daniel, I'm sick—not pregnant! And I would appreciate it if you don't mention this conversation to anyone—especially Peter."

"This will all stay between us."

I believed him, but it was obvious by the way he looked at me that he wasn't convinced. Once he left the room, I hid the little package in the bottom of my suitcase, determined not to give it any more thought.

We arrived home early in the afternoon on the twenty-ninth of December while Mom flew back to Naperville. Peter had several interviews and guest appearances scheduled over the next two days. The box office for *Night Shoot* was big and Peter's blue eyes were the talk of the town. Still tired and unable to eat, I wasn't feeling any better. I attributed the exhaustion to jet lag and the lack of appetite to whatever was left of the virus. Discarding Daniel's notion that I might be pregnant, I put his stupid package in my bottom dresser drawer and tried my best to forget about it.

Peter surprised me with airline tickets to San Francisco. He had made reservations for New Year's Eve back at the same oceanfront hotel in Halfmoon Bay where we stayed last year.

Other than a couple of short walks on the beach, we never left the hotel room. I didn't have the energy. I tried to eat the dinner Peter ordered, but I ended up in the bathroom shortly after. I didn't dare touch the champagne he had brought up. The cork remained unpopped as the bottle sat in a pool of water inside a silver ice bucket. The very thought of it made my stomach churn. Even if I did want it, Daniel's warnings replayed in my head though I tried my best to shut them out. This wasn't quite the New Year's Eve celebration we had in mind, but Peter never once complained as we lay in bed watching the ball fall in Times Square.

When the wake-up call came three hours later, signaling midnight on the west coast, he turned to me. "How do you feel, honey?"

"Like a party pooper."

"Well, Miss Pooper, at least you're not wearing that ridiculous-looking bathrobe. Do you feel up to a little midnight madness tonight or shall I take a rain check?"

"No rain checks," I told him. "It's New Year's Eve and we have a tradition to keep up, but please don't tell me you have a coconut cream pie hiding somewhere around here."

"Not even a bite." He shook his head with a grin. "But I could take a raincheck for that."

"You'd have to load me up with Irish coffee first." I grinned back at him. "And that is definitely not going to happen tonight."

"Are you sure you're ok, honey?" he asked as he clicked off the television. "You really haven't been yourself since Christmas."

"I'm fine." I slipped my arms around his neck and pulled him closer. "And I was really hoping we'd start the New Year off right."

"Since you put it that way…" He reached over and turned out the light. "Darlene?"

"Why are you still talking?"

"Because there are two things I want you to promise me." His tone turned serious.

"What's that?"

"First, if there's anything that makes you uncomfortable, you need to tell me, and second, you have to let me know when you're ready."

That night, Peter showed me his tenderest side, taking everything slow and gentle, making sure that I was all right with every kiss and touch. Afterward I cried—something that surprised even me as I'd never done that before. Maybe it was the fact that I didn't feel good or perhaps it was the way Peter put me first, or maybe a combination of the two. I never considered the possibility of raging hormones, or the fact that deep inside, something told me we were about to hit a bump in the road.

Chapter Eighteen

*P*eter *is still pulling double duty—working on* Fire in the City *and now promoting* Night Shoot. *I've hardly seen him in the last several days. It's just as well since I'm still not feeling good, but I can't possibly be pregnant.*

Children are something Peter and I have tucked away in some vague plan for the future. Not now. It has to be something else. Didn't Daniel say there were a million different things that could be wrong?

I was absolutely fine on Christmas Eve. It wasn't until the next morning that I started to feel sick. What was it Peter had said? He wanted to make the night unforgettable? I'm sure a baby was not what he meant.

This is stupid. I'm making myself crazy and I'm not even sure if I am pregnant. Just take the damn test. It will probably come out negative, and then I can call Daniel, tell him he was way off the mark, and ask him which one of the other 999,999 tests I should take next.

But what if Daniel's right?

Just do it, Darlene. Take the test now. There's no point in putting it off. If you're not, you can stop worrying about it. If you are, then you will have to find some way to deal with it and tell Peter that the magic he always talks about has suddenly and without warning left the building.

I was alone in my apartment on that Monday morning when I finally made myself open Daniel's note.

> *Darlene—*
> *Take the pregnancy test and call me with the results—either way.*
> *Daniel*

The word 'PREGNANCY' jumped off the page, screaming for attention. It seemed to be the only word I could see. 'PREGNANCY'—it dominated the paper. I sat there trying to collect myself as I held Daniel's message in my trembling hand. I was nauseous before I read it and now that sick feeling in my stomach forced me into the bathroom. After losing what little I'd eaten, I came back into the bedroom, sat down on the bed, and opened the package. Again the word 'PREGNANCY' printed on the box screamed at me.

There was nothing left to do, but take the test. Either I was or I wasn't, and I needed to know. The results? Positive!

The air escaped my lungs as if someone had given me a one-two punch in the gut. Now what? Call Daniel? What could he possibly do for me all the way from New York? Besides, my fingers were shaking so bad, they would never cooperate with a telephone. *Take a breath, Darlene. There's always the chance that the test could be wrong. But if it is wrong, then why do I still feel so awful? The flu should have been long gone by now.*

Daniel had written his beeper number on the back of the prescription paper. I took a deep breath, sat down on the bed and pulled the telephone off the nightstand. It took a few tries before my trembling fingers allowed me to correctly call the number. When my phone rang a few moments later, I grabbed it. "Daniel?"

"Yes, Darlene. It's me. I assume you took the test?"

"Yes," was all I managed to choke.

"And you're pregnant?"

"According to the test."

"I thought as much and I'm sorry," he answered quietly. "I know you aren't quite ready for this. Are you all right?"

"I don't know." My voice shook. "What should I do, Daniel?"

"Two things—you need to talk to Peter and you need to see a doctor. You're going to have to tell Peter yourself, but if you need a doctor, I can help you with that."

"I'd appreciate it," I answered quietly.

"Let me make a quick call, then I'll get right back to you. Sit tight."

The minutes dragged by as I sat on the bed waiting for Daniel's callback. I tried to process what was happening, but I couldn't seem to think. How would I ever tell Peter? It's the last thing he'd want to hear. I paced up and back, worrying myself into a frenzy. What was taking Daniel so long?

When the phone finally rang, I jumped. What if it wasn't Daniel? I couldn't talk to anyone else right now. I stared at it until the fifth ring and then I answered, trying to keep my voice from cracking. Daniel was on the other end and he came through for me big time. "Darlene, I have a friend from med school who's an ob-gyn in North Hollywood now. His name is Ed Shurloch. He knows Peter is my brother-in-law. He has several celebrity patients and he'll be discreet. You won't have to worry about anyone else finding out. Ed wants you to meet him Wednesday afternoon at one, when his office is closed. I promise you can trust him."

"Thank you, Daniel, and please don't say anything to anyone— not even Carmen—until I figure out how I'm going to tell Peter."

"Carmen doesn't know a thing. She doesn't even know that I saw you in Manhattan. And for what it's worth, I'm sure you and Peter will work through this."

"Peter isn't ready for a baby," I reminded him as well as myself. "And to be perfectly honest, neither am I."

"I think I know my brother-in-law, Darlene. Trust him. He'll do the right thing."

Ed Shurloch was a big man—well over six feet and on the heavy side and he insisted that I call him Ed. "I owe Daniel." He smiled warmly as I met him for the first time in his empty office. "And I'm glad if I can help you out." He took me into an examining room. "How do you feel?"

"Mostly awful. I can't eat anything and I'm so tired all I want to do is sleep. I don't have any energy."

"That sounds normal, but it should pass as the pregnancy progresses. How does Peter feel about all of this?"

"Do you know Peter?"

"We've met a few times, but you didn't answer my question. How does he feel about all of this?"

"He doesn't know," I reluctantly admitted.

"Are you considering alternatives without telling him?"

"What sort of alternatives?"

"An abortion for one."

"That's not an option!" I was surprised to find that the very thought of terminating my pregnancy horrified me. I'd never once considered it, but at the same time, I wasn't sure what to do.

"I want you to understand that you have choices, but you need to talk to Peter. You should be making these decisions together."

"I'm having this baby no matter what Peter thinks."

We talked a little more, and then he performed a general exam. The last thing he needed was my weight. My face fell as I looked at the scale. He knew that something was wrong. "You're going to have to help me out here, Darlene. I don't have a starting point. You've obviously been losing weight. How much have you lost?"

"Twelve pounds."

"Let's not panic yet. Some women lose weight in the beginning months. Do you have a scale at home?"

"Yes."

"Make sure you use it and if you don't start gaining weight, I want to see you back here in two weeks. In the meantime, no matter how hard it is, you've got to make yourself eat. Some antinausea pills might help and you need to start taking prenatal vitamins. I have some samples here so you won't have to fill any prescriptions at the drugstore just yet and, for the time being, we can keep meeting here when the office is closed."

Great! Something else to worry about! Not only did Peter and I have to deal with an unplanned pregnancy, but we also had to keep it from the media. A single prescription in the wrong hands could lead to serious trouble. I secretly blessed Ed Shurloch for his compassion.

Peter came home with his own news that same night. "Darlene, you wouldn't believe how many movie offers I've been getting. Last year, there were six. This year, it's more like sixty! I thought *Night Shoot* might be my first and final movie, but it looks like I might do another picture this summer. Maybe I'll find one with an exotic location so we could have some fun. What do you think about going to Tahiti or Monte Carlo?"

"That sounds nice, honey." I tried to be supportive, but my heart was breaking. If he had told me this before the holidays, I would have been thrilled. He had no idea that our charmed life was about to come crashing down around us.

"What's wrong, Darlene? You don't seem very excited about any of this."

"Of course I am. I'm just tired."

"Honey, you haven't been yourself since Christmas. We need to get to the bottom of this and fix it before I commit to anything. You really need to see a doctor."

"I did see a doctor today. He's running some tests, but the results won't be in until next week." I told him a half-truth. I left out the part about the baby. At least now he'd stop asking questions until I had a chance to tell him this weekend when we took our usual Sunday walk on the beach.

On Sunday morning, the first thing I did was weigh myself. I hadn't gained anything, but I was relieved to find I hadn't lost anything either. After a bite of breakfast that left me feeling queasy, we headed north on the Pacific Coast Highway under cloudy skies. I thought of a million ways to tell Peter my news, but none seemed right. I could only pray that the words I needed would somehow find their way to me.

We reclaimed our favorite spot just north of Malibu, but there was no sun and the air was damp. As was our custom, we walked in silence taking in the view, but today the view wasn't appealing. I zipped up my jacket as the wind began to blow and, despite our familiar surroundings, I was out of place. The view hadn't changed, but I had, and I felt like a time bomb was ticking inside me.

"Are you cold?" Peter asked.

"A little." I couldn't bring myself to look at him. I was about to turn his life inside out and he didn't have a clue.

"You're tired, honey." He stopped walking and pulled my hand. "Let's just sit here for a while?"

We wedged into the sand and I leaned into Peter hoping to get warm. Even though he slipped an arm around me, I didn't feel safe like I usually did.

"Darlene, you're shaking." He looked down at me. "Do you want to go back to the car?"

I shook my head. The moment I dreaded all week was here. We watched the waves as they rushed toward us and then pulled away.

"Talk to me, honey." Peter said. "Whatever it is, just tell me."

There was nothing left, but to say it. I took a deep breath and without looking at him, I quietly said, "Peter, I'm pregnant."

He never uttered a word. He never even moved. I turned my head slightly so I could look at him. He was staring straight ahead, but every bit of color had drained from his face. His silence was maddening. He never even turned to look at me. "Please, say something."

"When?" He finally spoke.

"September."

"How long have you known?"

"A few days."

"Why didn't you tell me right away?"

"I was trying to find the right time," I answered truthfully. "I couldn't exactly spring this on you when you got home from work."

"Who else knows?"

"Only Daniel."

"My brother-in-law?!" He seemed surprised and for the first time since I'd told him, he looked at me. I don't know what I would have done without him," I admitted as the whole story poured out, starting with Daniel's visit in Manhattan.

"How do you feel?" was all he asked once I was through.

"I'm scared."

"Do you want the baby?"

"Peter, this is *our* baby! How could I not want it?"

"Then you've already decided to keep it?"

"I never considered anything else!" I raised my voice as angry tears surfaced. "And if that's not what you want—"

"I never said that," he interrupted me. "All I want right now is for you to talk to me. Tell me what you want, Darlene."

"I want this baby and I'm having it—with or without you." Completely overwhelmed, I couldn't stop the tears once they started. "I'm sorry, Peter. I know it's not how we planned things."

"Let's get out of here." Peter stood up and pulled me to my feet.

I thought for sure we'd head home, but once in the car, Peter continued driving north. Eventually, he pulled off and drove into a small town near the highway. "Are you hungry?"

I shook my head.

"You need to eat," he insisted and pulled into the parking lot of a small sandwich shop. I watched him go inside where the patrons must have asked him for autographs. They wouldn't leave him alone—not even today. He brought back two sandwiches and sodas. We returned to the highway only this time we headed south. We went back to our spot north of Malibu and sat down on the little wall that separated the beach from the parking lot. I could only eat half of my sandwich and I was cold. Back in the car, we continued south as my stomach turned sour.

"Peter, can you please pull over?" I took a deep breath. "I feel sick." He no sooner stopped than I opened the car door and, leaning outside, I lost everything I'd eaten.

Other than to ask me how I was feeling, Peter never brought up the pregnancy once during the next week. He was still consumed with work, but I couldn't help wondering if he was avoiding me. When he stopped in at my place late Saturday night, I was laying on the couch in the middle of another crying session. It seemed like that's all I'd been doing lately. My insides were jumbled. I felt as if I was on my own with all of this because I still had no idea what Peter was thinking.

He squatted next to me and touched my hair. "Honey, I should have been here and I'm sorry. I needed a little time to think."

"And?" I sat up as he slid next to me.

"You seem pretty positive about keeping the baby."

"I am positive." I took a couple of deep breaths. "And there's nothing you could ever do or say to make me feel any different."

"But, Darlene, a baby changes things."

"And you think I don't know that?!" My voice rose a notch and the words spewed out before I could stop them. "You've never once talked to me. I don't even know how you feel about this baby. Do you even want it? Do you even want me anymore?"

"Darlene, of course, I still want you." He sat back, surprised at my outburst.

"But I feel like I'm all alone in this.' I choked on the words. "I need to hear you say it, Peter. One way or the other. I need to know. Do you want this baby or not?"

"Darlene, you're hardly alone." He reached for my hand. "And I'm sorry if I made you feel that way, but I have to be honest with you. I never saw this coming and the thought of having a baby is a little overwhelming. I've spent all week trying to come to terms with it."

"And have you come to terms with it?" I pulled my hand away. "Because I didn't have that luxury."

"Honey, I know this caught us both off guard." He took my hand back. "But according to my high school biology teacher, you didn't do this by yourself. I'm pretty sure I had something to do with it."

"But do you want the baby?" I asked again because he still hadn't answered my question.

"Darlene, what I want is for us to be a family." He laid his hand on my stomach. "But it's not just about the two of us anymore. We have to do what's right for the baby. Maybe we should get married. Have you thought about that?"

"I don't know." I swiped at the tears with the back of my hand. "The last time we talked about getting married neither of us was ready."

"Things are different now."

"But we wouldn't be sitting here talking about marriage if I weren't pregnant."

"I suppose not, but I don't want to be a part-time father and our baby deserves two parents."

"But I don't want to spend the rest of my life feeling like I forced you into something. I'd always wonder whether you married me because you wanted to or because you had to. How could I live with that?"

"So you want the baby, but you don't want to get married. I'm not sure where that leaves us."

"Maybe I could move in with you when the house is finished?" I brightened as the thought struck me for the first time. "That is, if you want us."

"Darlene." He pulled me closer and his fingers played in my hair. "When I bought the house, it was supposed to be for us—not just me. I never wanted to live there alone and if you bring along a little boarder, even better."

"You mean that?"

"Of course I mean it." He kissed the top of my head. "And tomorrow we should go over to the house and decide which room should be the nursery."

"Aren't you rushing things a bit?" I looked up at him, feeling somewhat relieved. "The baby won't be here until after summer."

"You're right. First, we need to find a spot in the yard for swings, then we can go inside and pick out the nursery."

"Then you're really okay with all of this?"

He laid his forehead against mine. "Honey, I know you had misgivings about moving in with me at first, but now we'll be together. This baby is our good luck charm—like a Lucky Penny."

And from that moment on, Lucky Penny became the center of our lives.

CHAPTER NINETEEN

P*eter passed up an offer to film in Rome. At first, I felt responsible for his choice to stay home, afraid he might resent me, but he assured me that no movie would ever be as important as our Lucky Penny.*

If I ever had any doubts about that, things were put in perspective today, when we heard about the awful death of Freddie Prinze. It's so hard to believe. Peter met him several times and the news hit him hard. Freddie was such a fun-loving, charismatic guy. He had the world at his feet and a new infant son whom he adored. This whole tragedy certainly woke us up and set our priorities straight.

Except for Doug and Helene, we're keeping the baby news to ourselves for now. I haven't even told Sydney yet and I'm not sure what to say to Mom. I doubt if she'll approve of our new living arrangements, let alone throwing a baby in the mix without a wedding in sight. I still can't keep much food down and that's another thing to worry about.

Peter has made it very clear he wants a girl. I have no preference—only a healthy baby. We visited the house and chose one of the bedrooms to turn into a nursery and Peter found the perfect spot in the backyard for swings. He is already spoiling Lucky Penny and she hasn't even gotten here yet. I can definitely see trouble down the road when he wants to buy her a red convertible for her first birthday.

By the end of February, I was eight weeks along with Lucky Penny, and Peter was moonlighting again, working on pre-production for a summer movie, as well as filming *Fire in the City*. Most nights, I didn't see him, but he always called and I always told him I was fine whether I was or not. I didn't want him worrying about me on top of everything else he was juggling, but I couldn't wait until *Fire in the City* wrapped for the season. Peter would have more time.

Maybe I would stop feeling so sick by then, too. I had gained very little weight and that was a concern.

Doug, on the other hand, was wonderful company. He stopped by two or three nights each week, cheering me up even when I didn't feel like smiling. I never knew whether Peter put him up to it or if he came over on his own. Either way, I looked forward to his visits. Doug was so easy to talk to and I believe, to this day, that those evenings cemented our friendship.

By mid-March, Peter was wrapping up season two of *Fire in the City*, and I had my next doctor's appointment. Ed Shurloch was still seeing me on Wednesday afternoons when his office was closed. Peter left work to meet me there.

"We need to get your weight, Darlene." Ed walked me over to the scale. My heart sank. I had lost the pound and a half that I had gained in February. Ed didn't say anything, but I could tell he was concerned as we followed him into an examination room. I lay down on the table so he could get a good look at my stomach, which seemed much rounder.

"Let's see if we can find a heartbeat today." The doctor pulled out what he called a fetal stethoscope and listened, but there wasn't a sound. "It may be a little too early for me to catch the baby's heartbeat with this." He held up the stethoscope. "But I am a little worried about your weight loss. Are you eating, Darlene?"

"I try, but I'm still having trouble keeping food down."

"She always seems to be sick," Peter offered, squeezing my hand.

"Are you taking the meds I gave you?"

I nodded.

"Good. Keep taking them and please, whatever you do, make yourself eat." He stood up to his full height. "I'd also like to do an ultrasound today if that's okay with you."

"What's that?" I wanted to know. After all, it was 1977 and ultrasounds were not commonplace.

"It's a way for us to take a look at the baby." Ed explained. "Ultrasounds are usually done at the hospital, but we have a machine in the office because of the celebrity patients we see. Like you, they prefer to keep things private so we decided to invest in one right here."

"Is it safe?" Peter asked.

"Totally safe," Ed assured us. "And we'll be able to see what's going on with the baby."

He took us to another exam room with a large machine in one corner. I once again lay on the table and Ed smeared some kind of cold gel over my stomach. He then took a wand that was connected to the machine by a cord and ran it over the gel. It gave me a chill and I shivered.

"Look at the screen," Ed told us. "We should be able to see the baby."

And just like that, a baby shape appeared. Ed pointed out the head, and other body parts, but the most miraculous thing of all was hearing our baby's heartbeat for the very first time. We listened in awe at the life we had created, but for one brief second, it seemed that the doctor was once again troubled. I glanced at Peter to see if he'd noticed. He hadn't. After I cleaned myself up, Ed ushered us back into his office.

"I was hoping by now you'd be feeling better and the problems you've been experiencing would have tapered off." He motioned for us to sit down. "Darlene, Peter, I have to be perfectly frank with you. The baby's heartbeat seems weak. Now that could change by your next appointment, but it does concern me at the moment."

"Should I be doing something different?" My breath caught in my throat and my mouth felt like it was coated with cotton.

"It's nothing you're doing or not doing, and I don't mean to scare you. Unfortunately, it's the way it goes sometimes. Make sure you get plenty of rest and, remember, you have to eat. I can't stress that enough. For now, we'll take one month at a time, but if anything seems wrong, and I do mean anything, I want you to call me immediately. Keep my beeper number handy."

The visit was anything but reassuring. Nevertheless, Peter had to go back to the studio and I went home. I tried telling myself that everything was fine—our next appointment would be better—but a feeling of dread that I couldn't shake began to take form.

When Doug stopped by that evening, I was in the kitchen packing up dishes trying to stop the doctor's words from racing through my mind over and over again.

"How did your appointment go?" Doug wanted to know as he rolled up his sleeves before pulling mugs out of the cupboard.

"Not so good." I busied myself rearranging the box so I wouldn't have to look at him. "I lost everything I gained last month and the doctor thought the baby's heartbeat sounded weak."

"Are you all right, Darlene?" Doug set the mugs on the table.

"I'm a little scared," I admitted.

"Peter should be here." He gave me a stern look.

"You know he's working."

"That's no excuse."

"He'll be here as soon as he can." I tried keeping my voice steady. "But I sure could use some company. Do you mind staying for a while?"

"What I mind is seeing you upset." He pulled out a kitchen chair. "You need to sit down and take it easy."

"I need to keep busy." I forced a smile. "But I promise not to overdo it."

"Why don't you take a break and go to dinner with me?" he asked. "Nothing fancy—just to get you out of here for a bit. And I'm pretty sure not a single soul will bother us."

"That sounds nice!" I told him, grateful for the diversion. "Give me a minute to change."

Doug and I went to dinner at a nearby eatery, where he had me laughing in no time. He was right. No one bothered us, but two days later, our picture was plastered everywhere along with a story proclaiming that we were having a torrid affair behind Peter's back. At first Doug was angry, and I was shocked, but it wouldn't be the last time we'd be fodder for the rumor mill. It was Peter who found the whole idea mildly amusing over Sunday morning coffee in his kitchen.

"If you two are having such a scandalous affair I'm not supposed to know about, that's one thing, but why did you go out in public and parade it around?"

"We thought you wouldn't notice," Doug told him as he bit into a bagel.

"Next time, we'll wear Groucho Marx glasses," I suggested. "Maybe no one will recognize us."

The house was finished the first week of April. Light and airy, it was a friendly and welcoming place. Our country kitchen was now oversized and completely updated with everything from microwave to dishwasher. It took up one side of the first floor. We even had a breakfast nook with a large window that looked out over the back-yard. Past the kitchen was a family room whose focus was a new canyon stone fireplace; to the right of that was a formal dining room that was, at the moment, empty. A new utility room had a built-in ironing board that swung out from the wall. For his den, Peter chose an antique rolltop desk that took three men to carry inside. I think it reminded him of his dad's desk back in Long Island.

Upstairs, in our room, we went with a hardwood floor and oriental area rug. Our new oak bedroom set reminded me of a 1940s movie. I could almost see Nick and Nora Charles having cocktails in the sitting area that held two oversized chairs with a large ottoman cen-tered between them. The expanded walk-in closet had a dressing room attached and our bathroom even had a hot tub—something I couldn't use until after the baby was born. For all the misgivings I'd had about moving in with Peter, I now looked forward to it.

Filming for season two finally wrapped up and Peter's schedule became more sensible. He even took time off so he could be there when the movers came. Physically, I couldn't do a whole lot so I tried to stay out of the way. Boxes filled every room of the new house, and I was overwhelmed with all the work it would take to unpack everything. Combining two households into one was harder than either of us had realized. The most important room to me, as always, was the kitchen, so I tried to get organized in there as best I could.

After an exhausting day, Peter and I went upstairs together. Once we were comfortable in our new bed, he turned on the TV looking for a late movie. "Are you happy, Darlene?"

"Yes." I smiled. "Are you?"

"I can't remember a better day."

We were both tired, but that didn't put a damper on the joy we shared as we stopped to watch Clark Gable hang the Walls of Jericho between himself and leggy heiress Claudette Colbert.

While Hollywood's King and his leading lady spent the night apart, we made love in our own home for the very first time, neither of us realizing that our joy would be short-lived. We were in the eye of the storm and we didn't even know it.

Three weeks later, Peter and I were unpacking boxes in the den on a Monday evening. It was the last room left to organize. I was sure I'd be feeling better, but I wasn't and my back was bothering me—something I wanted to discuss with the doctor at my next appointment, which was scheduled for Wednesday.

"Darlene, are you okay?" Peter asked as he unpacked a box of books.

"My back hurts." I stood on my toes and arched my back trying to stretch.

"You probably overdid it with all of this moving. Why don't you go upstairs and lie down for a while?"

"That sounds like a good idea."

"Call me if you need anything," Peter hollered after me.

I planned to go straight to bed, but when I got to the top of the stairs, my bladder had other ideas so I went into the bathroom first. A cold chill passed through me when I noticed blood. It wasn't a lot—just some spotting, but it scared me. I took a deep breath and found Ed's beeper number in my nightstand and I dialed. Before I upset Peter, I wanted to talk to the doctor. When he called, he assured me that a little spotting was normal. Heavy bleeding, however, would be another story.

"And there's one more thing—my back has been hurting an awful lot," I told him.

"Hurting how?" he asked. "A constant dull ache or periodic spasms?"

"A constant dull ache."

"Pregnancies often bring on back problems and I know that you recently moved. That can be both physically and emotionally demanding. Maybe you should stay off your feet for a while. Are you home alone?"

"No, Peter is here."

"Good. Get some rest and I'll see you Wednesday."

"Okay, and I'm really sorry I bothered you."

"I'm your doctor, Darlene. You're supposed to bother me and if you need me for anything, please don't hesitate to call."

Just as I lay down, Peter came in with a cup of tea. "I heard the phone. Were you talking to someone?"

"I called the doctor."

"Why? What's wrong?" His face paled.

"I'm spotting a little, but he said that's normal and I'll see him on Wednesday anyway so I guess I just panicked."

"Are you sure you're all right?"

"I think all I need is a good night's sleep." I sat up and took the teacup.

But the back pain persisted. I couldn't lie in bed so I got up and sat in one of the chairs, propping my feet on the ottoman. A few minutes later that wasn't comfortable. I changed into a nightgown, thinking maybe my clothes were too tight. Pretty soon Peter and I would have to tell people because I wasn't going to be able to hide Lucky Penny much longer. I still dreaded telling my mother. It was bad enough when I told her that I had moved in with Peter—something she accepted, but wasn't crazy about.

When Peter came up to bed that night, he found me pacing around the room. "Honey, I thought you were asleep by now. What's wrong?"

"I can't find a comfortable spot," I sighed. "My back is killing me."

"Are you still spotting?"

"A little, but if I could just lay down or sit somewhere with my feet up maybe I could sleep and then I'd feel better."

Peter took my pillows and propped them up against the headboard, then he pulled a small brown throw from the back of one of the chairs. He folded it in half and rolled it up. "Lean against the pillows, honey, and I'll slide this blanket behind your back."

I was willing to try anything, so I climbed into bed and when Peter placed that blanket at my lower back, it really did help. The pain was still there, but not nearly as bad, and I fell asleep.

The next day, the spotting stopped. I even managed to keep breakfast down, but the backpain persisted.

"Aren't you going to work?" I asked Peter when I realized it was after nine.

"I called the producers last night. There's no way I'm leaving you. I know we've been trying to keep Penny to ourselves, but I had to tell them why I wouldn't be there."

"What did they say?"

"They can shoot around me for a few days. Once we see the doctor tomorrow, I'll feel better about going back to work."

"Peter, you can't stay home indefinitely."

"That's something for me to worry about, not you. You just take care of Lucky Penny."

Severe cramps rolled through me early Wednesday morning, waking me from a deep sleep. Feeling weak and dizzy, something had changed. "Peter!" I shook him. "Peter, get up. Something's wrong! I need to get to the bathroom."

He was up in a flash and around to my side of the bed. He pulled the covers back and helped me up. Warm blood gushed down my legs. Lightheaded, I closed my eyes and my knees buckled. Peter caught me and gently sat me back down on the bed. "Don't move, honey. I'm calling the doctor. We need to get you to the hospital."

I couldn't focus, but I could hear Peter fumbling with the telephone. It rang one time and then I heard him talking, but he sounded like he was in a tunnel. I couldn't make out the words. The cramps seemed to come and go, but when they were at their worst, I could feel more blood oozing out of me.

He picked me up, but I didn't understand why. "What are you doing?"

"Taking you to the hospital." Peter carried me downstairs. "Ed says he'll meet us there."

"But I'm not dressed." I suddenly remembered I was only wearing a nightgown. I didn't even have a pair of slippers on.

"That's not important, honey. There's no time. Ed said I should drive you. We can't wait for an ambulance."

"Oooohh, Peter it hurts!" I gasped as another pain took hold. He carried me out the side door and I don't believe he even stopped to lock it.

"Hang on, honey!" Peter buckled me in and then laid the seat back since I could hardly sit up. "You're going to be okay. Stay with me, ok?"

He rushed around to the driver's side and when he pulled away, I distinctly remember hearing the tires screech. For some reason, I thought about the white interior. "Peter, your car." I started to cry. "I'm bleeding everywhere."

"Please, don't worry about the car, Darlene." His voice had an edge to it as he turned onto the street. "Just stay with me," he repeated as I drifted in and out. He squeezed my hand, and his fingers were cold.

"How much longer, Peter?" I moaned as another cramp took hold.

"A few more minutes." He sped up despite the winding roads he was trying to maneuver. "Try to hang on."

I don't remember how long it took us to get to the hospital, but the last thing I saw was a flurry of doctors and nurses as we pulled up to the emergency room doors. They must have been waiting for us. When I opened my eyes again, the cramping was not as intense, but I was tired. We were in some sort of cubicle and I was wearing a hospital gown. Several IVs were hooked into my arms.

"You're all right now, honey." Peter brushed the hair from my face. "The bleeding stopped and we're waiting to talk to Ed. He should be here any minute."

"What happened? Is Penny ok?"

"I don't know," he answered. "Why don't you try and rest until the doctor gets here?"

Whatever they gave me made my eyes feel heavy. I didn't want to sleep, but I drifted off for a few minutes until Ed arrived.

"How do you feel, Darlene?" he asked.

"I'm okay. I just want to know if the baby's all right."

"At the moment, I'm a little more concerned about you," Ed said. "You lost a lot of blood. We're going to have to admit you in case you start hemorrhaging again."

"What about the baby?" I asked once more.

"Let's get you out of here and into a private room, then we'll talk." He turned to Peter. "Is there someone who can bring you a change of clothes?"

Peter looked down at himself, surprised to see so much blood. The front of his shirt and his jeans were covered. I took in a sharp breath, suddenly realizing how heavily I must have been bleeding.

"It's all right." Peter stroked my hair. "I'll call Doug once we get you to your room. If he's not in court, he'll come."

I was soon settled in a hospital room and beginning to feel better. The pains had subsided along with the bleeding. A technician brought an ultrasound machine into the room and spread that icy gel over my stomach. Once again, we heard the baby's heartbeat. "She's still here!" I whispered, clutching Peter's hand, relieved that I hadn't lost the baby.

"She's tough like her mother," Peter smiled.

As he promised, Ed came back to talk to us. "Darlene, you haven't lost the baby, but you have to understand that the fetus has been through a great deal of trauma and stress. I don't want to give you any false hope, but to put it in layman's terms, your placenta is failing, and without that, the baby's life isn't viable. We're going to do everything we can, but if you start hemorrhaging again, you will most likely miscarry. I wish I had better news. I'm so sorry."

"But her heart is still beating." I closed my eyes, trying to take this all in.

"Darlene, I know this is hard." Ed sat down on the bed. "Most miscarriages happen during the first trimester. You're well into your fourth month now, which makes it all the harder and any more hemorrhaging could put you in jeopardy. No one here wants that."

"Honey, do you want me to call Ruth?" Peter asked.

"No. She doesn't even know about Penny and there's nothing she can do." I squeezed his hand, which felt even colder than it did before. "And I won't give Penny up without a fight."

Peter never once left me except to use the shower in my room and change into the clean clothes that Doug dropped off. He was strong when I wasn't, but his icy hands let me know he was worried. If I lost the baby, Peter would be devastated. If for no other reason, I had to fight this battle in order to spare him that pain. As hard as it had been in the beginning, we now embraced the idea of becoming a family and I wasn't about to let Penny slip away.

By evening, I was tired of lying in bed. I couldn't get comfortable. My head hurt and for the first time since the morning, the pains returned, only now they were more intense. All I remembered was the doctor saying that if I hemorrhaged again I would lose Penny. Once more I felt dizzy and faint, but I fought to stay alert. Penny depended on it. Then while Peter was on the phone with Helene, my entire body began to shake.

I looked under the covers and saw the pool of blood that was quickly growing around me. Peter dropped the phone and raced out into the hall for help. Nurses and doctors came running—some carrying blood, others pushing carts. I was vaguely aware of people working on me. The persistent pains were excruciating, but I was going to save this baby for Peter no matter what. They were still trying to get things under control when the doctor walked in.

"Peter, maybe you shouldn't stay," Ed quietly suggested. "This might not be easy to watch."

Peter hesitated and then let go of my hand. He stood up and I remember yanking the oxygen from my nose and trying to get up. Hysterical, I kept screaming over and over. "Don't leave me, Peter! Please don't leave me!"

Peter looked at Ed, not quite sure what to do.

"Will you be ok?" he asked Peter, who nodded in reply. "Then you can stay for now."

Peter sat back down and took my hand. I calmed down while they readjusted the oxygen and checked my IVs. The contractions grew worse, coming closer together. The pains were so sharp I could hardly breathe, and I started to feel the blood oozing out of me again.

"Darlene, listen to me." Ed stood directly over me. "You have to work with us here. Stop fighting. You're putting yourself in danger now. Talk to her, Peter."

"It's time to let go, honey," Peter pleaded, his voice cracking.

"No, Peter!" I sobbed, clutching his hand. "Penny's heart is beating. We both heard it. Please make them do something. Make them save our Lucky Penny. Please, Peter, tell them they have to save her. Please, Peter, please!"

"Darlene, it's not Penny they're trying to save," he whispered. "It's you. Our Lucky Penny is gone, honey. There's nothing we can do for her, but I can't lose you, too. Please, Darlene, stop fighting everyone and let them take care of you. Do it for me, ok?"

The last thing I heard was the doctor's voice. "We need to get her to the O.R. stat. She's bleeding out."

I'd seen many emotions in Peter's eyes since we'd met, but tonight was the first time I'd ever seen fear. Then everything went black.

I woke to the sound of a continuous beep, beep, beep. At first it was off in the distance, but the sound gradually grew louder and it wouldn't stop. Too exhausted to open my eyes, I was consumed by emptiness. I'd lost the baby. I lay there trying to put the pieces together, but it was all so overwhelming, I couldn't think. I finally forced my eyes open and the hospital room was dark. It was eerily quiet, except for that incessant beeping. I counted four hoses connecting me to IVs. Where had everyone gone? How long had I been sleeping? I tried to move, but whatever they had done left me hurting.

I turned my head to the right and saw Peter asleep in a chair. He looked so uncomfortable. He must have been distraught over losing Lucky Penny. There would be no nursery in the new house or no swings in the backyard—only the memory of a heartbeat. Devastated, my eyes welled up.

"Darlene." I heard my mother's voice and felt her gentle hand in my hair. "You're all right now, honey."

I thought I was dreaming until Peter woke up. He was out of the chair and taking my hand before I could speak. I kept looking from one to the other not quite sure what to think.

"I know you asked me not to, honey, but I called Ruth," Peter whispered. "I thought she should be here."

"She knows?"

"I know, honey," Mom said quietly, still stroking my hair. "And I'm so sorry you had to go through all of this."

"When did you get here?"

"Early yesterday."

How could that be? Peter was with me all afternoon. I purposely told him not to call my mother. Or, maybe, I had somehow lost track of time. "Peter, what day is it?"

"It's Friday, honey. I called your mother Wednesday night. She caught the red-eye and I had a car bring her straight to the hospital.

She's been here ever since."

Somehow, I'd lost a day and a half! "You were afraid." I looked up at Peter. "It's the last thing I remember."

"I was terrified."

"You two need some time alone." Mom kissed my forehead. "I love you, Darlene." She touched my face. "I'm going down to the chapel for a little while. Take care of my little girl, Peter." He gave her a silent nod.

"I should have tried harder." My voice broke as my mother closed the door behind her.

"You tried too hard as it was." There was the slightest tremor in Peter's voice.

"But Penny's gone," I cried.

"Not because you didn't try." He brushed my tears away with his thumb.

"Was Penny a boy or a girl?"

"A girl." His eyes were filling now, too.

"Did you see her?"

"No, honey, I didn't."

The pain on his face was too much. I turned away. I felt responsible. He tried to hold me, but I wouldn't let him. He tried to touch me, but I pulled back. Peter wanted a little girl and I'd lost her.

"I don't know what to do for you, honey. Do you want your mother?"

"I want Penny!" I wept, still refusing to look at him afraid to see the disappointment in his eyes. He left the room and I didn't even know it.

"Darlene!" Mom's voice got my attention a few moments later. "You aren't alone in this. It's Peter's loss, too. Do you have any idea what he's been through? Do you know how close we came to losing you?"

"What are you talking about?" I still couldn't pull myself together.

"Honey, the doctors worked on you most of Wednesday night." Her voice softened. "They'd no sooner get the bleeding stopped and it would start again. They gave you eight pints of blood. Peter called me when they told him how bad things really were. He was so upset he could hardly talk. Losing the baby was one thing, Darlene, but almost losing you was way more than he could handle. It was way more than I could handle. They finally had to sedate you because it was the only way they could get you to rest."

"But I never once felt like I was in trouble—only the baby. Nothing else mattered. I just wanted to save the baby."

"I know how hard you fought, honey." She stroked my hair once again. "But the worst thing you can do right now is shut Peter out. Share your grief with him like you'd share anything else. It's the only way for you both to get through this."

"Where is he?"

"I left him in the chapel. Why don't I go down there and tell him that you want to see him?"

When Peter came back, he just stood at the foot of the bed. He didn't reach for me or try to touch me.

"I'm sorry I put you through so much." I held out my hand even though the anguish in his eyes made me ache. "Somehow everything went wrong."

"Not everything." He came closer, taking my hand in his. "I still have you."

"But I know how much you wanted her." My voice broke.

"Watching you lose the baby was one thing." His voice cracked and his eyes filled. "But when the doctor said we were losing you, I couldn't take it, Darlene."

For the moment, Peter stopped being strong and I was anything but strong. Together, we cried for our Lucky Penny who we would never get to hold.

The night before I was discharged from the hospital, Peter and I, along with my mother, were in my room watching the news. A picture of Peter and me in my feather dress from the Emmys flashed up on the television screen as the news anchor announced the details of my miscarriage. Mom was shocked. I was devastated. Peter was livid. The leak had to have come from someone in the hospital, but it was impossible to know exactly who had given up the story. The media robbed us of all we had left of our Lucky Penny—the right to mourn her loss in private.

CHAPTER TWENTY

P*eter will be here soon and I'm glad to be getting discharged. It's been a hellish week. Our Lucky Penny's gone and it's such an empty feeling. Funny how you can miss someone you've never even met. Peter and I are trying to pick up the pieces. Physically, I'm better, but emotionally, the loss has been devastating and I'm still coping with it. I can't seem to stop crying. Any little thing sets me off. I keep telling myself it's hormones and maybe that's part of it, but I have to get a grip. I just don't know how.*

The doctor assures me that there is no reason why I can't have another baby. Realistically, however, another pregnancy isn't on the horizon and won't be for a long time, so that's little consolation. Besides, the future is a scary place, but after everything that's happened, the here and now haven't been so great either. I keep telling myself that at least Peter and I are together, but every time I look into those blue eyes, I see sadness and I feel responsible. Our charmed life seems to have collapsed around us and that so-called 'golden couple' has disappeared.

As much as I want to be home, I dread seeing the house. I don't want to go into the bedroom that would have been our Penny's nursery and I definitely don't want to see the backyard where Peter marked off a site for swings.

One good thing—Mom's still here. She's been an angel through all of this. I don't know what we would have done without her. I dread the day she has to leave.

The ride home drained me, but when Peter pulled in the driveway, I didn't want to go inside.

"What's wrong, Darlene?" Peter asked.

"The house isn't the same. I don't know if I can go in there. It's not our happy place anymore."

"Honey, wherever we are is our happy place. We were happy

before Penny and we'll find our way back there again. It'll take some time."

"I'd give anything to change all of this." The tears welled up and spilled over.

"So would I, but we can't just sit in the car. Your mother's waiting inside. Doug and Helene are coming by later. They've been worried sick about you."

When we opened the side door, the aroma of peach pie baking in the oven greeted us. Mom was sitting in the breakfast nook, reading, a steaming cup of coffee on the table in front of her.

"Darlene!" She got up and held her arms out. I fell into her, sobbing only this time my mother couldn't take the hurt away. "It's all right, honey," she whispered. "You need to grieve. Cry all you want. I'm right here."

She took me into the family room where we settled on the couch, while Peter got my things out of the car. Mom rocked me in her arms like she used to when I was little. I found that steady motion and her presence soothing. The tears subsided, but I clung to her, afraid to let go, and it didn't help that my hormones were all over the place.

Peter came in carrying two of the flower arrangements I'd gotten at the hospital. I watched as he placed first the white roses and then the purple orchids on the mantle above the fireplace. "Can I get you anything, honey?" he asked, and I shook my head in reply. He glanced at my mother and shrugged.

"Would you like to go upstairs and lie down?" He tried again.

I shook my head for the second time. I didn't want to go up there yet. It was too close to Penny's room. I might accidentally look that way and I couldn't risk it. Walking into the house was hard enough.

"You should really try and get some rest, honey," Mom said. "Doug and Helene will be here for dinner. They're really anxious to see you. Peter said he'd grill some steaks."

I closed my eyes and took a few breaths. *Get hold of yourself, Darlene. You can't keep falling apart like this. It's not helping anyone.* I looked over at Peter who was still standing by the fireplace. "Can you get me a couple of Tylenol and some water, please?"

He nodded without a word.

"I'm sorry, Mom," I turned to her once Peter was in the kitchen. "I didn't know coming home would be this hard."

"Honey, you've been through a terrible ordeal and no one expects you to come home and pick up where you left off. You need time to come to terms with everything and so does Peter. The two of you need to help each other. It's the only way."

"But every time I look at him, I see the hurt in his eyes, and I know it's all my fault."

"Darlene, none of this was your fault. Something went wrong— not because of anything you did or didn't do. Peter doesn't blame you and you shouldn't blame yourself."

"Are you sure, he doesn't blame me, Mom?"

"I was with him at the hospital and his only concern was you."

When Peter returned, Mom left us alone, saying she had to check on her pie. He handed me the glass of water and Tylenol, then sat next to me. As I set the glass on the coffee table, he laid his hand on my arm. "Come here." He pulled me closer and I nestled in against him, closing my eyes. For the first time in days, I felt safe again.

A couple of hours later, I was lying on the couch watching *Stage Door* with Katherine Hepburn, Ginger Rogers, and a very young Lucille Ball while Mom and Peter were in the kitchen prepping dinner. Doug strode into the family room carrying a small package, which he placed on the coffee table. I sat up, making room for him on the couch.

"You, young lady, scared the hell out of me." He narrowed his eyes as he sat next to me.

"I'm sorry, I didn't mean to."

"I'll never forgive you if you try anything like that again." He took both of my hands in his. "I mean it, Darlene. You have grown on me. When Peter first met you, I admit I was skeptical, but now I can't imagine a world without you in it and whether you like it or not, I will always, always look out for you."

The tears resurfaced as if they had a mind of their own. "I'm sorry, Doug. I think my hormones are all out of whack."

"You've been through a lot, honey." He slipped an arm around me and drew me in. "Cut yourself some slack."

"I don't know how to fix this, Doug!" For the first time, but certainly not the last, I clung to him for just a moment.

"You came home and that's a really good start."

"I'm sorry." I sat back and apologized again. "I can't seem to get it together." I pulled a crumpled tissue from my pocket and dabbed at my eyes, trying to regain control of myself.

"Here—maybe these will help." He handed me the package he had come in with and when I opened it I found a pair of Groucho Marx glasses, complete with bushy black eyebrows and matching mustache. They made me smile despite the tears.

"That's for the next time I take you to dinner. I got myself a pair, too." He pulled a second set from his pocket. "Let's put 'em on!"

We did just that and then burst into laughter at how ridiculous we both looked. The ruckus drew Mom and Peter from the kitchen.

"What in the world are the two of you doing?!" Peter tried his best to keep a straight face, while my mother, collapsing in a chair, could not contain herself.

"Getting ready for our next date," Doug answered, still wearing the glasses. "What do you think? Will anyone notice us?"

I wasn't really hungry, but once I started eating, everything tasted good from the steaks right down to Mom's potato salad. I couldn't remember the last time I'd enjoyed a meal, and best of all, it stayed down. By the time we polished off dessert, I was feeling much better. Mom's peach pie cures everything. Peter and Doug stayed in the kitchen to give Mom a hand with the dishes, while Helene kept me company in the family room.

"I'm so glad you finally got to meet my mother," I told her as we sat together on the couch.

"I wish it had been under happier circumstances," Helene said with a sigh. "But I'm glad to see you up and around. Are you feeling better, hon?"

"Still a little sore and tired, but I'm okay."

"You know you gave us quite the scare."

"I really don't remember much."

"It's just as well you don't." She took off her glasses and rubbed her eyes. "Peter was heartbroken when you lost the baby, but then when we almost lost you, he fell apart. All Doug and I could do was wait with him. I'll never forget the look in his eyes as long as I live. Peter felt responsible for you."

"But none of this was his fault."

"You were carrying his child, Darlene." She readjusted her glasses. "He blamed himself for everything you went through."

"I wish we could have saved the baby."

"But you still have each other. Don't forget that."

"But I feel like I let him down." For the umpteenth time that day, my eyes welled up.

"You did no such thing, hon," she assured me. "And now that you're home, things can get back to normal. Is Peter going back to work?"

"Tomorrow."

"And how long is your mother staying?"

"Till next Sunday."

"Good. Let's plan on lunch—the three of us. I'll look over my schedule when I get back to the office tomorrow morning and I'll call you. We have a few things to discuss, but you need to get some rest first. In the meantime, promise me you'll take care of yourself."

"I promise."

"Good, and if you need me to, I'd be glad to take care of Peter," she said with a wink. "You can send him to my place. I've got a saloon girl costume I think he might like."

"A saloon girl?" I asked, unable to hide a grin.

"Yes, you know, a soiled dove, and I have the perfect cowboy outfit for Peter!"

"With a ten-gallon hat?"

"And a lasso!" She laughed out loud. "Oh, Darlene, you have always been such a good sport. Can I take Peter home tonight?"

"You might want to wait a few days. He hasn't had much sleep this week and he might pass out before you get to the good part."

She laughed even louder and offered a hug. "Now you sound like the Darlene I know!"

Later that night when Peter took me upstairs for the first time, I was tired. I kept my eyes on the floor so I wouldn't have to look down the hall towards what would have been Penny's nursery. Once in our bedroom, I noted everything from the rug to the mattress to the bedding had been thoroughly cleaned. There was no telltale sign of blood anywhere. Despite that, I couldn't help but remember what had taken place there just the week before.

"It was good to hear you laugh today." Peter kissed the top of my head as we snuggled under the covers. "I was afraid I might never hear that sound again."

"I'm so sorry for everything I put you through," I whispered, feeling a little overwhelmed once more. "I never knew I was the one in trouble. All I could think about was saving Penny."

"It's all over now, honey." The familiar feel of his fingers in my hair was comforting. "And you're home. With me."

"Do you think she knew how much we loved her?"

"She knew."

"But I never got to tell her—she was just gone. One minute her heart was beating and the next minute it wasn't." The tears came quickly as I relived that awful moment. "Why did we have to lose her, Peter? Why couldn't they save our Penny?"

"It wasn't meant to be, Darlene. I wish things were different, but I'm grateful to have you. This house and everything in it would mean nothing without you." He suddenly pulled away from me, distress in his eyes. "You're not moving out because Penny is gone, are you?"

"I'm not going anywhere." I swiped at the tears with the back of my hand. "I'm right where I belong."

The next morning, Peter went to the studio, while Mom and I enjoyed a lazy day by the pool. We made lunch arrangements with Helene for Wednesday. She insisted on treating us at Musso and Frank. That seemed rather extravagant, but she thought Mom would get a kick out of it and it was a good place to discuss business—even though I wasn't quite sure what kind of business she meant.

By the time we arrived at Musso and Frank on Wednesday after-noon, Helene was already seated at a table. After the waiter took our order, Helene began the conversation. "Darlene, I know you aren't quite up to snuff yet, but we need to start thinking about dresses. The Emmys are coming up in September and Peter will have another movie premiere after that and then there's the Christmas Party."

"I don't know, Helene." I looked down at the table. "It seems like an awful lot."

"Exactly why we need to start talking about it now," she said. "You have a tradition to keep up and Peter gets such a kick out of it."

"It might do you good, honey," Mom agreed. "You need a diver-sion."

"I'm not exactly in a party mood."

"I know you're not, hon." Helene laid her hand on top of mine. "But you can't hide in the house forever. You and Peter have to come out sometime and everyone will be expecting you to dress like a star. You two are the golden couple, remember?"

"I don't feel very golden at the moment."

"I think Helene is right," Mom said. "You've been through so much. It's time you think about yourself—and Peter. You both de-serve a little fun."

"How many dresses did you say I need?"

"Three—one for the Emmys, one for the movie premiere, and one for the holiday party."

"Do you have any ideas because I'm fresh out?"

"Let's think about it for a week and we can meet back at my office next Thursday. We can brainstorm together. We'll start with the Emmys and go from there."

"I can't wait to see what you two come up with!" Mom smiled. "Maybe we should have a movie marathon before I leave."

And that is exactly what we did—musicals, dramas, love stories, you name it, we watched it. Mom even helped me take notes.

Mom flew out Sunday afternoon and I cried. From the airport, Peter drove to our favorite spot on the beach north of Malibu and we went walking. It was a warm spring day and the sun was so bright the water sparkled. It was the first time we'd been there since I'd lost Penny.

"Are you tired, honey?" Peter asked as we strolled along.

"A little," I answered. "But I'm glad we're here."

"Me, too."

"It was hard saying goodbye to my mother." I looked out at the water, squinting from the sun. "But I'm glad you called her. Thank you"

"I didn't do it for you," he said with a grin. "I did it for me. I really had a taste for one of her peach pies."

"I think she left you one in the freezer."

"No kidding?" He seemed surprised, but pleased. "Let's save it for when we get back from San Francisco."

"San Francisco?" I stopped walking.

"We'll be filming there for two weeks, remember?"

"I haven't really thought about it."

"I don't want to leave you, Darlene." He pulled me closer. "Come with me and we can take a long weekend for ourselves in Halfmoon Bay. Afterward we'll drive up to San Francisco. Between moving and everything else that happened, we deserve a break."

Since I'd lost the baby, I hadn't taken on any new work. I found it hard to concentrate and the only assignments I accepted were revisions of things I'd done originally. I needed some time to regroup—physically and mentally. I still hadn't set foot in what would have been the nursery. Luckily I hadn't bought anything for Penny so there were no toys or clothes to dispose of, but when I tossed out all the baby and parenting magazines that were stacked in the den, my insides ached.

I tried to take things slow, but before our trip, I had a million things to do. Helene and I got together for three brainstorming sessions and we finally settled on the gowns. It was a relief to have that out of the way, but I wasn't sure I would have the wherewithal to pull it off.

Despite our recent trauma, I was determined to make our house a happy, cheerful place. I wanted a peaceful home where I could have Peter all to myself, away from studios, photographers, reporters, and fans. I worked diligently making sure he'd want to come home at night, but Peter wasn't hard to please. He enjoyed a quiet dinner, a walk in the neighborhood, or a swim in the pool. I wasn't much of a tennis player, but Peter and Doug spent many Sunday afternoons hitting the ball back and forth over the net. Peter even installed lights so they could play after dark. We still continued our Sunday beach walks, but now took them earlier in the day.

Most importantly, Ed gave me the thumbs up to resume normal activities—things like driving, lifting, and other physical pastimes, as he put it. I thought Peter would be pleased, but he insisted on waiting until we got to Halfmoon Bay. I think he was afraid I might break.

CHAPTER TWENTY-ONE

We're flying to San Francisco tomorrow morning and from there we'll drive down to Halfmoon Bay. We sorely need some time alone. The rumor mill is churning. It was bad enough, that the press had found out about my miscarriage, but now the tabloids are saying that the baby was Doug's—all because he took me to dinner one night. I told Peter that I always seem to be the bad guy. First it was the fact that I was married when I met him. Then I left my husband for him. Now, I am cheating on him with his best friend. Peter pays no attention to any of it, but I find it disheartening. Doug doesn't say much, but I'm sure it bothers him. Peter insists the truth is boring and the media makes up their stories so they can sell their papers. He also reminded me that in a day or two, they'd find another story to focus on and we'd be forgotten—until next time. I only hope he's right.

The airports, both in L.A. and San Francisco, were nightmares. At LAX, we were hounded till we got on the plane and then in San Francisco, it happened when we disembarked. I was happy to reach the safety of our rental car and head south to Halfmoon Bay. Peter had booked the same room that we shared on New Year's Eve. It felt like a refuge to me and I didn't want to leave.

"Peter, can we call room service and have dinner here tonight?"

"Whatever you want." He tucked a stray lock of hair behind my ear as we stood together on the balcony looking down at the beach.

"I was pregnant the last time we were here, but I didn't know it."

"Honey, I never gave it a thought. I'm sorry. Maybe I should have booked a room at a different hotel."

"No, no, it's fine here." I assured him. "I'm a little tired and, to be honest, I don't want to share you with the world right now."

"It's a beautiful afternoon." He slipped an arm around me. "Why don't we enjoy it here—just you and me?"

We took in the vivid blue of the Pacific and the beachgoers that lined the shore—young couples, families, and a few loners. My eyes drifted to a group of children digging in the sand and I took in a sharp breath. Peter followed my gaze and saw the kids with their shovels and buckets. Another little girl in a pink bathing suit with a ruffle across her backside blew bubbles, watching intently as the breeze took them up and away. Any other time, I might have smiled at the sight of them, but today was different.

"Honey, are you okay?"

"I'm fine." I forced a smile, trying to shake my melancholy mood.

We walked over to the rattan sofa, where Peter lay down, pulling me on top of him, my head on his shoulder. His hand slipped under my t-shirt and rested against the small of my back. His other hand settled on the back of my head while his fingers played in my hair. "We'll get through this," he whispered. "We'll be that golden couple again, but until we are, let's try to let go of some of the sadness. I miss who we used to be. I want to see you smile and hear you laugh. I want you to be happy again, Darlene."

"I am happy." I picked my head up to look at him. "But sometimes I still ache for Penny."

"Close your eyes. Maybe the pain will go away—at least for a little while."

I nestled against him, taking several deep breaths in an effort to keep the tears at bay. The steady beat of his heart lulled me into a restful sleep.

Later that night, after dinner, Peter opened a bottle of champagne and poured us each a glass. "How do you feel, honey?" he asked.

"I feel like I've been missing you."

He tapped his glass against mine. "I've been missing you, too."

"Maybe we should do something about that." I took a sip and set my glass down on the table, then I took Peter's glass and placed it next to mine. I stood up and took three steps toward the bedroom, but Peter didn't move. "Are you coming?" I asked.

He got up, scooped me off the floor, and carried me the rest of the way. "One more thing," I said as he deposited me on the bed.

"What's that?"

"Don't hold back tonight." I unbuttoned his shirt. "Love me like you did that very first time."

"That's a pretty tall order."

"If you don't think you can handle it…" I began buttoning his shirt back up.

"I can handle it." He grabbed both my wrists with a grin. "But can you?"

And that weekend in Halfmoon Bay, Peter and I began to find our way back from the darkness.

While *Star Wars* made its debut, Peter kept busy filming *Fool's Romance*. Our two weeks in San Francisco couldn't have come at a better time. Normally, when we were home, I hardly ever visited Peter at work, but in San Francisco I didn't have much else to do, so I went to the set almost every day where everyone went out of their way to be kind. For the most part, movie people are a friendly group. They work long hours together, resulting in cast and crew jelling as a family of sorts. They were extremely kind and welcoming to me. They all knew what I'd been through.

Peter's leading lady was a lovely girl named Julie Dunbar. She was tall, shapely, and sported dark blonde hair that fell just below her shoulders. Prior to this film, she had some minor parts in a few other movies, but this was her first major role. Julie was single, but seeing Phil Becker, a policeman in L.A. Peter teased her mercilessly about being on his best behavior so he wouldn't have the L.A.P.D. after him. Julie told me she'd been nervous about working with Peter, but after the first couple of days, he put her at ease.

Julie and I spent a lot of time together. When she wasn't needed on the set, we'd sometimes go shopping or out to lunch. We both liked to read and, surprisingly, Julie also liked old movies. She was especially intrigued by my dresses and wanted to know how all of that came about, so I told her.

"I hope you're planning something special for the movie premiere," Julie said one afternoon as we sat in her dressing room.

"I am, even though my heart wasn't in it at first, but now I'm glad Helene persuaded me."

"Helene is a force to be reckoned with." Julie nodded with a smile. "When I got this part, she called to congratulate me and let me know that Peter is hers in case I had any ideas."

"She told me the same thing when I first met her!" I laughed at the memory. "I wasn't sure what to think, but she's been such a good friend and I appreciate all the time she makes for me."

"She must approve of you."

"She says she does, but I think she really does it more for Peter."

"Speaking of Peter"—Julie leaned in toward me—"Phil was a little worried about me working with him, so I had him come to the studio one afternoon and the two of them hit it off. I think it relieved his worries when Peter told him that going home to you every night is the highlight of his day."

As much as I liked Julie, I had to admit that watching Peter kiss another woman, even if it was for the camera, was not something I enjoyed. It wasn't that I didn't trust him, I just didn't like it. Julie said that I made her nervous during romantic scenes so we mutually agreed that on those days I would stay away. It worked out better for everyone.

Peter found my 'over-sensitive side', as he called it, mildly amusing. He liked to tease me, saying that we should rehearse his scenes at night so he'd only have to do it once the next day with Julie. It wasn't Julie I was concerned about. She wasn't after Peter, but a lot of other women were. That old insecurity resurfaced, making me wonder if I could really keep him happy. One night in our hotel room, I drummed up the courage to ask him about it, but only once we were in bed with the lights out.

"Peter, do you like kissing other women?"

"Are you talking about Julie?"

"No."

"I haven't been kissing anyone else."

"But would you like to?"

"Darlene, what are you getting at?"

"Peter, I know how women are. They practically take their clothes off in front of you. I could be standing right there and they don't even care. What man wouldn't like all that attention?"

"I don't go looking for it," he said a bit impatiently.

"Maybe you'd like to."

"Darlene, where is this coming from? What have I done to make you think I'm interested in other women?"

"Nothing, but if you ever get bored with me—"

"Bored?!" he echoed. "Honey, the last word I would ever use to describe you is boring. Stable, strong, and steady, maybe, but hardly boring"

"Stable, strong, and steady sound pretty boring to me."

"It might be, but then you throw in the magic. You make the chaos disappear, you keep the madness out, and at night, you add in the razzle dazzle."

"What does that mean?"

"It goes something like this…" He stirred me up with a kiss, then stopped. "That was the razzle and now we'll move on to the dazzle."

He kissed me again—only this time his lips lingered even longer before slipping down the side of my neck. "Have you got the picture yet?"

"I don't think so. You need to tell me again."

Fool's Romance wrapped in July. I was glad to see Peter growing his beard in time for our trip to Maui where, once again, the islands worked their magic. A few sharp-eyed fans recognized him, but for the most part, no one bothered us. It had been three months since we lost the baby and I finally felt like I was getting over it.

That summer, we also found a housekeeper, Estelle Connor. A tiny gray-haired woman in her mid-sixties, she was recently widowed and a neighbor of Helene's. When Helene heard that Peter and I were looking for a housekeeper, she brought Estelle around to meet us. Estelle had a soft southern twang that gave away her Kentucky roots. She wanted something that would get her out of the house a couple of days each week. She was the only person we interviewed. She was also the only person I knew who made her own hats. The first time we met her, she was wearing a bowler that sported a bright red rose. "It makes people smile," she explained in that sweet voice.

I think that hat is what convinced Peter to hire her.

Even though she only worked Tuesdays and Thursdays, it didn't take long for Estelle to become more than a housekeeper. I still did the cooking and laundry while she took care of the house and tried her best to take care of Peter. He relished her motherly attention as much as she enjoyed doling it out to him. Her diminutive size disguised a fierce lady who took extreme pride in protecting Peter from anything she deemed unpleasant. If he was sleeping, she didn't like noise. If he was busy, she allowed no interruptions. She even got upset with me if she thought I was giving Peter a hard time, but she never once complained if *he* gave *me* a hard time.

Despite her favoritism toward Peter, I looked forward to Tuesdays and Thursdays when Estelle and her hats would be there. She was good company, and I never could beat her at Scrabble. She also gave out the best hugs. Peter was completely enamored with her and the homemade cookies she always brought him. I had to ask for one, but Peter was welcome to scarf down as many as he could. With her guard-like housekeeping habits, Estelle was quick to become family.

August found Peter back at the studio for season three of *Fire in the City*. I braced myself for the whirlwind to come. Not only was he involved in the series, but also promotional efforts and post-production for *Fool's Romance* and the movie premiere itself. When he finally made it home at night, he was well beyond exhausted. Even our peaceful Sundays were no longer our own. I bit my tongue on several occasions. Besides, telling him to slow down had never worked in the past.

In September, we quietly celebrated our second year together. It was getting difficult for me to remember life before Peter. I certainly didn't think about Frank very often. When I did, I wondered how he was and if he ever sobered up. Of course, I never dared mention him to Peter. The least little reminder of my ex-husband still set him off.

Peter also won his second Emmy, in September, as did *Fire in the City*. That night I wore the first of my three dresses. A light gray, sleeveless gown with a ruffled bodice and a wide four-button cinch at the waist, the skirt fell gracefully over the hips to the floor. Based on a dress designed by Muriel King, it was worn in 1937 by Katherine Hepburn when she appeared as Terry Randall in *Stage Door*. Helene insisted the cinch be the same color blue as Peter's eyes. I insisted that the neckline be lowered a bit to accommodate my pearls.

Peter recognized it immediately since I'd made him watch *Stage Door* the week before. "I'm beginning to see a pattern here, Kate!" He gave me a once over before we left the house. "You make me watch a movie and the next thing I know you show up as the star. Maybe I could guess the next dress if I paid more attention."

"Maybe, maybe not." I twirled around. "Do you like it?"

"Katherine Hepburn can be a little intimidating." He gave a sigh. "But I hope she'll go easy on me tonight."

"Not a chance, mister!" I kissed him just as the car pulled up.

When we arrived at the Emmys, the reporters bombarded Peter, asking who his date was. "This is Kate!" He laughed. "But it's Ms. Hepburn to you!" And the flash bulbs flickered over and over. For the first time in a long while, we had a care free evening and Peter's win made it even better.

I had pretty much put the miscarriage behind me until September nineteenth, the day the baby would have been due. The thought of Lucky Penny hit me hard and I was unexpectedly consumed with her loss all over again. I kept wandering in and out of what should have been her nursery. It was now completely furnished, as were all the bedrooms, but to me this room was different. It should have had a crib—not a queen-size bed. Each time I set my foot through the door, the tears followed.

I was upstairs lying across the bed having my third good cry of the day when Peter's voice startled me. "Darlene? What are you doing in here?"

I quickly sat up, wiping my tears with a well-used tissue. "You're home early," was all I managed to squeak.

"It's a good thing I am." He sat next to me. "You've been on my mind all day."

"I'm all right." I wiped my eyes again.

"Honey, just because we don't talk about Penny doesn't mean I forgot. I know what today is and if I remembered, then I know you remembered." He laid his forehead against mine.

"I was fine yesterday, but today it's all I can think about." The tears returned. "Do you ever wonder how it would have felt to hold her or how she would have looked?"

"She would have been beautiful—like her mother."

"I would have given anything to keep from losing her."

"It wasn't meant to be, Darlene." He gently reminded me. "We have to accept that."

"I thought I had, until today."

"Honey, I promise you we'll fill this house with children—as many as you want, once the series is over." He slipped his arms around me. "Can you hang in there with me until then?"

"If you think you'll still want me."

"I want you to be the first thing I see every morning and the last thing I see every night."

"Those aren't exactly my best times of day."

By mid-October, the New York Yankees had wrapped up the World Series much to Peter's delight. My poor Chicago White Sox hadn't been in the running for years—neither had the Detroit Tigers, leaving Doug and me to compare our sorry baseball notes.

Peter finished with post-production, but soon started the talk-show circuit to promote the new movie scheduled to premiere the night before Thanksgiving. We were now past the 'tired' Peter, and the 'worn out' Peter was entering the picture. I tried several times to have the 'Peter, you need to slow down' conversation, but my words always fell on deaf ears. Doug tried talking to him, too, but Peter could be incredibly stubborn. He was losing weight again and his handsome face looked pale and gaunt.

I woke one night at the end of October and he was gone. I found him downstairs in the family room lying on the couch with blankets and pillows staring at the television.

"Honey, what are you doing down here? Why aren't you in bed?"

"I can't sleep. I have a headache."

"Peter, you don't get enough sleep as it is." I sat down on the edge of the couch. "How are you going to go to work?"

"I just have to get up and go."

"You need to stop this and take care of yourself!"

"Darlene, this will never stop as long as I'm committed to *Fire in the City*. It's taking everything out of me.'"

"Maybe you shouldn't make a movie next summer. Maybe you could use the downtime."

"When I'm through with this show I don't ever want to make another series. If I want a movie career, I have to keep my hand in it."

"Have you thought about dropping out of the show?"

"I did more than think about it," he admitted. "I asked Doug to review my contract. He's going to see if I can get out of it at the end of the season. Do you think I'd be making a big mistake?"

"I think you need to do what's best for you and if you want to do what's best for me, you'll come to bed."

It took Doug several days to thoroughly study Peter's contract. In the end, there was no way for him to leave the show without serious consequences. He was committed to playing James Dakota for another two years, whether he liked it or not. The subject of Peter's contract never came up again, but his restless nights continued.

CHAPTER TWENTY-TWO

Fool's Romance premieres tonight at Grauman's Chinese Theater with an afterparty immediately following across the street at the Roosevelt Hotel. Peter has no idea that Bette Davis will be going with him. Helene and I chose to copy the iconic gown that Bette wore when she played Margo Channing in All About Eve. *It was a stunning dress designed by Edith Head. The movie itself won six Academy Awards including Best Picture, Best Director, and Best Costume Design. The original dress was a chocolate color silk and when Bette tried it on, the bodice was too big. Tailoring the dress would have meant production delays, so she pulled it down past her shoulders and went back to work. For my dress, we went for the same color, but dropped the fur trim. A thin belt cinched the waistline and a full gown, with two side pockets, billowed out. I even found a crystal brooch to pin on the left front—much like Margo Channing wore, and of course, my pearls are a must. I am grateful to Helene for making me continue this movie star tradition.*

Peter was nervous about the film's premiere and his lack of sleep was getting to him—and to me. He was irritable and short-tempered. Even Estelle and her hats weren't enough to make him smile, although he never did turn down one of her cookies. To be truthful, we saw very little of him the week leading up to the premiere. He pestered me about my dress, but I refused to give up any information and instead of his usual good-natured responses, he grumbled. I wondered how he was coping at work, but he never talked about it and I never asked.

That afternoon before the premiere, Peter was supposed to be home by noon, but he didn't show up until after three. We had to be at the theater by five. The car would arrive to pick us up in less than an hour. I didn't say a word to him—just tried to stay out of his way as I finished getting dressed in one of the other bedrooms. After a last-minute check in the mirror, I patted my upswept hair. Maybe I should have worn it down like Margo Channing, but it was too late to worry about that now. I put on my pearls before stepping into my shoes, grabbed my purse, and raced down the stairs to the kitchen, where I considered having a quick cup of tea to calm my nerves. Margo Channing's famous line kept running through my head.

Peter soon followed in a black suit and multi-colored tie. "Darlene, will you—" He stopped abruptly, and I turned around from where I was standing at the stove waiting for my water to boil.

"Just when I think you can't possibly outdo yourself, you go and prove me wrong." He smiled, a genuine look of delight—something I hadn't seen in quite a while.

"I wasn't sure if you'd like it." I stayed right where I was. "You haven't liked much of anything lately."

"Darlene, let's not do this tonight." His smile faded.

"Peter, I don't want to argue with you, but I'm worried about you. I watch you, day in and day out, running yourself ragged. You can't keep going like this."

"Until I put James Dakota, and everything that goes with it, behind me, this is how it will be. You, of all people, should know that."

We stood there momentarily looking at each other until the teakettle whistled. I turned back to the stove and poured the hot water into a mug.

"Maybe we should try another take on this conversation." He strode out of the kitchen while I tried to collect myself. I didn't mean to snap at him or upset him—especially tonight—but he was running on fumes. I stood there in my Bette Davis dress holding a steaming cup of tea and waited.

"Just when I think you can't possibly outdo yourself, you go and prove me wrong." He came back with a smile. It seemed genuine enough, but then again, Peter was an actor.

"I wasn't sure if you'd like it," I repeated what I'd said earlier, but I still couldn't muster even something close to a smile.

He took the mug from my hand and set it down on the counter. "Darlene, I think we need a minute before the car comes."

He laid his forehead against mine. "Are we okay?"

"*We* are fine. It's *you* I worry about and, just to remind you, I'm not Darlene tonight." I slipped my arms around his neck. Those blue eyes again! Always drawing me in! Making me forget about my tea and the tiff we barely avoided.

"But are you Bette Davis or Margo Channing?"

"Who do you prefer?" I asked, finally able to come up with a smile.

"I'm not sure. They're both pretty scary, but not as scary as Darlene. She can be downright terrifying—especially when she rolls into guard dog mode."

"Maybe you don't kiss her enough."

"Maybe I don't." He looked perplexed for one quick minute and then he laid his mouth on mine, in a long, drawn-out kiss that not only sucked the air from my lungs, but stirred up things that were better left unstirred.

"Fasten your seatbelts," I whispered. "It's going to be a bumpy night!" And then I kissed him back.

We took advantage of the car ride over, using the quiet time to regain our equilibrium.

"I'm sorry if I upset you." I fingered my lucky pearls. "I didn't mean to."

"I probably had it coming."

"Not tonight." I looked toward the front of the car, thinking I had to make up for the earlier incident in the kitchen. "Do you think the driver can see us?"

"No."

"Do you think he can hear us?"

"No, but what are you up to?"

I took one last glance at the partition separating us from the driver and made a rash decision. I kicked off my shoes and hopped onto Peter's lap stretching my legs across the seat. "You're not really too old to make out in a car, are you?"

"Darlene—"

"The name is Bette! B-E-T-T-E! Bette!" I reminded him. "Try to remember that."

"Ok, Bette, but—"

"We have at least forty minutes before we get to the theater!" I kissed him. "Let's not waste time." I kissed him again. "Unless you really are too old."

A flurry of kisses followed, after which I found myself pinned between Peter and the seat, his hand under my skirt. "Peter!" I gasped. "What are you doing?!"

"Making out in a car," he said, his mouth still covering mine as I tried to catch my breath. He suddenly pulled back, but his hand continued sliding past my knee. "That is what you wanted, isn't it?"

My eyes grew wider, my mouth fell open, but no words came out. I only nodded my head.

"Good!" His lips once again made contact. "It's been a while, but it's like riding a bike. I'll show you how it's done." Still trapped underneath him, I tried catching my breath, but Peter made that impossible. I lost focus and gave in.

By the time we pulled up in front of the Chinese theater, things were way off-kilter. My dress needed adjusting. My hair, now completely down, begged for a comb. One of my earrings was caught in Peter's shirt. His suit was disheveled and he was scrambling to find a cufflink. I had one shoe on and, in a tizzy, dropped down to the floor searching under the seat for the other one.

"Darlene, do you see my cufflink down there?" Before I could answer, the driver opened the car door. Mortified, and still wearing only one earring and one shoe, I looked up at him from the floor where I was on my hands and knees trying to find my other heel and now a cufflink.

"Can you give us a minute?" Peter asked and the car door promptly slammed shut.

I retrieved the cufflink from under the seat and then my shoe. Peter helped me up. We swapped the cufflink and the earring.

"You're going to be the death of me, Darlene!"

"It's Bette. B-E-T-T-E! Bette." I reminded him and took another breath. I ran a comb though my hair, which now was long and loose, much more like Margo Channing's, then I slid the earring back into place.

"Is my tie on straight, B-E-T-T-E, Bette?" Peter asked.

Without a word, I fixed his tie, checked both of his cufflinks, re-buttoned his suitcoat, and removed the lipstick smudges that I could see. We made our exit and as we walked through the theater's fore-court, past the famous footprints, I still hadn't caught my breath. Fast-talking reporters and flashy paparazzi bombarded us.

"Peter, is that Margo Channing with you tonight?" one sharp-eyed woman called out as she snapped our picture.

"It's Bette, B-E-T-T-E, Bette!" Peter said with a sideways glance at me.

"Fasten your seatbelts!" she hollered back with a grin. "It's going to be a bumpy night!"

"If she only knew," Peter said under his breath, while shaking his head and pulling me inside the theater.

Doug, Helene, and Estelle, wearing an autumn-themed hat filled with silk, fall-colored mums, were already in the lobby. They must have been watching as we pulled up.

"What took you so long to get out of the car?" Helene wanted to know right after she kissed Peter.

"Ask B-E-T-T-E, Bette!" He rolled those blue eyes and Helene turned to me with an expectant look on her face.

"We had to make ourselves presentable." I rolled my eyes at Peter and Helene laughed out loud.

"You kids should know better than to wrestle in the backseat of a moving car." Doug frowned. "Didn't your parents teach you any-thing?"

"It was B-E-T-T-E, Bette! She started it and I had no choice but to finish it," Peter said and then put his lips to my ear with a whisper. "You can thank me later."

I was still trying to catch my breath when the lobby grew quiet. Julie Dunbar came in, looking like she'd stepped off a fashion runway in a backless blue gown. She was with her now-fiancé, Officer Phil Becker. Peter and I were the first to greet them. More flashbulbs popped and then Peter and Julie took center stage. Admittedly, they made a striking couple. I invited Phil to wait with us. He seemed a little overwhelmed by all the hullabaloo. I understood the feeling.

After we took our seats, Peter squeezed my hand and his fingers were freezing. He was more nervous than he let on. The lights went out, the music played, and the credits rolled. It was a date movie—light, funny, and romantic. Peter and Julie came across quite well. They enjoyed working together and it showed in the scenes they shared on camera. It made me feel a little inadequate, despite the earlier incident in the car.

The love scenes rattled me. I looked away a few times. My head kept telling me it was only a movie, but my heart skipped a beat every time I saw Peter holding Julie and kissing her. *You'd think by now you'd be used to it, Darlene, but how do you get used to something like that? Especially when the woman looks like Julie Dunbar!*

The rom-com itself was meant to be fun and to leave viewers feeling good. It did just that. There was little doubt, based on audience reaction, that Peter had another box office hit. As it turned out, the critics weren't especially kind, but *Fool's Romance* stayed number one at the box office for three weeks and remained in the top five for several more.

After a quiet Thanksgiving, I was home working. I had finally accepted a brand-new assignment—a personnel training manual for the human resources department of a well-established bank. It was challenging and I was deep in thought as Sarah Vaughan warbled on about 'Misty' when the ringing telephone startled me.

"Is this Darlene?" A familiar voice with a clipped speech pattern was on the other end of the line.

"Yes."

"Darlene, this is Bette Davis. I wanted to call about the dress you wore to Peter Chandler's movie premiere. My Margo Channing dress looked lovely on you. It's always been one of my personal favorites."

"Th-thank you, Miss D-Davis," was all I managed to say.

"Please call me, Bette. I feel like we're friends."

"Okay, B-Bette." My heart was about to thump out of my chest, as I tried to breathe.

"You also have exquisite taste in handsome young men." She went on. "I should know—I had my share of them."

"Yes, Ms. D-Davis, I mean B-Bette."

"If I were a little younger, I might try and take Mr. Chandler away from you!" She laughed that hearty, throaty laugh. "But will you promise me something?"

"Of course," I barely whispered.

"Do not follow up my Margo Channing dress with one of Joan Crawford's gowns. She never had any class. And one more thing before I hang up. Let that handsome beau of yours know that Bette Davis is watching him." The line went dead.

I sat there in a stupor, holding the phone. Was I dreaming or did I just talk to Bette Davis? I called Helene to make sure I was really awake.

It was a good thing, we had decided against a Joan Crawford dress for the studio Christmas party. Peter was dreading it, but he was intrigued by what I might wear. For that soiree, Helene and I settled on Audrey Hepburn's red gown from *Funny Face*. I'm sure it was the color that swayed us. The strapless silk, tube-shaped dress designed by Hubert de Givenchy, had a train attached, although I downsized it a bit. Audrey carried a matching red silk wrap so I opted to do the same. I declined the white gloves, but I did wear my pearls. Peter was delighted as he recounted all the different 'dates' he'd had, starting with Ginger Rogers.

"Who's it going to be next time, Darlene?" he asked.

"I'm not sure, but I guarantee it won't be Joan Crawford."

The week before Christmas, Peter was energized. He had invited his family, and my mother, out to L.A. for the Christmas holiday. Since it was our first Christmas in the house, he felt everyone should come visit us. I was disappointed that Sydney couldn't make it, but she promised to see me soon. Our long-distance telephone calls were not the same as an in-person pajama party involving wine. With only one week left before the holiday, Peter wanted to shop for a Christmas tree. I suggested an artificial one, but he insisted on the real thing. It had been quite a while since I'd seen him so relaxed and happy. He couldn't wait to decorate and put up the tree.

By Christmas Eve, we had a houseful. I was especially happy to see Mom. I also wanted to properly thank Daniel for all he had done when I first found out I was pregnant.

Peter enthusiastically took his family on a tour of the house while Mom and I manned the kitchen. Peter had requested one of her peach pies and we had to get it in the oven. Bobby and Timmy liked the pool best, but much to their disappointment, the December weather was a little too cool for swimming. Uncle Peter promised to turn up the heater so that they could cannonball later in the week. Taller and not quite as shy as they'd been the last time they saw their uncle, they couldn't wait to get him on the floor for some quality wrestling. I watched while Peter tossed them around as they laughed and squealed for more. My mother noticed the unhappy look that momentarily clouded my face. She reached over and patted my hand.

The next morning, we were ambushed as we slept in our own bed. "Uncle Peter! Wake up!" the boys hollered as they jumped on top of him. "It's Christmas!"

"Hey, you guys. Take it easy!"

"Aunt Darlene!!" They wriggled between us. "Make him get up. We want to go downstairs and see if Santa Claus came!"

"Where did 'Aunt Darlene' come from?" Peter was just as surprised as I was to hear that.

"Because you're the uncle," Bobby spoke up first. "And aunts go with uncles."

"That's right," Timmy agreed with his brother. "Like salt goes with pepper."

"Like moms go with dads!"

"Like grandmas go with grandpas!"

"Like—"

"Ok!" Peter tickled them both. "We get the idea."

"You boys shouldn't be in here!" Carmen stood, frowning, in the doorway, interrupting our fun.

"Carmen, it's ok." Peter glared back at his sister. "I told them to come and get me when they woke up."

I suddenly felt very awkward. I was probably the reason why Carmen didn't want the boys to come into our room. Her eyes briefly met mine and her glaring disapproval was apparent. As far as she was concerned, I didn't belong in her brother's house, let alone his bed.

"Come on, boys," she ordered them. "Your Uncle Peter will meet us downstairs."

"Hurry up, Uncle Peter," they hollered as they left with their mother.

"I need to have a talk with my sister." Peter got out of bed. "And straighten her out about a few things."

The boys woke the entire house with their shrieks and shouts. They couldn't wait to see what Santa had left under the tree. Mom put a pot of coffee on and placed a French toast bake in the oven. It was the easiest thing to do on a busy Christmas morning since we had prepared it the night before. In what seemed like an instant, the family room was littered with shredded gift-wrap, limp ribbons, and empty boxes. While Mom and Peter picked up the holiday debris, I slipped back into the kitchen to check on breakfast and set the dining room table. Unfortunately, Carmen followed me.

"Do you need a hand, Darlene?"

"No, thanks. I've got it."

"Can we talk then?" She sat down at the edge of the breakfast nook. "I'm worried about my brother. He looks terrible."

"He's been working some very long hours."

"Why aren't you taking better care of him?" Her voice rang with sarcasm.

"I try, Carmen, but he won't listen. I'd appreciate it if you could get him to slow down."

"We didn't appreciate hearing you were pregnant on the evening news."

"Neither did we. Someone from the hospital talked to reporters."

"Peter should have called and told us about the baby right away."

"It wasn't like we planned to have a baby."

"You mean Peter didn't plan it." Her eyes accused me.

"What are you getting at?"

"We both know you're trying to hang on to my brother any way you can."

"You are out of line, Carmen!" John's angry voice boomed through the kitchen. "Darlene went through hell. What's wrong with you?!"

She strode past her father and out the kitchen door without another word.

"I saw her come in here and I knew there'd be trouble." John gave a loud sigh. "Again, I apologize for my daughter. She had no right to talk to you like that! I will remind her that this is Peter's house and she should respect that."

"It's Christmas, John, and Peter has been looking forward to it. I don't want to spoil it for him."

"You two have had a rough year," he said, as he helped himself to a cup of coffee.

"We're fine now." I pulled the French toast bake from the oven and set it on the counter to cool.

"Darlene, I really am sorry about everything that happened to you." John sat down in the breakfast nook. "My son should have done the right thing and married you long before you lost the baby."

"He asked me, but I turned him down."

"Why?" John seemed surprised.

"I never wanted to feel as if I'd trapped him," I answered with a shrug. "I couldn't live with that."

"Darlene, I know that times have changed since I was courting Joyce, but you seem like the kind of girl who wants a husband and children—not a living arrangement."

"I do want a husband and children one day, but for now, Peter and I are together, and that's all that really matters."

"My son should not be asking you to put your life on hold."

"He's never asked me to do that, John," I assured him and, at the same time, tried to convince myself. We weren't getting any younger, and every once in a while, I felt a twinge of emptiness. It didn't happen often, but sometimes I longed for a baby—mostly at night when it was dark, and Peter was asleep.

CHAPTER TWENTY-THREE

With a houseful of people, I don't have much time to write. I'll catch up after the New Year. Mom left earlier this afternoon. I wish she had stayed longer and that I'd had more time to visit with her. Doug called from Michigan to see how things were going. I told him that handling Peter's family takes a lot of energy and now something's up with Peter and his sister. They've been arguing a lot since Christmas Day and it's making me wish that we'd taken a slow boat to China for the holidays.

Peter announced that he was taking the boys to Disneyland. Bobby and Timmy screeched with excitement. Sometimes Peter didn't think.

I called Helene despite Peter's protests. She'd know what to do. She came through by getting a limo to pick us up and arranging for Disney security to meet us at the entry gate. Peter didn't like it, but that's how it had to be.

When the stretch limo arrived, Peter was still not happy about having a security detail. "I don't know why Helene went through all this trouble. It's not necessary. All I want to do is have fun with the boys."

"We can still have fun." I assured him. "But we have to be smart about it. Honey, you can't wander through Disneyland and expect no one to notice. Don't be so grumpy."

"Grumpy is one of the seven dwarves!" Timmy piped up.

"Yeah, Uncle Peter," Bobby chimed in. "You don't wanna be like him!"

Peter's frown slowly turned into a smile. "I'm never grumpy."

"We can debate the grumpy part later." I told him.

With the help of security, we really did have a good time despite one incident at Fantasyland when Mickey and Minnie Mouse appeared. While the kids were getting autographs from and pictures with the famous mice, the adults converged upon Peter, but security kept things in check. Besides, having them around had other advantages. They knew the park inside out and made sure we didn't miss a thing—including lunch in the Trophy Room at the prestigious Club 33.

Disneyland made quite an impression on Bobby and Timmy. That night, the boys pored over every detail of every ride. They thought it was cool to have a security escort throughout the park, which made Uncle Peter very cool in their eyes. They knew he was on television, but didn't everyone have an uncle on television? That's what uncles did.

On the last day of their visit, the adults opted to see John Travolta's new movie, *Saturday Night Fever.* Peter thought he'd take this opportunity to spend more time with the boys and volunteered us to baby-sit while the rest attended a matinee. Carmen was reluctant to say yes, but Daniel stepped in, giving us the go-ahead.

We packed a few snacks and walked to a neighborhood park. Peter spent the afternoon chasing after his nephews, pushing them on the swings, and hoisting them in the air after a trip down the slide. I think he had even more fun than they did.

"Uncle Peter, we don't want to go home tomorrow," Bobby told him as they walked toward the picnic table where I was pouring some apple juice. "It's too cold in New York."

"We want to stay with you." Timmy still agreed with his big brother on just about everything.

"But I have to go back to work in a few days." Peter picked them up, one under each arm.

"You don't work," Timmy laughed. "You pretend you're a fireman on TV."

"It's hard work pretending you're a fireman." Peter swung them both around until they hollered.

"Can we come back another time when you're not pretending?" Timmy asked as Peter deposited them at the picnic table.

"We'll have to talk to your parents."

That evening, I suggested a takeout, but Peter insisted on going out to dinner—his treat. We picked an Italian restaurant because the boys wanted spaghetti. When we first arrived, there weren't many customers, but by the time we ordered, and our food arrived, the restaurant was filling up. A parade of autograph seekers and picture takers soon began making their way to our table.

"Uncle Peter, you sure know a lot of people," Bobby observed.

"Your food's cold," Timmy said. "My mom gets mad when I fool around and my food gets cold. Aunt Darlene, do you get mad at Uncle Peter when he fools around and his food gets cold?"

"Yes, I do." I would have laughed, but I noticed Carmen bristle when Timmy called me 'Aunt Darlene.' "Your Uncle Peter fools around a lot when we go out to dinner. That's why I make him eat at home most of the time."

"Peter, you shouldn't let people interrupt you like that," Joyce scolded.

"Mom, there's not much I can do about it." He sighed as another fan walked up. "If I don't give them an autograph or take a picture, they won't leave."

Before the airport car came to pick everyone up, Peter and Carmen were quarreling in the kitchen. I stopped just outside the doorway when I heard their heated voices.

"At least think about what I said!" Carmen demanded.

"No, and the sooner *you* stop thinking about it, the better off we'll both be."

"I know how badly she hurt you, but she still loves you and she misses you. She's even willing to come to L.A. All you have to do is ask her."

"Why should I?"

"Because she's in your league. She models and people notice her."

"Then she doesn't need me."

"Stop being so stubborn and give her another chance."

"I said no."

"There was a time when you wanted her back."

"That time is long gone, Carmen. Kathleen made her choice."

"A woman can always change her mind."

"And Kathleen changes her mind like some women change their clothes."

We only had a couple of hours to pack and get to the airport ourselves. In keeping with our New Year's Eve tradition, we were flying to San Francisco later that same day. After a hectic holiday, we were ready for some time alone.

I didn't care if we ever left our room at Halfmoon Bay, but Peter wanted to drive to Monterey for dinner. Sitting at a table near a window that overlooked the water, we watched the sunset as dusk turned to dark. A few autograph seekers interrupted us, but over dessert, I broached the subject of his sister.

"Did you and Carmen have a fight?"

"No. She has this crazy idea in her head about—" He stopped abruptly.

"About what?"

"Kathleen. The girl I was seeing in New York."

"The one you wanted to marry?"

"Yes. Evidently, Kathleen got married and now she's divorced. Apparently, she kept in touch with Carmen all this time."

"Do you want to see her?" My stomach tightened.

"No, Darlene, I don't."

"What if she calls you?"

"She already has. She found me at the studio two weeks ago."

"How come you never told me?"

"It was a five-minute conversation hardly worth mentioning."

"Do you think she'll come out here?"

"She won't waste her time. Knowing Kathleen, she's probably already sleeping with her next victim."

I was curious about Kathleen, but I let the subject go. She was not a threat no matter what Carmen wanted. Once we were back in our room, I didn't want to play by Peter's silly rules, but he insisted. By midnight, Kathleen was long forgotten. I was more than ready for Peter's touch. Light and gentle, that first kiss turned into a second and then a third—each one more intense than the one before. I gave in to him like I always did, losing myself in the feel of his body against mine.

We were on an even keel for a change, and I wanted to enjoy it. After being with Peter for more than two years, I knew that it was only a matter of time before our lives would once again spin out of control. It was just the way things were with him.

As was my custom on Peter's birthday, I had a large cake delivered to the studio. Afterward, Doug, Helene, and I took him to Wu's Room for lunch.

"Peter, I don't care how many birthdays you have," Helene sighed after we ordered. "There's not a better-looking fireman in all of California."

"How do you feel about urban planners?" Peter asked her.

"I've never thought about it. Why?"

"Because I'm considering a play this year. It's called *Something to Live For* and the main character is an urban planner."

"What's it about?" Helene wanted to know.

"Two people, an urban planner and a doctor, who meet at a support group for widows and widowers."

"Who would play the doctor?" Doug asked.

"Karen Updyke already signed on."

"Interesting choice." Helene sat back, passing Peter one of her odd looks. "Are you willing to work with her for the summer?"

"It's only twelve weeks." Peter shrugged, but he returned 'the look'.

"That can be a very long time," she commented. "Are you sure you wouldn't rather do a movie?"

"Nothing's interested me so far. I thought a play would be a nice change of pace and I'd get to spend a little more time with Darlene."

"Live theater can be pretty intense," Helene cautioned him. "On stage and off."

Peter asked us to stick around that afternoon. They were filming a fire scene on the back lot. To him, it was just another day at work, but I rarely visited Peter on a set like that. The fires made me nervous. I knew from experience that two paramedics with their ambulance always stood by in case of an emergency, but the sight of them only increased my anxiety.

Helene had a meeting, so she had to get back to her office. I had a restaurant brochure and a job aid to edit, but Doug's schedule was clear and he talked me into staying. Out on the backlot, the technicians lit the flame bars and Gene yelled 'action' as Peter, fully dressed in fireman gear, raced inside, followed by two cameramen carrying handheld equipment.

My eyes were riveted to the burning structure waiting for Peter to come out when I noticed black smoke billowing from the backside of the hollow building.

"Something's wrong." I clutched Doug's arm. "There shouldn't be that much smoke."

"They've done this a hundred times, Darlene." He tried reassuring me, but his eyes remained fixed on the smoke-filled structure. "They know what they're doing." The seconds turned into minutes as the black smoke thickened and stung our eyes.

Gene picked up his megaphone. "You guys need to come out of

there! Can you hear me? You need to come out of there, now!"

The crew stood motionless as if on alert. The technicians were on the ready while the paramedics quickly donned their oxygen masks and tanks. My knees shook. My mouth felt dry, and my heart pounded harder than a high school drumline. There was still no sign of Peter or the cameramen. No actual flames were visible, but the smoke was now so thick it was getting hard to see and the sickening stench made us cough.

"We need to go in!" Gene yelled frantically and motioned to the paramedics, who rushed inside, while others worked furiously to put the fire out. Every minute that passed seemed longer than the one before, while the smoke billowed upward. As the two cameramen finally stumbled outside, coughing, the back of the façade collapsed. Still no sign of Peter.

Gene was the first to reach them as the other crewmembers gathered round. I only heard bits and pieces of their conversation in between their fits of coughing.

"Too much smoke."

"Hard to breathe in there."

"Couldn't see a thing."

"Where's Peter?"

"Never saw him."

Doug caught me as my knees buckled. It seemed like hours had passed before the two paramedics called out loud enough for everyone to hear: "We've got him!"

My relief was short-lived. I wasn't prepared for the sight of Peter being carried out, unconscious. I grabbed Doug to steady myself before taking a step toward them, but he held me back. "Let them do their job, Darlene. They'll take care of him." His voice was calm, but the color had completely drained from his face. I started shaking as I watched them affix an oxygen mask on Peter then take his vital signs.

"What is it?" Gene demanded.

"He took in a lot of smoke," one of the medics replied after removing his own mask. "We need to transport him to the hospital."

His partner pulled a stretcher from the back of their ambulance. Doug let go of me and I dashed over to Peter. Today was his birthday.

We were just celebrating and now he was lying here, out cold, his lungs filled with smoke.

"Peter, please wake up!" I grabbed his hand as they put him on the stretcher. Panic set in and I couldn't hold the tears back any longer.

"We'll take care of him," the taller of the two said as he gently moved my hand away.

"Will he be all right?" I took several deep breaths in an effort to gather myself.

"We need to get him to the hospital. You can ride with us if you like."

"Go on, honey." Doug was right behind me. "I'll meet you there."

With the sirens blaring and the flashers turning, we were on our way. It was almost like a scene right out of *Fire in the City*. Only this was all too real. I prayed all the way there, but Peter didn't wake up.

When we arrived at the hospital, I tried to follow them, but the doctors directed me to a small, private waiting room. I was relieved to finally find Doug and Gene. "Where is he?" Doug wanted to know.

"I'm not sure." I couldn't stop the trembling in my hands.

"He'll be fine, honey." Doug slipped his arms around me.

"It's his birthday, Doug," I choked, clinging to him as I tried pulling myself together.

"I know," he whispered. "When you see him, make sure you tell him that the hospital is not the place to party."

I smiled despite my shattered nerves, and then I turned to Gene who was visibly shaken. "Do you know what happened?".

"I'm not sure, but I intend to find out."

Shortly after, The Brothers Grimm showed up.

"Any word on Peter?" Eric Cox asked in a perturbed tone.

"No, nothing yet." I couldn't help but wonder if they were

genuinely worried about Peter, or their investment in him.

"This is exactly why we don't want him doing this kind of thing!!" John muttered. "It's too risky. We should have put a stop to it a long time ago."

"Peter never listens to anything we tell him." Eric echoed the same irritated tone as his brother. "And now he's shut down production."

"Production?!" My nerves finally snapped. "That's all you can think about? Production?! What's wrong with the two of you? Peter got hurt today and we don't even know how serious it is!" The words came out of my mouth before I could stop them, but I didn't care. "Maybe you should go back to the studio since you're more worried about your show than you are about Peter!" Silence filled the waiting room as the three of us faced off.

"Let it go, Darlene," Doug whispered.

"But Doug—"

"Let it go," he repeated firmly, and nodded toward the entranceway, where reporters were approaching with Helene hot on their trail. "We have bigger things to worry about right now."

"There's no story here." Helene pushed her way to the waiting room entrance. "The studio will issue a formal statement later today when we have more information."

"Was Peter Chandler hurt on the set today?"

"Peter Chandler is fine," she replied. "He's only here as a precaution and that's all we are going to say right now. I will ask you to kindly leave."

They refused, so Helene had hospital security show them out. Once the reporters disbursed, Gene left to go back to the studio and check on the investigation, but only after we promised to call him as soon as we had any news.

"Doug, maybe we should call the Chandlers," I suggested. "I don't want them to see this on TV. We should probably call your folks and Estelle, too."

"But we really don't have anything to tell them yet," Doug said with a shake of his head. "Let's talk to the doctors first."

"Doug's right." Helene agreed as she sat in the chair next to mine.

"We should hear something soon." She glanced over at The Brothers Grimm who were sitting at the opposite end of the waiting room and shook her head. "I have half a mind to throw them out of here, too." She looked at me, made a quick decision, and then strode over to them.

"Why don't the two of you go back to the studio? You're upsetting Darlene and you're irritating the hell out of me."

"We're waiting for word on Peter," John Cox replied.

"I'll call you when we know something," Helene said, her voice flat.

"We have a lot riding on him." Eric Cox stood up.

"Then go back to the studio." She gritted her teeth. "And check on your show since that seems to be your main concern. Maybe you should call your writers together in case you need a quick revision."

"We've told Peter a thousand times—"

"Get out!" Helene fumed. "No one wants you here—least of all me. Your show would be nothing without Peter and you know it. Hell, everybody knows it. Now I suggest you find your way out of here and if you're smart, you'll be praying that Peter makes a full recovery so he can continue making the two of you look good."

She stood there, arms folded, staring them both down. The brothers looked at each other and then walked out. Helene reclaimed her seat next to me. "I'm sorry, Darlene, but I couldn't stand the sight of them for another minute."

I was tired of sitting so I paced for the next half hour. My head hurt and my nerves were stretched about as far as they could go. Doug finally made me sit down again. I rubbed my temples with my fingers, trying to stop the pain from getting worse. What was taking so long?

"Honey." Doug 's voice made me look up as a man wearing a white coat walked toward us.

"You must be Darlene." The doctor stopped in front of me. He was an older gentleman with gray hair and glasses. "I'm Dr. Constantine. I've been taking care of Peter. He's asking for you. Would you like to see him?"

"Is he all right?"

"He took in a little too much smoke this afternoon, but he'll be fine. We'd like him to stay overnight for observation and keep him on oxygen for his own comfort, but he says today is his birthday and he refuses to spend it here. Maybe you can convince him to stay."

"I doubt it." I shook my head. "He's incredibly stubborn, but I really do want to see him."

"I'll take you to him."

"Go on." Doug nodded. "I'll make those calls."

"And I'll let everyone know at the studio." Helene looked as relieved as I felt.

"We have a couple of IVs in him—one to keep him hydrated and one to offset infections," Dr. Constantine explained as we walked down the hall. "If he won't stay overnight, he has to be here long enough to finish taking in the IV fluids. The oxygen is helping him breathe, but once we release him, he'll need to take it easy. He definitely shouldn't be working or doing anything strenuous for the rest of the week."

"Did you tell him that?"

"I did, but I got the impression he wasn't listening."

"He probably wasn't. Is there anything else I should know?"

"He's going to experience some discomfort for the next few days. Breathing may be difficult. His chest and throat will be sore."

Seeing Peter lying in a hospital bed with IVs and oxygen startled me, but at least he was awake. "Honey,"—I took his hand and leaned over to kiss him—"you scared me half to death."

"I've had better days, myself." His voice sounded raspy and his breathing labored.

Chapter Twenty-Four

P *eter didn't sleep at all last night. His throat is sore, his chest hurts, and he's having a hard time breathing. I wish he had stayed in the hospital where they might have made him more comfortable.*

He sure gave me a deadly scare yesterday. I'll never forget the sight of him being carried out of that fire. He was lucky—things could have easily turned out different. News of the accident is all over the radio and television, as well as in the newspapers. He'll be home for the next couple of days. Thanks to some quick rewrites, they'll shoot around him.

Gene assured us that the accident is being taken quite seriously and a full investigation is underway. He'll get back to us as soon as he has some answers.

"Peter, honey, you should be in bed." Estelle wasn't happy to see him in the kitchen early Friday morning. She shouldn't have been there at all, but she insisted it was her job to take care of him.

"I'm tired of lying around." It was still an effort for him to talk.

"How's your throat?" I asked him.

"Sore."

"You're not thinking about going to work today, are you?" Estelle frowned at him.

"Not today," he answered as he took a seat in the breakfast nook. "But I have to go in tomorrow for a couple of hours." He stopped to take a breath. "Gene is going to call and let me know when."

"Peter, the doctor wants you at home," I reminded him.

"I can't shut down production. I'll never hear the end of it."

"You need rest." It was Estelle's turn to scold him.

"I promise you ladies that I won't be there long," he said with a sigh.

I drove Peter to the studio Saturday afternoon to keep tabs on him. He was feeling better, but nowhere near one hundred percent. Gene met us in Peter's trailer to go over the shooting schedule. He promised that Peter's scenes would be quick.

"I have some other news you may find interesting," Gene told us. "Someone left a pile of wood stacked in the back of the building where we were filming. It caught fire and that's where all the smoke came from. You collapsed before the cameramen even got close. They tried to find you, but they couldn't see for the smoke. Thank God everyone was okay."

"We were lucky," Peter agreed with a nod. "I wish someone could rescue me from The Brothers Grimm. I'm sure I'll hear about it next week."

"I already have." Gene nodded. "You're next."

Peter had no break in between filming *Fire in the City* and starting work on the play. After filming the final show of the season, he immediately began rehearsals at the theater. Unlike the studio, he seemed superstitious about me coming to the theater. A couple of times, I asked him about watching rehearsal, but he always said no— something about bad luck. He wanted me to wait until opening night when I could wear my pearls. I respected his wishes even though I thought it was pretty silly. I never even met his leading lady. I had no idea who Karen Updyke was, but Peter assured me I'd probably recognize her once we met. Other than that, he never said much about her.

Something to Live For was a drama concerning a widower and a widow and their developing relationship as they overcome first grief, then guilt, to find hope in a life neither of them expected they would have. The characters were opposites, which kept their story from being trite.

Even though opening night would not be a formal affair, Helene insisted I continue my tradition of dressing like a star. This one was tricky. No gowns. No fancy dresses. We talked about it for two full weeks and then Helene hit upon the perfect outfit—a white jumper made for Ingrid Bergman's character, Ilsa Lund, in *Casablanca*. Designed by the Australian-born Orry-Kelly who was the top costumer at Warner Bros., the white, square-shouldered, sleeveless dress had an open neck all the way down to the waist. It was paired with a short-sleeved black-and-white-striped blouse underneath. I had the neckline altered just enough so I could wear my pearls. Peter expected to see them.

The opening night of the play was nothing like a movie premiere. Peter had to be at the theater early to run through a final dress rehearsal.

"Are you coming as Darlene tonight?" he asked as he grabbed his car keys.

"What fun would that be?"

"Let me guess—Scarlet O'Hara at the barbeque?"

"Not even close."

"Cinderella at the ball?"

"I would look ridiculous coming to the theater in a ball gown."

"You would look ridiculous riding in a pumpkin." He bussed my cheek.

"I guess you'll have to wait and see." I sent him off with a good luck kiss.

"It wouldn't have anything to do with *Casablanca*, would it?" he called from outside. "I think you made me watch it three different times."

I closed the door without answering.

"Darlene!" I could still hear him hollering. "Whatever you do, please don't show up as Humphrey Bogart!"

Doug was picking me up and Helene was bringing Estelle. We all planned to meet in Peter's dressing room prior to Act One.

Doug and I arrived first, and we found Peter alone in his dressing room with the door open reading over some last-minute changes. He laid down his notes and smiled. "You're early!"

"Darlene, had some crazy idea that she wanted to see you before the curtain went up." Doug rolled his eyes.

"Except I don't think that's Darlene." Peter shook his head. "Somehow you got mixed up and brought Ingrid Bergman here instead. Darlene is going to be furious with you if she's late."

"I wanted to keep it simple." I gave a spin.

"I think Bogie was a fool to let you go!" Peter pulled me down onto his lap and in the worst Bogie voice I ever heard, he said, "Of all the dressing rooms, in all the theaters, in all the world, she walks into mine!"

"Darlene!" Helene came in, followed by Estelle wearing a straw boater with daisies, and carrying a large tin. "You're in my spot." Helene yanked me off Peter's lap and promptly sat down. "Are you ready for tonight, darling?"

"About as ready as I'll ever be."

"I'm not talking about the play." Helene frowned at him. "I'm talking about my place afterward. I have big plans for us tonight once we're alone."

"Let's not talk about it in front of Ingrid." Peter shook his head. "You know she has a jealous streak and it could get ugly in here."

"Are you nervous?" Estelle asked, setting the tin down on the dressing table.

"A little."

"Don't be." She gave him a smile and patted the tin. "I brought you some cookies in case you get hungry. I bet you didn't have dinner.

"I grabbed a bite." Peter smiled at her. "But I missed dessert."

"Speaking of dessert---how's Karen?" Helene seemed to know her.

"Karen's Karen," Peter shrugged. "But everything should be fine now that Ingrid and her lucky pearls are here."

"Ingrid, are those pearls really lucky?" Doug wanted to know.

"Yes, they are," Peter answered for me. "And sometimes when she takes them off, I get even luckier."

"So, tell me Peter—" Helene stood up—"what kind of uniform are you wearing?"

"No uniform."

"You mean you're not wearing anything?" She sounded hopeful.

"Now, there's an idea, honey." A striking red-head in a way-too-short beige bathrobe appeared in the doorway. She sashayed across the room and stood directly in front of Peter. I did remember her! She had presented an Emmy with Peter the night he won his first Best Actor Award. I didn't like her then and I certainly didn't like her now.

"Hello, Helene." She smiled, not acknowledging the rest of us. "I think you came up with a great idea."

"It was a joke, Karen." Peter stood up immediately, on the defensive.

"Whatever, honey." She shrugged. "I wanted to see you before curtain call."

"Is there something you need?" Peter seemed impatient.

"What I always need from you." She quickly stood on her tiptoes, kissing him full on the mouth.

"Karen!" He pushed her away. "You should be getting ready."

"Oh, I'm ready, honey. The question is: are you?" She winked at him and left the room without a word to any of us. So this was the woman Peter had been rehearsing with for the past several weeks.

"Why don't we wait for Darlene in the hall?" Helene shepherded Doug and Estelle out the door.

"Now I see why you haven't wanted me to come to the theater all this time," I said to Peter once we were alone.

"I didn't want you to be upset like you are now. I've told Karen a million times to knock it off, but she won't."

"I'm sorry if I don't appreciate seeing some woman crawling all over you." Those old insecurities were resurfacing once more.

"Look, honey, I have to be onstage soon. I don't want this hanging over my head while I'm out there. I'm really sorry if Karen upset you. I wish she hadn't."

"All this time I thought you didn't want me here because of some silly superstition." The harshness in my voice surprised even me.

"That was part of it."

"But not all of it."

I tried to clear my head and enjoy the play, but as soon as Karen appeared onstage, my stomach tightened. I studied her every move. She leaned against Peter unnecessarily. When they kissed, she enjoyed it a little too much. She constantly touched him. By the end of the first act, I'd seen enough.

"Take it easy, Darlene," Doug whispered. "You're getting all worked up over nothing."

"Maybe I need to get some air." I started to get up.

"You can't just leave," Doug held onto my arm. "Peter will notice."

So I stayed and watched some more. I thought about Julie Dunbar. Her scenes with Peter in *Night Shoot* didn't bother me half as much. Julie was different. She never chased after Peter. She did her job and that was it. Once filming was finished, it was over. But this play wouldn't be over for another eight weeks and who knows what had gone on during rehearsals.

As the players took their final bow, applause rang out. Peter came out last, carrying red roses. As he handed them to Karen, the audience rose to its feet, cheering. They roared even louder as she kissed Peter with an obvious passion. I was seething.

"Calm down, Darlene." Doug squeezed my hand. "Look at Peter. He's furious with her." Doug was right. Even though Peter was smiling, his eyes were angry. Maybe no one else in the theater noticed, but those of us who knew him couldn't miss it.

As the final curtain came down, Doug pulled me into the lobby and out the front door. We took a few steps down the street and stopped. "Take a deep breath, honey. Get it out of your system, now, before we go back inside."

"She got to me, Doug, and it's only opening night. I can't do this for eight more weeks."

"But Peter isn't interested in her."

"She's more than interested in him. Has he ever mentioned her to you?"

"Not once."

"Would you tell me if he had?" I felt bad as soon as I said it, knowing I shouldn't be taking this out on Doug.

"Maybe the problem isn't really Karen at all." Doug was quick to catch on. "Maybe the problem is you."

"Maybe it is." I paced in a circle. "Peter meets fascinating women everyday. If it's not Karen, it will be someone else. Sooner or later, he's bound to get bored with me and want one of them. I don't know how we lasted this long."

"Darlene, take a breath. We have to go back inside, and Karen will probably be there. The best thing you can do is ignore her. Don't give her the satisfaction of knowing she can get a rise out of you. Do you really think that she's the kind of woman Peter would even be remotely interested in?"

"I suppose not. I'm sorry, Doug. I let her get to me."

Back in Peter's dressing room, it was crowded—mostly with people I didn't know. He didn't see us come in, but Helene did. "Peter's been looking for the two of you. Are you all right, Darlene?"

"I'm fine."

"If it's any consolation, when I got back here Peter was telling Karen off. You should have heard them. It got pretty loud and ugly. Karen left here in tears."

Somehow, I couldn't feel sorry for her.

Outside the theater, the press was waiting. Obviously, they had not heard about the rift between Peter and Karen. They were more interested in what I was wearing. I tried putting on a happy face, but without a chance to talk with Peter, my nerves were still a bit raw.

"Who's your date, Peter?" one of them asked.

"Ingrid Bergman!" Peter smiled and flash bulbs popped. "She stood up Humphrey Bogart and Paul Henreid to be here tonight, but she has to catch a plane back to Casablanca before they notice she's gone. Victor Laszlo is the jealous type, and I definitely don't want to get on Bogie's bad side."

"Peter, what's it like going out with all of these different women?"

"It's exhausting," Peter said with a grin. "I spend weeks trying to figure out who is going to show up and then I have to find a way to get rid of Darlene. Tonight, I sent her to the wrong theater. She's going to be furious with me when I get home."

As the press drifted away, one by one, cast and crew wandered across the street to a local restaurant that had seen its share of opening night celebrations. Karen Updyke was noticeably absent. She and Peter seemed to be the hot topic of conversation around the room. Almost everyone inside the theater had heard them arguing after the play. They were all speculating whether Karen would be a no-show.

With hors d'oeurves and wine on every table, the chattering voices in the room suddenly fell silent. All eyes turned toward the door. Karen stood there in a very low-cut black gown with thigh-high slits on either side. She held the red roses Peter had given her, which brought a splash of color to her otherwise austere appearance. No one spoke as she strode across the room directly to the bar, perched on a stool, and demanded a whiskey.

Karen never left her seat. She didn't eat, but continued drinking. Occasionally she turned to watch Peter. She was obviously agitated and the more she drank, the more it showed. After she downed her fourth shot, she slowly got up from the barstool, using it to steady herself. Once again, a hush fell over the room as she left her roses and slowly made her way to our table. She stood behind Peter on wobbly feet.

"Peter, you had no right to say those terrible things to me." Her voice was slurred from the alcohol.

"I had every right."

"I only took this job because rumor had it you were interested." She put her hands on his shoulders.

That seemed to set him off and he stood up, facing her. "Karen! You've had a few too many!"

"Maybe I have." She looked directly at him. "Maybe you should take me home."

"I'll call you a cab."

"I don't want a cab!" She stubbornly folded her arms. "I want you!"

"Karen, you're drunk," Peter told her quietly, well aware that all eyes were on the two of them.

"Then take me home."

"I told you before, the only lady I take home is this one." Peter rested his hand on my shoulder.

"I've pulled out all the stops, Peter. What does a girl have to do around here to get your attention?"

"You're making a scene here, Karen." Peter was losing his patience.

"Then take me home."

"Karen, I think Peter has made himself perfectly clear." Helene stepped in. "You need to go home and sleep it off."

"The only sleeping I want to do is with Peter!" She grew louder. "Take me home and these could be yours!" She yanked the front of her dress down exposing herself.

"Say good night, Karen!" Helene rushed around the table, pulled the front of Karen's dress back up, and pushed her toward the door.

Peter was livid. The color drained from his face while anger flashed in his blue eyes. He sat down, trying his best to calm down while the shocked production company looked on in silence.

"I'm sorry I gave you a hard time about Karen." I felt I had to apologize as we lay in bed in the dark.

"I'm sorry about Karen, period." He reached for me.

"Can we talk first?"

"About what?"

"About us."

"I thought we were okay."

"We are, but do you ever wish you had someone a little more exciting in your life?"

"Darlene, how many times do we have to go over this?"

"I'm not trying to be difficult, Peter." I sat up. "But sometimes I feel like I fall short. I wish I didn't, but I do. I'm not tall enough, or thin enough, or glamorous enough. My hair's not blond—"

"Darlene!" Peter pulled me back down. "I don't know how many more ways I can say it, so how about if I show you?" He quickly covered my mouth with his, effectively ending our conversation, but my insecurity remained firmly wedged in place.

CHAPTER TWENTY-FIVE

What the critics say doesn't matter because as far as box office is concerned, every performance is sold out. Their verdict, however, is important to Peter's career. They describe his portrayal as moving and forceful. Someone wrote that as much as they enjoyed the play, Peter's blue eyes were meant for the big screen. I have to agree. Peter's best feature doesn't quite come across on television or stage, the way they do in the movies. According to one critic, 'Chandler and Updyke make a sparkling stage couple'. If they only knew what caused those sparks!

Peter limits any contact with Karen to their work onstage. Outside the theater, he refuses to see or speak to her. Publicly, Peter praises her ability as an actress and compliments her on the way she plays her part. Karen, on the other hand, complains that Peter is cold and distant. Sometimes she blames me, saying I'm the jealous girlfriend.

Peter had been performing in the play for almost three weeks when his brother-in-law, Daniel, called. He wanted to surprise Carmen with a week in Hawaii—just the two of them—as soon as the boys were out of school if their uncle agreed to keep them. Needless to say, Peter was delighted. We stocked up on everything they might like. Peter talked about nothing but his nephews for days. He wanted to cram a year's worth of fun into one week.

Peter had a matinee performance, so I headed out to the airport alone on Saturday afternoon. Carmen and Daniel had a connecting flight to Honolulu and I picked up the boys during their two-hour layover. Carmen had a hard time saying good-bye to her sons. Bobby and Timmy, on the other hand, never looked back, but they didn't hide their disappointment when they saw me. They thought their uncle was coming to get them. I was a sorry second. Of course they were hungry. They were boys. We stopped for burgers, but what they really wanted was Peter.

"What time does Uncle Peter get home?" Timmy dipped his french fries in mustard, making me grimace.

"He'll be home for dinner, but he has to go back to work after we eat."

"Can we go with him?" Bobby took his hamburger apart looking for pickles.

"Afraid not, but the three of us can do something. How about a movie?"

"Can we get popcorn?" Timmy laid his straw on the table and sipped his chocolate milk, leaving a dark mustache under his nose.

"Yep." I smiled, wondering if I would have enough energy to keep up with the two of them all week.

After a swim in the pool, we came inside to make dinner. I put the boys to work setting the table. While they were busy with that, I heard Peter's car in the driveway. "Your uncle's home."

"Come on, Timmy, let's hide!" Bobby raced for the stairs with his brother close behind.

"Where is everybody?" Peter asked as he laid his keys on the counter. I pointed upstairs.

Peter called out to them as he climbed the stairs. It was obvious they were in our bedroom by the noise they were making. Peter made a big production out of looking for them—first in the closet, then the bathroom. He looked behind the curtains. From under the bed, their muffled giggles grew louder as he kept searching, but didn't find them. Peter sat down on the bed, trying not to laugh. "You don't think they changed their minds and went to Hawaii instead, do you, Aunt Darlene?"

"If they did, they forgot all their clothes."

Their laughter grew louder. They weren't even trying to be quiet anymore. "Aunt Darlene, did you bring stray elephants home again?" Peter dropped to the floor and looked under the bed. The boys rolled out from their hiding place, jumping and climbing all over him. There hadn't been this much noise in our house since Christmas.

Dinner was a nuisance. The boys were more interested in wrestling on the floor. All three of them were disappointed when Peter had to leave. "I'll be here in the morning when you get up," Peter gave them one last tickle.

"Aunt Darlene, can we still go to the movies and get popcorn?" Bobby never forgot a thing.

"If you boys aren't tired."

"Watch your popcorn around Aunt Darlene," Peter picked up his jacket and keys. "She likes to eat it all up."

That night I took the boys to see the latest, but not greatest, Disney movie, *The Cat From Outer Space*. I couldn't tell what they liked more—the movie or the popcorn. By the time we got home, they were both yawning, but didn't want to go to bed.

"We want to wait up for Uncle Peter," Timmy told me.

"He won't be home till late."

"Please, we'll be good," Bobby pleaded. "We'll watch TV and when Uncle Peter gets home, we'll go right to bed."

I couldn't tell them no, and within minutes, they were both sound asleep on the couch.

When Peter came in, he carried them upstairs one at a time. Neither of them opened an eye.

Sunday morning gave us a preview of the week to come. The boys hit our room like kangaroos, jumping on the bed. They screamed in delight as Peter tickled them both. "Let's go downstairs and wrestle!" Timmy hollered.

"We have to have breakfast first," Peter told them. "Us men have to keep up our strength."

"I'm hungry," Bobby agreed.

It seemed to me that they were always hungry. It was a good thing we had stocked up before they came. I went downstairs to put on a

pot of coffee and start breakfast while the boys stayed upstairs hors-
ing around with their uncle. As I was pouring my first cup, their
squeals grew louder. Peter carried them into the kitchen—one under
each arm. One at a time, he deposited them in the breakfast nook and
then poured them each a glass of orange juice.

"Do you have to work today, Uncle Peter?" Timmy took a bite of
toast, leaving a streak of jelly around his mouth.

"I have to go to the theater this afternoon, but I'll be back for
dinner."

"Then can you stay home with us?" Bobby flinched as he spilled
most of his orange juice on the table in front of him.

"No, I have to go back after dinner." Peter mopped up the mess
with napkins. "But tomorrow, I'll be home all day. I won't have to go
to work until Tuesday night."

I was exhausted and they hadn't even been up for an hour.

Peter planned something every day. On Monday, it was an es-
corted tour of Universal Studios; Tuesday, the zoo; Wednesday, a
picnic; Thursday, the beach; Friday, Peter made arrangements to take
the boys to a real fire station, compliments of some of the real firemen that he knew. Everyday was an adventure to them. They never
once asked for their mom or dad. When their parents called, they
only talked to them because their uncle said they had to.

They tolerated me because I took care of them when Peter wasn't
around. I wasn't much good when it came to roughhousing. They
really came alive when they were with their uncle. Having children
around agreed with Peter and our house was energized.

The boys begged Peter to call their parents and have them stay in
the islands another week. If Peter thought for a moment he could
have talked his sister into it, he would have, but Daniel and Carmen
came back the following Saturday while Peter was at the theater for
a matinee performance. Timmy and Bobby gave them a rather cool

welcome. They both knew the arrival of their parents meant that in a couple of days, they would be going home. In contrast, when Peter arrived for dinner, they greeted him with wild enthusiasm.

Once again, Daniel was friendly while Carmen was distant. I should have been used to it by now. At least, she and Peter seemed to have forgotten their differences from Christmas.

"I hope the boys weren't too much trouble," she told Peter over dinner.

"Uncle Peter, tell Mom how good we were so we can come back!" Timmy urged.

"You guys were terrific. You can come back whenever you want."

After Peter left for the theater that night, the boys wanted to swim. Carmen and Daniel took them outside while I cleaned up the kitchen. She must have been trying to avoid me because she sent Daniel in for drinks.

"I don't know how we're going to get the boys to leave on Monday." Daniel poured soda into plastic cups.

"Peter's going to be lost without them. We've had more fun this week than I can remember in a long time. I'm so glad you decided to leave them with us, but how in the world did you talk Carmen into it?"

"I never gave her a choice." Daniel looked me over thoughtfully. "You're good with the boys. Mothering becomes you. From one outsider to another, may I ask if you and Peter ever think about trying for another baby, or is it none of my business?"

"From one outsider to another, Peter wants to wait until his run with *Fire in the City* ends."

"Are you okay with that?"

"I suppose." I forced a smile. "But to be honest, ever since I lost the baby, I've felt like something was missing."

"Perfectly normal. Have you told Peter that?"

"I've never told anyone that—until now."

Sunday night, Carmen and Daniel went to the theater with Peter. I stayed with the boys who once again wanted to swim in the pool. After a quick shower, they asked to play cards—Go Fish was their current favorite. As had become their custom, they fell asleep on the couch waiting for their uncle to get home, but not before telling me that they wished their parents would go back to Hawaii—forever.

After the boys left, the house was depressingly quiet. It reminded me of the day I came home from the hospital. Our Lucky Penny would have been crawling by now. I never realized how much I wanted a family. We weren't getting any younger, and although my biological clock hadn't started ticking yet, that didn't stop the feeling that something was missing.

Monday was Peter's only day off, so we opted for a walk on the beach at our favorite spot. He didn't say much during the drive, and he remained unusually quiet as we strolled along the water's edge. Even the bright summer sun did nothing to lift his spirits.

"Do you miss the boys?" I asked him.

He stopped walking and looked down at me. "More than I thought I would. After spending a week with my nephews, they made the house come alive. There were toys and coloring books and cartoons—."

"And dirty clothes and messes to mop up and faces to wash." I finished his sentence with a grin. "They were a handful, but they were fun. Maybe Carmen will let them come again."

"Maybe, but after having Bobby and Timmy with us, the house seems too big for you and me. I always figured that we'd grow into it, but it seems so empty now."

"Maybe if I hadn't lost Penny—"

"That was not your fault." He wrapped his arms around me, and we stood there for a moment drawing comfort from each other. "Are you happy, Darlene?"

"Of course I'm happy. Are you?"

"Yes." He laid his forehead against mine before he spoke again. "But I thought we had it all—maybe I'm wrong."

Peter had one more week left in the play. The tension between him and Karen had grown worse. He didn't talk about it, but it was obvious that the situation was taking a toll on him. It had been quite a while since he'd done live theater, but this was not what he anticipated. To his credit, Peter never once said anything unkind about Karen publicly. Karen, however, had no qualms telling the press that Peter was hard to work with—and that possessive girlfriend of his only made matters worse.

I had long gotten over my worries about Karen Updyke. I never brought her up unless Peter did. She wasn't worth the energy. With only seven performances left and several sleepless nights, Peter was tired and irritable. Then on Wednesday morning, when he spotted a handwritten note from Estelle, he went off the rails.

"What's this?" Peter snatched a small piece of paper from the refrigerator. We'd just been planning our annual trip to Maui over coffee, but now, he was obviously upset.

"I don't know. What is it?"

"It's for you," he snapped, shoving the paper at me.

It was Estelle's handwriting: "Darlene—Frank called. He'll call back later."

I shuddered. It had been a while, but now it was unavoidable. We were about to have another Frank episode.

"When did he call?" Peter demanded.

"I don't know."

"How did he get our number?"

"I don't know, Peter. I haven't talked to him in over two years."

"So he's had two years to sober up." He glared at me. "It looks like you'll finally have your chance to talk to him when he calls back."

"What's that supposed to mean?"

"You always said that you wanted to talk to him before the divorce, but you never did and that bothered you." Peter grabbed his car keys. "For all I know, it still bothers you."

"Where are you going?"

"Out!" The door slammed behind him. It was best to leave him alone. He'd work it out for himself sooner or later. He always did. I crumpled up the note and threw it away. Somehow I must have missed it. I wished I'd seen it first. This whole thing could have been avoided.

Peter stayed out much later than usual that night and when he did come home, he didn't come upstairs. I found him early Thursday morning asleep on the couch—the television babbling in the background. When I turned it off, he woke up.

"Why didn't you come to bed?"

"I prefer the couch." He gave me a disapproving look.

"You mean you didn't want to sleep with me."

"It was a long night." He turned his back on me. "And I'm tired, Darlene."

"I don't want to argue with you, Peter—especially over someone that doesn't even matter to me."

"You obviously matter to him." He kept his back to me.

"Frank is ancient history. I thought you knew that by now."

"He called you and that doesn't sound like ancient history to me."

I left him downstairs. If Peter didn't trust me by now, maybe he never would. I couldn't imagine what Frank wanted, but I resented him for causing this rift between Peter and me. If Frank did call back, I'd definitely make it clear to him that he shouldn't call again. But what if Peter picked up the phone first? The thought of that brought on a chill.

Normally, Peter's silence never lasted more than a day or two, but this time was different. I think it was the 'call back' that loomed over us. By the time the weekend arrived, I couldn't tell which was worse—Peter's silence or the headache I'd been living with.

He came home after three that Saturday morning, surprised to find me lying awake on the couch. "We need to talk," I told him.

"It's late, Darlene, and I'm tired."

"So am I." I stood up, looking directly at him. "I'm tired of sleeping alone."

"And I'm tired of walking in the door every night wondering if you've been with Frank."

"Why would I be with Frank? He hasn't called back; he may never call back. If he was drunk, he may not even remember he called here in the first place."

"And if he does?"

"It doesn't matter what Frank does or doesn't do!" The pain in my head sharpened.

"I think it does."

"I'm going to bed, Peter. I have a terrific headache." I turned to go upstairs more hurt than angry. "Sleep on the couch if that's what you want to do."

"I know you, Darlene." He caught my arm and whirled me around to face him. "You married him, and you wouldn't have done that if you didn't have some pretty deep feelings for him."

"Why are you dredging all this up?"

"Because I'm afraid of losing you—like I lost Kathleen!"

"Kathleen?!" I didn't understand. "You said Kathleen didn't want to move to L.A."

"She didn't! She wanted to stay in New York because she was still seeing her ex-husband, but I didn't know it. As soon as I left, she married him again."

"How come you never told me that?"

"I'm telling you now." His grip on my arm tightened. "And if you decide to give Frank another chance where will that leave us?"

"Let go of me, Peter." It didn't matter what I said when his moodiness took over.

"I'm afraid to let you go." He kept staring at me with those searing blue eyes.

"I said, let go of me!" I tried pulling away, but his grip tightened. "Please, Peter! It hurts!"

He opened his hand, and I rushed upstairs. The migraine, now surging through my head, made me sick to my stomach.

Sunday morning, my headache and I were still alone. Maybe some caffeine and a couple of Tylenol would help. I glanced in the family room on my way to the kitchen. Peter was gone. He was probably out canceling our trip to Maui.

Once the coffee was brewing and the Tylenol taken, I went back upstairs and hit the shower. The steam felt good and the pain in my head eased. Afterward, I slipped on my robe and stepped into the bedroom. Twelve long-stemmed white roses lay across the bed with a tiny envelope propped against them. The note inside read:

> *Darlene—*
> *I hate it when we're broken.*
> *Peter*

"I'm sorry, Darlene, but Frank gets to me in the worst possible way." Peter's voice came from the doorway. "I wish he didn't, but he does. When I found out that Kathleen was still sleeping with her ex-husband behind my back, I was bitter."

"But after all this time, you still don't trust me." I didn't turn around. I stood there for one long moment trying to push back the lump in my throat as Peter came closer.

"It's not that I don't trust you." He placed his hands on my arms.

"Then what is it, Peter?" I finally turned to look up at him.

"I'm afraid of losing you, Darlene. I'm afraid of coming home to an empty house."

"Peter, I—"

He silenced me with a kiss and that damn cologne went to my head, while those blue eyes drew me in. His lips brushed against my ear and his breath felt warm.

"Peter, we need to talk." I quietly protested as his lips traveled along my neck.

"Not now." His mouth was next to mine. "I need to fix this, Darlene. You're the only one who keeps the balance."

"But Peter—" He muffled my words with another kiss, but I knew if we didn't stop right then, we never would. Nothing would be resolved and next time would be worse.

"Please don't do this, Peter." I tried once more to stop him, but he wasn't listening. Each time he kissed me, I gave in a little more. Before long, I found myself kissing him back, my arms around his neck. Peter wanted me and, for the moment, nothing else mattered.

That night, I attended Peter's final performance. Afterward, there was a cast party catered at the theater to celebrate the play's successful run. Peter and Karen stayed at opposite ends of the room. There was no interaction between them and Karen left early, much to everyone's relief. I was relieved that Peter and I were back on track. Or were we? It was hard to be sure.

This was the worst Frank episode we'd ever had. I was even more careful not to mention Frank in front of Peter. I even ordered Estelle not to leave a note like that again. If Frank called, she was to tell me privately. She was never to say Frank's name out loud if Peter was in the house. It may not have been the answer, but I was so glad to regain the momentum we'd had, I didn't care. Deep down, however, I knew that nothing had changed.

I didn't realize it at the time, but Peter's insecurity over Frank was similar to my own self-doubts about keeping him happy. Our fears weren't rational, but based on emotions we didn't quite understand. The only way to stop them was to face them head-on, but neither one of us was willing or brave enough to take that chance.

Worst of all, it was only a matter of time before Frank came back to haunt us.

CHAPTER TWENTY-SIX

The last few weeks have been so hectic, I've hardly had any time to write. Once Peter and I got back from the islands, Sydney came to visit for a week. I just dropped her off at the airport. She's always so much fun and now that she's gone, I really do miss having a girlfriend in L.A. Peter isn't much for girl talk and I sure can't take him shopping.

Speaking of Peter, things are good between us again. After that last Frank fiasco, two weeks in Maui were exactly what we needed. The Maui magic refreshed us. I wish we could have stayed there forever. Now, Peter is back to being James Dakota and we're once again on that wild ride for yet another season.

I'm a little tired of the technical writing. I'd like to try my hand at something more creative, but I'm not sure what. It must be that need to nurture—whether it's a baby or something else I've created. I shouldn't complain. As a technical writer, I work my own hours at home, keeping only the clients I like, and I make good money. I especially like the freedom it gives me.

And one more thing I'm grateful for—Frank never did call back.

Besides our August birthdays, Doug had another reason to celebrate. He made senior partner at the law firm where he worked. A substantial raise came with having his name included as a partner. Peter and I wanted to celebrate big, but Doug preferred a quiet Sunday dinner at our house. He worked hard and deserved the recognition, but I never liked the fact that he was still alone. Just before dinner, Peter went into the den to make a call, leaving Doug and me in the kitchen.

"I'm thinking about buying a house." Doug leaned against the counter with a beer in hand while I snapped and washed green beans at the sink. "Would you help me out?"

"I'd be glad to, but are you sure you want *me* to do it?"

"Why not? You did a great job finding this place."

"But isn't there anyone you're interested in? Because if there is, maybe *she* should help you look for a house."

"I'm only interested in you, Darlene," he said with a grin.

"But any girl would be lucky to have you." I dropped the last of the green beans into a pot and dried my hands. "I hate seeing you alone all the time."

"I'm fine, thank you very much. I got burned once and I'm not going for twice. Getting serious with anyone is off the table."

"But you must know some interesting lady lawyers."

"Lady lawyers bite." He took a swig of beer. "Some of them have fangs."

"They don't have fangs." I rolled my eyes. "I think some great girl is out there looking for a terrific guy like you and if you don't open your eyes, you might miss her."

"I'm not missing a thing—except maybe teeth marks."

In September, Hollywood was abuzz over the death of Jack Warner, the youngest and last of the four original Warner Brothers. Peter had never met him, but everyone knew that Jack, despite his movie-making prowess, was not known for his personal ethics or integrity. Although he'd been ill for quite some time, his passing marked the end of an era.

While Jack Warner made the news, Helene and I finished up the final touches on my dress for the Emmys. This time, we picked Elizabeth Taylor's famous white gown from *A Place in the Sun* when she played high society debutante Angela Vickers. At seventeen, Taylor was transitioning from child to adult movie star. Designed by Edith Head, the strapless gown had tiny silk flowers covering the bodice and a full tulle skirt dotted with more silk flowers. It became one of the most favored dresses of the early 1950s and several versions were seen at various formal parties throughout that era. I chose to wear it in light pink with matching shoes.

Peter pestered me for two full weeks about what I was going to wear to the Emmys. Even though I made him watch *A Place in the Sun*, I also threw in a few different films to keep him guessing. He honestly had no idea, until just before we left the house.

"Darlene, the car is here!" Peter called from the kitchen.

"I have to put my pearls on," I hollered back before rushing down the stairs.

"Darlene!" Peter smiled when he caught sight of me. "Or should I say La Liz?"

"Liz will work fine tonight. Do you like it?"

"Like it?! I'm going to be the envy of every man there."

"Somehow, I doubt that." I shook my head and then looked outside. "I thought you said the car was here."

"I lied. It's not here. I just couldn't wait to see what you had on."

When we arrived at the Emmys, the red carpet awaited, along with the reporters. "Who's your date tonight, Peter?" one of them asked.

"Elizabeth Taylor," he answered. "How lucky can a guy get?"

"Are you going to be Liz's next husband?" another voice called out.

"Oh, no." Peter shook his head with a wink. "We're just good friends! At least that's what I told Darlene before I left the house, but I'm not sure she was buying it. She has a jealous steak a mile wide. For all I know, she may be in the closet right now cutting up my clothes."

"Really, Peter?" I shook my head while everyone else laughed.

"Don't worry," he whispered as we walked toward the theater entrance. "I won't let crazy Darlene anywhere near you."

Peter collected another Emmy that night. When we got home after the studio party, we headed straight to the den, and he placed the statuette alongside the first two before turning to me with trouble in those blue eyes.

"And now the moment I've been waiting for my entire life." He pulled me closer. "I've always wanted to kiss Elizabeth Taylor." He followed through with such a hot-blooded kiss, my knees went weak.

"Don't stop now." I curved into him for more. "Unless you want me to go straight to the closet and cut up your clothes."

House hunting for Doug came to an end when we found a sprawling, gated, art deco-style ranch complete with wooden floors throughout in Bel Air. The three-bedroom, four-and-a-half bath home was perfect—plenty of room for family visits. The backyard had a fenced-in pool and an oversized patio. Doug loved it, but I let him know in no uncertain terms that he should be looking for a lady to share it with. As usual, he didn't listen.

That fall, I spent more time writing creatively—especially in the evenings after my technical work was done and before Peter came home. I wrote about whatever happened to be on my mind at the moment. I was sure no one would be interested in my ramblings—not even Peter—so I kept them under wraps.

A few weeks before Christmas, I was home working on a glossary of medieval terms for a college professor when the telephone rang.

"Darlene?"

"Frank?!" I gasped at the sound of his voice.

"I keep thinking about you." He sounded depressed and his voice a bit slurred. "But it took me awhile to get up the nerve to call you back."

"How did you get this number?" My stomach tightened.

"I have connections. I know more about you and Peter Chandler than you think. I fell on some tough times and he took you right from under me."

"What happened between us had nothing to do with Peter. You were drinking. You still are and you need to leave us alone."

"I can't do that, Darlene. I want you back."

"Frank, we've been divorced a long time. You should have moved on by now. I don't want to see you and I don't want to talk to you, so please leave us alone."

"I hate the way you look at him," he said, ignoring what I'd just told him. "You never looked at me that way."

"How do you know how I look at Peter?" A chill crept over me.

"I've been watching you."

I never did tell Peter about that phone call. As the holidays approached, I tried putting it out of my mind. I had plenty to keep me busy. With Estelle's help, I got the house ready for Christmas. Doug was in his new home and the Lassiters were coming in from Michigan. Peter's parents were getting older and wanted a break from the cold New York weather and the boys were begging for another trip to L.A. Mom also liked the idea of getting away from the Windy City so our house it was. I also had several fittings for the dress I planned on wearing to the studio Christmas party. As usual, Peter had no clue, and the suspense was killing him.

My inspiration for the holidays was Nora Charles played by Myrna Loy in *The Thin Man*. In the movie, Nora and her husband, Nick, portrayed by William Powell, attended a Christmas party. Myrna wore a striped dress created by famed British designer, Dolly Tree. With large sheer ruffles cascading at an angle just below the hips and at the very bottom, the back of the dress had an open vee with a ruffle attached to each shoulder. The spaghetti straps and scooped neckline worked perfectly with my pearls and the red-and-white striping hollered holidays. Best of all, the stripes on the ruffles went the opposite way of the stripes on the dress so when I walked, the gown formed a checked pattern illusion where the ruffles were placed.

As usual, I got ready in one of the extra bedrooms so Peter wouldn't see my dress. He kept calling down the hall asking if I was done. I kept calling back NO!

"I need to know who you are tonight, Darlene." He finally stood outside the closed bedroom door.

"Let me get my shoes on," I told him, but he opened the door anyway.

"If it isn't Nora Charles!" He grinned. "I should have guessed."

"Nicky, you could have brought me a drink!" I walked over to him and slipped my arms around his neck.

"Who thought of this one?" Peter laid his forehead against mine. "You or Helene?"

"It was me, but Helene loved the idea."

"Do you think I could pass for William Powell?" he asked as he pushed me out in front of him for a second look.

I eyed him carefully. "No. He was definitely more debonair—not to mention charming."

We arrived at the Beverly Hills Hotel on Sunset Boulevard where the party was being held and were greeted by a band of reporters and photographers. "Peter, is that Myrna Loy you're with tonight?" one of them asked.

"No, this is Nora Charles. Her husband, Nick, is working a homicide case at the moment so he asked me to bring her, but he did warn me not to let her drink too much because she has to take Asta for a walk after the party." He looked me over for a minute and then turned back to the reporters. "Nora Charles never lets Nicky get away with anything. Women like that are very hard to live with—kind of like Darlene!"

I gave him a swift kick in the shin.

"Ow! What was that for?"

"Nora Charles didn't like what you said about Darlene." I scrunched my face up the same way Myrna Loy always did.

"And that's another thing about Nora Charles and Darlene," Peter addressed the reporters with a shake of his head. "Even Nicky will tell you—keeping them happy consumes all of our energy."

By Christmas Eve, we had a fully decorated house filled with people. With so many holiday guests, including the Lassiters, Peter and I had Christmas dinner catered. Mom, however, insisted that something be homemade, so she got busy in the kitchen making peach pies for dessert. No one attempted to change her mind.

The next morning at breakfast, with only family present, Peter dropped his bombshell. "I suppose this is as good a time as any to tell you all that I'm not renewing my contract with the series. I'm out after next season."

The clatter of forks stopped as Peter's announcement sunk in. "Geez, it's not that bad. I didn't say I was turning to a life of crime. I just thought you should know that James Dakota and I are parting ways."

"Peter!" Carmen threw me an accusing look. "Have you seriously thought this through?"

"I've been thinking about it for the past four years and I'm tired of the long hours."

"What will you do, son?" John seemed disturbed by Peter's decision.

"I'd like to concentrate on movies for awhile."

"What if they offer you more money to stay on?"

"They already have, but it's not about the money, Dad. It never has been."

"What do *you* think about all this, Darlene?" Carmen seemed to imply that this was my idea.

"Peter makes his own decisions. Whatever he does is fine with me."

"Would you consider another series?" my mother asked.

"Absolutely not. Our lives have been on hold long enough. It's not fair to Darlene. I don't know how she puts up with it."

"Can you afford to walk away?" Joyce found her voice.

"We're fine," Peter assured her. "But I need to get off this roller coaster ride and breathe."

"Uncle Peter, does that mean you won't be on TV anymore?" Timmy asked. The boys were finally figuring out what their uncle did for a living.

"What it really means is that I'll be home more, and you guys can come and stay as long as you want, whenever you want."

Bobby and Timmy were the only ones—other than me—who were happy about Peter's news.

Later that same evening, John found me in the kitchen packing up leftovers from dinner. "Darlene, do you have time to take a walk with an old man?"

"I don't see any old men—just a handsome guy from Long Island."

"Once around the pool?" He held out his arm with a smile and I took it. We stepped outside where the December night was cool.

"So what do you really think about Peter leaving the series?" John's limp seemed more pronounced than usual, but he refused to use a cane.

"I think Peter's tired."

"He's turning his back on an awful lot. Does he have work lined up?"

"He's been looking at scripts, but nothing definite."

"I don't know about this business Peter's in. There aren't any guarantees. Has he considered the consequences?"

"Believe me, John, Peter has given this a lot of thought. He didn't make his decision lightly, but he really needs a break from the series so he can try other things."

"And if these other things don't work out, then what?

"We'll deal with it like we always do—one day at a time."

"We, huh?" John raised an eyebrow. "Sounds like you plan on sticking around."

"I think so. Handsome men from Long Island don't come along every day."

"I hope Peter's cavalier approach to his work doesn't apply to you." John finally smiled. "And that's the other thing I need to talk to my son about. He's been dragging his feet a little too long where you're concerned."

After our annual New Year's trip to Halfmoon Bay, Peter went back to work. The following Sunday, we drove to our favorite spot on the beach just north of Malibu, where the afternoon air was brisk.

"Do you think I'm making a mistake, honey?" Peter asked as we huddled on one blanket and wrapped another one around us.

"Are you having second thoughts about leaving the show?"

"I'm having second thoughts about a lot of things. My dad thinks I'm pretty foolish to walk away from *Fire in the City*. If I didn't know better, I'd think The Brothers Grimm got to him. They are none too happy with me for not extending my contract."

"But we've been over this a hundred times. I thought that leaving the show is what you want."

"It is what I want and it's not that I'm ungrateful, honey. I know better than anyone that I wouldn't be where I am without the show, but I think it's time to move on—no matter what they offer me. Is there something wrong with that?"

"Of course not."

"And then there's you," he said with a sigh. "My dad thinks I'm—

"

"Dragging your feet?" I finished for him.

"Oh, so he got to you, too!" Peter shook his head.

"He did, but someone has to keep you and your blue eyes in line."

"And you volunteered for the job?"

"I like the fringe benefits." I slipped my arms around his neck, and he laughed.

Peter eventually signed on to film another comedy over his upcoming summer break. This time, however, he made a bold move and requested a director of his choice, Gene Sutherland. Gene had never directed a feature film before and there was a lot of hesitation from the producers about hiring him, but Peter prevailed. He and Gene had developed a good rapport over the past four years and, more importantly, Peter trusted him.

Peter also discovered my secret writings and encouraged me to take a chance and submit some of my essays to various publications. I still had my doubts whether anyone would be interested in my words, but Peter cheered me on. It was nice to know, he had so much faith in me—more than I had in myself.

Right after Peter's birthday, he and Gene began moonlighting in the preproduction phase of the movie, which was, as of yet, untitled. Peter played a Walter Mitty-type pediatrician, who, after being in his practice for several years, felt that he had made some very wrong professional choices. He escaped into a world of daring daydreams triggered by either his patients or their parents. Since Peter liked kids, and they almost always liked him, he was a natural for the part.

As a result of the double duty, the tired Peter moved back into our house. Most nights he didn't get home until after midnight and was gone again by six a.m. As March rolled around, not only was he irritable, but he was also losing weight. I hated it, but I held my tongue knowing that his schedule would ease up once *Fire in the City* ended its fourth season.

CHAPTER TWENTY-SEVEN

Peter continues moonlighting. He's hardly ever home and when he is here, he's either exhausted or crabby—sometimes both. I could use a break myself so I'm flying out to New York this afternoon to spend a long weekend with Sydney. She met a guy named Roy Conway at a holiday party in December. He's a photographer, self-employed, and according to Sydney, he's been divorced for almost two years. As far as she knows, his ex-wife isn't in the picture, so Roy has full custody of his four-year-old daughter, Megan. I can't imagine Sydney as anyone's stepmother, but she really likes this guy and wants me to meet him.

Now, if we could only find someone for Doug…

I liked Roy the moment I met him at the airport. His slender frame and long blond hair pulled back into a ponytail gave him an artsy appearance. Sydney glowed every time she looked at him. Little Megan glowed every time she looked at Sydney. She didn't say a word, but her head full of light brown curls peeked out from under Sydney's arm while I waited for my bag. After dinner and banana cream pie at the Carnegie Deli, Roy and Megan dropped us off at Sydney's apartment where she had wine chilling.

"I'm so glad you're here." Sydney filled two glasses once we changed into our pjs.

"Me, too. I miss you so much and once you told me about Roy— I had to meet him for myself."

"So what do you think?"

"I like him, Syd, but what matters is what you think."

"To be honest," she said as she sipped her wine. "I never imagined I'd fall this hard for anyone—especially a man with a ready-made family."

"It's obvious Megan's crazy about you. What's the story on her mother?"

"She walked out on them not long after Megan was born. She decided that life behind the white picket fence wasn't what she wanted."

"How does a mother walk away?"

"I don't know, but Roy isn't even sure where she is."

"So how does he manage?"

"His folks help him out a lot."

"And now he has you."

"We're a couple of lucky ladies, wouldn't you say?" She tapped her glass against mine.

"Maybe." I hesitated as I finished the wine and then poured us each a second glass.

"That didn't sound very reassuring."

"Nothing's perfect." I gave a sigh and shrugged.

"Is something bothering you, Darlene?"

"I don't know." I took another good long drink. "Maybe it's the wine talking, but sometimes when I let myself really think about it, I still wonder how long a girl like me can keep Peter's interest."

"Girlfriend, big hair and big boobs do not make the woman."

"I know, but Peter keeps saying he doesn't want to get married until his commitment to the show ends. Maybe that's his way of saying he doesn't want to marry me at all."

"Why would you say that?"

"Maybe it's just me being insecure, as usual." I tried shaking off that melancholy feeling. "Tell me more about Roy."

Peter surprised me after *Fire in the City* wrapped for the year by taking a long weekend off. He rented a cabin up in the mountains in Northern California. It was a beautiful, tranquil spot where we reclaimed some of the peace we'd lost. We hiked and took in some spectacular views.

On our last full day, we followed a trail that led to an impressive waterfall where we found ourselves alone. Peter took some pictures before we sat down on the rocks to simply enjoy our surroundings.

"I haven't felt this relaxed in months." He slipped an arm around me.

"Maybe we should do this more often."

"I intend to. Things are going to be different after next year. We're going to have a lot more time to do the things we want to do—like get married."

His words made me shiver and Peter sensed the sudden tension. "I thought that's what you wanted."

"It is what I want." I assured him, trying to push away the anxious feelings. "But promise me that whenever we decide to get married, we do it—no long engagement, no fanfare. Just something simple."

"Whatever you like." He smiled, but that troubling sensation lingered.

When we returned home, Peter began filming *The Pediatrician* with Gene whose biggest challenge was getting the child actors to cooperate. By the second week of production, Gene complained to me that Peter was worse than the kids when it came to fooling around. I could have told him that. Obviously Gene had never seen Peter in action with his nephews and unlike a lot of other actors who consider children scene-stealers, Peter liked being around them.

I'd been worried about who might play Peter's wife, afraid he might have another Karen Updyke on his hands until Julie Dunbar, Peter's costar in *Fool's Romance*, accepted the role. Julie and her husband, Phil, had recently had a baby and she was reluctant to take on long-term work. She liked Peter and because she only had to be on set for three weeks, she agreed. I was relieved. Julie was all right. She not only played Peter's wife, but her little girl played one of his patients.

In the midst of her filming, Julie and I met for lunch. Afterward, she talked me into coming back to the studio with her. Dressed in a white coat with a stethoscope hanging from his neck, Peter was talking to a couple of crew members when he spotted us. "What are you doing here?"

"I thought maybe Darlene could straighten you out," Julie said and then turned to me with a grin. "It's like a three-ring circus around here when Peter gets with the kids."

"It's like a three-ring circus wherever he goes." I gave a sigh. "Kids or no kids."

While Julie excused herself, saying she had to call her mother to check on the baby, I noticed a little girl with long dark curls standing directly behind Peter.

"Who's your friend?" I asked him.

He turned around, surprised to see her. "Good Golly Miss Molly!" He took her hand. "Are you following me?"

She smiled, but didn't say a word as Peter picked her up. "Darlene, this is Good Golly Miss Molly."

"I don't know why he calls me that," she said with a shake of her curls. "My name is just Molly."

"How old are you, Just Molly?" I asked.

"Six." Her brown eyes looked me over rather coolly. "How old are you?"

"A little more than six." I couldn't help but laugh.

"I'm sorry, Peter." A frazzled woman, obviously Molly's mother, walked over. "I told her not to bother you, but when she saw you, she took off running."

"She's fine," he said with a wink, and then kissed Molly on the cheek before setting her down. She rolled away into a series of cartwheels.

Peter turned to me. "Why don't you do that when I kiss you?"

To my delight, I had my own success that summer. One of the many magazines I sent articles to contacted me. After tons of rejections, *World of Wonder Magazine* wanted my piece on Maui. A relatively new publication, they were also looking for a fresh voice to develop a monthly column focusing on different places throughout the world. They provided guidelines and asked me to write three sample features on Monte Carlo, Tibet, and Thunder Bay.

I was ecstatic. I could hardly wait for Peter to come home that night so I could share the news with him. Determined to make it an evening to remember, I put a roast in the oven, fresh flowers on the table, and slipped into a little black dress. When I heard Peter's car in the driveway, I dimmed the lights and lit the candles on the dining room table.

"Honey, where are you?" he called from the kitchen.

"In the dining room."

He came to a complete stop when he saw me. "All right, Donna Reed—what have you done with Darlene?"

"Donna Reed?! I go to all this trouble and all you can think of is Donna Reed?!"

"I can't help it. Ever since I was a kid, I've always wanted to come home to Donna Reed. You should have put on your pearls."

"I wasn't going for the Donna Reed look," I told him flatly.

"Indulge me, Donna—I mean Darlene," he said and followed up with a kiss.

"This isn't working out the way I planned. We're supposed to be having a romantic dinner to celebrate, but you aren't cooperating."

"What are we celebrating?"

"You'll find out later!" I pushed him into a chair and went into the kitchen.

It wasn't until after we cleared the table that I made him sit back down and then handed him the letter before settling on his lap.

He opened the envelope and a broad smile spread across his face. "Honey, you should have been doing this all along."

When Peter wrapped up filming for *The Pediatrician*, we took our annual getaway to Maui. The island was still so magical. I never wanted to leave. I knew that once we returned, Peter would be back to filming *Fire in the City*. It was his last season with the show and a chapter was closing, but I wondered where the next one would lead.

Peter was not nominated for an Emmy that year because, as he put it, people were getting bored with James Dakota. There weren't many original stories left to tell. As a presenter that night, however, he had to appear. That meant Helene and I had to come up with a dress and she picked a winner—the black satin two-piece gown worn by Lauren Bacall when she played Marie 'Slim' Browning in *To Have and Have Not*.

The sultry Bacall showcased the dress when she sang 'How Little We Know' accompanied by Hoagy Carmichael on the piano. Designed by the Chicago-born Milo Anderson, the dress set a fashion trend for bare midriffs. With a vee-neck, the gown had long sleeves and the top was connected to the skirt by a small black ring just above the navel, exposing an inch or two of midriff. The very front of the skirt also had a slit to the knee—all quite modest by today's standards, but scathing in the 1940s. Nonetheless, audiences loved it and I hoped Peter would love it, too.

Per usual, the night of the Emmys, I got ready in one of the extra bedrooms so Peter wouldn't see me. On my way downstairs, I tried sneaking past our room where Peter was putting on his tie, but the door was open, and he spotted me. "Whoa! Hold on, Darlene! What are you wearing?"

"This one was all on Helene." I stood in the doorway. "What do you think?"

"I have no words." He stood there looking at me.

"Then maybe you ought to whistle." I slipped my arms around his neck. "You know how to whistle, don't you, Peter? You just put your lips together and blow."

"You are absolutely terrifying. Maybe I'll ride up front with the driver tonight."

"What are you afraid of?" I pulled him a little closer.

"Getting in the backseat of a limo with Slim Browning—or have you forgotten what happened on that ride with Margo Channing?"

We drove to the Emmys without incident because Peter made me sit at the opposite end of the car. Once we arrived at the auditorium, we took our turn on the red carpet. A lady reporter stepped up, holding a microphone. "Peter, is that Lauren Bacall you're with?"

"Yes, she showed up out of nowhere and she's been trying to teach me how to whistle."

"And has she succeeded?"

"No, I need more practice."

"Can you show us how you practice?" The reporter gave him a mischievous grin and if I didn't know better, I would have thought Peter put her up to it.

"It goes something like this…" He bent me back over his arm and kissed me.

"How was that, Ms. Bacall?" the woman asked as I straightened myself up.

"He needs a lot more work," I answered.

"Darlene, you're ruining my image!" With a shake of his head, Peter yanked me away.

"And there you have it, folks!" The reporter smiled into the camera. "The golden couple!"

We were so busy we hardly noticed as the fall months zipped past. I had a two-volume training manual to complete plus my new monthly column, *Let's Escape*, to write. It was challenging, but creatively, nothing gave me more satisfaction. Each month, the editor assigned the place, and I took it from there. Our arrangement worked and so far, I hadn't gotten any complaints. In October, I wrote about the Panama Canal and my November article focused on the Isle of

Capri.

The Pediatrician was scheduled to premiere in New York on Christmas Eve. Peter was in high demand—everyone, from reporters to talk show hosts, wanted interviews about the movie. They also asked what his plans were once *Fire in the City* was over. His standard answer was that he hoped to make more movies. When asked about his personal life, he only said it needed some serious attention.

My immediate concerns were my December article on Montreal and dresses--one for the Christmas party and one for the premiere. Helene had to do a lot of talking to convince me to try Rita Hayworth's black Gilda dress designed by American costumer Jean Louis. It's said he was inspired by the *Portrait of Madame X*, a John Singer Sargent painting. Hayworth famously shimmied in it as she sang 'Put the Blame on Mame'. The strapless satin sheath had a slit on the side and a large bow on the left hip. We opted to change the black color to dark green since it was the holidays, and I eliminated the long, matching gloves. I also lifted the neckline and downsized the bow. I wasn't sure if I could pull it off, but Peter had fun with it, assuring me that Gilda was indeed the most dangerous woman he could think of, and that was all that really mattered.

Two weeks later, we were settling in at the Waldorf on Christmas Eve. We lunched on sandwiches from room service, but Peter was nervous and only picked at his plate. Afterward, he went downstairs for a scheduled interview. I gladly let him go. I was never comfortable around the press. They weren't really interested in me anyway—unless I wore a dress that intrigued them. I much preferred staying in our room with my mother, watching *Miracle on 34th Street*.

By four o'clock, Natalie Wood believed in Santa and I had to get ready for the evening. Mom went back to her room and I went to work. Tonight, I was wearing a full-skirted, cocktail-length dress based on an Edith Head design for Doris Day when she played Jo McKenna in Alfred Hitchcock's *The Man Who Knew Too Much*. The sleeveless dress was white with large green tropical flowers and a square neckline—perfect for my white pearls. Doris Day wore it when, for the very first time, she sang what would become an Oscar winner as well as her signature tune, 'Que Sera Sera'. I thought it was appropriate given all the children that would be at the premiere.

Our room soon filled with animated voices belonging to the Chandlers and the Lassiters. Mom, Sydney, Roy, and Megan rounded out our crew. A call from the lobby let us know that our cars were waiting outside. Peter still hadn't put his jacket on, and I was barefoot, rushing around in a robe.

"Why don't you all head downstairs?" Peter suggested to the group. "Darlene and I will meet you at the theater."

In a moment, the room quieted and we were alone.

"When do I get to see your dress?" Peter grabbed his jacket off the bed. "Or are you wearing that robe tonight?"

"Sit down and close your eyes," I told him as I walked over to the closet. I unzipped the garment bag and pulled out my dress. "And no peeking!"

I slipped it on, put on my pearls, and then my heels. "You can look now."

He didn't answer, pretending to be asleep as he leaned against the headboard.

"I know you're awake!" I tugged on a curl.

"Not now, Darlene!" He opened one blue eye. "I'm dreaming about Doris Day singing 'Que Sera Sera'."

"You peeked!" I poked him in the shoulder.

"Maybe a little." He pulled me down on his lap with a grin. "But it was worth the risk."

"Your hands are cold." I shivered at his touch, before slipping my arms around his neck.

"Doris," he whispered, pressing me close for a moment. "I couldn't do this without you."

The theater bustled with reporters, photographers, critics, and other industry people. Flashbulbs popped and a roar erupted when we arrived. Gene was already there, along with most of the children and their families. Molly squealed when she saw Peter and broke ranks with the other kids, racing straight to him for a hug. The cameras swooped in, taking advantage of just one of the evening's many delightful photo ops.

"Good Golly Miss Molly!" Peter squatted down to her level. "You've grown ten feet since I saw you last, but what happened to your front teeth?"

"They fell out and the tooth fairy's got 'em!" She took a spin and her red holiday dress twirled around her. "Do you like my dress?"

"You look stunning!"

"I'm seven now and all grown up." She slung an arm around his neck. "And I want to marry you."

"Good Golly Miss Molly!" Peter said, obviously caught off guard, and the shocked look on his face made me laugh. "Maybe we should talk about this later."

"After the movie?" Molly blinked.

"About twenty years after!" Peter shook his head.

"As long as you don't forget," Molly said as her mother stepped up and grabbed her hand.

"Molly! You're supposed to be taking pictures with the other kids!" She turned to Peter. "I'm so sorry, but the only thing she talked about all week was seeing you tonight."

"Peter says we can get married in twenty years!" Molly grinned. "I asked him!"

"Oh no you didn't!" Her mother was horrified.

"She doesn't mince words." Peter shook his head. "Now I have to square things with Doris here and that won't be easy!"

Julie and Phil chose not to come since it was their baby's first Christmas. I actually missed Julie that night. Of course, the tabloids proclaimed that the real reason she hadn't come was because she and I were feuding. Evidently, the scandalous version was more intriguing than the fact that we actually liked each other.

Once again, I sat in a dark theater with Peter's icy hand squeezing mine. Superstition had prevented me from seeing the final cut of the movie until now, so I was watching it for the first time along with everyone else. Within fifteen minutes he knew—we all knew—the audience approved. Slowly, Peter's grip on my hand relaxed and his fingers turned warm again.

The excitement followed us back to the Waldorf where dinner and dancing awaited in one of the reception rooms all decked out for Christmas. There was even a train display that looked as if it had been delivered straight from Santa's workshop. When Peter and I walked in, the band started playing 'Que Sera Sera', so he took me for a spin on the dance floor before we even sat down.

It was late when we finally returned to our room, but we were still reeling from Peter's success. All that was left was to read the reviews in the morning papers, which Doug promised to bring to brunch. Peter was pleased when he found a bottle of champagne chilling in the bedroom—compliments of the Waldorf. By the time I changed, he was under the covers with two glasses of champagne bubbling on the nightstand.

For a fleeting moment, I thought about that Christmas Eve when we stayed at the Waldorf for the very first time. I'd gotten pregnant that night. It seemed so long ago, but at unexpected moments like now, I still ached for the baby we lost.

"I know what you're thinking." Peter's voice brought me back to the present as he handed me a glass.

"I'm sorry." I tried to shake it off. "This hotel…the premiere…the holiday…it all reminds me—"

"Don't say it." He placed his finger over my lips. "Not tonight." We drank our champagne in silence and Peter set our empty glasses back on the nightstand.

"I didn't mean to spoil the moment."

"You didn't." Peter pulled me closer and covered my mouth with his, effectively silencing me. Shivering, I wrapped my arms around him, unwilling to let go.

The next morning we met everyone downstairs in a private dining room for Christmas brunch. Bobby and Timmy insisted they each sit on either side of their uncle, so I sat next to Mom. Doug carried a stack of papers and handed one to Peter before sitting down at the table with a wink toward me.

Peter took a deep breath as he found the entertainment section. He held it out in front of him. All the articles were cut out. Peter looked at Doug through one of the holes. "Were they that bad?"

"I was trying to spare your feelings," Doug said with a shrug. "But if you must know—here!" He pushed the rest of the papers toward Peter. The critics gave *The Pediatrician* high marks. They thoroughly enjoyed Peter's performance and credited Gene with keeping the storyline on track, preventing the movie from turning into something silly. Instead, it was funny, touching, and entertaining.

As Peter passed the papers around, Sydney quietly tapped me on the shoulder. "Can I see you outside for a minute?"

She had the oddest look on her face as we stepped into the hallway—almost as if she didn't know what to say.

"What's wrong, Syd?"

She took a deep breath. "Roy asked me to marry him last night." She held out her left hand, revealing a princess-cut diamond. "I said yes!"

"Oh, Sydney!" I squeezed her. "Now we have even more to celebrate!"

"We haven't talked about the details yet, but will you be my maid of honor?"

"Of course I will."

I pulled her back inside the banquet room still filled with noise as the waiters began serving. Walking directly over to Roy, I stood between him and Megan. "I think you've put Santa to shame with that ring!"

"How about a nightcap?" Peter caught me off guard in the hotel lobby that night as we returned from Christmas dinner at his parents' house. Mom was tired and had gone directly to her room. It seemed odd that he wanted to go to the lounge for a drink. The room was practically empty—after all, it *was* Christmas. Peter's serious face made me wonder what was wrong. By the time the waiter returned with two martinis, he still hadn't said a word.

"Peter, you're scaring me."

"I'm sorry." He reached for my hand. "That's not what I'm trying to do." Another moment of silence passed before he spoke again. "Honey, we've talked about this before, but I think we should talk about it again. *Fire in the City* will wrap up soon." He hesitated once more.

"And now you're not so sure about moving on?"

"I'm positive it's time to move on." He looked directly at me with those magical blue eyes. "I want to marry you, Darlene. I almost bought you a ring for Christmas. The only thing that stopped me was something you said a while back. You said that whenever we decide to get married, we should just do it. You didn't want a long engagement."

"I don't."

"But Roy giving Sydney a ring for Christmas made her happy. I want to make you happy."

"You do make me happy, Peter."

"But last night—"

"Last night, I slipped, and you caught me."

"No more slipping." He squeezed my hand. "I promise you, the day my commitment to *Fire in the City* ends, you'll have that ring and everything that goes with it."

But as we finished our drinks that unfounded fear crept over me once again.

Peter had a full schedule promoting *The Pediatrician*, so Mom and I hit all the after-Christmas sales in Manhattan, stopping long enough for lunch.

"Aren't you tired, Mom?" I kicked my shoes off and dropped onto the couch once we got back to the hotel.

"My feet hurt." Mom fell next to me. "I haven't walked that much in ages."

"Are you up for dinner at Carmen's later?"

"The question is—are you? After all this time you've been with Peter, Joyce and Carmen should appreciate you by now."

"What matters is, Peter appreciates me."

"Does he?" Her question surprised me.

"Yes, Mom. What makes you think he doesn't?"

"I thought by now you two would have gotten married."

I hesitated for a moment, debating on what I should tell her exactly. "We both agreed to wait until Peter is done with *Fire in the City*, then we'll have time to concentrate on us."

"And while you're concentrating, will you be making wedding plans?"

"I don't know, Mom." I finally had to tell someone. "Every time I think about marrying Peter, I get this terrible feeling inside and it scares me."

"What kind of feeling?"

"I can't explain it, but I'm afraid that when it comes down to it, maybe I'm not meant to be Mrs. Peter Chandler."

"Why on earth would you say that, Darlene?"

"Because sometimes I don't think that happy endings are in the cards for me."

"What's Peter done to make you feel that way?"

"It's not Peter. It's me. I keep wondering when he's going to realize that he wants more than a plain, everyday girl."

"I know I'm your mother, Darlene, but you're hardly a plain, everyday girl."

"Did you look around the theater last night? Did you see the women there? Flashy…glamorous…sexy—"

"And I never once saw Peter looking twice at any of them." Mom interrupted me. "So get those thoughts out of your head, Darlene!"

"I wish I could," I told her. "Because they're eating me up inside."

Peter and I once again flew out to San Francisco for New Year's Eve and then drove down to Halfmoon Bay. I was ready for some down time with him—even willing to follow his stupid New Year's Eve rules.

We had a leisurely lunch in Monterey and a peaceful walk along the ocean, which was welcome after the hectic week we'd spent in New York.

That evening, at the hotel, the New Year's Eve celebrations were loud and lively. We bypassed them all, preferring the quiet of our room so we could celebrate in what had become our own custom. White roses and champagne were waiting next to the bed.

"Honey, do we have to have rules tonight?" I asked.

"Yes, we do." His blue eyes were full of mischief. "I love how it drives you crazy."

Finally at midnight, he kissed me as if it were the first time and my knees turned weak. I still found Peter's kisses exciting and our love-making exhilarating. In the wee hours of the morning, we finally got around to our second glass of champagne.

"This is going to be our year, Darlene," Peter announced as he took a drink.

Out of nowhere that dreaded feeling erupted, starting in the pit of my stomach and working its way up.

"What's wrong, honey? You're not changing your mind, are you?"

"No, but I'm afraid, Peter."

"There's nothing to be afraid of." He nuzzled the side of my neck. "We have so much to look forward to this year—a new beginning for us, and a family. Just think about it, honey. Maybe by next Christmas we'll even have a new baby to love." His kisses abruptly stopped. "That is what you want, isn't it?"

"It's all I ever wanted. I never thought it would really happen."

"Ten more weeks." He returned to the spot where he left off and his lips brushed my ear. "James Dakota will be a memory and we'll have our happily ever after."

Instead of feeling reassured, however, his words made me shudder.

CHAPTER TWENTY-EIGHT

The eighties are here, and I just finished drafting my first article of the new decade. This one's about Quebec. I've always wanted to go there. Sainte-Anne-de-Beaupré Basilica would be amazing to visit in person, but I might have to brush up on my high school French. I'll have to ask Peter if he can speak le français. Or is it la française?

I wish The Brothers Grimm would stop pressuring him about signing on for one more season. Peter refuses to even consider it and they should get that by now. The Pediatrician remains strong at the box office, and he is receiving new scripts everyday. He hasn't committed to anything specific yet, but since he won't be returning to the series in August, he can take his time choosing. There's no reason to rush and no tight schedule to follow.

Maybe he'll be able to take those French lessons with me! Ooh-la-la!

"Meet me for lunch, Darlene?" Peter called one morning from the studio. "Something's come up and we need to talk. It can't wait."

"Wu's?" I suggested.

"Perfect!"

I arrived first and ordered. Nervous, my imagination got the best of me. Maybe Peter decided to extend his contract with the brothers after all. Maybe he had accepted an offer to do another series—there were plenty of those. When he finally walked into the restaurant, he slid next to me into the booth. It seemed odd that he didn't sit across from me. We never sat on the same side of a booth when we were alone.

"What's going on, honey?" I braced myself.

"I got a call this morning." He took my hand. "Remember the movie I turned down earlier this year because of the show?"

"The murder mystery?" I recalled Peter's disappointment at the time.

"That's it." He nodded. "Harrison Ford dropped out of the lead role. They're scheduled to start production next month and the producers want me to fill in."

"But you'll still be working on *Fire in the City* next month."

"They know that, and they offered to work something out. I'll have to moonlight for a few weeks—just until the series is over. I really want to do this, Darlene."

"There's more, isn't there?" I looked down at the table, not quite sure I wanted to know.

"A little more." He paused. "As soon as the show is over, I'll have to fly to Rome for three months."

"Rome?!" The waitress brought our food and left, but suddenly, I wasn't hungry.

"I know it's not what we planned, honey, but we could get married while we're there and when I'm through filming, you and I could take an extended honeymoon in Europe."

"But what about my mother and your family?" I pushed my plate away.

"We'll fly everyone in for the wedding."

"All the way to Rome?"

"Why not?" Without taking a bite, he fidgeted with his fork, nervously tapping it on the table. "Once we get there, you can plan whatever you like. We could even get married in one of the old cathedrals."

"I don't know, Peter. Do you really think everyone will want to come to Rome?"

"Why wouldn't they?" Peter kept on talking while I tried to grasp everything he'd just thrown at me. "Think about it, Darlene. We've put our lives on hold long enough. I don't want to wait anymore. If you don't want to get married in Rome, I'll turn down the offer, and we'll get married here. They're waiting for my answer."

My thoughts tumbled over each other. Rome seemed so far away…neither of us wanted to postpone the wedding…this movie was obviously important to Peter or he wouldn't have brought it up to me…we could fly everyone in…it would be so romantic—something we'd never forget…I could plan whatever I wanted…we could honeymoon indefinitely…Peter wanted to marry me…he was willing to pass up a big professional opportunity so we could get married at home if that's what I wanted…how could I ask him to do that, especially when he was at such a crucial crossroad in his career…did it really matter where we got married…the people that were most important to us would still be there…

"Darlene?" Peter interrupted my disconnected thoughts as our lunch cooled. "Darlene, will you marry me in Rome?"

His words jarred me. Peter wasn't talking about a movie, he just proposed! How could I say no to this man when he was all I ever wanted? "Peter, I'll marry you anywhere you want."

We forgot where we were as he pulled me close. His kiss was so intense, I could barely catch my breath. "Please tell me you don't mind getting married in Rome because if you do—"

"I should know by now," I interrupted him. "With you, nothing ever happens quite the way we plan."

"You can have any kind of wedding you want." He went on. "Once we get to Rome, you can pick the date, the time, and the place. We'll get someone there to help you. They can drive you around, interpret, whatever you need. Once it's all set, we'll call everyone and make arrangements for them to come."

That anxious feeling returned, but I managed to push it away as I looked into Peter's blue eyes, wishing he had come home for lunch instead of meeting me at Wu's. Neither of us had taken one bite of our food so we took it to go.

The more I thought about it, the more I liked the idea of our very own Roman Holiday. When Peter came home, he carried white roses in one hand and a script in the other. He laid the script on the kitchen counter and handed me the flowers with a kiss. "Do you still want to marry me in Rome, or have you changed your mind?"

"I haven't changed my mind. Have you changed yours?"

"Not for a minute. As a matter of fact, I could hardly wait to get home tonight."

"You're in?" I nodded toward the script.

"I'm in."

"You never did tell me what happened to Harrison Ford."

"He's slated for some action movie about Indiana, but let's not talk shop tonight. You've been on my mind all afternoon."

We had so much to look forward to—a trip to Europe, getting married in Rome, and starting our life together as husband and wife. Over our reheated lunch, we talked about a family.

"Honey, what if we started trying for a baby now?" Peter asked me.

"Now? As in today? Now?"

"Why not? We'll be getting married anyway and if it happens sooner rather than later, would it really matter?"

"I don't know, Peter." I hesitated. "What if there are complications like before?"

"The doctor told us that was highly unlikely, and we've waited long enough. Besides, it probably won't happen right away."

"I'd feel better about it if I talked to Ed."

"Then make an appointment and see him as soon as you can."

That night, as we lay next to each other surrounded by darkness, Peter took me in his arms. "I had no idea when I got up this morning that I was going to ask you to marry me."

"Does this mean we're engaged?" The thought suddenly struck me.

"Not officially. I asked if you would marry me in Rome. I had to know if you would. As soon as *Fire in the City* is over, I'm going to officially propose."

"You're going to ask me to marry you again?" I giggled with delight.

"I might ask you a hundred times, because I like hearing you say yes."

I did see Ed Shurloch later that week and he assured me that the difficulties I'd experienced with Lucky Penny were unusual. He thought I should be fine if we tried again. He even gave me a ninety-day supply of pre-natal vitamins and advised me to pack a couple home pregnancy tests in case I needed them in Rome. With the doctor's assurance, Peter and I threw caution to the wind.

Peter's moonlighting began immediately. Script changes had to be made, as well as some adjustments to the character Peter was now playing. We hardly saw each other. Peter worked seven days a week splitting his time between *Fire in the City* and *Frame of Mind*. By the time his birthday rolled around, he was dragging. Maybe he shouldn't have taken on so much all at once. If he kept up this pace for another six weeks, he might not make it to Rome.

We agreed to keep our wedding plans to ourselves. I even decided to wait until we got to Rome to look for a dress. I almost slipped a few times with Estelle. I thought for sure that Peter would tell Doug and Helene, but he didn't, and, as much as I wanted to, I never called Mom or Sydney.

For Peter's birthday, I ordered a large cake and had it delivered to the studio as usual. This was the last birthday he would spend with the *Fire in the City* crew, so I wanted it to be special. I invited Doug and Helene to lunch with us. Peter opted for the diner's backroom so we could talk without a thousand interruptions.

To my surprise, Helene grew dewy-eyed over her Caesar salad. "I'm sure going to miss you when you leave, Peter."

"I'm not leaving the planet. We'll still see each other."

"But the studio won't be the same without you and your uniform." She dabbed at her eyes with her napkin.

"How much longer can I possibly wear that uniform without everyone getting bored?" Peter took a bite of his cheeseburger.

"You're right," she said with a sigh. "But no one will ever wear that uniform the way you do. Lucky for me, I was paying attention when I saw you in New York. The show had a great run thanks to you."

"People, please! Can we lighten up here?" Doug waved his arms over his BLT. "Peter has another month and half of work left on *Fire in the City*. We can mourn the passing of James Dakota six weeks from now!"

"But being another year closer to forty doesn't seem like much to celebrate," Peter said chewing on a French fry.

"There must be something we can all be glad about." Doug looked at me. "How about you, Darlene? Is anything exciting going on in your life?"

Peter and I exchanged glances. He wanted to tell them, so I nodded my agreement as I sipped my soda.

"Maybe there is something to celebrate," Peter began. "But it's unofficial, and you have to swear you won't tell anyone."

"Ok," Doug agreed. "What deep, dark secret are we unofficially celebrating?"

"Darlene and I are getting married in Rome." Peter smiled, delighted with their shocked expressions.

"Explain the 'unofficial' part," Doug finally spoke.

"I asked Darlene if she'd marry me in Rome. I had to know before I accepted this movie offer, but I'm not officially proposing until next month. I was hoping you'd come to Rome and be my best man."

"Officially or unofficially?"

"That depends on Darlene. If she officially says yes when I officially ask her that would officially make you the best man."

Doug leaned across the table. "Darlene, didn't I tell you not to get mixed up with him? He never does anything the way he should! He can't even propose the right way."

"I'll marry you, Peter." Helene finally found her tongue. "We can go to Rome, Germany, England, Spain, wherever. I'll marry you once in every country if you want."

"If Darlene turns me down, I might take you up on that," Peter said with a grin.

As we left the diner that afternoon, we used the back entrance to avoid the crowd. A small blue Ford Escort pulled out of a parking space. The driver waved and I choked back a gasp when I realized it was Frank!

"Someone you know?" Doug asked as he opened the car door for me.

"No." I glanced across the roof of the car to see Peter conversing with Helene. Thankfully, she had his undivided attention.

"I could have sworn he was waving at you." Doug insisted.

"No one ever waves at me." I quickly slid into the car. "It's always Peter."

"If you say so." Doug shrugged, but I could tell he didn't believe me.

CHAPTER TWENTY-NINE

I*t's been over a week since I saw Frank in that parking lot. Just the thought of him sends me into a panic. Peter is so tired and short-tempered lately, the least little thing provokes him. If Frank calls or comes around now, there's no telling what might happen.*

Every time the phone rings, I'm afraid to answer it. I reminded Estelle that under no circumstance was she ever to mention Frank in front of Peter. For once, I'm glad that he's working so many hours. If Frank does call, Peter probably won't be here. We hardly go out so the chances of running into Frank are slim.

Rome is looking better and better. Frank won't follow us there. Everything will be all right once we get to Rome.

The third Sunday of February was a cool, but sunny day in L.A. I was writing at the kitchen table when I heard a car pull in the driveway. I glanced at my watch—four o'clock—too early for Peter. I thought it might be Doug, but to my surprise Peter walked in.

"I'm exhausted, Darlene, and my head is killing me." He leaned against the counter, dropping his keys. "I had to come home."

"Why don't you take something for your headache and lie down? I'll call you when dinner's ready." He obviously wasn't feeling well. It was not like Peter to leave work early.

"I'll shower first," he said with a sigh. "Maybe that will help."

He went upstairs and I went back to work. Moments later, another car pulled into the driveway. This time it had to be Doug. He must not have had his key because the doorbell rang. I opened the door, ready to tease him, but shock replaced the smile on my face, when I found Frank standing there instead.

I stepped outside so he wouldn't come in. "Frank, you shouldn't be here."

"I need to talk to you." He looked almost respectable. I actually saw a hint of the man I married. He wore a neat pair of Levi's with a dark sports coat. He'd put on some weight and his hair was styled the way he used to wear it when we lived in New York.

"If you want to talk, I'll meet you somewhere—anywhere! Just not here! Peter's upstairs and he won't like it if he finds you here."

"But I'm doing better, Darlene. I've even got a steady job playing at a club in Beverly Hills." He reached into his pocket and handed me a business card. "Maybe you can come up there sometime. I really want to talk to you."

"Not here." I repeated. "I'll call you tomorrow, but you have to leave before Peter sees you."

"Can't I have five minutes?"

"No, you can't!" Panic was setting in. "You have to go!"

"But I've been thinking."—it was obvious he intended to stay—"we had a good marriage until I messed it up. I'd like to try and make things right between us."

"There's nothing left to make right."

"Then tell me why Peter never married you?"

"That's none of your business." I turned my head and glanced back toward the kitchen. Peter should be out of the shower by now. "You really need to leave."

"Not yet." He took a step closer, backing me into the house's brick wall. "You and I have some unfinished business."

"No, we don't." I tried pushing him away.

Frank seemed to be looking over my shoulder into the house as a broad grin spread across his face. "One kiss, Darlene," he whispered, and pulled me against him. "And then I'll leave." He pressed his mouth against mine, while one hand held my head firmly in place and his other hand slipped under my sweater. He took his lips from mine and said, in a louder voice, "I knew if I could prove myself, you'd come back to me."

"What the hell is going on here?" The side door opened and Peter stepped out, his face white with rage.

"Tell him you want me, Darlene." Frank kept one arm around me. With a sick feeling, I glanced from one to the other. Frank, now defiant, was almost daring Peter to hit him. Still holding his business card, I realized that Frank had set me up.

"Get out of the way, Darlene," Peter spoke quietly, too quietly. The coolness in his tone unnerved me. I had never seen him this angry.

"Frank, you said you were leaving." I jerked away from him without taking my eyes off of Peter.

"Maybe I changed my mind."

"Get out of the way, Darlene," Peter repeated way too calmly.

"Please, let him go, Peter. He only came here to cause trouble."

Frank pushed me aside before taking a step toward Peter. I watched in horror as Peter pulled his arm back, hitting Frank with so much force, Frank fell backwards.

"No, Peter!" I screamed, jumping in between them. "Stop it!"

"Get out of the way, Darlene." Peter warned me once more.

"Frank!" I turned in time to see him getting up, his face bloody. "You said you would leave."

"You had your chance," Frank taunted Peter, ignoring my pleas. "And you can't ever change the fact that I slept with her first."

Horrified, I turned to Peter who was rearing back to punch Frank one more time. "No! Peter! Don't hit him!" I tried to shield Frank from his wrath.

Peter stopped mid-swing. "Are you protecting him, Darlene?"

"No! I'm trying to protect you! Just let him go, Peter! Please!"

"She'll never marry you!" Frank kept on. "Because she's still in love with me! Tell him, Darlene! Tell him, how you used to like it and how you wanted more!"

Peter shoved me aside, lunging at Frank, but this time Frank hit him.

"Stop it! Both of you! Stop it!" I tried getting between them one more time.

Once again, Peter pushed me out of the way, as he fought with Frank who went down. While I frantically pulled on Peter's arm, Frank had the chance to get back on his feet.

"Go, Frank!" I screamed. "Get out of here!"

This time, Frank listened as he realized he was no match for Peter's rage. "This isn't over," he called out as I held on to Peter. "She doesn't want you because she still wants me! You saw how much she liked that kiss!" After Frank's car pulled away, Peter slowly turned to look at me. He was bleeding.

"Peter!" I gasped, reaching up to touch his face. He grabbed my wrist, and roughly pushed me away. My knees shook so hard I couldn't hold myself up and I sank to the ground.

Peter went back inside the house for his car keys. He walked right past me, and then drove off. I sat there trying to collect myself. He needed to cool down; he'd come back and I'd make him listen. I'd explain. I'd make him understand. Once he calmed down, this would blow over and everything would be all right.

Eventually, I made my way back into the house. My head throbbed so I went into the bathroom for Tylenol. When I saw my reflection in the mirror, my hair was matted with blood. At first, I thought it was from Peter, but then I realized my head was bleeding and the palms of my hands as well as my knees were scraped raw. I dragged myself upstairs and into the shower, but not before I tore up that damn business card.

Daylight turned into darkness, but Peter never returned. He was in such a rage when he left, he could have easily lost control of his car. The very thought was terrifying until the hammering in my head finally forced me to lay on the couch. I couldn't go upstairs to our empty bed.

I found some comfort with the rising sun. Peter had to be at work, or someone would have called looking for him. This was the first time that he stayed out all night, but it wouldn't be the last.

Come Tuesday morning, I couldn't face Estelle. I had to get out of the house before she arrived. I was desperate to talk to Peter so I drove to the studio. We needed to put this behind us and if we couldn't, I would never, ever forgive Frank for what he'd done.

No one answered when I knocked on his trailer door so I let myself in. Our Fred and Ginger frame lay face down on the floor, the glass cracked. I picked it up and put it back where it belonged.

The bed had been slept in so Peter must have been staying here. I should have guessed. I sank down on the bed, picking up his pillow in an effort to pull myself together. I had to be able to think when Peter came, but the miserable pain in my head was making it impossible. Leaning back against the headboard, I closed my eyes. A little while later, the front door opened.

What if he didn't want to see me? What if he wouldn't talk to me? What if he refused to listen? All I could do was try. As I sat there struggling with myself, Peter walked into the bedroom, surprised to find me there.

"You shouldn't have come here, Darlene."

"We need to talk."

"Maybe it's Frank you should be talking to."

"You know better than that. Frank is pathetic. I tried my best to get rid of him, but he wouldn't go!"

"It looked to me like you wanted him to stay."

"That's ridiculous, Peter!"

"Then why didn't you call me? I was right upstairs."

"He said he'd leave if he could have one kiss and then he grabbed me." The tears began their escape. "I was afraid if you saw him, you'd lose your temper and then—"

"What did you expect?" Peter grew angry all over again. "Your ex-husband shows up at our house, and was not only kissing you, but had his hands all over you and I'm supposed to just stand there and watch?!"

"He only came to cause trouble."

"Then he got what he wanted."

"Don't let him come between us, Peter."

"He already has. Be honest, Darlene. Do you want him back?"

"No, I don't want him back! How can you even ask me that?"

"Because *you* never filed for the divorce!" Peter exploded. "And I always wondered whether you really wanted it."

Lowering my voice, I gave it one last try, mustering up all the strength I had left. "You asked me to marry you, Peter. You said you wanted to have a baby!"

"And I'm sure as hell glad *that* never happened!"

It took a moment for his furious words to sink in. "Does that go for Lucky Penny, too? Are you glad we lost her?"

"It was a different time, Darlene."

"Tell me how it was different!" I screamed at him. "Tell me what changed, Peter!"

"Nothing changed and that's the problem. Admit it, Darlene, you never got over Frank."

I had to stop and catch my breath before I spoke again. "After all this time, after everything we've been through, you don't think I love you?"

"I'm not sure what to think after seeing you kiss him on Sunday. It makes me wonder what else you two have been doing while I've been working."

His words stung, but I tried one more time. "You know better. I love you, Peter and if I ever meant anything to you at all, you'll come home so we can fix this."

"Darlene, some things can't be fixed." He stormed off. I heard a crash, then the front door opened and slammed shut. The entire trailer shook.

On my way out, I found our picture lying face down on the floor again—another crack in the glass. I picked it up once more and put it back on the side table before I left.

I couldn't go home. Estelle would be there, so I drove up the coast to our spot, but I found no peace. Instead, I sat in the car and cried. By the time I got home, it was dark, the house empty. Unable to sleep in our bed, I chose the couch as I tried grasping everything that happened the last few days. Shortly after midnight, a car pulled into the driveway. Peter!

He went straight upstairs. He must have thought I was in bed, so I went after him. When I reached our room, he wasn't there, but I noticed a light in one of the other bedrooms.

"Peter?" No answer so I walked toward the light. I stopped cold when I found him standing next to the bed, minus his shirt. He had no intention of sleeping with me tonight. "What are you doing?"

"Getting ready for bed." He never even looked at me.

"You're sleeping in here?" I knew the answer before I even asked the question.

"You asked me to come home, Darlene." He pulled the covers back. "I'm home."

I never heard Peter leave for work Wednesday morning. I spent the day alone at home trying to write my next column, but the pain in my head kept me from concentrating. I tried everything to rid myself of the migraine, but nothing worked.

Once again Peter came home around midnight, sleeping down the hall. He never said a word to me. Devastated, I couldn't bring myself to see or talk to anyone, but I had no choice concerning Estelle. I couldn't keep leaving the house every time she came.

When Estelle arrived Thursday morning, I was already sitting at the kitchen table with my coffee, waiting for her.

"What's the matter, Darlene?" She set her purse and hat down on the kitchen counter.

"Something's happened that you should know about."

"From the look on your face," she said as she poured herself some coffee. "I'd say you and Peter had a fight."

"It was worse than a fight. I'm not sure we'll ever get past it."

"It probably seems worse than it is."

"No, Estelle. This is bad." She listened sympathetically while I told her what happened.

"I'm so sorry, honey." She squeezed my hand. "No wonder you didn't want me to mention Frank's name in the house."

"I don't know what to do, Estelle. I can't get through to him and my head hurts so bad, I can't think."

"Come with me." She took my hand and led me upstairs. Estelle pulled down the covers and made me get into bed. Then she closed all of the shades so the room was dark.

"I'll be right back." She patted my hair. She returned with some Tylenol and a glass of water. I'd lost count of how many pills I'd already downed, but I took them from her anyway.

"Close your eyes and relax." She sat next to me, her fingers gently massaging my temples. "You need some rest."

"I miss my mother, Estelle." The tears built up once more. "Will you stay with me?"

"As long as you need me."

Eventually, I drifted off to sleep and I was grateful to find her still there when I woke up. The migraine wasn't gone, but it remained as a dull ache.

"What time is it?" I asked wondering how long I'd been sleeping.

"Almost one. Are you feeling any better?"

"A little."

"Were you dreaming?" She stroked my hair with a tender hand.

"I don't think so. Why?"

"You were crying in your sleep."

Oddly enough, I couldn't remember dreaming a thing.

Chapter Thirty

I t's been one week since Frank was here. Peter is still sleeping down the hall. His unrelenting silence is wearing on my nerves—not to mention my throbbing head.

Estelle is the only person who knows what happened. I've come to know her in a different light these past few days. Her maternal presence is comforting. I wouldn't be able to manage without her.

"I'll come if you need me," Estelle said when she called early Sunday morning.

"I've imposed on you enough. Take a day for yourself. I'll be all right."

I tried to write, hoping it would distract me, but it didn't. It was hard to concentrate and the longer I sat there, the more frustrated I grew. The house felt chilly, so I slipped on one of Peter's sweaters. My constant headache worsened and once again, I was sick to my stomach. I wandered into the bedroom where Peter had been sleeping and lay down. I no sooner closed my eyes when I heard a car in the driveway and the side door open.

It was early afternoon, but maybe Peter had a change of heart and came home to talk. I felt hopeful for the first time in days. "Peter?" I called out.

"No, honey, it's Doug. Where are you?"

"Upstairs."

"Can I come up?"

"Yeah. I'm in the last bedroom on the right."

"What are you doing in here?" he wanted to know as he walked in.

"Trying to get rid of this headache."

"Darlene, what's going on?" Doug sat on the edge of the bed. "I've been calling Peter all week, but he hasn't called me back."

Obviously, Peter hadn't talked to Doug. Now it was up to me. I slowly sat up and leaned against the headboard, closing my eyes trying to think of what to say.

"Are you all right, honey?" he asked.

I silently shook my head, keeping my eyes closed and rubbing my temples in an effort to clear my head. The relentless pain was once again becoming unbearable. "It hurts so bad, Doug. I can hardly think."

"Talk to me, Darlene. Tell me what's got you so upset."

"Frank was here last Sunday." I felt a catch in my throat as another flood of tears threatened.

"Frank, as in your ex-husband, Frank?"

"Doug, it was awful." My voice shook. "I've never seen Peter so furious. They had a terrible fight. I tried to stop it, but I couldn't. Afterward, Peter left and he never came back. I waited two days for him and then I went to the studio. All I wanted was for him to come home."

"Honey, I'm not making excuses for him, but Peter's been under a lot of pressure lately," Doug offered. "He's working way too hard, and you know how he gets when he's tired. Give him a chance; he'll come around."

"But he thinks I still want Frank."

"He what?!"

"I'm afraid Peter's always had that thought somewhere in the back of his mind because I wasn't the one who filed for the divorce." I tried to explain to Doug as well as to myself. "I just never knew it, but now when I think about it, the signs were all there. He'd get so angry whenever Frank's name came up, but I never understood why. I always made it a point not to mention Frank in front of him."

"Honey, you have to be wrong about this. You and Peter have

that quirky connection. Anyone who knows the two of you knows that."

"Things are different now." My headache intensified. "He won't even look at me."

"Then I'll talk to him. He's not thinking and one of us needs to set him straight. If he won't listen to you, I'll make him listen to me."

"I'm so tired, Doug." The unwelcome tears finally got the best of me. "My head hurts and I've been so cold all day. I can't seem to get warm."

"How about some hot tea?"

Doug took me downstairs and into the kitchen. He put on some water and then he wrapped a blanket from the family room around me.

"Have you eaten anything today?" he asked as he pulled the mugs out of the cupboard.

"I can't remember." Everything seemed a bit foggy. With the headache, it was hard to think about even the simplest thing. "I don't know what's wrong with me."

"It's all right, honey. We'll get something hot in you and you'll feel better. Have you been alone all week?"

"No, Estelle's been here."

"She knows what happened?"

I nodded, but then questioned my judgment. "Do you think it was okay that I told her?"

"It was fine. I'm sure she took good care of you. Was she here today?"

"I think I told her not to come." I continued shivering, but couldn't focus. "It's Sunday, isn't it?"

"That's right."

Doug and I drank our tea in silence. It felt good going down, warming me up enough on the inside to let the blanket slip from my shoulders. I held the mug in both of my hands trying to warm them, as well. We each had a second cup, and by the time I had finished it, the headache eased.

"Feeling better?" Doug asked.

"I'm not so cold."

"Good. How about something to eat?"

The thought of food was nauseating so I shook my head.

Doug gave me a skeptical glance and then looked at the kitchen clock. It was going on seven. "I thought Peter came home earlier on Sundays."

"Maybe he's not coming home."

"Darlene, if I weren't sitting right here, looking at you, I'd never believe any of this."

Doug gave me two more Tylenol before we went into the family room. Sitting together on the couch, we stared at the television, neither of us saying much until Peter's car pulled up.

"Go upstairs, honey." Doug's tone was sharp.

"I don't want you arguing with Peter."

"I don't intend to argue with him." He looked down at me with a stern face. "He needs to hear some facts. Now, go upstairs, put the TV on, and close the bedroom door."

I hesitated as Peter walked in, not sure what to do.

"Go upstairs, Darlene," Doug said for the third time, but now he was frowning at Peter.

I stopped at the top of the stairs, debating whether or not I should go into the bedroom. I could still hear their voices.

"How could you break that lady's heart?" Doug began.

"If you came here to talk about hearts," Peter answered. "Let's talk about mine. First it was Kathleen. She went back to her ex-husband and now, Darlene is doing the same thing."

"How can you even compare them?"

"What makes you think Darlene's any different? She's talking to Frank again. As a matter of fact, I saw it with my own eyes—there was a whole lot more than talking going on between the two of them."

"What's wrong with you!?" Doug raised his voice. "Darlene loves you—God knows why, but she does. She's stuck with you every single step of the way. Good times. Bad times. Her name's been dragged through the tabloids more than once because of you, but she's never complains. Where do you think you'll ever find another woman like her?"

"Maybe I need to find a woman who's not carrying an ex-husband around her neck."

That was it! I'd heard enough and escaped into the unwelcoming silence of our bedroom.

Nothing changed as each day dragged by. Peter came home late every night and slept down the hall. We barely spoke. Estelle and Doug kept tabs on me. My headaches came and went. I was hardly sleeping or eating, and I couldn't keep warm even though I constantly wore one of Peter's sweaters.

One night, I woke up shaking from the cold despite the several blankets I was under. As I stumbled to the linen closet for another cover, I stopped to watch Peter soundly sleeping in the other bedroom. Without thinking, I stepped inside. Maybe if I lay down next to him for a few minutes, I might warm up. I quietly moved the covers and got into the bed. Peter moved toward me. Maybe somewhere deep down he was missing me a little. I only meant to stay a few minutes, but his warmth relaxed me, and I fell asleep.

When the alarm went off early the next morning, Peter was surprised to find me next to him. "What are you doing in here?"

"I was freezing. I thought that if I lay next to you for a little while, maybe I wouldn't be so cold. I never meant to fall asleep."

Without a word, he got out of bed and pulled the covers up over me. He left the room and came back with two more blankets. "Are you warmer now?"

I nodded.

"Go back to sleep." He touched my cheek. "I'll turn the heat up before I leave."

Later that same morning Helene came by. "Something's off, Darlene." She sat down in the kitchen. "Peter hasn't been himself for days. As a matter of fact, he's been so difficult lately that everyone is complaining. That's not like him. He won't talk to me so I thought I'd come to you. What's going on, hon?"

At first I hesitated, but Helene insisted so I poured out the whole story one more time. It wasn't getting any easier to talk about, but somehow confiding in Helene was calming. She simply listened as I crumpled tissue after soggy tissue.

"You're leaving for Rome soon." Helene patted my hand. "Once you get there, the two of you will work this out."

"I'm pretty sure Peter wants to go to Rome alone."

"Maybe neither one of you should go. Maybe you both need to stay home and take care of each other."

"Peter has a professional commitment. He has to go."

"Then so do you."

"He doesn't want me, Helene." I took a deep breath. "I'm afraid now that *Fire in the City* is almost over, Peter wants to put all of it behind him—including me."

"I don't believe that for a second, hon." She shook her head. "Peter could never just put you behind him. Things may not seem quite right at the moment, but the two of you will never let go of each other. You're the golden couple."

"Not anymore. Once Peter leaves for Rome, I'll have to decide what I need to do for me."

"Promise you'll talk to me before you do anything rash?"

"Okay, but—"

"No buts, Darlene," Helene interrupted me. "And when I get back to the studio, I have a few things to say to Peter."

"He won't listen."

"He's going to hear it anyway."

After Helene left, I'm not sure whether it was the Tylenol or the sheer exhaustion that sent me back upstairs. Curled up in Peter's bed, I slept until rummaging sounds from our bedroom woke me. I found Estelle standing in our closet. Peter's half-filled suitcase lay open on the bed. "Estelle, you shouldn't be here! This is your day off."

"Peter called and asked me to start packing for him."

The reality of the situation hit me. Peter was going to Rome this week. We were supposed to be planning our wedding, but instead, he was leaving me! I finally admitted defeat. There was no way to make things right. I'd somehow have to let him go, but where would I ever get that kind of strength? Inconsolable, I dropped to the floor, sobbing, refusing to listen to anything Estelle said, but she was a trooper. She stayed with me until I was empty and the last tear shed.

Over the next several days, Estelle continued packing for Peter. She even put some things together for me, but I knew in my heart that I wouldn't need them. Peter came home late every night, continuing to sleep in the other bedroom. He rarely spoke. I dreaded as each day passed and his departure for Rome grew nearer.

On the final day of filming, a party was planned at the studio to celebrate the end of *Fire in the City*. Helene wanted me to come, but Peter never brought it up. He went alone and I stayed home staring, at the suitcases that Estelle had so carefully put together. His contract with the series was over. This was the night Peter was supposed to officially propose. Instead, he'd be leaving for Rome in the morning, without me.

What went wrong? How had everything changed so drastically in what seemed like an instant? We had to talk before he left. There was no way I could let him go if we didn't. I needed some finality and closure. I needed to feel his arms around me one last time. I needed to hear him say good-bye.

For the first time in weeks, an eerie calm came over me. The pain in my head dulled and I didn't feel quite so cold. I refused to see Peter off in silence, so I opened one of the suitcases that Estelle had packed for me, pulling out a nightgown that I knew he liked. I showered, put it on, and fixed my hair. I lay in bed, surrounded by darkness waiting for him to come home.

Shortly after two, I heard his car pull in the driveway. The lights in the hallway went on and he came upstairs. The day must have been an emotional one for him. Maybe, I prayed, he'd be a little vulnerable tonight.

"Peter? Can you come in here, please?" I held my breath, hoping he would.

The light from the hallway cast into the bedroom as Peter stood in the doorway, looking me over rather intensely from head to toe.

"What is it?" he asked quietly.

"I need you." I felt as if I was exposing my soul to him. "Please, Peter, you're leaving in the morning. Will you stay with me tonight—just one more night? That's all I'm asking."

"I don't know, Darlene." He hesitated.

"Please, Peter." My voice broke. "I'm begging you for one more night. I don't know how else to let you go."

He slowly walked over and sat next to me, placing his hand on my cheek. I felt myself tremble, only this time it wasn't from being cold. "I'm sorry about all of this, Darlene," he said quietly. "But we both know that under the circumstances, it's best if I go to Rome alone."

"What happened to us, Peter?" It was all I could do to keep myself together.

"I don't know." For the first time in a long time, his eyes weren't angry. "Darlene, I've tried. I've tried to get the picture of you and Frank out of my head, but I can't. It plays over and over in my mind. I've even dreamt about it. It's not that I want to hurt you. I can't get past it."

I knew he was telling me the truth, but I didn't want to spend our last night arguing or trying to change his mind. "Please don't leave me tonight." I looked into his blue eyes. "I don't know how I'll ever manage if you do."

He was so close I could feel the warmth of his breath and see the desire in his blue eyes. "Please, Peter," I asked again. "Stay with me?"

I slipped my arms around his neck and instead of pushing me away, he pulled me closer. I had to remember every touch, every kiss. I never wanted to forget how Peter made me feel. I would live forever on our memories and this, our last night together. Nothing could be forgotten, no matter how small or insignificant. If only he didn't have to leave in the morning, maybe we could have found our way again. As it was, I was grateful to be with him one last time.

Afterward, I lay awake memorizing him as he slept. I glanced at the clock, counting the minutes I had left to be near him. I could sleep forever once he was gone, but while he was here, I had to stay up in order to hold on to each and every second.

It ended too quickly when the alarm sounded. Peter used our shower for the first time in weeks, while I lay in our bed still trying to comprehend the fact that he was leaving. I watched him dress and throw a few last-minute things in one of his suitcases. Hot tears eased down my cheeks as he sat next to me.

"I really am sorry, Darlene"—he took my hands in his—"but I think it's best if we don't call each other for the next three months—no matter what. Let's use this time to regroup. Maybe when I come back, we'll both see things a little differently."

I only nodded in reply as the tears continued spilling over and my body shook with disbelief that he was really leaving. Peter pressed his lips on mine one last time, picked up his suitcases, and walked out. He never looked back.

Of course, neither of us could have predicted the future or grasped what we set in motion that morning. It would have been too much to even imagine the devastating events to come. We couldn't have known about the long road we both would travel, each on our own separate path, now that the James Dakota years were over. I had no idea more than ten years would pass before I looked into those blue eyes again. A decade later, fate would step in, forcing us to face each other and the life-altering choices we both made. No one could hurt us like we hurt each other. Likewise, no one else could give us the strength and comfort we needed during the worst of times. There was never a choice—we were indeed connected and always would be no matter how hard we tried to fight it.

As it was, that March morning, everything inside me ached over the mistakes we'd made. I thought my heart might stop beating. I drew my knees up, put my head down, and cried. A car pulled up in the driveway. Doors opened and closed. The engine gunned once before driving off. I listened for the side door hoping that maybe just maybe, Peter might come back, but all I heard was screaming…and screaming…and screaming. I covered my ears, but the screaming continued, growing louder and louder until I thought I would lose my mind.

**THE END OF BOOK ONE
TO BE CONTINUED IN**
***THE CHANDLER CONNECTION – BOOK TWO:
DREAMIN' WITH DEE***

Acknowledgements

Writing this story has been a very long journey. Thanks to my best friend, Linda Wells, it was not a journey I took alone. She has been there every step of the way. Her input and friendship have both been invaluable—not to mention the laughter we shared as we went along.

I would also like to thank the other members of my team—my writing partner Cheryl Bartlam DuBois who designed this fabulous cover and our technical guru Christopher Staser who works magic that I can't begin to understand.

In addition, I want to thank my writing group. They are the best--Becky, our fearless leader; Christy; Dan; Dawn; Karla; Steve; and Vicki for their endless support and patience as this book unfolded. You all rock and you are all gifted writers—each with a unique voice.

I also want to thank Alberta Asmar for always telling me that I can do it! You have been a part of my life as long as I can remember and I plan on keeping you for a whole lot longer!

And then there is the family, my daughter, Rachel, and my son Jonathan, along with their respective spouses, Jon and Stacey. They always cheer me on when I need it most. I also have to mention my four little people (who are not so little anymore) Madeline, Olivia, Michael, and Lucas. I love you to the moon and back! You are all so special to me in your own unique way. Lastly, I have to thank my husband, Michael, who puts up with an eccentric wife who is often preoccupied by the characters in her head.

The whole idea of this story came about in a dream. The characters seemed to shout out and demand that their story be told. Twenty-five years ago, I drafted the entire series—all except for the very end. And then it sat…and sat…and sat…until the characters once more insisted that they be heard.

So who is Peter Chandler? I would like the reader to come up with their own version of Peter Chandler, but for me he is based on an old-time English actor who never made it big in classic Hollywood. He had more success in England, but I can assure you he was one of the handsomest fellows ever to grace the silver screen—here or across the pond. He had dark curly hair, much like Peter, but I am not convinced his eyes were blue since the movies he made were all black and white. I did see a color portrait of him once and he did have striking blue eyes in that particular photo so I took it from there. The name, *Chandler*, is a nod to handsome actor Jeff Chandler, who always had a commanding screen presence, but tragically left us way too soon. *Peter* is a nod to Clark Gable who won his only Oscar when he played Peter Warne in *It Happened One Night* (1934). Peter Chandler and Clark Gable also share a birthday—February 1st. It was easy for me to remember.

Darlene, on the other hand, is not really modeled after anyone in particular, but she is most like actress Marion Davies in personality—without the stutter. Loyal to the man she loved (William Randolph Hearst), Davies, a favorite Hollywood figure among her peers, was known for her kindness and big heart. She was pretty, but not glamorous, and she only made movies because it pleased Hearst, and yes, he built San Simeon for her. As for the name, Darlene, it just seems to go with Peter.

As a couple, Peter and Darlene showcase the magic that always seemed to surround Clark Gable and his third wife, Carole Lombard. They were truly Hollywood's golden couple until tragedy struck on Mt. Potosi taking thirty-three-year-old Lombard to an early grave.

Google them sometime and I guarantee that you will see a couple who genuinely glowed when they were together.

The other characters, like Doug and Helene, are strictly products of my imagination and not based on any specific person. I must admit, however, that Estelle is patterned after my sweet neighbor who lives above us in our Florida condo. She is almost ninety and has two speeds—fast and faster! I often run upstairs for a hug!

The story of Peter and Darlene will continue in *Book Two of The Chandler Connection: Dreamin' with Dee.*

And never fear, their story now has an ending, but you will have to wait a while before we get there!